JOYCE VERRETTE

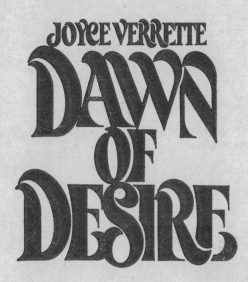

DAWN OF DESIRE

AVON
PUBLISHERS OF BARD, CAMELOT, DISCUS, EQUINOX AND FLARE BOOKS

DAWN OF DESIRE is an original publication of Avon Books.
It has never before appeared in book form.

AVON BOOKS
A division of
The Hearst Corporation
959 Eighth Avenue
New York, New York 10019

Copyright © 1976 by Joyce Petratur.
Published by arrangement with the author.

ISBN: 0-380-00562-X

All rights reserved, which includes the right to reproduce
this book or portions thereof in any form whatsoever.
For information address Avon Books.

First Avon Printing, June, 1976

AVON TRADEMARK REG. U.S. PAT. OFF. AND
FOREIGN COUNTRIES, REGISTERED TRADEMARK—
MARCA REGISTRADA, HECHO EN CHICAGO, U.S.A.

Printed in the U.S.A.

PART I

Chapter One

The gathering heat had already begun to reach into the palace courtyard. The air above the stone walks was shimmering, forecasting the day to come. In the courtyard there was no breeze to relieve the steadily climbing temperature. The trees and shrubs were unmoving.

Amenemhet could see beyond the courtyard walls, the Nile flowing green and brown, its placid surface reflecting the mid-morning sun. Boats of all kinds moved both ways, manned by the deeply-tanned Egyptians, whose skins were used to the ever-present sun. The constant wind from the north filled the sails of the boats traveling south. The deceptively quiet surface of the water held a strong current which carried those who traveled north at a surprisingly rapid speed.

The sound of the sailors' voices carried to Amenemhet as he contemplated his problem. It was one of the most perplexing problems the young prince of Tamera's southern kingdom had ever had to face. It was surely a new problem to him regarding women.

Being heir to the throne had never hindered Amenemhet's opportunities for learning the art of love, and like most Egyptians, he hadn't been shy about enjoying its delights. Their religion didn't hinder them. Its teachings held that life was to be enjoyed as long as a certain balance—avoiding excess of any kind—was maintained. But, upon his return from the center of learning at

3

Anu, Prince Amenemhet had found himself facing marriage!

The days before the ceremonies for the inundation had been long and dull, with little to occupy Amenemhet's mind besides the contemplation of his approaching marriage. Like tiny, silver fish leaping at the summer flies, thoughts of his bride-and-princess-to-be darted past his half-closed eyes. Although his father and the priests had painted a bright picture of new strength for Tamera resulting from the marriage, Amenemhet was unconvinced. His father had reminded him that the marriage contract would allow him a harem if Nefrytatanen didn't please him. But Amenemhet was still disturbed.

He wondered how Nefrytatanen looked and if she wondered about this marriage as he did. To him it was an extraordinary idea to marry a woman he had never met, in order to join their kingdoms into one country. He had heard that she was beautiful but he reflected skeptically on such reports. Would any woman allow disparaging descriptions to be brought to her intended husband? She was his own age, not quite twenty, and already she had ruled her land for several years since the accidental death of her parents. But her youth might mean only he would have to endure her longer. He was sure she must be willful, having ruled alone for that long a time at so early an age.

Amenemhet rubbed his brow, stretched once more, and fell back against the cushions. Already his linen tunic felt damp and limp against his skin.

Absently he watched a fat blue fly soar lazily over the brick wall and head for the bowl of fruit on the table beside him. The fly landed and rubbed its wings together in joy over its good fortune, then began to roam the area, seeming to measure the extent of its new wealth. Sensing a human nearby, the fly paused, considering Amenemhet, who smiled as the fly dismissed him as unimportant, and began again to inspect the fruit.

Amenemhet was vaguely irritated with himself for wasting time on an insignificant creature when he had his own thoughts to untangle. He considered then put aside the idea of speeding the fly's final destiny, and he closed his eyes again.

Sounds of shouting drifted across the wide expanse of river and dispelled his hopes for a peaceful day. Everyone's patience would be diminished with the rising heat, and he knew his own temperament was unlikely to be even. Impatiently he waved the fly away and sat up. The fly buzzed overhead and clung to the ceiling. Amenemhet stood then paced the room for a moment or two before turning to the terrace.

He blinked in the sudden brightness and instantly regretted not wearing sandals against the sun-heated terrace rock. The morning breeze carried the warm, yeasty smell of baking bread, and his stomach rumbled ominously, muttering about his late-eating habits.

His thoughts turned again to Nefrytatanen. He wondered how she would feel about giving the rule of both lands to his father until his death and afterwards ruling with Amenemhet. He knew she was nearly to the point of desperation. Her high priest, Hathorbes, spoke openly against her, and enemies to the east eyed her land.

King Mentuhotep's spies had informed them that bands of Hyksos made forays frequently across Nefrytatanen's borders. Although her army had clashed with them and sent them flying, it was impossible to keep an effective guard on the borders continually. She needed the strength of the Upper Kingdom to combine with her own. And they, Amenemhet knew very well, needed her Lower Kingdom's resources and its outlet to the Great Green Sea. It was nearly an even trade, but no treaty could join the Two Lands as effectively as marriage. When Nefrytatanen produced an heir— and Amenemhet had mixed feelings on the events that must lead to this—the land would be whole.

He reflected on the separate elements that had cast

him into this predicament and wondered if she, too, had mixed feelings. Queen or not, she was a woman, and a woman must have strong feelings regarding so personal a matter as marriage. He reminded himself it had been Nefrytatanen, who had proposed, and he began to doubt that she had any longings of her own. The thought depressed him further.

Although Amenemhet had been anything but enthusiastic, he had decided that, in order to make the best possible beginning, he might have his apartments rearranged. Keeping as much as possible a feminine point of view in mind, he had long ago ordered the changes made. As the next morning was to be Nefrytatanen's arrival, he was dismayed at the confusion and impatient for everything to be finished. After weeks of work, his rooms seemed a marvel of disorganization. As he worried, he heard workers bickering over some minor matter, further slowing their progress. He lost his temper and stepped back into his chamber abruptly.

'Silence!" Amenemhet shouted above them. There was an instant hush. "Stop your endless quarreling and get back to work," he commanded. "The time is short, and if everything isn't accomplished by tomorrow morning, I'll have all of you carted out and left on the desert."

The workers stared at him in surprise. He rarely spoke in such a fashion.

"Master, this one—" Yazid began.

Amenemhet held up a hand to stop him. "You know my orders," he said and turned his attention to the worker Yazid had been arguing with, who now stood in uncertainty, wondering about his fate. "Yazid knows my wishes, and you'll do as he tells you. I'm tired of this whole nuisance. I'll hand you over to the first Babylonian slave trader who passes the city gates if I see even the slightest frown cross Nefrytatanen's brow." He glared at them a moment then shouted, "And someone drive this fly out!"

He turned from them to face the river again; there

was a smile on his lips he wished to conceal. He had no intention of carrying out such threats. He was often too lenient with them, and he knew it wasn't a bad idea to remind them of his status from time to time. He could hear work progressing behind him at a faster pace, and he knew they were being as quiet as possible. He also knew that after the evening meal Yazid would try to distract him from his black mood. Amenemhet decided he would relent somewhat then. It wasn't Yazid's doing that he must marry this female from the north.

Suddenly Amenemhet remembered that the statues he had ordered hadn't yet been set in their places. His face again implacable, he turned to look at the workers and said in a soft but clear voice, "I do not see the statues."

Yazid's thin face turned to Amenemhet. "The artists have not yet delivered them, master. They sent word they aren't finished."

Amenemhet was seriously concerned by this news. "Send a messenger immediately," he said. "Tell them the pieces must arrive before sunset. No doubt they're ready now, but the crafty artists probably hope that bringing them at the last moment will enlarge their value. Pay them exactly what was already decided and no more. If they hesitate, tell them I'll send soldiers to deal with them."

Amenemhet knew the truth of what he said. The statues had been made at his order, by the best artists, and the price agreed upon had been generous. He wouldn't let them smile behind their hands thinking their prince foolish enough to fall for such a ruse.

He glanced at the work being done and was satisfied that it would be finished on schedule, after all, as he inspected with admiration the polished alabaster walls and granite floors. They glowed like mirrors. The new gold-decorated furniture made the apartments more comfortable and luxurious than the rather severe rooms they had been before. He decided he would enjoy the changes even if Nefrytatanen didn't.

"Ra," Amenemhet muttered shaking his head, "keep from me a haggling, ugly wife."

He knew that marriage should afford happiness and companionship, but he was wistful thinking of that now. It was too much to hope that Nefrytatanen would please him. Concubines would provide physical compensation should Nefrytatanen prove undesirable, but such arrangements, he was sure, couldn't bring the emotional fulfillment of love. Despite the amatory freedom he had always enjoyed, he had always looked forward to the day he would have one loving wife. He sighed, impatient with his disobedient emotions. Dreaming of impossibilities wasted time.

Amenemhet passed most of the long evening in the Temple of Asar and Aset. Finally dragging himself to bed, he found he was unable to sleep, so he wandered restlessly into the garden.

As he gazed absently at the countless bright stars in the cloudless sky, he was amazed to see twin streaks of blue suddenly appear in the blackness. They raced across the silent arch of the sky and disappeared at the eastern horizon, leaving their passage etched upon his closed eyelids.

The astronomers had predicted no comet's passage, he had never heard of them in pairs, and he had certainly never known that comets had so strange a color. He wondered if they were an omen, and he felt a peculiar thrill.

He sat on a marble bench and tilted his head to the sky, continuing to gaze at its dark veil. Before he returned to his chambers, a faint blue dawn had begun to light the horizon.

The eye of Ra had become a glowing disk of orange fire as it set, turning the sky into a fantasy of streaming orange and violet. It seemed that Ra greeted the spirits of the afterlife, welcoming their nightly travels with this splendor of celebration.

The water on which the ship silently moved turned to unfathomable blackness touched only in the distance with the gold of fading light. The sandy shores were transformed from the shimmering blaze of the afternoon to the softness of pale gold and long purple shadows.

Nefrytatanen stood on the deck before the doorway to her compartment, watching the moving landscape, During the day the cabin had been cool, and she hadn't stirred from it. With the coming night, the compartment —though fragment and furnished with every convenience—had become stifling. She wondered if it was only her own restlessness that made the place seem airless; as the ship came nearer her destination, she grew less calm and more worried. She told herself once again that she was not the first, nor would she be the last, queen to marry for unsentimental reasons. But she wondered if it had always been so hard for the others.

The delicacies Sira had brought for Nefrytatanen's evening meal hadn't tempted her, and, although she knew Sira worried about her withdrawn manner and lack of appetite, Nefrytatanen couldn't help herself.

She saw a bird looping in joyous circles through the air, and she wondered why so lowly a creature should be free while she, queen of Tamehu, was little more than a prisoner. She envied the bird its wings as she watched and whispered to the skies that *she* had wings *she* longed to use. She was filled with sorrow and the bitter knowledge that her royalty was like a chain dragging after her.

Nefrytatanen began to scold herself again for her unqueenly attitude. Just then she heard several of the ship's crew joking and laughing over some matter of significance only to them, and she was unreasonably jealous that they might laugh. It was the catalyst to loose her anger.

"Stop the ship!" Nefrytatanen ordered sharply. The

sailors stared at her rare flash of temper. "I won't sleep one more night on this river," she added. "I feel sick with the motion."

"We're not prepared to spend the night on shore," the ship's commander reminded her cautiously.

"We will manage," she replied coldly. "Put in to the shore and prepare to stay the night." The captain hesitated, and she added, "At once!"

Nefrytatanen knew she wanted only to delay the journey. At least they wouldn't be traveling as she tossed in yet another useless attempt at sleep. She knew a makeshift bed on the sand would hardly compare with the ship's fragrant compartment, but it wouldn't really matter. She anticipated another restless night wherever she laid her head.

When she stepped upon the river bank, the sun was almost out of sight. The first cool breeze of the coming night swept her heavy hair from her eyes, and she turned her face deliberately toward it, savoring its fresh scent and the softness of its touch, allowing herself a moment's pleasure with it. But she couldn't distract her thoughts for long.

How is it possible, she wondered, to put aside all your feelings and marry a man you've never seen, simply because he's a prince and you're a queen? Since the death of her parents, she had carried not only the burden of personal loneliness, but the added weight of ruling Tamehu under the most trying conditions, and she was tired. She thought, with satisfaction, that even Hathorbes, her high priest, had sometimes been surprised and impressed with her decisions—though he disapproved of her. Now, though, she was truly desperate. Marriage to Prince Amenemhet had been the only solution she could devise.

Too well Nefrytatanen remembered the day her messenger had returned bringing King Mentuhotep's gifts and the acceptance of her proposal. How humiliated she had felt! Although it had been a matter of politics, the thought of having proposed to her future husband still burned her face with embarrassment. She wondered what the prince felt. It had been his father who had answered. Her future husband had sent neither gifts nor greetings.

Thinking of Amenemhet made her face grow warm, for her thoughts invariably dwelt on their wedding night. As she waited for the servants to prepare the camp, she burrowed her foot in the sand and wondered how it would be possible to share intimacy with a stranger. She dreaded the first meeting, though she realized she had prepared herself for the worst possible circumstances.

Nefrytatanen imagined life with Amenemhet and shuddered. His parents would probably treat her like a beggar. And the palace at Wast was, doubtless, a most hideous heap. If all the worst of this came true, how would she ever find the strength to endure it? She wistfully remembered her parents and the profound love they had shared. She straightened her back and resolved that, whatever this union brought, she would do her part to make the best of it and, if possible, keep some remnant of dignity. When the proof was before Hathorbes, she reasoned, he must stop denouncing her. And the Hyksos would disappear like smoke in the wind when the combined strength of all Tamera faced them.

Seeing that Sira had finished with her bed, Nefrytatanen lay down fully clothed. Sira lay on some pillows near her feet, as usual ready for her mistress to call. As Nefrytatanen turned, trying to find a comfortable position, she sighed. At least, she reminded herself, she would still have her faithful Sira.

Nefrytatanen stared at the glittering stars in the blackness of the sky for awhile, and then she shut her eyes with determination. She decided she *must* sleep. If only orders given her own emotions would be obeyed as quickly as the commands she gave others! She realized they would have to travel half the next day because of this stop. It would be hot and tiresome, and her arrival would be late. She wondered how she could endure this final part of her journey.

Long after she closed her eyes, she finally drifted into sleep, still chiding herself that queens shouldn't weep over so trivial a matter as a political marriage. But the stars shone on glistening trails along her cheeks.

Ra began his journey with a burst of crimson rays, and Amenemhet gloomily began his day thinking of Nefrytatanen. After his morning bath and a hasty meal, he called together those who had prepared for her arrival and gave each of them a reward for his help.

Knowing the prince's uneasy mood, Yazid waited until Amenemhet had left the room before giving the servants their final instructions. Pausing outside the door, Amenemhet listened and smiled as Yazid said, "Anyone making a noise greater than the beat of a fruit fly's wings will bring joy to his departed relations, for he will quickly join them in the afterworld."

Meeting his father in the hall, Amenemhet struggled to smile convincingly. Correctly reading his son's expression, Mentuhotep said casually, "We think this meeting will be strain enough on Nefrytatanen and you without having your mother and me present. We've talked it over. Ameni and have decided to stay in our own apartments until you send word that she's ready to meet us. Then, we'll be informal." Amenemhet gave Mentuhotep a grateful look, but before he could speak Mentuhotep smiled and left.

As the morning dragged on and there was still no sign of Nefrytatanen's ship, Amenemhet began to worry that an accident had befallen it. He couldn't imagine that anyone would dare threaten the heavily guarded ship.

The sun climbed higher, and Amenemhet grew irritated. Was Nefrytatanen so pampered she disdained time and left others to wait and wonder? He was chilled as it suddenly occurred to him that she might not come at all. Her absence would be highly embarrassing at best.

As the time for the noon meal approached, Mentuhotep and Meresank sent a message that they would remain in their apartments. Amenemhet was chagrined that they waited patiently while no message came from Nefrytatanen. He turned his face from his food and would not touch it. It was the custom to nap after the noon meal when the sun was at its highest, but he didn't rest. He paced his room in irritation until word finally came that the ship had been sighted.

From his terrace he grimly watched the great red and gold sails with their cobra and lotus insignia nearing the palace moorings. Nefrytatanen's arrival at this time of day insured even more privacy than she had planned when she had first requested docking at the palace and not marching through Wast. Amenemhet wondered glumly if she were so ugly or misshapen that she deliberately avoided a procession through the streets. A lavish display would have been more in keeping with the arrival of a queen.

The ship's sails formed a graceful arch against the bright blue sky and even from his distance Amenemhet could see the sheen of the vessel's golden trim.

When the sails had been lowered and the ship was finally in place at the quay, he heard the noises of unloading. Finally all was quiet, and he knew this was the moment Nefrytatanen would step upon the soil of Tashemau. He wondered if she was offended that he had sent no one to greet her but decided she deserved it for being late. Following upon the heels of this decision came the realization that she might have had a good reason for the delay, and he was dismayed at his own peevishness. This was no time for such nonsense. Grimly Amenemhet reminded himself that he would be spending the rest of his life with her, and it might be difficult enough without provoking her at the beginning. He hurried down the stairs to greet her at the entrance, trying to appear calm.

Amenemhet was surprised at how little time the party took to organize itself. Only moments passed before the retinue was at the doors of the palace courtyard.

As the great main gates slowly opened. Amenemhet watched a number of servants enter. His heart began to pound, his head ached, and his new red tunic fastened itself to his damp back.

A woman cloaked in purple richly trimmed with gold moved out of the group and toward Amenemhet. The others followed slowly, some distance behind her.

The heat beating against the stones caused Nefrytatanen's distant form to shimmer as though she were aflame. The hood of her cloak hid her face. She walked quickly, and the loose cloak billowed against her body with her steps. Amenemhet could see a white gown through the front opening of the cloak. Its shifting folds gave him increasingly tantalizing glimpses of her figure as she moved nearer.

With growing amazement he began to perceive that the messengers who had told him of the beauty of her form had lacked sadly in eloquence. Amenemhet found himself thinking of all the women he had ever thought beautiful. As he watched Nefrytatanen's feline grace, he felt a certain pity for those women. From this day, they would feel they had been cheated by the gods. If Nefrytatanen's face was comparable to her body, then he had been given a goddess instead of a woman. The silence thundered in his ears. Nefrytatanen's sandals were strangely soundless on the stones. She stood before him at last, her face yet concealed by the shadow of the hood. A servant stepped close behind her, slipping the cloak back. Catching the garment before it touched the ground, the girl melted silently away.

Although Nefrytatanen held her head high, she couldn't look at Amenemhet; she kept her eyes fixed on her feet. She was afraid to see him, but her face held no expression.

Amenemhet caught his breath at the sight of her.

The beat of his pulse seemed to fill the courtyard. He stared at her. He saw a golden, oval face with delicate high cheekbones, a long and slender neck, full and soft-looking lips, and a long stream of black silken hair. Finally her black lashes lifted, and Nefrytatanen gazed up at him.

He stared at the great sapphire eyes that met his, feeling the power that poured from them radiating through him, penetrating his very soul. He smiled automatically at her and almost shivered at her slow returning smile.

Nefrytatanen stared into the slanted golden eyes that looked at her with so strange a light. Here was Asar or Sutekh, she was unsure which. Good or evil, she was magnetized by Amenemhet, and when he held his hand out to her she took it and walked up the two low steps to him. Wherever that hand would lead her, she would willingly follow.

Nefrytatanen stood beside Amenemhet, looking up into his eyes. He found he had to make an effort to compose himself. When he spoke the traditional words of welcome, his voice had softened almost to a whisper.

Nefrytatanen took the arm he offered and, as he led her into the shady hall, she decided they shared a secret. The others could watch and listen, the whole world could watch and listen, but no one could ever really know this thing between them.

The hall was peaceful and cool with soaring ceilings and polished alabaster walls. Nefrytatanen wondered how the palace was so well-lit—she saw no lamps or window-openings—for it seemed the walls themselves gave off light. The corridor was lined with exquisitely carved statues and vases. Even the air she breathed held a light and pleasant scent.

When she looked up into Amenemhet's eyes, he felt again the exciting sensation he'd first experienced when he had seen the fiery blue streaks in the sky, and he imagined a new, more beautiful, palace with lapis lazuli walls and ceilings that would match the color of her eyes—a palace decked with gold to reflect her golden skin—a palace to last forever.

Nefrytatanen was sharply aware of Amenemhet's guiding hand on her arm. She felt she must be trembling and found herself making an effort not to betray it. Those golden eyes that gazed at her sent unfamiliar but compelling urges through her, and she found she must look away from him.

As they walked, Amenemhet said softly, "Although your chambers are actually part of my private apartments, they have been temporarily separated. You'll have as much privacy as if you were on the other side of the palace."

Nefrytatanen made no comment. But thinking of the closeness of his rooms made her renew her efforts to steady herself.

"This is my half," Amenemhet smiled and stopped at a door. "We can wait here in comfort while the servants put your things in order."

Nefrytatanen was surprised at how large, how light and yet how cool, the chamber was. One side held several red couches strewn with cushions, chairs of black, red, and gold intricately carved and delicately painted, and tables with polished stone tops that might have been mirrors. The walls were covered with gracefully draped white silken hangings. On the other side of the room was a large bed of gold leaf on a circular dais draped with white silk and scattered with heaps of pillows. Nefrytatanen self-consciously turned her attention from this area to a white and gold cabinet covering one wall's length and height.

Smiling slightly Amenemhet watched Nefrytatanen, knowing she was pleased. When she turned to look at him and put her hand on his arm, he thought his heart hadn't enough room for his feelings. Gently he laid his hands on her shoulders, and seeing the growing light in her eyes, he knew she wouldn't protest, so he slowly leaned closer.

Yazid entered the room. Amenemhet said nothing

but drew away from Nefrytatanen, though he kept one arm around her waist. Ti and Zaroya followed Yazid, bringing some of Nefrytatanen's belongings. Amenemhet could feel Yazid appraising his feelings and gave Yazid the secret sign he had used since childhood to indicate his approval of Yazid's efforts.

Nefrytatanen thought Amenemhet seemed amused at the tiptoeing of the servants. They were so elaborately unobtrusive that she realized they must be burning with curiosity about her. Amenemhet pressed her slightly closer to him, sending a shiver through her, and when the servants noted this they seemed happy. Nefrytatanen was glad of this because she knew Amenemhet must treat them well to have earned their affection. It spoke favorably of his character.

Remembering her dread of meeting Amenemhet, Nefrytatanen thought wonderingly of how wrong she had been. Had she searched through all eternity, her choice would have been no better than this man who was thrust upon her by chance. Or did destiny choose them for each other? With no more than a few formal words, she felt she had always known him. She couldn't —and had no wish to—conceal her awareness of their strong physical attraction. Every look she gave him, she knew, must reveal her feelings. Each gesture, the very pores of her skin, must shout her desire, and she was unembarrassed. Breathlessly she wondered what Amenemhet would do when the servants had left.

Amenemhet was startled by the strange look on Yazid's face as he bowed out the door. It was a look of neither envy nor respect. Suddenly Amenemhet realized it must be the same look he himself had worn when he'd seen the falling stars. It was awe.

Nefrytatanen was watching Amenemhet with an open, warm expression that was intoxicating. He put his arms around her and leaned closer. She stood motionless, waiting for his kiss. They lips were almost touching when there was a soft tap on the door. Before they could move, the door opened, and King Mentuhotep and Queen Meresank swept in.

Amenemhet realized he hadn't informed them of Nefrytatanen's arrival, and he surmised that they had seen her ship from their terrace. He felt guilty for neglecting them, and he quickly stepped away from Nefrytatanen.

Nefrytatanen was surprised to see them. She had anticipated a formal presentation to them later.

Mentuhotep approached Nefrytatanen immediately. He was of medium height, lean and fit, with granite-grey hair. His eyes had the same golden glow of his son's eyes.

"We welcome you to our house, Queen Nefrytatanen," Mentuhotep said softly, "and to our family. May your days at Wast be filled with joy."

Nefrytatanen smiled and murmured her thanks. He had used her title deliberately, she knew. He might have referred to her only as their future princess. She was grateful for his acknowledgement of her rank. She liked him already.

Meresank, small and slight with dark eyes, was serenely beautiful. She smiled warmly as she took Nefrytatanen's hand. "There was no trouble, I hope?" Her voice held genuine concern.

Nefrytatanen realized Meresank was referring to the delay in her arrival, and a flood of embarrassment rushed through her.

"I hope you weren't too inconvenienced by the delay," she apologized. "There was no accident. I must confess I stayed last night on the shore." She lowered her eyes because when she thought of her reason for staying on shore she felt doubly foolish. "I felt I couldn't sleep another night floating on the river," she finished softly.

Meresank's eyes were wise and smiling as she regarded Nefrytatanen. "It was no inconvenience, but we were concerned for your safety. We're relieved you had no difficulties." Her glance at Mentuhotep was a signal passed between them.

"We're sure you'll welcome a chance to refresh yourself," Mentuhotep said, "and no doubt you have much to discuss. We'll leave now and see you again tomorrow."

Amenemhet thought he saw a small but significant look pass between Mentuhotep and Meresank as they left, and he realized, smiling to himself, that he had done so badly disguising his joy that the whole palace must know how he felt!

Nefrytatanen welcomed being left alone at last with Amenemhet, and she wondered what he would do. Although she would initiate nothing, she secretly hoped he would kiss her. Her heart fluttered strangely with the knowledge that it was unlikely she could refuse him anything.

"A bath has been prepared for you," Amenemhet said courteously. He noted the look of disappointment in her eyes and couldn't prevent a faint smile as he added, "Surely you must feel dusty, having traveled in the morning's heat."

"Thank you," Nefrytatanen murmured. "I had forgotten the dust." She couldn't look at him when she admitted this. Quickly she turned to follow a servant he had summoned.

When the doors had closed behind her, Amenemhet fell back on the bed cushions and stared at the ceiling. His reflection on its polished copper surface gazed back, smiling widely. Then the ceiling blurred, and he lost himself in dreams of endless adventures together with Nefrytatanen, of an eternity of nights to share.

He became so lost in his visions that the time Nefrytatanen was gone passed quickly, and he was startled by her return. His surprise quickly turned to pleasure when he saw her standing just inside the doorway wearing the white and gold robe he had ordered set out for her convenience. He had dreamed of how she would look in it, and her appearance surpassed those dreams.

Nefrytatanen's wide eyes staring at him reminded Amenemhet that he still sat on the bed. He leaped to his feet, wondering what she must think of him.

"Please sit down," he invited, moving toward one of the couches. "Make yourself comfortable." He turned and called for the servant Tarya. The girl entered immediately, carrying a container and two golden goblets.

As Tarya poured the wine, Amenemhet wondered what perfume Nefrytatanen wore, for he had never known another like it. It held the warm sweetness of a lotus in the sun, but it was elusively tangy and subtly spiced in some way he couldn't recognize, and he found it both innocent and provocative.

Tarya left, her garments softly whispering, and closed the doors carefully behind her.

"The wine is most refreshing," Nefrytatanen murmured and fell silent. When Amenemhet's golden eyes met hers, her mind went blank. She knew of nothing to say.

Amenemhet wondered what thoughts were passing behind her eyes. They were warm and, at the same time, reserved. She was so close to him, yet she seemed beyond his touch. He watched the cloth of the robe she wore rise and fall gently with her breath, and he wondered if some special element she exhaled was the reason for his feelings. They were unlike any he'd known before. He felt as light-headed as if he'd drunk too much wine, but he had not. He continued looking at her silently, enjoying the pleasurable feeling he couldn't resist. Conversation didn't occur to him.

Nefrytatanen decided that if Amenemhet intended to silently study her in this manner she would also look at him; she was fascinated by his expressions, which continually changed with his thoughts.

His face was like none she had seen before, and she decided it was his eyes which were so arresting. Their shape was unusual, pointed and tilted up at their outside corners, almost triangular, and their color shifted from gold to amber. They seemed to see more than other eyes were capable of seeing, and his gaze was that of a golden-eyed lion. His hair was dark and very thick, so neatly in place he reminded her of a small boy dressed for a special occasion. It looked so soft she felt like drawing her fingers through it, but she didn't dare. He was no small boy. His lips were full and sensuous, but sensitively shaped, and she wondered how his kiss would feel. She was growing more anxious to experience it. He gave the impression of strength. He could make one feel safe—or threatened. Amenemhet was a singular man, more than merely pleasant to look upon, but whatever qualities she might yet discover in him, she knew she would always be sharply aware that he was a man.

"Is it not a little unusual for a girl to be named after Tatanen?" Amenemhet asked, startling Nefrytatanen from her thoughts.

"In Noph," she answered slowly, "Tatanen is highly regarded and thought of more as a divine being than a male spirit. In the north my name means beautiful earth spirit." She looked directly at him because a question of some importance had occurred to her. "How is it you are the heir?" she asked. "There was another son, older, wasn't there? And are you the child of the king and queen?"

"My half-brother died as a child. I'm of the house of Intef by my mother, who is also dead." He added quickly, "My mother was not a harem woman, but queen until she died. Meresank has been like a mother to me." His voice had a sharp edge.

"I asked not out of idle curiosity, Amenemhet," Nefrytatanen said quickly. I heard the story and asked only so I may know the truth." He was silent. "Now that you've answered me, I don't doubt your word."

Amenemhet's quick temper baffled him. It wasn't a point that ordinarily wounded him. He couldn't understand his sensitivity to her question. She had the right to know about the man she would shortly marry. He looked into her eyes, which were level and cool upon him, but he didn't apologize.

"Let us not have differences so soon," he said, smiling sweetly. When he saw that Nefrytatanen's coolness had subsided, he changed the subject. "As we were discussing names, my parents call me Ameni. It's a little less formal and less a mouthful to say."

Nefrytatanen softened then, realizing he was as unused to the situation as she and that they must learn to know one another.

"I will call you Ameni," she replied.

Her slow smile threw his mind into disorder, and he fervently wished all these formalities were over and he could take her in his arms. He knew his inability to concentrate was for that very reason. He couldn't remember ever having felt such desire for any woman, and this restraint was becoming an effort. He wanted to kiss her until that composure deserted her. He wanted to see how those eyes looked when they were lit with fire. He wanted to strip that clinging robe from her and see what its folds only half concealed. He wanted to twist his hands in her hair and learn if it were as silky as it looked.

He wanted to toss aside his crown and title along with hers, forget the protocol accompanying their status, walk with her in a forest or a field of wild flowers, and sit beside a lotus pond gazing at their reflection in the water.

Although Amenemhet didn't realize it, these thoughts were reflected on his face, and Nefrytatanen watched him with mixed emotions. Some of his expressions almost frightened her. Yet, at the same time, she felt an echoing response that exhilarated her. Then his face suddenly grew gentle and wistful, and she stared at him in wonder.

Seeing Nefrytatanen's expression subtly changing with his own thoughts, Amenemhet continued staring at her, his strange eyes revealing clearly that he wished to wait no longer. His eyes were sunlight that warmed her, shifting suddenly to a piercing gold that wanted more than warmth. Nefrytatanen didn't know what to do or say. She realized that if he touched her she would melt without resistance. She began to chatter of various innocent matters, refusing to look at him at all, then chided herself for her confusion.

Amenemhet really heard nothing but the sound of her voice. He was imagining how it might be to make love to her. He was thinking about how soon he would discover this. Then, realizing how far his thoughts wandered, he tried to pay attention to what she was saying.

Nefrytatanen fell silent. Amenemhet was appalled. What had she said? He decided the most tactful comment would be a smile. He didn't realize he was smiling after her account of a particularly bloody Hyksos raid. Nefrytatanen realized Amenemhet hadn't been listening. She also thought she knew what he had been thinking about. To save him embarrassment, she smiled in response. In an effort to compose himself. Amenemhet began to tell Nefrytatanen about refurnishing his apartments. His speech reflected his distraction, and she listened intently in an effort to help him, making polite remarks from time to time.

The sinking sun cast long blue shadows over the floor, reminding Nefrytatanen it was time to leave. Reluctantly she told Amenemhet she must go, and he walked with her to the doors. He stood looking at her a moment before he opened them.

He smiled. "We've had a strange beginning," he commented. "It isn't easy for us."

Nefrytatanen sighed. "Yes," she admitted, meeting his eyes, "and I'm as confused as you must be." She found herself unable to look away yet not knowing what else to say, though Amenemhet neither opened the doors nor stepped aside.

He put his arms around her. Her heart beat faster. He was going to kiss her, she knew, and she didn't know quite what to do about it. But she had little time to wonder as he tilted her face to his and kissed her gently but thoroughly. At last he knew what he was doing, and he didn't intend to hurry through this moment. He closed his eyes and savored each sensation.

Nefrytatanen wondered at this warm delight and enjoyed his kiss without pretense. Amenemhet held her even tighter, and she pressed closer of her own accord. It was not possible to think. It was possible only to feel this strange sensation that made her warm and want to be even closer. The feeling was yet too new to become true arousal, but it was exciting. When he released her, he stepped back with a pleased look that lit his eyes to gold fire. She didn't want to leave the room. She wanted to explore these sensations further.

Rather hastily Amenemhet opened the doors to the servant waiting in the hall. With one last glance at him, Nefrytatanen followed the servant to her own chamber. She forced herself to appear calm until she turned a corner and was out of sight. Then she recalled her behavior with him, and her face flushed.

What made her fall so easily into his arms? Why was she silent one minute and chattering senselessly the next? She didn't understand herself. Neither did she understand the strange weakness in her knees and the fluttering that had invaded her stomach.

Bewildered and chagrined, she walked swiftly through the corridor. Her gown, sweeping behind her and catching the edge of a carving, stopped her abruptly. Before the guard had a chance to aid her, she wordlessly wrenched the cloth free and marched from his sight, leaving him gaping and curious.

In her room she dropped into a chair without looking and miscalculated its position. She found herself on the floor.

"Oh, Wadjet, protectress of the crown," she moaned in disgust. "What a regal crash I might have made for that guard to hear. He would have come to the aid of his princess-to-be and found her royal person sprawled upon the floor! What manner of thing is this that now comes over me? In Amenemhet's presence, I'm reduced either to dumbness or foolish chatter. I, who have calmly dictated decisions regarding the fate of an entire kingdom! I, who give orders to the commander of my army! With Amenemhet I am an idiot, scolding myself inwardly for a tongue which is silent altogether or else will not stop. How he must marvel at the extraordinary good fortune which has turned my errors into wisdom, for he surely must be convinced that what I have accomplished has been by accident, and not by wit. His touch, however casual, confuses and empties my mind. I'm no longer an adolescent. Aset, must I again be reduced to that miserable and clumsy state?"

Nefrytatanen saw herself in her imagination as she was convinced Amenemhet must see her, and she was filled with despair.

Amenemhet had watched Nefrytatanen until she was out of sight. Then he had gone back into his room and closed the door slowly behind him. Again he had lain on his bed, staring at the ceiling, a blank look on his face, an ache in his body.

Was not the king the most powerful of men, he reflected. Did not the prince, then, also have some authority? Amenemhet shook his head in wonder. If he had been born a farmer's son and Nefrytatanen the daughter of a weaver, they would have had more freedom. They could go where they pleased and do what they wished and not have to wonder at the propriety of their activities. They could say what they wished without others listening. He groaned softly. Must he endure two more days of this torture before the wedding? He wondered how he would retain his sanity.

When Yazid came to prepare his master for the night, he saw the glazed look of Amenemhet's eyes but said nothing to tease him. Amenemhet was silent all the time Yazid was with him, and his mind was not on what he did. When Amenemhet stepped into his bath, he was thinking of the difference in his feelings since that morning. He remembered Nefrytatanen's eyes and a sharp, sweet pang went through him. "I am in love with her," he suddenly realized. This discovery brought his head up sharply, and he stared into space for several minutes while Yazid waited patiently for his master to step from his bath.

Leaving the prince, Yazid went down the hall muttering his gratitude to all the gods and goddesses he knew that *he* wasn't stricken with the affliction of love.

Sira, coming to prepare Nefrytatanen for the night, found her mistress sitting, her eyes focused far in the distance. When Sira went silently into the adjoining chamber, Nefrytatanen was barely aware that she'd left.

Nefrytatanen realized later, as she lay with eyes wide open, that she had spoken not a word to Sira, and Sira hadn't broken the silence with her customary light chatter. It was strange to think of Sira's sleeping in another room. Having grown up with Sira, Nefrytatanen regarded her servant as a sister. But Nefrytatanen dwelt only briefly on her maid for her senses could not erase the touch of Amenemhet's kiss.

She couldn't sleep. Each time she closed her eyes Amenemhet looked at her. She got out of bed and stood in uncertainty. Finally she stepped out onto the terrace.

In the courtyard below, the torches danced with the evening breezes. The night wind was warm and soft, caressing her shoulders. The moon was bright. She felt the stillness of the night as intensely as if she were a part of it. It wasn't the calm of peace, but the stillness of anticipation. Every sense was aroused, and the sensation was so exciting it was almost painful. She longed to run through the gardens in the damp grass and touch the smooth leaves of the plants. She wanted to slip into the shadows and become one with them. She longed to pull off her nightdress and stand naked in the moonlight, absorbing it into her very skin. She wanted Amenemhet to come to her.

She counted the window openings to his room. Its coverings glowed softly with a faint light. Perhaps he, too, could not rest tonight. She watched and wondered if his mind were as full of turmoil as her own. Abruptly the light was quenched, and she saw a shadow moving near the window. Was it his? A figure stepped from his doorway onto the terrace and walked slowly to the wall overlooking the courtyard. A flicker of torchlight caught his face, and, with a catch of her breath, she recognized Amenemhet. He turned toward her. She knew she should return to her room immediately but she was unable to move. They stared at each other as if they could do nothing else. In truth, they could not.

When Amenemhet saw her, pale and glowing in the moonlight, he thought at first that she was a wandering spirit of the night. Then he realized it was Nefrytatanen, and he knew only too well she was no spirit—but warm flesh and blood.

The breeze rippled through Nefrytatanen's hair. It seemed part of the sky's blackness. Her eyes were glowing pools of starlight. Through the flimsy veil of her gown, clinging softly to her body in the breeze. Amenemhet saw plainly the curve of her hip and the line of her legs, and he wished with every part of his being that he could lead her now into the shadowy gardens and make love to her in the silver light. He was afraid to move, afraid that she might run back into her room. He wished he could look at her until dawn came.

"Don't go, Nefrytatanen," Amenemhet mused. "Let me watch the night breeze caress you as I dare not. Your hair looks like the sea's black water glimmering in the moonlight. Please stay a moment more, so I may take the memory of you to my bed and make a dream of it."

Nefrytatanen stood silently looking at Amenemhet, wishing he would take her to his bed, wishing they could live his dream together. She watched his dark hair ruffle in the breeze and longed to feel the warmth of his body in this cool night.

Neither of them knew how long they watched, but Amenemhet turned silently away at last and melted back through his doorway.

Nefrytatanen sat on the wall, looking at the sky, thinking of their afternoon of solitude in his chamber. It had been like a fire lying within embers, blooming into the flower of flame. The intensity of her feelings amazed her. She hadn't known such sensations were possible for her, and she fervently hoped the days before the wedding would hold many distractions for them both.

She continued sitting there until the last hour before dawn, unwilling to return to her room, and thinking she would look like a wilted weed on her wedding day unless she soon mended her ways and got some sleep.

She smiled, recalling her father's jesting remark of long ago that she was better suited to be a dancer than a queen, so undignified was her manner. With the discovery of her new and powerful emotions, she wondered if he had been right, although he'd been teasing. Perhaps Aset could give her peace; the goddess of women must understand these feelings. Nefrytatanen went into her chamber and, throwing a blue cloak over her nightdress so she wouldn't be so readily seen, she started for the temple.

After restless hours thinking of Nefrytatanen, Amenemhet, too, had decided to implore peace from Aset. As he was leaving the temple, he saw a dark figure moving from the apartments toward him, and he recognized Nefrytatanen. On impulse, he stepped back into the deeper shadows and watched her as she passed.

Amenemhet held his breath, unwilling to dispel the charm of the moment, while he watched her through the open door. Each gesture she made as she lit the incense and made her devotions, seemed unearthly and graceful. In the silence her whisper wafted to him through the echoing temple, much like the sound made by the wind. Hearing his name, he was deeply moved.

When Nefrytatanen emerged from the temple, Amenemhet stood unconcealed on the path, watching her come toward him. When she reached him she put her hands on his arms. Although her flesh was warm against his, she still seemed unreal. Her eyes glowed with a blue light, like the eyes of animals in the dark.

His lips softly brushed against hers in a kiss as gentle as the tremble of a butterfly's wings. Even at that slight touch, powerful feelings again rushed through him. He wondered whether he kissed a spirit or a mortal. Did Nefrytatanen enchant him? Her lips remained offered to him, and he kissed her many more times in the same light way, tasting the feeling again and again, wondering. Finally, drowning in the strange sensation, he stepped away to the side of the path. Nefrytatanen said nothing, merely looked at him for a moment, then walked past him and continued on her way.

When Amenemhet entered his own chamber, Yazid stood waiting, and told him Sinuhe had requested that Amenemhet meet with the priest and arrange his portion of the dedication to Asar. Amenemhet agreed to see Sinuhe later.

After Yazid had left, Amenemhet smiled to himself. He was very tired, but he knew he would only nap lightly. Nefrytatanen's scent still clung to his mouth and garments, and he could taste her lips and feel the nearness of her body under the soft cloak. He saw her eyes, full of their strange, blue light.

Chapter Two

Nefrytatanen awakened to the sound of Sira's pleading. "My lady, forgive me, but Ra is looking upon you from very high. I knew you'd wish time to prepare for the day's ceremonies."

Nefrytatanen leaped out of bed. "Get my robe, Sira," she ordered. "Where do I bathe? Do you know the way, for I've forgotten." She took the robe Sira produced and, not waiting for her servant's help, quickly put it on.

"Everything is ready, my lady," Sira said as she opened the door. She waited for Nefrytatanen to pass into the corridor, then led her toward the bathing room.

"I've seen to everything," Sira said. "Your bath is waiting. Yazid has told me Prince Amenemhet will meet you at the table when you've dressed. He'll explain today's ceremonies. He's had clothes prepared for you that will be fitting for the occasion."

Nefrytatanen blanched at the thought of Amenemhet's waiting for her all this time.

She followed Sira into the bath chamber, where several other servants waited for them. As they entered, the girls lowered their eyes and bowed. Nefrytatanen suspected their eyes were filled with the echoes of giggles.

When she was dressed in the robe Amenemhet had provided for her, she stepped in front of the polished gold mirror and examined her reflection. She wondered if the deep green gown with its heavy beaded sunburst collar was meant to look modest before the wedding. It wasn't suited for hot weather. She had already refused the wig she was offered, but had allowed her hair to be dressed in separated strands bound at their ends with tiny gold beads that twinkled attractively with her movements. But the weight of the beads added to her coronet felt exceedingly heavy. She gathered her already weary dignity into as regal a bearing as possible and wondered briefly how she and Sira would find the dining room.

Without hesitation, Sira led her to the door and turned into the corridor to show her the way. Nefrytatanen was relieved that Sira had already managed to learn her way around, for she herself was completely lost.

Sinuhe, accompanied by two other priests, entered the room where the palace books were kept. They opened the new scroll and spread it out the length of the table. Amenemhet examined the proclamation of marriage. He suggested a copy be made and sent to Tamehu for their records, then drowsily listened while Sinuhe reviewed the inundation ritual once more.

Immediately after the priests left, Yazid came to announce that Nefrytatanen was ready for the morning meal. As Amenemhet walked with Yazid to the dining room, the servant related everyone's favorable impression of Nefrytatanen. Amenemhet seemed to hear the servant through a mist while he thought again about the events at dawn. He wondered anew at himself and considered consulting a seer about his strange and intense feelings for Nefrytatanen. He wondered if she had somehow cast a spell on him.

When Nefrytatanen entered the room Amenemhet rose from his chair. Looking at her, he decided that if she *had* woven a spell to enchant him, it was all right with him.

"Please sit down," he invited. "I'll explain what will

take place at the ceremonies." When she was seated, he added softly, "You are beautiful in the morning, but you're Aset herself in the night."

Nefrytatanen gazed at him, and, seeing the familiar glow in his eyes, she felt warmth flooding through her. Once again her mind was befuddled and she smiled, not knowing what to reply. She glanced at the food without enthusiasm, but, knowing the day's ceremonies would require strength, she nibbled.

Amenemhet was still speaking when a company of guards arrived. He hastily finished his explanation and stood to signal the beginning of the procession.

In the hall, they were joined by Mentuhotep and Meresank, who greeted them briefly and then preceded them in a retinue of priests, officials, servants, and guards. As Amenemhet walked beside Nefrytatanen through the maze of corridors, he smiled at her encouragingly. "All you really need do is be present," he whispered. "Everyone will be at your feet without your doing more."

The palace doors swung open slowly to the sound of trumpets, and the murmuring of the crowd outside was silenced. Nefrytatanen reminded herself that she no longer addressed only her people, as their queen, and presented herself as princess of both lands. She stood very straight and took Amenemhet's arm. He put his hand on hers and pressed it reassuringly as the procession began.

The throng was silent as they walked to the front of the great stone platform known as the Place of Appearances. King Mentuhotep and Queen Meresank said nothing, only pausing at the platform's front a moment before moving to the side to sit in chairs beneath an awning. Amenemhet and Nefrytatanen were left standing in the sun, and her costume was as uncomfortable as she had anticipated.

As if some signal had been given, the crowd began to cheer as though the sound came from one throat. Amenemhet felt a surge of pride. He knew it was Nefrytatanen's greeting. He looked over the crowd and saw on many the garments of her people, which differed slightly from those of the southern kingdom, and he realized many had traveled far from home to be there. Despite her trouble with the Hyksos and with her high priest, it seemed her people were loyal to her. His ears rang with the noise, and he gazed at Nefrytatanen. Seeing her happy smile he teased, "We'll have to post guards to keep you from being stolen away from me."

Nefrytatanen laughed, and at her laughter a new crescendo rolled from the onlookers. She noted a discreet smile on Mentuhotep's face and suspected he had heard Amenemhet's comment. Then the high priest Sinuhe came forward, and the crowd grew quiet.

"Queen Nefrytatanen, true of speech, living forever, ruler of Tamehu, daughter of Ra, soon to become princess of the White House by marriage to Prince Amenemhet, true of speech, living forever, son of Ra, sole inheritor of the crown of Tashemau, great is our joy and our thanks to the divine beings who have brought you safely here, uniting the Two Lands and bringing peace and prosperity to all. The hearts of both peoples swell with wishes for happiness and strength for our land and for your marriage."

Sinuhe began a long and eloquent prayer to each divine being and every force of nature, invoking sundry blessings and expressing gratitude. Amenemhet and Nefrytatanen continued to stand motionless in the sun. Though Nefrytatanen listened dutifully to Sinuhe's words, she wished them shortened. Although she'd often stood uncomfortably in the sun while a long speech or prayer was said and had been well-trained by such occasions, she longed for a lighter and looser garment made of linen. It might not appear as rich as the silky cloth she wore, but she knew it would be cooler. She thought enviously of the shade under the awning where the king and queen sat and wondered if the throng below might not also wish a swift end to the prayer.

A sudden loneliness came over her. The recent events

had so occupied her that this was the first chance she
had had to reflect. She dwelt on her father and mother,
and she wondered if they were aware of what was
happening to her. She wished they could have met
Amenemhet. They would have been pleased with him,
she was certain. Seeing again, in memory, the places
she had known and loved since childhood—the pools
and fountains, the cooling kiss of the sea breeze, the
majestic pyramids blazing white in the sun, the slender
obelisks of Ptah's temple reaching toward the sky—she
was filled with longing and pride. She wanted Amenemhet to see these things she loved. She wanted him to
meet the northern people and for them to see him.

She thought, too, of a land she'd never seen—her
mother's home. For the first time in many years, she
longed to visit Atalan and perhaps, then, understand
Issella better. She recalled how many people had
avoided her mother, fearful of her. The people of
Tamehu had heard strange tales of Atalan, and some
had called Issella a sorceress. Many of them had
shunned her when she had come to Tamehu as Tefibi-
Siut's bride.

Issella had been different in many ways from the
people of Tamehu. And there had been envy among
families who had hoped Tefibi-Siut might choose to
wed one of their own daughters. Many priests, too,
had hated Issella, for she had had knowledge they had
not. Nefrytatanen recalled a time when, as a child, she
had heard an angry priest at court accuse Issella of
casting spells. Issella had answered sweetly that spells
were being cast by his own mind. He had accused her
of performing strange and unholy rituals, and she had
laughed and replied that all women did things incom-
prehensible to men. She had graciously forgiven him
for his accusation, but that night Nefrytatanen had seen
Issella's expression drained of mirth as she, unaware of
her daughter's spying, had stood before the open sky
speaking in a language Nefrytatanen didn't understand.
Now Nefrytatanen smiled to herself as she recalled

that the priest had never bothered Issella again after that night.

Later Issella had taught Nefrytatanen her secrets, and Nefrytatanen found them neither strange nor evil. She couldn't have explained them to that particular priest either and wouldn't have bothered trying.

Nefrytatanen wished she could visit Atalan and see for herself what her mother had so often described when she'd been homesick and had no one to listen to her but her child. Nefrytatanen wished she could see Atalan with Amenemhet as her father had seen it with Issella before he had taken her from it forever.

At the renewed cheering of the crowd, Nefrytatanen realized the prayer had ended and wished her voice might be added as enthusiastically to theirs. Now she was allowed to sit under the awning, but Amenemhet remained standing in the sun. It would be her first time seeing him perform an official duty in public, and she watched him carefully, both curious and anxious that he do it well.

Amenemhet stood very straight, and, with head held high, he stared at the crowd for a long moment. Their attention captured by that compelling golden stare, he raised his hands outward toward them. It was a dramatic and impressive gesture when done well, and Nefrytatanen noted with satisfaction that he did it very well.

Amenemhet spoke to Asar, directing that the inundation be good and bring to Tamera's next planting the excellent nourishment of the Nile so that the land might once again be lush and rich with the beauty of growing things. He took a gold container filled with water from the river, and while Sinuhe blessed it in sonorous tones, Amenemhet poured it over the soil he held in his other hand. As the water and soil mingled and ran from his fingers, he entreated Asar to hear the son of Ra and give his people life.

From a green jar he took seeds of grain then sprinkled them over the heads of the people. The seeds fell on them like a golden shower in the sun, a symbolic offering of food for Tamera's life.

Amenemhet removed his loose white robe to reveal a short green tunic edged in gold; exclaiming as he did so that Tamera would be green and prosperous. He ended his part in the rite with praise to Amen-Ra, Asar, and Heru and then lit a torch as tall as he was, which was fixed to a richly decorated gold stand. Finished, he declared he had been heard by Tem and all the divine beings.

When Amenemhet turned to walk back to Nefrytatanen, he saw she had risen to her feet, her eyes shining in approval, and his head rose even higher than before.

Sinuhe addressed the people once again, but neither Amenemhet nor Nefrytatanen listened to his words. Their attention was so completely on each other that they were startled when King Mentuhotep brushed past them. He walked to the front of the platform with Queen Meresank and gave his blessing to the people. Without further ceremony, the procession reentered the palace, the watching crowd sinking to its knees as the royal party left.

After the evening meal, Amenemhet and Nefrytatanen sat in his apartments talking quietly of the day's events. Amenemhet still basked in the glow of Nefrytatanen's eyes, which had continued to reflect her admiration. He saw that a servant stood in a corner of the room taking note of all that passed between them and he wondered what the servant was doing there because he had ordered none.

After a time Amenemhet also noticed they were often interrupted by other servants passing in and out, and he began to wonder impatiently if they mistook his private chamber for the marketplace. Even Yazid seemed unconcerned with Amenemhet's increasingly obvious signals to be gone for he shamelessly darted in and out with endless pieces of useless information.

Finally Amenemhet began to suspect they followed

orders, and, after his first flush of irritation subsided, he became amused at his father's vigilance. He resigned himself to the presence of all these others, irksome as their intrusions were, and made no comment.

"It has been an unusually active day," he sighed, sinking into the soft cushions on the couch, "and I hope you haven't been too fatigued."

"No," Nefrytatanen answered softly. "My habits lately have been so changed, I find myself forgetting being tired, not even worrying over my loss of sleep."

Amenemhet began to speak of plans he had made for the future and related some of the wedding details. Gradually he began to describe some of his political aspirations and his hopes of expanding Tamera's authority by a series of treaties. He found Nefrytatanen an enthusiastic listener, and he was encouraged to disclose his private dream, an irrigation system to enlarge the area on which crops were grown and livestock grazed.

He fell silent from time to time, noticing the look in her eyes, which was the same she had worn when he had finished his part of the ceremony, and he felt much less weary. He was so distracted by her fragrance, the drift of black hair that lay on her shoulder, and the immensity of her eyes, that he forgot the presence of the vigilant servants. Twice he rose to approach her and a servant, seeing the look in the prince's eyes, coughed discreetly. Both times Amenemhet gave the man a cold stare but sank back onto his couch.

Again Yazid crept into the room, this time accompanied by Nefrytatanen's servant. Amenemhet rose, and Nefrytatanen followed his example. Meanwhile Amenemhet flashed Yazid a piercing look that made the servant shrink.

Amenemhet turned to Nefrytatanen and said lightly, "Today was long and tiring." He smiled easily at her. "Tomorrow will be soon in coming. Perhaps we should end this evening so we may rest." Taking her arm as they walked to the door, he ignored both Sira and

Yazid. He looked at her meaningfully and said, "Sleep well, little night spirit. May the moon's light bring you peace."

His message wasn't lost on her, and she smiled, replying, "May Aset bring beauty to your dreams."

Amenemhet's heart sang with hope, and he resolved he would swiftly rid himself of Yazid and all the rest of them, even if he had to carry them out bodily.

When Nefrytatanen prepared for bed, Sira didn't leave the room as she had the night before. Nefrytatanen found it necessary to order her to go. Sira left, looking unhappy, and Nefrytatanen suspected she'd also had orders from Mentuhotep. But Sira was Nefrytatanen's servant, and her direct order forced Sira to go.

Soon Nefrytatanen looked from her door to see if Amenemhet stood on the terrace and was disappointed to find it vacant. Had she taken his words for more than he'd intended? After what seemed an eternity of waiting, she stepped out on the terrace boldly, not bothering to disguise her footsteps. She sat on the terrace wall in the fresh, cool air staring sadly into the courtyard shadows, embarrassed that she had presumed so much.

Suddenly Amenemhet was beside her. He had come without a sound. "Whatever Father may think or arrange," he whispered, "I didn't think that it was a proper way to say goodnight."

He put his hands at her waist and drew her to her feet and, pulling her against him, brought his mouth to hers. Fire surged through their bodies, as if from a strong, sweet wine. They seemed to melt into each other's flesh, and they kissed with shivers of steadily growing flame flaring within them, compelling them to press closer until the flimsy fabrics of their garments might as well not have existed. He touched his lips to her cheek, her ear, her throat, her shoulder, leaving a trail of fire with soft kisses, and she clung to him in wonder.

He moved back and looked at her a moment with

glowing eyes. His mouth took hers again, urgently but gently, caressing and nibbling, exploring, until she was a harp singing to his touch. Finally he held her away from him. "We must part now," he whispered, breathing rapidly, "or I will not go at all."

She couldn't say go, but she dared not say stay. She watched him silently while her eyes told him her true feelings. Amenemhet backed away slowly with an expression of regret. Then quickly, he left.

With shaking legs, Nefrytatanen went back to her bed, so awake she thought she would never sleep. But she fell asleep almost immediately, having dreams that, before this night, would have made her blush. She would never blush again.

Amenemhet awakened slowly, drifting from a pleasant dream he couldn't remember. He lay for a few moments reflecting on the previous night.

Nefrytatanen's kisses were all he had hoped for. Although he knew from her inexperienced lips that she was still untouched, he could see she was eager. He smiled, giving silent thanks to Aset that he would be the man to awaken her sleeping fires. Recalling her body trembling in his arms he shivered, then sighed, and sat up.

He put on a short tunic of white linen and stepped out onto the terrace, where Ra extravagantly showered him with warmth and light. The air was fresh with mingled scents from the garden, and the breezes played about him, changing the fragrances from tangy to sweet to spicy.

Amenemhet leaned against the terrace wall feeling the rough warmth of the bricks against his arms. Glancing over, he saw Nefrytatanen step from her doorway, smiling at the day. She still wore her nightdress and, with Ra's help, Amenemhet could see through it quite clearly. He watched in silence for a moment until he decided to greet her.

Nefrytatanen turned to see him smiling at her from

the end of the terrace. Then he straightened and walked toward her, his golden eyes examining her, smiling slightly, still saying nothing. At his expression, she remembered how she was dressed and realized she should feel shy. She did not and this knowledge made her uneasy.

"I've just awakened," Nefrytatanen said lamely.

Amenemhet blinked, startled by her voice, then smiled in understanding. "I don't mind," he said softly. He had no intention of allowing her to distract him from his desire but wished to make her even more aware of it. Finally he asked, "Is there anything particular you plan to do today? There are no obligations upon us." He was pleased that she smiled and shook her head. "If you wish, there is a place, serene and beautiful, which I would like to show you."

"That sounds like the kind of place I was just dreaming about."

"To get there," he said, "we must travel by horse for an hour. We needn't hurry, but we shouldn't delay too long. I'll arrange for a basket of food, and, if you wish, we may also swim. There's a pond ringed with lotus." As he spoke, he could see she was pleased, and he congratulated himself on his idea. It was a favorite place of his and one he wished to share with her. And it was a place where they could have some privacy.

"I'll prepare now," Nefrytatanen replied and turned promptly to her room, knowing he watched her intently. She tingled with the idea of having a day free and alone with him.

Later, when Nefrytatanen and Sira joined Amenemhet in the courtyard, Nefrytatanen was disappointed to see him accompanied not only by Yazid, but also by six guards.

"I, too, wish it need not be so," Amenemhet said, sensing her sentiments, "but we'll be away from the city. There's not only the danger of wild animals and thieves, but an occasional Hyksos spy passes through. They'd be interested in knowing that we sometimes go unguarded outside the palace walls."

Although Nefrytatanen was disappointed, she understood his reasoning only too well. In Noph it was impossible for her to travel anywhere unescorted.

When they reached their destination, Nefrytatanen saw that Amenemhet hadn't exaggerated its beauty. Between protecting rock formations, in which there grew numerous leafy vines, was a small area shaded by trees and carpeted with grass and flowers, where bees flew lazily from blossom to blossom and a sun-spotted pond was cool and inviting. A breeze, laden with the scent of lotus, spoke softly in the treetops, and small birds sang their separate songs, which blended into music as brightly colored as their feathers.

While Amenemhet was supervising Yazid's arrangement of the things they had brought, Sira unwound Nefrytatanen's robe and removed it. Beneath Nefrytatanen had worn only a length of white linen, tied and twisted simply. Slipping off her soft riding boots, she walked slowly toward the water.

Amenemhet turned his eyes from Yazid to her. What he hadn't seen in last night's moonlight had been hinted at further by her sheer nightdress in the morning sun. Now her golden body was further revealed, and his eyes widened at the sight.

Abruptly shortening his instructions, he took off his tunic without waiting for Yazid's help. He, too, was wearing a simple length of linen wrapped and tied around his hips. As he approached Nefrytatanen, she dove, slipping between the waters with barely a sound. She glided just beneath the surface to emerge among the lotus plants. With eyes the color of the blossoms, she watched him dive as she had. She stood in the neck-deep water, waiting until he reached her side.

"I thought swimming was a pastime left mostly to boys," Amenemhet said, facing her, watching her loose hair streaming in the ripples.

Nefrytatanen smiled. "I'm an only child," she replied. "I was both son and daughter to my parents." Her face grew more serious as she added, "My father thought I would be safer, particularly as a child, knowing how to swim. We lived with much water nearby." A hint of her previous smile returned as she said, "He thought it wise to teach me many things not usually taught to girls. He wanted to be sure, in case I never married and had to rule alone, that I could do it well."

"But you won't have to rule alone," Amenemhet said softly. He put his hands on her waist, feeling its smallness, and looked down into her eyes. She was unmoving as if hypnotized, and his hands slid around to her back and drew her to him. Holding her close, he closed his eyes and laid his head against hers, enjoying the touch of her body's whole length against him. He bent to kiss her. Nefrytatanen's lips were cool and wet from the water, and his head reeled as he kissed her long and deeply.

When he released her, her eyes were as dark and shadowy as the water. She stared at him, and he felt again that strange power her eyes held for him. Then, thoughtfully, she turned and swam slowly away.

For a time they glided quietly side by side, drifting in a private world of floating lotuses, blue water, and bluer sky, sharing easily their silence. Finally Nefrytatanen stood up and began to wade out, and Amenemhet followed her, taking her hand as they went. He kissed her wet shoulder lightly and inhaled the scent of her cool, clean skin.

On the bank Sira had fixed a place for them in the lacy shade of a tree. Nefrytatanen sat while Sira combed her hair dry, and, seeing it loosened to the sun, Amenemhet reflected that even now it seemed a part of the night's black skies.

After Sira had finished and stepped discreetly away to settle herself under another tree with Yazid, Amenemhet touched Nefrytatanen's hair. Stroking it gently, he said, "It feels like unwoven silk, and it shines like silk. How do you make it so?"

Settling herself more comfortably to lay on her side, Nefrytatanen answered, "When the moon is waxing,

Sira washes it at night to gather moonlight, but when the moon is waning, she washes it in the day so Ra may smile upon it. It's as my mother taught me."

Amenemhet leaned toward her and kissed her again. It occurred to him that she had never yet protested his advances in any way. What difference, he wondered, should a wedding make when it was clear they loved each other? He pressed her gently but firmly, deciding he wouldn't wait for tomorrow. If Nefrytatanen hesitated, he would persuade her.

He bent over her, kissing her with more intensity than before, until he felt her body shivering beneath him. Amenemhet felt himself tremble, and he slowly kissed her closed eyes, her face, her throat, moving down her neck until he reached the swell of her breast. She breathed much faster.

Then she stopped him. She pushed him away and sat up, breathless, her glowing and darkened eyes staring at him.

Amenemhet looked at her silently a moment. Then he sat up also. "Yazid and Sira know better than to stare at us now," he said a little sharply. "The guards are here to be alert for others. Their eyes are turned away from us." His face clearly showed his disappointment. "Why do you push me away?" he asked more gently. "Last night you clung to me and didn't want me to leave."

He waited for her answer, but she said nothing. She only looked at him, torn by her emotions. He sighed.

"You're right," he admitted. "My passion drowns my judgment." He drew her robe around her shoulders, smiled faintly, and lay back, looking at her from the corner of his eye. "Cover yourself, so I'm not further tempted," he added a little gruffly. He closed his eyes. He was very shaken and needed time to regain his composure.

Amenemhet was quiet for awhile, thinking very carefully. When he finally spoke, it was with some hesitancy. "I've been wondering if you'd think it well for us to travel to Tamehu after the wedding."

"It would be reassuring for the people to see you," she agreed.

"That's as I thought," Amenemhet said. He sat up and looked at the water for a moment. "I want them to know Tashemau doesn't intend to rule Tamehu—that Tamera is one."

"If I went before you to prepare for your coming as you did for mine, it would be easier, perhaps."

"I think so, too," he replied. He was quiet once again. Then finally he said, "I wonder if it might be good for you to leave the night of the wedding. To go to them that soon would make them feel more a part of the celebration."

Nefrytatanen was silent. She had anticipated spending that night in joy with him.

Amenemhet continued, "The party would last through the dawn and we would have to stay—unless Father gave you permission to leave on this trip. If you left by ship that night, you could rest from all these last hectic days. I would meet you in Noph after you had prepared for my arrival. It would be only perhaps a decan until we'd be together again." Nefrytatanen lowered her eyes, not wanting Amenemhet to see her thoughts. He knew them and said, "I don't wish to let you go from me at such a time, but I think it would be easier that night than the next or the next after. To wait will make our first night sweeter."

"You're right, Ameni," Nefrytatanen said slowly. She lifted her eyes to meet his. "I think it wouldn't be possible to leave your arms later, but I'll miss you terribly, even so."

"I'll think and dream of you often," Amenemhet whispered close to her ear. "Surely you know how I hunger for you."

She turned her eyes to the water. "Ameni," she said clearly, "had I known these plans a short time ago, I wouldn't have stopped you; for I barely had the strength to do so."

Amenemhet took a deep breath and smiled. He

caught her hand in his. "Ten days of waiting won't be long when we have all our life before us."

"It will be long," she replied.

They sat beside the pond watching the rushes sway in the wind and the bees sipping the nectar of the lotuses. The sweet smell of the grass mingled with the warmth of the sun as it began its downward journey.

They held hands and spoke softly of light and often foolish things, kissing frequently, but with a new tenderness. The birds sang, but they heard little of the music for it was the music of their own soaring hearts that sang in their ears. The scent of the flowers was also lost to them, as was the caress of the breeze. They were aware only of each other's scent and touch.

They walked awhile on a shady path, the long, soft grasses bowing beneath their bare feet. As they strolled, each noted the grace of the other's steps, a turn of the head, a gesture, a look. It was a quiet and peaceful interlude in which they shared each other's dreams. When the hour came for leaving, they had learned much about each other.

The shadows were lengthening as they mounted their horses. Nefrytatanen paused and turned to look once more at the place and sighed.

"We can return again, often if you wish," Amenemhet said softly, placing his hand on hers.

"Yes, Ameni, I wish it." Nefrytatanen's shining eyes turned to him. "But as pleasant as later visits will be, they'll never be quite the same as this. I want to remember this day."

Amenemhet nodded for the guards to begin the trip back to Wast. He was very pleased with the day's results. Thinking of it and smiling, he decided he would also put this memory in a special place.

The early evening birds continued their singing as the darkness gathered softly about them. But as Amenemhet and Nefrytatanen, still holding hands, rode through the deepening twilight, the song of the birds went unheard. They were too dizzy with their own song.

Chapter Three

That night Amenemhet found himself too exhilarated to sleep. Although he remained in a pleasant frame of mind, he found himself also thinking of the responsibilities of marriage and of eventually being king. He began to realize how unfettered a life he had lived until now. He also began to wonder how it would feel to be married, to have children one day, to have a son whom he would teach to be king after himself. This sobered him and made him realize the importance of his station. On an impulse, he went down to the throne room.

It was silent in the immense, darkened room, for the household was sleeping. The enormity of the shadowy chamber staggered Amenemhet. He thought of those who had ruled before his father and felt as if they were all around him, present in this, their inherited place. He felt that they all waited to guide him.

He sat on the edge of the dais, below the golden thrones, watching the soft light from the window openings flowing in elongated patterns along the alabaster walls, catching the shimmer of gold here and there, then disappearing into the ceiling's soaring shadows.

Amenemhet was still reflecting when he heard a soft footstep and the rustle of cloth. He looked up to see the lean form of his father.

"What are you doing up at such an hour, Father?" he asked. Mentuhotep sat beside him on the dais edge.

"I sometimes come here to think," Mentuhotep answered. "You are doing the same?"

Amenemhet smiled. "I wasn't sleepy, and the thought of the new life beginning tomorrow brought me here."

Mentuhotep returned the smile. After a pause, he asked, "Ameni, how do you find Queen Nefrytatanen? I wish you to be happy, my son. You seem so, but I've wondered. Do you like her?" Mentuhotep put his hand over Amenemhet's. "Beauty fades, Ameni, and it fades sooner if you're unhappy with your wife. I know you desire her, but I hope this hasn't blinded you to her character. Remember, it will someday be her child who will sit upon this throne. Other arrangements could be made with the Lower Kingdom if you think this marriage unwise. They wouldn't be as binding, but it could still be done. Be candid, Ameni. Tell me what's in your secret heart."

Amenemhet was quiet as he collected his thoughts and arranged them with great care. Finally he said, "Father, the gods plan events in strange ways. Although the marriage was agreed upon for political reasons—and I must admit I was unenthusiastic about this—I am glad now. Nefrytatanen is not only beautiful to look upon, but her character shines as well. Passion she has, and for this I thank Aset. But no tales of her adventures will be whispered sneeringly behind hands. Father, she's of a gentle disposition, but she's not without spirit. She's also wiser for her years than one would expect." He looked at Mentuhotep with shining eyes. "She's worthy of the double crown in every respect."

"So had I also thought, but I'm glad to know your feelings." Mentuhotep's face shone with pleasure as he looked at his son. "It seems you've found treasure beyond counting."

Amenemhet sat quietly, satisfied that his father thought so highly of Nefrytatanen. Then he remembered her journey.

"Father," he said, "Nefrytatanen and I thought it would be well if I visited the Lower Kingdom and met her people as she has met ours. Perhaps it would lessen any suspicions of our motives here, and it would be a demonstration of our respect for Tamehu. We talked of it this afternoon and decided it would be best to do this without delay. We thought it would be good for her to leave tomorrow night, and, after she's made preparations, I'll follow her. "It would make her people feel more a part of the wedding celebration if the marriage were consummated there. Will you give us your permission?"

"That's a wise decision," Mentuhotep said. Then he chuckled softly. "Ameni, you have more restraint than I'd thought!" Amenemhet made no comment. "You have my permission," Mentuhotep said. He paused then said softly, "My son, I've seldom spoken to you of the day when you'll take my place, for Meresank and I have always been of the opinion that we could teach you more by example than by lectures. I think, though, that now is a good time for me to say some of the things I've been thinking about lately."

"Are you not well?" Amenemhet asked, alarmed.

"I am well, Ameni. Fear not. But we must always face the moment when we leave this life. And when I do, I'll pass on to you a far heavier burden than others leave their children. I give you the crown, Ameni, and the Two Lands are beset by many problems I haven't solved. If these things are not yet resolved when you become king, I ask that you try to accomplish what I could not."

Mentuhotep lifted his eyes to regard Amenemhet solemnly. "Build Tamera into a land of happy people if you can, and your name will live forever," he said. "If the lands can be successfully joined despite the difficulties that some will cause, then our enemies beyond the borders will greatly fear Tamera's strength and will bargain with us peacefully. If the nobles can be persuaded to follow you without jealousy and struggling for power among themselves, the land can truly be made to prosper."

Mentuhotep no longer looked at Amenemhet. "I hope for a kingdom where even the lowliest of people believe that life is good—as is right and in accordance with the most ancient of our laws," he said softly. "I dream of a land where a man can labor in his fields or at his bench singing and have food enough to feed his children well. I dream of a land where none need be afraid to rest by the roadway from their travels, for they are assured an army protects them. I dream of a land of beauty and learning." Mentuhotep's eyes focused on Amenemhet once more. What I cannot accomplish, perhaps you can."

"Father, I'll try. And I'll teach my children, if we're fortunate enough to have them, as you've taught me," Amenemhet promised.

"Thank you, Ameni. I know you're just and merciful. You'll gain wisdom with time, as we all hope to do." Mentuhotep sighed. "I look forward to the day I see your children myself, but it's good to speak to you of these things now. Our people have always been proud of their land, rightfully holding themselves above others, because there is no other land or people like those of Tamera. It should always be so."

"I, more than all of them, am proud of our land and our people," Amenemhet whispered.

They sat quietly a little longer, their thoughts the same, king and king-to-be, as Asar and Heru. Their company was the whispering of those rulers long gone from the throne.

They said their goodnights more affectionately than they had in many years and returned to their separate chambers, leaving the golden throne room quiet except for the soft voices in the night air.

Nefrytatanen was glad it had been the task of others to arrange the details of the wedding. Amenemhet had already been careful to explain the arrangements and had sought her opinion in all things; but she was convinced that to plan such an elaborate celebration combined with the ceremony for the inundation would have been more than she could have managed.

She had thought, with some humor, while examining the list of beverages, that every head in the land would be aching after this celebration. It seemed as if the combined resources of both lands couldn't have produced the quantity and quality of food and drink that would be available that night. She also marveled that the lands could grow as many flowers as now decked the palace. And the servants. There were armies of them rushing through the palace. She could barely turn a corner without risking collision with a hurrying worker or enter her own chamber without startling someone.

Every piece of jewelry carrying her insignia and the crown as well had been redesigned to symbolize both kingdoms combined. There was only one item that nothing could change and which had been kept a carefully guarded secret—her wedding garment.

She had bathed with the help of several attendants, but only Sira would help dress her. After a maid had arranged her hair to fit the new crown, the servants had been dismissed. Nefrytatanen reclined, naked, oiled, and perfumed, very careful lest one coil of hair fall loose and upset Sira again.

She was grateful for this moment of rest because Sira had caused her some consternation by her extreme vigilance. Now the servant was placing Nefrytatanen's wedding garments in order, and Nefrytatanen smiled as she reflected on Sira's behavior. The servant had been like a lion guarding her, ordering servants about in all directions. And though she had wondered whether Sira would drive the whole household mad, she had made no comment. For once, Sira was in charge, and her queen, Nefrytatanen, remained silent. She knew Sira did these things out of love, and she had caught glimpses of Sira's eyes looking suspiciously wet.

Nefrytatanen turned her thoughts to the coming ceremony and wondered how Amenemhet would look when he first saw her enter the temple. She grew excited, and her hands felt cold while her face flushed hot.

When Sira finally gave Nefrytatanen a signal, she rose from the couch feeling that she moved in a trance, and distractedly watched Sira begin the ritual of dressing her. No one but Sira knew how to place the folds and drapes of this gown because a gown like this had never been seen in Tashemau or in the Lower Kingdom. It was the gown her mother, Issella, had worn for her wedding. She had brought it from Atalan, her mysterious home, and it was made of a silk-like cloth with so sheer a texture that no hands but Sira's dared touch it. It was woven of fine silver threads combined into a web that clung to Nefrytatanen as she moved. Gathered high on one shoulder and baring the other, the gown drifted like the mist of a waterfall to the floor.

Even when Sira's critical eye was satisfied, Nefrytatanen didn't turn to a mirror. She waited while Sira's own hand painted her eyelids, mixed colors on her palette until she had obtained the same blue of Nefrytatanen's eyes. After this had been applied, she sprinkled her queen's lids with silver dust until her eyes were a fantasy of stars.

Sira placed the red crown carefully over Nefrytatanen's hair, muttering her hopes that the hair wouldn't be disarranged when the red crown was exchanged for the new double crown. Still Nefrytatanen said nothing.

When Sira was finished, she sighed and took her to the mirror saying, "My lady, it is done. The prince will be enchanted by the sight of you, or else he's blind."

Nefrytatanen inspected the image before her. But for her father's inheritance of high cheekbones and slightly slanted eyes, she looked exactly like Issella. Wordlessly she turned to Sira and opened her arms to the servant. They embraced silently a moment, each knowing her life would never be the same after this day.

Finally Sira stepped back a little. "My lady," she whispered, "may your marriage be graced with every beauty of love. May you and Prince Amenemhet be as Aset and Asar in your happiness."

Then Sira released Nefrytatanen, went to the door, and opened it. She stood aside letting Nefrytatanen pass, and Nefrytatanen paused to give Sira's hand one more squeeze before stepping into the corridor.

A company of palace guards waited in the hall staring stiffly ahead as Nefrytatanen stepped between their ranks. Though not one of their heads moved, she knew their eyes examined her curiously.

No one else was in the corridors as they walked; no one was in the courtyard. Nefrytatanen and her escort crossed the stone pavement in the sun, alone except for a bird who, perched on a low-hanging branch, silently watched them pass. Nefrytatanen felt as if all the cosmos held its breath until she was before the entrance to the temple which had been built by Amenemhet's family generations ago and dedicated to Asar and Aset.

Then the temple doors opened, and a mass of faces swam before her. The waiting crowd silently parted for her. Palace guards formed a cordon on each side and stood like two rows of painted statues holding upright beside them their elaborately decorated lances. Lamps blazed everywhere, and the scent of flowers and spices was as heavy as water in the air. The statues of Aset and Asar towered before her. Beneath them stood the priests—and Amenemhet.

Nefrytatanen was dressed in the silver of moonlight, and Amenemhet's robe was the gold of the sun, its light reflected in his eyes. He watched her so intently that Nefrytatanen felt as if she were being drawn to him by the light emanating from his eyes. From narrow openings high above, the sun fell on the table of offerings. As she entered the bright circle, the warmth of Ra welcomed her.

Sinuhe spoke the words in a level voice. Amenemhet and Nefrytatanen responded in whispers. They drank the sweet, spiced wine and ate the consecrated cakes. They moved and spoke. They lit incense and

scattered flower petals and fragrant herbs. They put
their seals upon the scrolls. Their crowns were removed
and the new ones placed on their heads. Incense rose
in perfumed clouds. During all of it, they moved as in
a dream, barely aware of the motions they made.

With every movement, Amenemhet managed to
brush close to Nefrytatanen in some way. Tilted golden
eyes looked down to meet those of glowing sapphire
until King Mentuhotep gave his formal approval and
turned to leave the temple, Queen Meresank's arm in
his. Amenemhet took Nefrytatanen's hand and followed, each of them intoxicated with the other.

They were amazed by the great mass of people who
had managed somehow to crowd into the area before
the temple. The noise deafened them, and while they
stood silently staring, a shower of fragrant leaves and
flower petals rained over the wedding party.

In a moment they all were covered with petals
and leaves. Smiling, Amenemhet took a petal from
Nefrytatanen's shoulder and placed it in a slit in his
robe, as if to save it. Nefrytatanen smiled and plucked
a leaf from his hair to do the same, brushing his hair
lingeringly, desiring to touch him even in this small
way. This slight contact made them both dizzy.

Someone in the crowd began to sing, and soon the
whole throng delightedly joined in a song of celebration. King Mentuhotep began to smile with pleasure.
Queen Meresank had been sweetly smiling all the while,
but Amenemhet and Nefrytatanen were too caught up
in each other's presence to notice.

As the royal party began its return to the palace, the
song ended, though echoes of it still remained, and the
crowd began to sing another. Amenemhet wondered if
his welcome to the Lower Kingdom would compare
with Nefrytatanen's here. He grasped her hand even
tighter as they entered the palace, the air yet filled with
the scent of flowers and with song.

As they approached Nefrytatanen's door. Amenemhet put his arm around her waist, determined to brush

closer. Thinking of her journey renewed his need to wring from these moments all he could.

The royal family went separate ways after the ceremony, passing the next several hours resting and preparing themselves for the evening's banquet. While Amenemhet spent most of this time making last-minute arrangements for Nefrytatanen's journey, she spent the hours in her chamber, supervising packing.

When she was finally alone, she didn't feel like resting. She went out on the terrace to think about all that had happened in so short a time. Although she wished to dwell on the happiness that lay in her future, she felt uneasy and strangely fearful. What could be wrong?

The cooling breeze of the approaching night caressed her. She watched the the shadows in the courtyard below lengthen as one met another, joining until the area was almost dark. A servant entered the enclosure, and she watched him lighting the torches.

Nefrytatanen at last decided her uneasiness might be relieved by a moment of meditation in the temple. She knew that if she went right away, she would have time before the party began. She picked up her cloak and, throwing it loosely over her shoulders to cover the glistening of the silver gown, walked quietly down into the courtyard, through the shadows, to the temple.

The great doors were closed, and it was necessary for Nefrytatanen to thrust her weight against them before they swung silently open. Noiselessly the doors closed behind her, and she stood alone in darkness. Cautiously she found her way to the front of the temple, relying more on memory than on the faint light coming from the window openings high above.

Nefrytatanen found a lamp, its glow surrounding her with a pale circle. She felt very small standing before the massive statues. The weight of the stone ceiling seemed to crush her despite the many rows of columns supporting it.

The silence was so deep it seemed that she could

taste it. The wedding incense yet floated on the still air.
She looked up at the face of Aset, but the features of
the goddess were hidden in the shadows beyond the
realm of the little lamp. Nefrytatanen composed herself
and tried to open her mind to receive whatever thoughts
came to guide her.

Nefrytatanen's skin prickled with the awareness of
someone's presence. Turning quickly she saw that
Sinuhe had silently approached her.

"Why are you here?" she demanded, her voice echoing in the stillness.

"My princess," Sinuhe inclined his head, "I saw the
light and came to inquire if someone wished my presence. If I'm disturbing your meditation, I'm most
humbly sorry for my intrusion. I'll leave at once." He
turned to go.

"Wait, Sinhue," Nefrytatanen said. He turned again
to face her. "I would ask you something," she whispered. He waited silently. "I am troubled. I fear this
journey for I see frightening things connected with it.
But I also feel it is necessary, as if it's part of my
destiny. I feel that the darkness I see ahead will touch
many with sorrow and will influence the whole kingdom."

Sinuhe studied Nefrytatanen's face carefully for a
long while as he considered her words. "If I may suggest it," he began, "the natural emotions of a bride
make you anxious. To leave your beloved on this night
isn't easy." He was silent, as if searching for words,
then added, "The journey would seem to be a good
thing. Surely the divine beings would find favor in so
unselfish an act as delaying your wedding bed for the
good of your people." He smiled encouragingly.

"I am, no doubt, foolish in these fears," Nefrytatanen conceded. "You must be right. My emotions are
greatly disturbed." She felt hesitant to say more.

"Whatever your destiny," Sinuhe murmured, "it
must be fulfilled. I predict it will be a happy one."

Nefrytatanen's smile felt stiff, but she didn't wish to

alarm the priest. She pulled her cloak tighter around her, thanked Sinuhe, and wished him a pleasant evening. As she left the temple, she felt even more uneasy than before.

When Nefrytatanen entered her chamber, the strange feeling persisted, but she resolved not to spoil Amenemhet's evening with her gloomy mood.

Sinuhe remained where he stood as he watched Nefrytatanen close the doors. The lamp she had lit inexplicably died and left him alone in the darkness. When he tried to relight it, he could not. Finally, feeling uneasy and disturbed, Sinuhe gave up and found his way to the door. He shuddered, remembering Nefrytatanen's words. The unseen eyes of Aset seemed to pierce his back like daggers.

The air was filled with laughter, conversation, and music as the royal party approached the banquet room. A fanfare of trumpets announced their arrival, abruptly silencing the other sounds.

Two very young girls came through the doors, as softly silent in their steps as a drifting summer breeze. They wore lotuses in their hair, and their slight bodies were adorned with robes of pleated white gossamer. They scattered flower petals whose fragrance lingered behind them.

King Mentuhotep and Queen Meresank, dressed in richly decorated white and gold robes, their faces serene with dignity, swept into the room. Prince Amenemhet and Princess Nefrytatanen followed, still wearing their wedding garments but having replaced the heavy double crowns with more comfortable coronets. Whispers ran through the room like ripples in a lotus pond, and the officials and their ladies sank to the floor in a gesture of deep respect. The prince and new princess were followed by fan bearers and numerous other attendants. Royal guards marched after the company, resplendent in colorfully decorated uniforms and gleaming ornamental weapons.

When everyone was seated, Mentuhotep gave a signal, and the music resumed, along with the murmur of conversation. During the evening guests would consume many courses of rare and beautifully prepared dishes, drink countless goblets of exquisite wine, converse, and be entertained at intervals both by slaves and paid professionals. Those guests who were particularly favored would be called to approach the royal family and allowed to say a few words to the newly-married couple. Everyone present hoped he or she might be thus honored. They stared at the royal table, noting carefully each gesture and every detail of the royal family's garments. These observations would be recounted endlessly to friends and acquaintances not fortunate enough to have been invited.

Shortly after dinner began, a dancing girl from Kenset in a costume of bright orange decorated with gold pieces and a headdress of long, floating orange feathers appeared in the center of the floor. Like a shimmering flame of orange and gold, she began to dance with skillful grace.

The king and queen watched the entertainer, intermittently conversing with those who came forward. Amenemhet and Nefrytatanen courteously acknowledged the greetings and made polite conversation, but it was obvious that they were more interested in each other than in the entertainment, food, wine, or their visitors.

The scene was luxurious beyond the dreams of those who lived in humble cottages far from the palace. But the peasants were having their celebration, too. The royal family had sent gifts of food and beer to the people. Many danced in the fields and streets, and if their celebration wasn't as elegant as that in the palace, they were as gay.

Amenemhet and Nefrytatanen teased each other, laughing at their mutual struggle to absorb every sight and sound as if to engrave each memory forever on their souls. But more than any other sight, they gazed at each other. For over both of them hung the shadow of their impending separation.

"This is," Amenemhet whispered smiling, "one more moment to save in that special place in our hearts." Nefrytatanen turned her eyes to meet his. At the expression he saw in them he added, "When you look at me that way, I glimpse a future so filled with joy, today is pale by comparison."

Nefrytatanen made no reply, knowing that whatever she might say couldn't be said here.

An hour before Nefrytatanen's scheduled departure, Amenemhet rose from his chair and stood silently looking down at her with a strange expression, as if he had a secret of great importance to share. He took her arm, gently pulling her to her feet, and drew her away from the others, who stared in surprise. He ignored the curious looks and, still saying nothing, led her into the hall—then toward his chamber. The sentry outside Amenemhet's door followed them with speculative eyes as the door closed. He smiled, wondering.

Once inside the room, Amenemhet released Nefrytatanen's arm and went to a cabinet. She watched him take a container from it, noting his tension. He returned to her almost hesitantly.

"Beloved," Amenemhet began softly. He stopped, as if in confusion. He'd never called her this before. At the sound of the endearment, a soft glow entered her eyes. He continued, "I wanted to give you something that would have meaning to us both—so you would always be reminded of me." He hesitated again, as if searching for words.

Nefrytatanen looked at Amenemhet, not knowing if she should speak or what to say if she did. She remained silent, not wishing to spoil this moment, for his eyes were solemn.

At last Amenemhet sighed. "The night before you came to me, I was in confusion. I was disturbed about marrying someone I'd never seen before—as you probably also were. Thoughts tumbled through my mind like sand blowing over the desert. I wondered what you'd be like, and I anticipated the worst. I wished I hadn't consented. I didn't know what to think."

Nefrytatanen's faint smile admitted her own emotional turmoil.

Amenemhet went on, "As I stood in the courtyard just before dawn—for I couldn't sleep—I raised my eyes to the night and saw two stars traveling together. It was a rare sight to see two, but, even stranger, they were blue! I marveled at them. They were so beautiful I was staggered with emotion. I was filled with awe. They seemed to be an omen, and I have often wondered about them since that night. The next day when I awaited you, you walked toward me with your eyes downcast, and I thought you were the most beautiful woman I'd ever seen. When Sira took your cloak and I saw your face, I thought the whole world trembled beneath me. Then you looked up. As your eyes met mine, I understood the omen at last. Your eyes were surely the stars I'd seen. My gift is poor in comparison. I wish I could capture those falling stars for you, but I cannot."

He held out the box, and she took it, her eyes still on him. He smiled. "Open it."

Nefrytatanen's fingers trembled as she obeyed. Within the box, wrapped in soft cloth, lay a necklace of silver links. Suspended from it were two silver lotus blossoms encircled by the shape of the full moon, and in the heart of each of the flowers lay a blue gem, a star glowing in its heart. Nefrytatanen had never seen such stones. Speechless and wondering, she looked up at Amenemhet.

He said, "They're the same as your eyes and the same as those stars, the same as the lotus blossoms we swam among."

"They're beautiful," she whispered, touching them with a fingertip. "I've never seen such gems, and I've never heard of such an omen." She looked up at him. "No man ever gave a woman so beautiful a gift. Surely all our lives before this moment have been but a preparation for now. A message from the divine beings, who arranged our meeting, is captured in your gift." She picked up the necklace and detached one of the silver blossoms offering it to him. "I would give one of them to you," she whispered, "that you'll have something of me to keep. When we're apart, you can look at it and know it's part of me, as when I look upon mine I'll know it reveals your heart. My beloved," she whispered, "put my necklace on for me now and know I'll never remove it."

Amenemhet took the necklace, and Nefrytatanen turned away so he might fasten it. When it was secure, he kissed her shoulder gently, and she turned into his arms.

"I'll put this lotus on a chain like yours," he promised, "and I, too, will wear it always."

Amenemhet put his arms around Nefrytatanen and held her tightly. Close to them both was the understanding that they need not leave his room now but could delay her journey for a few hours. Dwelling on this, Amenemhet's mind reeled, but then he thought of saying good-bye afterwards.

"Let us return to the party," he whispered reluctantly into her hair, feeling drunk with her perfume. He forced himself to back away from her.

Nefrytatanen put her hand on his arm as if to detain him. Her face held not passion, but solemnity. She began to speak in a voice strange to him, as if she was someone else. Her eyes held his face, but they appeared not to see him.

"In the time of King Seneferu," Nefrytatanen began, "there was a man named Neferu, who was so greatly favored by Bast that she gifted him with prophecy. He said, 'I will show thee the land wailing and weeping. A man's spirit will be concerned with his own welfare. Every mouth will be full of "pity me." All good things will have departed. The land will be destroyed.' "

Nefrytatanen paused to regard Amenemhet with eyes

that were unfamiliar and a bit frightening. "And then, beloved, Neferu said, 'A king shall come forth from Tashemau called Ameni, the son of a woman of the south. He shall receive the white crown and wear the red crown. Be glad, ye people of his time! The son of a high-born man will make his name for all eternity. They who would make mischief and devise enmity will suppress their mutterings through fear of him. There shall be built the walls of the prince, and those to the east shall not again be suffered to go down to Tamera. They shall beg again for water for their cattle, after their custom. And maet shall come into its own again, and wrong shall be cast out.' Whom did he foretell?" she asked.

The eyes that rose to meet Amenemhet's were hers once again. She was silent a moment, allowing him to reflect on her question. Then she asked, "Is it you he spoke of?" Amenemhet said nothing. She looked at the jewel in his hand. "I think it's you, beloved," she whispered, "and I, I am your wife and will see these things accomplished in my time also."

"If I do them," Amenemhet declared, grasping her shoulders as he spoke, "I'll do them with you. You'll be part of them and so your name shall live with mine."

Nefrytatanen's eyes clouded. She said sadly, "I think not, beloved. I think my name, if not forgotten, will be of no significance." A faint smile alighted on her lips. "I would be glad enough to see these things accomplished. I'll be glad enough—and proud—that I was your wife and, loving you, was loved by you, though my name and all memory of me be erased for all time."

"This will not be," Amenemhet said with determination. "I shall build temples and other places of great beauty, unsurpassed by any others. Deeply carved in their enduring stone, your name will be linked with mine. I'll have statues made of you. When we leave this life, we'll lie together in our burial chamber with our seals set side by side in the stone. I'll have songs in praise of you carved in granite for all to see. Those who come after us will know us both. It is one of my deepest wishes for the Two Lands to be united, peaceful, and prosperous. If we can accomplish this, I'll build a new palace wherein we'll rule together. It will be our own palace, and it will last forever."

"All this will be done," Nefrytatanen said softly. "The palace will be named Ithtawe."

Chapter Four

Amenemhet had arranged Nefrytatanen's departure so she would be well on her way before dawn lit the eastern skies. He had foreseen a restless night for her on the ship and had thought she might finally be able to sleep awhile before daylight came.

As they walked to the quay, Nefrytatanen was silent. Although she had managed to brush away some of her uneasiness during the party, her dark forebodings were steadily growing stronger. Amenemhet walked with one arm around her, and she was much tempted to beg him to delay the voyage, despite Sinuhe's reassurance. Amenemhet couldn't refuse, she knew, but she felt foolish to think of trying to explain her intuitions.

When they finally stood on the deck, Nefrytatanen's puzzling fears grew so strong she was hesitant to say good-bye. She almost feared they would not meet again. The ship was ready to leave, but Amenemhet hadn't given the order. They stood in silence delaying, for a few precious moments, their separation. Nefrytatanen decided not to tell him of the gloom that hung over her, but to tell him again of her feelings for him. If there was significance to her premonition, she wished to leave Amenemhet the sure knowledge that she loved him.

"Ameni," Nefrytatanen began so softly that only Amenemhet heard her words. She saw his eyes, filled with longing, turn down to meet hers. If she asked him to let her stay, he would agree. She thought of the reason for her leaving. Was she a ruler or a bride? Realizing this would be the question in the minds of the northern subjects, she knew she couldn't stay with Ameni. "Beloved," she began again, "I truly came to you with a sorrowing heart thinking I'd left all hopes of love behind me, but I dragged my heavy feet to more than I'd ever dreamed of. Beloved, if all the men of the world paraded past me and I had my choice of them, it would be you I'd run to. My beloved, I will love you always, whatever fates the gods may choose for us. My heart shines with love for you."

The moment held a sweetness that filled her completely. He held her tightly to him as if, in that embrace, they sealed themselves together for all time. She clung to him, locked in the strength of his arms, wanting nothing more of life. When he finally held her a little away from him to look at her face, crystal drops sparkled in the moonlight on his lashes, and she didn't know if they were his tears, hers, or theirs combined.

Amenemhet whispered, "I care no longer for the reasons this marriage was arranged. My life would be empty without you." He held her face gently between his hands and looked deep into her eyes, saying softly, "Whatever path may be ours, we will always be together. Nothing can ever truly separate us, for you take with you part of my soul."

"And I leave you mine," Nefrytatanen whispered.

He brought his lips gently to hers, in that kiss expressing all that words were never made to say. With no other words, mistrusting himself and knowing she had no will but his, he turned away and leaped to the shore, giving orders quickly for the ship to sail.

When Amenemhet knew the ship had moved into the river, he turned to watch it draw away. Nefrytatanen stood in the same place, wearing an expression that twisted his heart.

As she watched the water between them widen, she wished to leap into the Nile. Amenemhet's love would weave a water spell protecting her from crocodiles and snakes. She would swim back to him, her bewitcher.

The moon slid behind a cloud, and the sudden darkness brought all her fears vividly back.

"That's an evil omen," muttered one sailor to another. Nefrytatanen shivered and looked at the black sky until the moon returned. By then Amenemhet was too far away to see. The omen was, indeed, very bad.

When Nefrytatanen dragged herself into her compartment, she sent the serving women away. She wanted only Sira's company. The attendants passed with sympathetic looks, bidding her fair dreams as they left.

Nefrytatanen and Sira sat in silence a long while. Knowing Nefrytatanen's mood, Sira waited patiently. Finally, at Nefrytatanen's signal, Sira rose to help her take off the wedding gown, knowing all the while how deeply Nefrytatanen wished Amenemhet's hands were undressing her this night.

"The prince's love for you is great," Sira murmured as she helped Nefrytatanen with the garment's intricate folds. "He'll join you quickly."

Nefrytatanen looked at her and whispered, "If at this very moment he stood in that doorway, it wouldn't be too soon."

"Time will pass, my lady," Sira murmured. "However long it takes to drag by, the decan will pass as surely as do all other days. And think how great your joy will be when you see him once again."

Nefrytatanen smiled at Sira's sweetness. The dress had become a shimmering cloud of silver stars in the lamplight. As Sira laid it down, Nefrytatanen noticed her eyes held a wistful look that sent a pang through Nefrytatanen. She reflected that Sira would never have all she herself now possessed.

Aloud, Nefrytatanen said, "Sira, will you put on the dress for me? I would like to see how it looks on you."

Sira's eyes widened, shocked at the idea. "My lady, I cannot!" Her expression was as if such a suggestion was akin to sacrilege.

"Of course you can," Nefrytatanen replied. "I've just asked you to." Sira's eyes were bottomless blackness, and her hands trembled slightly as she lifted the gown. "Let me help you with it," Nefrytatanen offered, smiling. "Let us pretend as we did when we were children. We'll exchange places." She fell silent. Looking at Sira with a plaintive expression, Nefrytatanen added, "It would distract me for a moment, perhaps, Sira. I *asked* if you would. I don't order this."

Sira relaxed at Nefrytatanen's coaxing, her heart melting at her mistress's expression. She recalled King Mentuhotep's order that she watch Nefrytatanen the nights before the marriage so the attraction between her and Amenemhet might not prove too much for their control. Sira bit her lip. Had she known the true depth of their emotions, she mused, the king might have ordered her head sliced from her shoulders first. Sira wished she might have devised some way that they could have stayed together. Although Sira had known Nefrytatanen like Amenemhet, she hadn't realized the attraction had grown into love. Now Sira understood the fires that lay behind Nefrytatanen's eyes, and her heart was filled with regret.

Sira turned to Nefrytatanen with a warm smile and said, "Sira, will you help me with my powder?" Nefrytatanen stared at her in surprise. Sira added softly, "Make me beautiful for Ameni."

Nefrytatanen smiled slowly then assumed her role. Her imitation of Sira ordering imaginary servants about, as Sira had done that morning, sent both of them into uproarious laughter. Nefrytatanen could see that Sira's sharp eyes had missed nothing; Nefrytatanen could well imagine herself in Sira's performance. When she had carefully applied Sira's eye paint, it was her turn to stare.

Nefrytatanen bowed low and whispered, "Princess Sira, you are beautiful."

While Sira gazed wonderingly at her transformation in the mirror, Nefrytatanen realized how different life could have been if their positions had been reversed. She wondered if Sira thought of this for her eyes were misty. Nefrytatanen resolved to speak to her of a husband for, if Sira longed for someone, it would be like her to remain silent. Nefrytatanen didn't wish Sira to be lonely. She would tell Sira that arrangements might be made for her happiness.

"Princess Sira," Nefrytatanen began. Her words were halted by peculiar, muffled, struggling sounds outside. They were astounded when the compartment was suddenly filled with men carrying daggers and swords. Before they could move or speak, one man took Sira in his arms, covering her mouth. Her terrified eyes were all Nefrytatanen saw as the man dragged Sira out on the deck.

Nefrytatanen struggled and kicked and heard her captor laugh softly at her efforts. She wasted no breath on screams, realizing that if these men were in the royal compartment, the guards had already been overpowered.

Nefrytatanen was outraged. Blind with anger, she bit the hand in reach of her and stamped on a booted foot. For the slightest instant, her captor released her. But before she could take a step, he struck her.

As she fell she watched the floor coming closer and was curious that she didn't feel her body strike it. She lay for a moment wondering at this, until she could see or think no more.

Nefrytatanen became partly conscious and was dimly aware of being carried through the night over someone's shoulder like a sack of grain. She could hear a low, moaning sound. As she wondered, dazed, who could be making so forlorn a noise, she realized the sound came from her. Rough hands dumped her unceremoniously on the sand, and she lay where she had fallen, too dizzy to move. She heard herself moan again.

"Silence her!" A hoarse whisper sounded nearby, and she felt a blow that sank her into darkness.

Nefrytatanen opened her eyes slowly. A sweaty face

with red-rimmed black eyes peered at her. She tried to move, but her hands and feet were bound. She found her efforts useless.

"Where am I?" Nefrytatanen gasped. "Who are you?" He ignored her questions.

Suddenly Nefrytatanen realized she did not understand her situation. She could remember nothing. She lay quietly, trying to keep her rising panic under control, her head aching with the effort. She tried to think calmly and found she couldn't remember her own name.

"Who am I? Who am I?" She heard the fear in her voice. The black eyes looked at her with renewed interest. "I cannot remember. Who am I?" Shivering she stared at the eyes until she grew a little calmer and added more quietly, "I truly remember nothing. Please tell me who I am, at least! Please!" The eyes continued to stare with increasing curiosity.

"What does it matter what a slave's name is?" he finally muttered coldly.

Nefrytatanen considered this a moment. She didn't feel like a slave. She wondered if there were some special way a slave should feel and found she didn't know. She couldn't think at all. She decided to try again.

"It matters to me, if that's what I am," she sighed. The man turned to consult with someone out of Nefrytatanen's view. She heard him mumble that she didn't talk like a slave. His accent was coarse, and she wondered how she knew this. An impatient voice answered him.

"She's a slave of the highest station. Would a noblewoman have a personal attendant who is as stupid as the women you're used to? Fool." The voice muttered, "I don't like the smell of this whole affair. I didn't like the looks of those guards either. Now I have to contend with a slave's pestering." The voice came nearer. A booted foot prodded Nefrytatanen until she turned over to face him.

From where she lay, he seemed like a giant. He wore

a sword and a dagger, and, although he wasn't poorly dressed, he looked dusty and was unshaven. He was scowling.

"Untie her," he ordered. "She can't escape now." He watched as the other man loosened her bindings.

Nefrytatanen was in a tent of medium size. It looked to her as if it had been put up hastily and contained only the barest essentials. A shield hung on one wall. She got to her feet painfully and gently touched her red and aching wrists.

"Who am I?" she persisted. "Can't you tell me that? Where am I? How have I come to be here?"

"Be silent," he ordered. "You provoke me with your endless questions." There was a faintly military air about him, and she wondered if he'd lost his rank through some dishonorable act. He didn't behave like a peasant. He pulled back her hair which had straggled over her face.

"Don't touch me," she commanded, surprised at the authority in her voice. It didn't seem likely to her that a slave would think of speaking so, but it felt natural to her. He looked at her, surprised for a moment. Then his expression changed, and he studied her thoughtfully.

"Why not?" he inquired, in a very soft voice. His smile was menacing. "You're my property. I won you in a battle. I own you. I can touch you however I wish." He ran a finger over her cheek, and she shuddered.

"What battle?" she asked. She was far from giving up. "At least tell me my name, tell me about the battle —something!" She thought that hearing something, anything at all, might help her remember.

"I don't know your name," he replied, then commented brusquely to his companion, "If we clean her up a little, perhaps I'll find some use for her." He laughed.

She grew angry at this. She didn't think her impudence would matter now. "Who are you to decide my use?"

He looked at her in renewed surprise. "I'm Kheti,"

he said. His face broke into a smile, and he laughed with genuine humor. "You have spirit," he remarked, still laughing softly. Then his humor faded. He became quiet, reflecting on this. He observed, "You also have very poor manners for a slave."

He's getting angry, Nefrytatanen decided. His grey eyes had grown hard, and the look in them frightened her.

Kheti reached out suddenly, and grasping a handful of her robe he tore it. The garment fell around her feet; as she quickly bent to pull it up, she saw his hand move to his dagger. Seeing the warning in his eyes, she straightened up, leaving the robe in a heap on the floor. She was angry and ashamed, but too afraid to move. She stood motionless, naked before his piercing gaze.

Kheti walked slowly around her, inspecting her as though she were a horse he might or might not buy. He leaned closer to stare intently into her eyes.

"Perhaps I'll let her live to amuse myself with later," he commented.

The other man had stared at her all through this, and she realized it was a deliberate demonstration that Kheti could kill her if he liked. She wasn't sure which fate she preferred, but she remained obediently motionless until Kheti stepped away and gestured for her to pick up her robe. She quickly gathered up the material and covered herself as well as she could. It was now little more than a rag.

"Don't try to sneak away," Kheti advised. "The guards will kill you."

Then they left her alone.

Nefrytatanen stood in the same place, still holding the robe to her. She stared down at her hands. She felt the material of the robe and thought about it, hoping something familiar would prod her memory. She touched the silver lotus on her necklace, and she lifted it to study it carefully. It had a strange blue stone in it. Nothing came to her. She vowed that, if she never remembered more, she would always remember Kheti and his insulting look.

Finally she lay on a mat on the tent floor considering how she might kill Kheti should she get the opportunity. She fell asleep with these thoughts.

In another tent nearby, Kheti was laughing softly. "Rakkor, would you care to share your tent with me?" he asked. "I think you'll have to put up with my company tonight, like it or not. I'd as soon sleep with a cobra than spend the night with that one. Did you see the fury in her face?"

Rakkor grumbled about his missing blanket and rolled over to sleep.

Nefrytatanen had just opened her eyes when, without warning, Kheti walked into the tent. He looked at her in a manner that made her jump to her feet, still grasping the ragged robe around her.

"Get ready," Kheti ordered, smiling faintly. "We're almost ready to leave."

"Get what ready?" Nefrytatanen snapped. "I have nothing, not even a sip of water. And how can I go anywhere when both my hands must be occupied holding together these rags you made of my garment?" She was sure she would kill herself with her own sharp tongue, but she spoke the truth.

Kheti examined the tattered robe. He seemed amused by her this morning, and he left the tent smiling. Soon he returned carrying a water bag, a bit of meat and fruit, and a strip of cloth.

"I'm not carrying a selection of garments for women," he remarked, "although I wish I did have a proper robe for you." His eyes hinted at what he might have liked to see her wear. He added, "Perhaps you can do something with this sash." Nefrytatanen looked at the sash in dismay, and Kheti left the tent, smiling and shaking his head.

Nefrytatanen put the sash aside to wash her face and eat the food. Then she took it up and, finding that she could turn the robe and arrange it another way, she wound the sash around her waist. She was just finishing tying it when the black-eyed man she had seen the night before came in. Taking her arm roughly, he pulled her into the sun's searing heat. She stood blinking, looking around.

There were no other women. There were only men standing around, all of them staring at her. She silently observed that if Kheti had seemed no jewel he surely rose head and shoulders above these others. They seemed a treacherous gang. Fear chilled her, but she decided she must not let them know how afraid she was. She stood very straight, giving them an icy glare. One of them held a horse which Kheti motioned her to mount.

Already on his own horse, Kheti leaned close to Nefrytatanen and whispered, "You needn't be afraid of them. You're mine, and they know it. Just stay near me."

If he'd meant his words to soothe her, she didn't feel any better. Disgusted, she realized her brave show hadn't fooled him.

As they rode she observed Kheti and the way he managed the men. He was alternately tough and diplomatic with them, keeping them entirely under his control so skillfully she couldn't help but admire him. She was sure it wasn't an easy task. She found herself wondering about Kheti.

She noted they rode northeast and realized that, if she should find some means of escape, she would have to go southwest to find the threads of the tapestry of her past. She noticed, too, that they used horses for speed rather than camels for distance and stopped only when the animals needed rest. She was sure they were pursued by someone or feared they were. She concluded that someone, then, must hope she was alive, and she found comfort in this. Later it occurred to her that Kheti might merely be continually pursued, and her hopes that her abduction had caused concern somewhere grew fainter.

The hours passed slowly. They rode all day; when night approached, they stopped to set up a rough camp. Again Nefrytatanen was placed in the tent, and no one came to see her except to bring food. When she lay on the mat, she wondered how long it would be before Kheti decided to amuse himself with her. She finally slept, uneasily.

Chapter Five

Amenemhet stared at the prime minister, his face frozen in incredulous horror. Time crept by, and he said nothing, only continued to stare. Meri, not happy to be the bearer of such news, was alarmed by Amenemhet's reaction. He had expected the prince's anger, but this paralysis stunned him. Meri wondered whether Amenemhet had gone mad with shock. Finally Amenemhet's eyes focused, and he seemed to regain his faculties.

"It isn't true!" Amenemhet exclaimed. He shuddered, and Meri was embarrassed at having to watch his prince in so emotional a state.

"It may be wrong," Meri offered. "Commander Korusko is gathering soldiers to investigate."

"It must be wrong. It must!" Amenemhet seemed to speak, not to Meri but to himself. His golden eyes were alive with fury. "Tell Korusko I will also go." Amenemhet turned away, calling over his shoulder, "Tell me when he arrives. I'll be in the temple."

Amenemhet strode away. When he reached his private chambers, he found his face was wet with tears he couldn't remember shedding. He changed from his wedding garments like one sleepwalking. Tears continued to fall, spotting his clothes as he moved. Now he felt nothing; he was hollow. Yazid looked in quietly and, saying nothing, stood by the door waiting. Even when Amenemhet was dressed, his sword at his hip, they both said nothing. Amenemhet wiped his face with his hands before he went back into the hall.

The party was as gay as when Amenemhet had left. No one at the palace yet knew what he knew. He could hear the laughter and music celebrating his wedding. And Nefrytatanen might even now be dead.

Amenemhet went to the temple with dragging steps, looking at his feet as he walked through the flower petals and leaves that had been strewn through the courtyard in the afternoon. Yazid followed him silently, his grief for his master overcoming worry for Nefrytatanen. He had never seen Amenemhet look so lost.

Amenemhet knelt alone in the quiet darkness before Aset. Exhaustion drained his strength, and sorrow his senses. Through a shimmering mist, he could see Nefrytatanen again in his feverish mind, like hope held before the hopeless. He couldn't bear to think of her dead. He turned the thought aside and lit incense.

The wavering light of one small lamp cast streaks of color on the walls around him. Amenemhet could almost see Nefrytatanen standing in the shadows, and he closed his eyes, visualizing her clearly. He heard in his memory the sounds that had heralded her arrival, and he remembered how his heart had lifted when the doors had swung open. She had stood before them like a silent silver goddess. He thought life could bring no moment of greater happiness.

"Nefrytatanen," Amenemhet whispered into the emptiness of the temple. The sound ran like wine through his veins. He remembered the hush that had come over them all when she walked forward slowly and proudly, despite their stares, until she stood in the golden light beside him.

He remembered glancing at Sinuhe and noting that the priest's eyes had held a peculiar gleam. Amenemhet wondered briefly at the expression. It hadn't been respect or admiration Sinuhe's eyes had shown. Startled, Amenemhet realized it had been fear. Why should Sinuhe fear her, he wondered. Or had Sinuhe feared *for* her? Had the high priest foreseen tragedy? A shudder ran through Amenemhet's body.

He remembered the ceremony. He felt again how he had brushed lightly against Nefrytatanen and she had looked deep into his eyes with a feeling that had made him shiver. He had thought, then, of the days and nights before them. Now—perhaps they had none. Amenemhet turned this thought aside. He could see again the subtle tones of her golden skin beneath the silver gossamer of the gown. The gown had looked like moonlight captured in a lotus pond. He had leaned closer and breathed the sweet fragrance that was Nefrytatanen's alone, until he'd felt almost drunk with it.

"Master, I beg your pardon, but Korusko is returning."

Amenemhet opened his eyes and saw Yazid waiting in the doorway. They hurried out to the courtyard.

Mentuhotep and Meresank waited, together with Sinuhe and the commander of the army. Amenemhet could no longer hear the music and laughter of the party. It must have been interrupted by now.

Commander Korusko looked terribly disturbed. He was grimy with soot and blood. Fear passed through Amenemhet like a cold wind over the desert. He urged Korusko to speak, even as he dreaded what the commander would say.

"We found the ship," Korusko stared quietly.

"You found the ship!" Amenemhet could barely control his voice. "What of Nefrytatanen?"

Korusko's voice was soft with fear and horror as he described the scene. "The vessel was burned and half-sunken. All the men were dead, and we found the mutilated bodies of the women in a grove of trees nearby. I fear one of them is the Princess Nefrytatanen."

Amenemhet grasped Korusko's arms tightly and stared into his eyes, feeling that his own life was slipping away. "Are you sure it's Nefrytatanen?" he begged.

Korusko looked at him sadly. "It's very difficult to recognize any of them."

Amenemhet stared through him, shivers running through his body. Finally he turned to Yazid. "Bring my horse immediately. I'll go there now."

Yazid dashed away, shouting and waving to the guards. Amenemhet and Meresank stood quietly as Mentuhotep gave instructions to Korusko for continuing the search for whoever had done this thing.

Yazid led Sekhmet, Amenemhet's horse to him. The horse sensed the tension and danced nervously. Amenemhet leaped to Sekhmet's back and, joining the guards, raced through the gates, and then north along the river.

News of Nefrytatanen's disappearance had spread through the countryside even as the palace heard of the attack. The people, who had begun their evening in celebration, were now fearful and silent, anxious not to be noticed lest the wrath of the king and his son fall upon them.

As they rode along the curving bank of the Nile, Amenemhet cursed himself violently for suggesting that Nefrytatanen leave his side. He couldn't believe that anyone, however hardened, could bear to kill so beautiful a woman and close forever those sapphire eyes. But a lonely ship, so richly appointed, would indeed make a tempting target. If Nefrytatanen's beauty enchanted an attacker, he might take her alive. Amenemhet shuddered anew at the fate she might suffer. And he devised, in his darkest imagination, methods of execution that would make those responsible beg for death.

Already small bands of men were trying to flee the country in fear of being accused, and Mentuhotep had sent soldiers to wait in the desert around the waterholes and in the mountain passes.

In the east the hills were becoming purple as Ra began his journey for a new day. As Amenemhet neared his destination, he wondered if Nefrytatanen would see the same sunrise, and he urged Sekhmet to a faster pace.

The sun cast a soft, clear light over the grisly scene. Bodies lay in the rear of several carts gathered from

nearby farms, and they were covered with the soldiers'
cloaks. Heartsick, Amenemhet inspected each body.
Although they had been hacked and burned, he didn't
believe any of them could be Nefrytatanen. He promised each would receive a proper burial and goods
enough to take them handsomely into the afterworld.
Then he ordered the bodies covered. He turned away,
unable to look at them any longer, and silently went to
inspect the ship.

The vessel had been dragged to stand in the shallow
water. Amenemhet waded through the compartments
looking for some clue. In Nefrytatanen's cabin he saw
articles of her clothing floating in the dirty water. He
began to weep, and he turned away. When he could
speak, he instructed Korusko to salvage what he could
and have it sent to the palace.

On a small table that bobbed gently in the water lay
a silver container. Absently Amenemhet lifted the lid,
and Nefrytatanen's perfume surrounded him. He covered it quickly, unable to endure the pain it gave him.
He took the container with him and left the ship.

Korusko's men had gathered people from the surrounding countryside for questioning, and they stood,
huddled and silent, awaiting their fate. When the questioning began, Amenemhet could see them whispering
fearfully among themselves.

Finally a boy who called himself Necho summoned
enough courage to step forward and ask if they were to
be killed. Amenemhet looked at him in surprise.

"Those who did this will be punished," Amenemhet
answered slowly. "If anyone has seen them or a sign of
them, he will be rewarded for his help."

Slowly Necho's story came out. A band of men had
camped beside the river the day before, as if in waiting, not anxious to make themselves conspicuous. They
had left during the night without leaving a track. Amenemhet instructed Korusko to take Necho to the palace
so he might identify any men captured in the next several days. Necho's family was afraid until Amenemhet

gave them his ring as a token of good will and Necho's safety, a gesture they received with gratitude.

As they rode back to the palace, Amenemhet began to see that this was no commonplace robbery. Someone had calculated the attack most carefully. Someone had deliberately schemed against them. The implication was staggering. Someone hated them so much that he would risk everything to commit this crime. Whoever was behind this needed considerable wealth to pay the men responsible. This indicated someone in a high place. Amenemhet couldn't help but suspect those in his court, even in the royal household itself! He realized many, perhaps hundreds, had assisted in the hurried preparations for Nefrytatanen's voyage and knew every detail of the plans.

The sun was high when they reached the palace. Amenemhet's clothes were filthy with dust, sweat, and blood. As he marched through the entrance with Korusko and Yazid, his eyes were filled with a strange, distracted look, and he seemed startled when a waiting servant offered him a cool goblet of wine. When he'd drunk half of it, momentarily slaking his thirst, he motioned impatiently for the servant to serve the others. Then he leaned one hip against a table and wiped his forehead, leaving a grimy streak. He stared at the goblet, not really seeing it, fingering its rim absently until Mentuhotep's footsteps were heard coming toward them.

The king saw a sorry picture. Heads hanging, Korusko and Yazid both stood staring at their feet. At Mentuhotep's entrance, they began to kneel, but he motioned their dismissal. They went gravely away. Yazid limping painfully.

Amenemhet didn't change his position. Mentuhotep put his hand on his shoulder gently.

"The news is not good, my son?" Amenemhet's upraised eyes held grief. "Is she one of the dead, Ameni?" Mentuhotep asked softly.

"No. No!" Amenemhet stared at him. "I cannot believe it. I won't believe it." Amenemhet paced the small area. "It happened almost in sight of Dendera. The women lay hacked and burned almost beyond recognition, but two bodies, we think—it wasn't easy to tell— were missing. It's my conclusion that the bloody work was done so we couldn't be sure if she'd been carried away, perhaps with her woman, Sira. Mutilating the bodies can be explained no other way, unless we have a gang of madmen running loose."

Amenemhet shuddered. "There's no sight of the wedding gown, which would certainly be conspicuous whether Nefrytatanen still wore it or had changed. There was no sign of the lotus pendant I gave her before she left." He held up his own that hung from his neck. "It matches this, and she said she'd wear it always." His vehemence passed, and he again became the weary man Mentuhotep had seen when he'd first entered. "Korusko has assigned search parties," Amenemhet said, dully. "We've offered rewards. We'll make arrangements for the burial of those who were killed. I'd still be searching, but Sekhmet was exhausted. I was reeling with dizziness myself."

Mentuhotep's anger now became too much to be contained. "Who did this? Who could hate her or us enough to do so ungodly a thing?" He slammed his fist on the table, and a vase jumped. Amenemhet looked up, startled. Seldom had he seen his father lose his temper. As Amenemhet took out a small silver container and looked sadly at it, Mentuhotep vowed, "Who did this had better know he has written his sentence himself. We'll find them, Ameni. They'll pay fully."

Amenemhet was quiet in his sorrow. "It will mean nothing to me, Father, if she's dead," he said lifting the container's lid. Perfume drenched the air.

Mentuhotep recognized its scent and swore softly in his fury, but Amenemhet hadn't heard him. He sank into a nearby chair, his head back and his eyes closed.

A glance told Mentuhotep that Amenemhet had collapsed, and the king clapped his hands for help.

Servants, who had been out of sight, came running from nearby and lifted Amenemhet up to carry him to his room.

Mentuhotep picked up the perfume container which had fallen from Amenemhet's hand. He covered it carefully and followed the servants.

Now accompanied by Meresank, who had been waiting, Mentuhotep swept up the stairs, issuing orders for the continued search and for the care of Amenemhet, interspersing vivid curses on those who had done this thing.

Meresank said nothing as they walked. Her head was high, and she kept her eyes straight before her. They ran with tears.

Still dirty, the exhausted Yazid limped after them. In Amenemhet's room Yazid began, with shaking hands, to undress his master.

Mentuhotep noting Yazid's weariness, said, "Go and tend to yourself, Yazid. He'll be cared for. Come later to watch over him, if you wish, when you've rested." Mentuhotep turned to Meresank. "I'll wait awhile with him here."

"I'll wait with you," she replied promptly. "Have the others go. I'll care for him myself."

Mentuhotep motioned to the group, who left whispering, while Meresank went about her task.

Amenemhet was watched over my Mentuhotep and Meresank all afternoon until Yazid finally came, looking a bit less weary than before. Mentuhotep, having urgent business, left. Meresank went with him, asking to be called when Amenemhet awoke.

Yazid settled himself near the bed. It was not very long before Amenemhet began to stir. Yazid quickly got up to summon a guard, but Amenemhet called before he reached the door.

"Don't call them as if I were on my deathbed. I'll go downstairs." Amenemhet's feet were already on the floor.

"A thousand pardons, master, but your father said to

call if you wanted to leave here." Yazid was hurrying to stop Amenemhet, though he wasn't sure how he would accomplish this.

Amenemhet waved him away muttering, "I'll go see him myself. I'm not sick or a cripple." He dressed, wavering slightly, but when he left the room he felt steadier.

When Amenemhet entered the dining chamber, where the king and queen stared at their untouched food, they looked up, startled.

"I'm all right," Amenemhet said brusquely. Then, realizing the harshness of his tone, he added more gently, "What have you heard?" Meresank signaled for a plate for him, but he sighed, shaking his head. "I have no appetite," he said. A servant poured wine for him, and he sipped it slowly. At first it made him dizzy; but after a little more, he began to relax and felt strengthened. He looked at them more calmly.

Mentuhotep, who had been observing his son carefully, pushed away the plate and picked up his goblet. "It's the same," he sighed. "The area has again been carefully searched, and it's as you said. There's no sign of the wedding garment or the pendant. Two bodies are missing."

"There's a chance, Ameni," Meresank offered.

Hope rose in Amenemhet's breast like a small bird for her words echoed his own thoughts. "Anpu," he said softly, "may not have her yet. I'll find her. I swear it. If she's dead, they won't leave her in a nameless grave." He remembered Nefrytatanen's words when she'd predicted her name would be lost forever, and he was silent a moment, unable to speak. Finally he said, "I must turn this thing over in my mind to see what might make sense here." He drank the rest of his wine slowly and thoughtfully, and when he was finished he stood up abruptly.

"Where are you going?" asked Meresank. "Ameni, I was hoping you'd rest a little longer."

"Where is there to go? I'm all right now. Shall I lie

in bed staring at the ceiling when I have the strength to search for her?" he asked.

Seeing his face, they did nothing to stop him. He left and didn't come back for several days. When he returned, dirty and exhausted, he left the door open behind him. He said nothing, his despair clearly written on his face. Mentuhotep watched him pass and commented to Yazid, "Her parents are fortunate to be dead and spared this torment."

Yazid watched the prince for a moment then looked meaningfully at the king and trudged after Amenemhet.

Unaware of Yazid and even Mentuhotep, Amenemhet climbed the stairs silently. As he passed the door that had been Nefrytatanen's, he paused and looked into the room. His eyes traveled from the chair where she had sat, to the bed where she had slept, to the terrace where she had waited for him in the night. He said nothing, but his expression was grim as he turned away and continued slowly to his own room.

Another day passed in the same fashion. Nefrytatanen stayed near Kheti as they traveled and, although the other men often looked furtively her way, they never touched her or spoke to her. Kheti ignored her. He was occupied directing the men. Nefrytatanen often wondered what the end of this journey would bring, but she dared ask nothing.

She had begun to feel less cautious about Kheti because he seemed to have more interest in their traveling than in her, leaving her alone in the tent at night and not entering even to speak.

The following day a sandstorm was sighted in the distance. It was traveling toward them, and they made camp early to afford them shelter. Kheti sent Nefrytatanen to the tent and went to see to the safety of his men and the animals.

Nefrytatanen listened to the wind, which was beginning to rise from a low moaning to a thin shriek. The tent made peculiar noises from the pressure of the wind. Soon she heard no longer the ordinary sound of sand blowing against the fabric. Instead she heard a strange roaring noise.

She was afraid of the storm. She wondered why no one came to see to her safety, at the same time dreading what might happen if someone did. Her fears vied for prominence until Kheti came through the tent flap with a cloud of sand and the wind's shriek accompanying him. He secured the opening carefully and, after shaking off the cloak he wore, removed it. Then he turned to face her with a look that made his intentions clear.

Nefrytatanen slowly backed away, resolving she wouldn't beg but would fight with teeth and nails if she must. Terrified she glanced quickly around for something to serve as a weapon. There was nothing. There was no escape she could devise. She wouldn't consider surrender.

Observing Nefrytatanen's panic, Kheti smiled. She stared at the hand that reached to touch her hair, hypnotized by the glitter of his ring. Surely, she thought, this must be how a rabbit feels when confronted by a cobra.

Suddenly Kheti pulled Nefrytatanen to him and kissed her firmly. She squirmed to free herself. Some voice in her mind asked if this was how she would first taste love. The sounds of the storm increased, ascending to a vicious roar, distracting her attention.

Still holding Nefrytatanen tightly, Kheti was encouraged by the pause in her struggles and bent to try another kiss. As his lips touched hers, a fresh gust of wind rose above the rest of the noise and struck the tent a blow. Nefrytatanen began to struggle again. At that moment there was the sound of shouting outside.

"By Asar!" Kheti exclaimed, stepping away and listening, "We've been attacked!" Releasing Nefrytatanen, he drew his sword and rushed from the tent.

Nefrytatanen caught up his cloak and, throwing it

over her head, took a water bag and ran out into the storm.

The blowing sand was like a solid wall against her, taking away her breath with its force. She wavered in her steps but struggled on, taking a direction which led her away from the sounds of fighting.

She was thinking that, whoever the attackers were, she had no desire to meet them, and she searched for a way to conceal herself. She didn't think the attackers meant to rescue her. Had that been so, they would have advanced more cautiously to insure her safety. She concluded they must be thieves and might treat her worse than Kheti had.

Nefrytatanen knew she couldn't hope to go very far in the storm. When she found a small pile of stones she crouched behind them. They afforded some shelter from the wind and blowing sand. She hoped that if she remained motionless the sand might cover her. Then, when the fighting and the storm were over, and if she were still alive, she might not be seen.

Making herself as small as possible and grasping the precious water bag close, Nefrytatanen covered her head with Kheti's cloak, thus forming a small air pocket. Meanwhile she prayed to every divine being she could remember that she might be spared.

The furious roar of the storm blotted out the sounds of battle. When the noise of the storm finally stopped, there was only silence. Gradually she realized she was completely covered with sand. She wondered if she could hear nothing because of this. At the idea of being buried, she felt she would smother, but she pushed the feeling inside. She dared not move lest the sand sift away and reveal any part of her. She hoped that if anyone was still nearby, they wouldn't notice a new drift in sand. Nefrytatanen's limbs ached from her cramped position, but she willed herself to remain motionless, scarcely daring to breathe.

The sand gradually grew cool against her skin, and she realized night had come. She decided that whoever had been left alive after the battle must have left the camp. She had no choice but to get up since her supply of air was almost exhausted. She was beginning to grow lightheaded.

Nefrytatanen tried to rise, and her stiffened limbs collapsed. The sand rolled off with her movement. There was no one standing nearby. Although she was still half-covered with sand, she could see the sky and stars, and she gasped, hungrily taking in great breaths of air. She managed to sip a little water, but each movement was agonizing, and her hands shook with the effort. When she could endure it, she turned over on her stomach, and, rising to her hands and knees, she crawled until life slowly returned to her limbs. Finally she managed to stand.

Nefrytatanen looked around more carefully and was horrified by what she saw. Hacked and mangled bodies, sodden with their own congealing blood, lay scattered —some heaped upon others. Shadows moved outside the circle of the camp, and she knew them to be jackals kept back only by her living presence. She shuddered. The tattered tents were like banners of the dead.

She limped around a bit looking at the nearest bodies, recognizing some of Kheti's men and seeing many strangers. She decided Kheti's men had made a good account of themselves because they must surely have been outnumbered.

Nefrytatanen found herself staring at the dead eyes of one sand-caked face whose body seemed to have been trampled. Feeling sick, she quickly turned away. She wondered which, if any, was Kheti. She reasoned he must lie somewhere among his men, but she couldn't bring herself to look further. She felt pity for him and the others, whatever they had been. Jackals were waiting for their bodies, instead of proper burial. It struck her that she might have just remembered something of her past—why did she feel so strongly about a proper burial?

The thought sobered her for it turned her mind to

her own slim chance for survival. She lifted the water bag to her ear and shook it. It was almost full. Grimacing, she cautiously took a water bag from a body and filled hers to the top. She searched the body and found a dagger which she tucked into her sash. She could see no food, and the thought of searching further among the dead filled her with fresh horror.

Involuntarily Nefrytatanen straightened to her fullest height. In that moment, she resolved she wouldn't die nameless. She would know, before she left this life, what she was leaving behind.

Then Nefrytatanen turned and walked with a firm step toward the southwest, knowing only that she must travel as far as possible at night and rest during the day when the sun became too hot to walk. She put aside thinking about her loss of memory. Having resolved to stay alive, she became concerned solely with survival.

As she walked through the pale moonlit silence, her eyes glowed an eerie blue, and the creatures that roamed in the night avoided her.

When dawn began to light the skies, Nefrytatanen found a small formation of rocks in the sand. Although they offered little shadow, she lay down close beside them. Tangled thoughts raced through her mind, and she tried to sort out the recent events. Finally she gave up and stared at the brightening sand until the glare became too strong. Then she closed her eyes—sure she couldn't sleep in the heat that already seemed to sear her skin. But her body was exhausted, and she slept fitfully, moving often.

Nefrytatanen awoke when the sun was low in the sky and sipped a little water. She lay for awhile longer, fighting the desire to drink more. Finally she dragged herself to her feet and walked again, her hollow stomach aching.

Sometime before dawn, Nefrytatanen fell and slept. When she awoke, the sun was high and the heat intolerable. She drank a little water, savoring the wetness in her mouth before she swallowed. Its taste left an almost irresistible temptation she struggled with and overcame. There was too little water left. She decided to walk on, though the sun was high, for she'd wasted time sleeping at night. She was newly grateful that Kheti had given her boots for riding. The sand's heat crept through their bottoms, but walking barefoot would have crippled her.

Nefrytatanen had no idea how far she had walked. She didn't know for sure if she continued in the right direction because she walked both in daylight and at night, and she couldn't read the stars. She lived in an endless agony of aching thirst and anguished limbs. When the water bag was empty, she carried it for a time—as if it were an amulet, as if in refusing to drop it she could refuse to acknowledge its emptiness. Hunger no longer troubled her.

She no longer noticed her skin was raw with burns. How many times she fell and dragged herself to her feet she couldn't count. How long she remained down she didn't know. She was dimly aware that each time was longer than the time before it. She knew she was sometimes unconscious. The swirling sands that lay ahead seemed endless.

Oasis after shimmering oasis appeared. After the first few joyful times she'd run toward them she no longer bothered, knowing them illusions. Her lips were cracked and swollen, but the pain was too trifling to notice. Her entire body, once smooth and translucently golden, had peeled and blistered and peeled again. Sand had become imbedded in the open wounds, and she began to believe she was a person made of sand—that she was not flesh and blood—but part of the desert. She vaguely recognized the strange sound she heard as her own mad laughter, and a small, still rational, part of her mind forced her to stop, to control herself, aghast at her state.

For a time she began to wonder if life was worth fighting for. Death would be relief from struggle. She thought of the bodies of Kheti's men waiting for the jackals, of herself moldering on these sands while the jackals and vultures tore at her flesh. She shuddered and dragged her feet forward.

She fell and lay gasping. In that moment she saw with sudden, sharp clarity her desperate loneliness. It was abysmal. It stretched as far as time. It was as high and as deep as forever. She was suspended in the midst of it. She raised herself on one arm and, desperate to confirm her being, she turned to look at the tracks she'd made. For a moment part of her pitied the poor creature who walked so unsteadily with wavering steps, who fell and crawled. She watched as the wind silently erased the marks of her passing. Her soul was filled with desolation. She lay on her face on the searing sand, the pain of her face merging with the pain of her body and soul. Had she tears, she would not have wept, for her grief was beyond weeping over.

Finally, knowing she could no longer stand, Nefrytatanen gathered her rags together and drew herself up until she knelt as straight as strength permitted, so those she addressed might see her in some semblance of dignity. She shut her eyes.

Not knowing she did this out of long habit, she lifted her arms toward the sun in the gesture of a child reaching for a loving parent—as was the custom of her people in prayer.

Nefrytatanen's voice was gone, and her moving lips were soundless as she spoke. "Oh divine beings, whose presence I feel near, my strength is gone. I can go no farther. If it is in this manner I must pass from this life, then so it must be. I know not who I am or what I have done with my life. If I'm evil, I cannot say, and now it is perhaps too late to seek pardon, if indeed pardon be necessary . . ."

She reflected for a moment on the fast approaching time when she would meet Asar, and she wondered how she would answer his questions if she had no memory. Perhaps he'd consult the records of Tehuti for her deeds.

Nefrytatanen looked into the endless blue of the sky

and begged, "Look upon this poor, mindless creature who now faces eternity, and if I deserve any favor, ease my suffering with the granting of but one request. If anyone would mourn for me, I beg that he not learn how I died. Spare him this pain." Her lips faltered. She wondered if she presumed, if anyone would care how she died. She sank from her knees and sat staring at the small grains of sand that slid with her movements.

After she had sat for a time, she gradually began to feel hope again. Slowly some strength seemed to seep back into her body. She was surprised to find in herself a renewed wish to struggle on. She was even more surprised when she dragged herself to her feet and began moving feebly forward.

Nefrytatanen managed to go a little farther, to the crest of the hill on which she'd fallen, and she stood, wavering, looking below. To her amazement, her blurring vision revealed swaying palms and the sparkle of water.

She stared for a moment before she decided it was yet another illusion, and she wondered if this fancy of her mind was, perhaps, the memory of a place she'd seen before. She savored the sight, thinking it might be a link with her past, sure it was the last she would see of any green and living things. Perhaps this was the final mercy the gods would show her in this life, thus making her death a little easier. She tried to absorb the beauty of the illusion, hoping it would last for the eternity facing her.

Nefrytatanen's loneliness struck at her again, almost a physical blow. She looked bitterly at her precious illusion. She could almost smell the trees and taste the coolness of the water.

She hadn't allowed herself, until now, to give full freedom to such longings, knowing she would become mesmerized by the dream and never rise to walk. Now she was convinced she would go no farther, and she allowed the luxury of her imaginings to wash over her. How real it seemed! She could smell the water, almost feel it running coolly through her fingers. She believed she was mad in her last living moments, but her pounding heart and increasing excitement urged her to run toward the dream.

What harm is there in it, she thought. Where else can I go? If I must die now, why spend my last moments groveling in the sand? If I see a dream, let me die as I run to it.

Nefrytatanen's efforts at running were but a pitiful staggering, not much faster than she had crawled, but she saw the trees coming nearer, and she saw the glimmer of a pool. She imagined tents set in the shade, and people moving among them. The madness that filled her couldn't be resisted. With strength she hadn't known she still possessed, she struggled on toward them.

"A ghost!" The trembling servant pointed. "A ghost of the desert, Drankma!"

Drankma turned heavily in the chair and looked with incredulous eyes as a small figure stumbled down a sand hill toward them. He leaped to his feet and ran in its direction, surprisingly swift for a man his size. As he reached it, it stumbled and fell in a heap at his feet. He knelt and turning it over, saw the burned and fevered face of a woman.

"You're a fool, Kassim," he muttered and took her up in his arms to hurry to his tent. He lay her on the pillows of his own bed and roared at Kassim, who had followed wringing his hands, "Oils! Cloths! Water! Move, you fool, move!" Kassim ran out and returned in a moment with what Drankma had ordered.

Drankma touched a dampened cloth to Nefrytatanen's lips, and she licked them feebly. He lifted her head on his arm so she might drink and allowed her a small sip. Then he tore away the shredded cloth she wore and cleansed her burns of the coating of sand. She was too deeply unconscious to do more than moan softly. He wrapped her from her head to toe in cloths soaked in cool oils and let her sleep.

For a day and a night Drankma kept watch, send-

ing his servant for more oils and fresh cloths and
changing them, letting Nefrytatanen sip a little fruit
juice when she could. Drankma was reeling with sleeplessness when her eyes fluttered and opened. Her lips
moved, but she couldn't speak.

"Don't try," Drankma said gently.

Nefrytatanen saw brown eyes looking at her, kindly.
She did not understand his language.

"Who are you?" she finally managed to whisper.

In her own language, Drankma said, "Thank the
gods you'll live. You came from the desert half-dead,
but you're safe now. I'm Drankma. Sleep and don't be
afraid." His voice was gentle and soothing.

Nefrytatanen was very tired and needed no further
urging to close her eyes. She slept immediately.

When she awakened, finally refreshed, she had the
clear memory of a dream in which eyes, filled with love
and sorrow, looked at her. They were strange eyes,
tilted and golden in color, but she couldn't see the rest
of the face. She held the memory close to her, wondering.

When Drankma saw she was awake, he came to her
at once. "You've slept long," he said. "It's almost night,
but after what happened to you, you need much rest."

"You've been very kind to me," she said with
genuine gratitude. She managed to sit up slowly.

"You may feel better," Drankma cautioned, "but
don't try to stand. You're still weak." He was silent a
moment, watching her. Then he said gently, "Now,
Lotus Eyes, tell me how you came to me from the
desert. Tell me who you are."

Nefrytatanen studied him a moment. He wore a
strange look. "I cannot tell you who I am," she answered. "I wish I knew myself. I cannot remember.
I awoke, with all my memory gone, in the hands of a
rough-looking band of men in the desert." Drankma's
eyes widened slightly at this. "The leader told me I was
his slave, captured in a battle. What battle I cannot
say." She told Drankma what she could remember,

omitting Kheti's name, trying to appear a little simple-minded because she felt something—a slyness perhaps—about this Drankma that made her distrust him, although he'd saved her life.

When she was finished, he was silent a moment. Finally he said, "Perhaps your memory will return in time. In the meanwhile you must travel with us. Perhaps at the next village we'll hear news and find a way to discover who you are."

"You're very kind to me," she said humbly, "for as my captor said, I am but a slave."

"Perhaps he lied," Drankma replied peering at her again.

Although she was startled that he echoed aloud what she had privately thought, she merely glanced down in a dejected attitude.

"That may be," she said looking at him again, "but I don't know. If I could only remember something, anything! It's a fearful thing to know nothing of your past, not even your own name."

Drankma smiled and patted her hand. "You may remember later. In the meantime, have no fear. We're your friends." He rose to leave. "Until we know your name, we'll call you Lotus, and you can stay with us."

Nefrytatanen thanked Drankma enthusiastically several times. When he was gone, she thought about him carefully. There was a look in his eyes that made her cautious. He'd seemed almost relieved that she had no memory. Was it possible he knew her and pretended not to? Her heart leaped at the thought. He acted suspiciously in any case, she decided.

She hadn't mentioned her dream to him, feeling that it was private. She was convinced that those strange, golden eyes belonged to someone real. If he lived, he must be searching for her.

After she'd laid down for the night, she continued to think of the eyes, and she dreamed of them again. They were veiled by a silver web, and a rainbow of colors sparkled from a gem she couldn't see. When she awakened in the morning, the dream was still vivid.

Nefrytatanen felt much stronger and was able to stand with only a slight weakness, which faded slowly. Her skin, she observed, was almost healed and firm again, although it was no longer golden. She had the complexion of the sand-dwellers and could easily be mistaken for one of them, except for her eyes. They were startling in contrast to her brown face.

Drankma's wife or serving woman—Nefrytatanen couldn't know which, for she didn't understand her—gave her a robe. It was of heavy, coarse cloth and had a hood that would shade her effectively from the sun. The woman acted as if she was uncertain of Nefrytatanen's status, and Nefrytatanen didn't understand it herself. Although she had been told she was a slave, Drankma treated her more as if she was his guest. She decided to take advantage of his attitude.

When she had first awakened, she had looked out of the tent and decided she didn't much care for the tasks she saw the women of the camp laboring at, although there were few enough women to do them. It seemed to Nefrytatanen that the women were younger than first impressions gave, and she thought their lives must be very hard for them to age so quickly. She had no wish to share their lot. If she could avoid it, she would.

She had just finished dressing when Drankma came. He held out his closed hand to her.

"There was nothing left of your garments to save," he said, "but you wore this around your neck." He opened his hand, and Nefrytatanen's heart leaped. As she looked at the necklace, something stirred in her memory, but, like the shadow of a cloud passing the sun, the memory escaped before she could grasp its substance. Drankma dropped the necklace into her hand. "It would seem valuable," he commented. "Does it look familiar to you?"

She stared at it with so pitious a look he was moved. Nefrytatanen murmured, "I don't know why, but I feel it's important to me for some reason other than its value."

As Drankma fastened the chain around her neck, another shadow moved in her mind. He was saying, "Perhaps wearing this will help you remember something later."

Nefrytatanen touched the silver lotus, and a sudden, inexplicably exciting sensation rushed over her. "I must wear it," she exclaimed, her eyes wide. "I cannot lose it!"

"You won't lose it," Drankma said comfortingly. "Have no fear of that. The fastening is very good and won't open of its own accord."

When Drankma left, Nefrytatanen sat down and looked at the pendant for a long time, wondering at the strange feelings the touch of it stirred in her.

As the day wore on, Nefrytatanen found she had nothing to do. No one spoke to her and she wondered if they didn't understand her language or if they had been told not to speak. When she met Drankma from time to time, he said nothing of importance but asked her many sudden questions, as if testing her memory. Whoever these people were, decided Nefrytatanen, their manner was somehow furtive. They carried weapons, but she was sure they needed them in the desert. Although they appeared to go about normal daily activities, they had an air of expectancy that made questions arise in her mind. She asked Drankma nothing. She said as little as possible, keeping deliberately simple. She didn't know with whom she dealt, and she decided she would prefer that they underestimated her intelligence. She didn't know why she harbored such suspicions. She knew only that caution harmed nothing.

The next day, after the noon meal when the sun was high, Nefrytatanen went into the tent, pretending she wished to nap. She had become familiar enough with her surroundings, and she wished to be left alone to think. She closed her eyes and lay quietly, pretending

to sleep. After some time she did sleep, and again she
dreamed.

The dream was about a voyage on a ship with a great
red and gold sail unfurled above her. The ship was
sumptuous, and she commanded those who sailed with
her. The dream was pleasant but held an air of uncertainty, as though she was unsure what her destination
held.

When she awoke, she lay quietly thinking about the
dream and wondering if it revealed something of the
riddle of her past. Eyes closed as she mused, she eventually became aware of voices outside the tent speaking
in her own tongue. One of the speakers had a heavy
accent. It was difficult to understand them, but she
caught a little of it. They spoke softly and rapidly.
She strained to hear, for it seemed they spoke of her.

One voice, whispering in cultured accents, seemed
vaguely familiar. It repeatedly referred to "she" in what
seemed to be many questions. Nefrytatanen caught a
bit of a report that "he" was searching everywhere.
"He" had spies at all the watering places and passes
and was searching whole villages house by house. The
people were terrified of his wrath. The voice mentioned
her necklace, and she grasped it tightly, her heart
pounding. The voices moved farther from the tent, and
she was unable to hear more.

Nefrytatanen marveled at what she'd learned, thinking again of her dream and the faceless golden eyes.
With their vision before her, she resolved to continue
playing her role even more carefully. Although Drankma had acted openly, thus far, as if he meant her no
harm, she doubly distrusted him after what she had
heard.

The now indistinguishable murmur of the voices
came to an abrupt end, and Nefrytatanen lay quickly
back on her pillows feigning sleep. It was well she did
because she heard the flap of the tent pulled softly aside
for a moment, then let fall back in place. She lay

breathing softly, moving no muscle, until long after she was sure he'd left.

Nefrytatanen relaxed and thought about the bits of conversation she'd heard. Whoever was causing so much turmoil with his search seemed to have armies of men and endless wealth at his disposal. Who would have such power? Perhaps a noble—even the king? Her mouth fell open at this idea. Why would someone in so high a place search so zealously for a slave? Perhaps she wasn't a slave. Could she possibly be a member of an important family? Surely she was no favored concubine because she knew, from her panic at Kheti's advances, that she must be as yet untouched.

The voices she had heard had mentioned that people were in terror of this man who searched every house. He must be exceedingly powerful, she decided, and obviously most determined. She thought of the eyes in her dream and concluded they might very well have belonged to such a man. She trembled, thinking of those vividly glowing eyes and hoped he did search for her, whatever her status.

Nefrytatanen was a prisoner here and wondered who she preferred as her captor, Drankma with his oily words and peering eyes, or Kheti, who was at least direct. With some intuition, she decided that it would be easier to manage a man who hungered for your body than one who schemed over you as if you were an object.

She began to plot how she might escape Drankma. She had no intention of going back to the desert alone, if she could avoid it. She resolved she would find a means of discovering her past. She knew Drankma had no intention of helping her.

The next day passed without incident, and Nefrytatanen continued playing her part. Two more days passed in the same fashion. When she was alone, her publicly blank expression changed to concentration. She was trying to remember, and her head ached with the effort.

Long after the rest of the camp was sleeping, Nefry-tatanen lay awake, endeavoring to drag some small morsel from her mind in the hope of building on it. Suddenly she heard the beat of hooves racing into camp. No one had left the camp at night so she decided the rider must be an outsider. If he could arrive by horse at such a pace, they couldn't be far from a settlement. She wondered if she could steal an animal and escape into the direction from which he'd come.

Her fancies were interrupted by voices not far from her tent. She heard clearly a speaker of her own language. His voice was rising gradually in anger, and, at its unguarded sound, the obscuring veil swept from her mind.

She knew him. Once she recognized him, she knew his place. Once she remembered this, she began to realize her own place. As shock after shock of memory swept over her, each memory falling into its proper order and contributing to the next, a fury such as she had never known assailed her, growing until she almost writhed with anger.

Sinuhe! Sinuhe, the high priest, who had bid her a fair journey and had brushed aside her premonition with honeyed words. It was he who had taken her from Amenemhet. Sinuhe, also behind the fate of Sira, who must surely be dead. The despicable creature stood just outside the tent and was telling someone to put her to death.

From Nefrytatanen's almost uncontainable fury was born a calm like that of a lioness watching her prey, too cunning to allow her excitement to betray her. Nefry-tatanen listened as the hated voice ordered her death, and she resolved to make sure of his.

"I'm surrounded by fools!" Sinuhe said. "They take her maid for her and don't know who she is."

He was silent a moment, and Nefrytatanen could picture him tapping his teeth with a fingernail as he considered the matter. As she made this small observation, she rejoiced in her new-found memory.

Sinhue began to speak again, but more softly. He seemed to consider his decision. "She truly knows nothing, Drankma? Nothing at all? We shall soon see. If she is as you say, you'll continue to hold her here awhile longer."

"But I'm afraid!" Drankma's voice was indeed flooded with fear, and Nefrytatanen smiled without humor. "What if he finds us?"

"He won't. If I thought his eyes turned in this direction, I wouldn't leave her here with an ass like you. She's far too valuable for me to risk." Sinuhe sounded calmer now. "You said she sleeps? Let me see her myself. I can trust none of you. I must take the risk and be sure it's not a servant you hold here."

As Sinuhe spoke, Nefrytatanen lay quickly on her mat, and when they entered the tent she tried to look as if she had been startled from sleep.

"Drankma," she asked, "is something wrong?" She stared at Sinuhe as if he were a stranger. "Who is this man, Drankma?" she asked, pulling her blanket up modestly.

Sinuhe peered at her and turned to Drankma. "She isn't the one I search for," Sinuhe said while Nefrytatanen continued to stare at him blankly. "I'm sorry to have disturbed you from your slumber," he said politely as they left.

Once they were outside, Nefrytatanen strained her ears because Sinuhe spoke very softly, instructing Drankma to continue holding her. He followed this with a list of dire threats to be carried out if Drankma failed. She could imagine Drankma's terror and almost laughed. Sinuhe would keep her alive to use as a last threat in dealing with Amenemhet.

Nefrytatanen fell asleep that night smiling because she contemplated a variety of penalties for Sinuhe.

The sun had barely begun to light the horizon, casting a faint pallor in the tent, when Nefrytatanen was awakened by another voice nearby. It was Drankma and he sounded furious.

"Those crafty river people are like the golden snakes they wear as ornaments. Snakes are fitting for their seals." Drankma spat the words contemptuously. "We'll bargain with the others for her. We'll take their gold, be rid of her, and disappear into the desert."

Nefrytatanen heard another rider leave the camp. He rode fast. She wondered to whom Drankma had now decided to pass her. She could sleep no more. Instead, she lay thinking grimly of her circumstances.

Nefrytatanen's thoughts turned again to Amenemhet, and she grieved for his pain. Silently she spoke to him—hoping Tehuti would feel compassion and carry her message to him.

"I long for you, beloved. My heart is filled with tears as I await your coming. Gladly would I go back into the desert if I might find you waiting for me. Until we are together, beloved, Ra has left the skies empty above me."

When Drankma came to Nefrytatanen in the morning, he explained that the visitor had been someone who had thought she was his slave. He'd been mistaken. She forced herself to be appropriately disappointed but noted that Drankma had apparently not slept at all. His eyes looked tired and revealed both anger and fear.

Life continued in the camp for the next several days much as it had before Sinuhe's visit. Nefrytatanen could find no way to leave the place without detection. It seemed, however, that under the surface of normal activities, everyone was quietly packing, preparing to leave quickly. Casually she asked Drankma how long they'd stay until they moved on to a village. As casually, he answered that he was undecided. She asked nothing else.

It was far more difficult to play at being Lotus now, but Nefrytatanen found the strength to do it. During the nights, when she was alone and waiting for sleep, she thought of Amenemhet. She felt sick thinking of his torment. Sometimes she wept for him, taking care to be silent as her tears flowed for she knew she was watched constantly. She touched her necklace, remembering how he had held her close when he had given it to her, and she wondered if she would ever have those arms around her again. She thought of Sira playfully taking her place and surely giving her life. Nefrytatanen stared into the darkness and mourned for her friend.

During the days she could see that Drankma's fear of both Sinuhe and Amenemhet was so great he couldn't fully conceal it. He seemed to be holding his breath waiting for salvation. She soon learned what form his salvation was to take.

One morning they again had visitors. Nefrytatanen had learned caution, and she looked carefully around a corner when she heard them ride into camp. She almost fainted with relief to see Ankhneferu, one of her own priests from Tamehu, riding with an armed escort. It was well she restrained her joy and didn't run out openly to greet them because she then saw him pay Drankma in gold for her and promised to keep their bargain a secret.

Her own priest had plotted against her. Nefrytatanen was weak with shock. How many others were tangled in this evil? She could believe in no one except Amenemhet. She resolved she would continue to act as if she remembered nothing, concluding that memory would mean instant death. Perhaps she could still buy a little time.

When Drankma brought her to Ankhneferu, he told her only that he had a surprise for her, someone to help her. She went docilely and met Ankhneferu with so blank a look she could see he was shocked.

"You remember nothing of your past? Nothing at all?" Ankhneferu looked at her with the stare of a cobra.

"Nothing," she said sadly.

Hesitantly he said, "I can tell you by your features you're of my land."

She thought she would see where his land was at her

first opportunity. Allowing some hope to creep into her voice, she murmured, "Do you truly think so?"

He smiled encouragingly. "I'll take you back with me. Perhaps we can find your past."

Although it was most disgusting to her and she could well imagine the triumph he must feel. Nefrytatanen sank to her knees and kissed his hand humbly, thinking it a proper gesture for Lotus facing a superior. She forced herself to keep her eyes downcast as she rose, because she dared not let him see them.

Ankhneferu said gently, "Come, Lotus, and gather your belongings, if you have any. We'll leave now."

With tears of anger they mistook for joy, she said, "I have nothing but that which Drankma has given me. Even what I wear is his." She turned to Drankma with uncertainty, as if he might demand the robe back and send her away naked.

Drankma said quickly, "Keep it, Lotus, and remember only that you have a life to discover." She reflected on his cruelty—telling her of life when he knew he was probably sending her to death.

As Ankhneferu led her away, she called back to Drankma, "May you be properly rewarded for what you've done for me!" Silently Nefrytatanen prayed the gods would reward him properly in the afterlife, if she were unable to do so in this one.

During the journey Ankhneferu said little to Nefrytatanen, other than that they would stop for water and food at a small village. No one seemed to watch her very carefully, she noticed, and she decided they must be confident of her empty head. To reinforce that confidence she frequently mentioned her gratitude for their help. She thought Ankhneferu must be amazed to see how far his queen had fallen, but he said nothing, only looking solemn as he rode. She thought his solemnity fitting: it was a solemn deed to kill his queen.

By the time the sun had nearly completed its journey, they approached the oasis Ankhneferu had mentioned. Nefrytatanen realized that he must have decided to wait before killing her. If he hadn't done it before reaching the village, he must wish to have a full day's traveling between other people and the spot where she would be murdered. She reasoned he must not want to kill her before the eyes of the people of this village, and she decided she must somehow escape that very night.

When Ankhneferu commented that she looked tired and feverish, Nefrytatanen knew he spoke the truth. The fever was from her thoughts of escape and her weariness from the endless plots that swirled around her. She knew that, even if the villagers recognized her under the hooded robe, they wouldn't be able to help her. She hoped only to steal a horse or a camel from the village. Enough blood had been shed already, and she wished to bring no reprisals on innocent people. She resolved not to approach anyone in the village unless she could see no other possible solution.

As Ankhneferu arranged for their night's lodging, the group milled about in the road waiting for his bargaining to be concluded. Nefrytatanen had so convinced them of her harmlessness that they paid her little attention. She dismounted, and, while she appeared to be gazing at the fading light, she studied the village carefully. Not only did she wish to acquaint herself as much as possible with the situation and possible use of the few buildings, but she was examining the place to discover where a horse or a camel might be found. She didn't intend to be in Ankhneferu's hands when morning came.

Only a slight stiffening of Nefrytatanen's body was noticeable—had anyone been watching—when she saw Kheti walking toward her leading a horse in the dusty road. For a moment, she was shocked. Then she decided he might be her only chance. The prospects of the village seemed bleak.

Nefrytatanen wandered a few steps from the group in Kheti's direction and dropped the hood of her robe. She smiled her most beguiling smile at him. He stopped and stared. Noticing, then, the gesture that she carefully concealed from the view of the others, he resumed walking as if unconcerned with her. She strolled casually toward him and, meeting him, admired his horse, stroking the velvet muzzle in genuine appreciation.

"Please take me away from these people," Nefrytatanen whispered quickly. "They seem to know me and wish me harm." Kheti looked at her speculatively, both his interest in her and his curiosity aroused. "Please, Kheti," she begged. "If you won me, will you not claim your property?" She looked at him from beneath her lashes and didn't drop her eyes when she saw the light that grew in his.

Kheti seemed to be considering Nefrytatanen's story most carefully, and when he glanced at the guards, he startled her with the glow of hatred in his eyes.

He smiled at her and whispered, "I'm ready to leave this place. Can you stay in the road while I get my other horse?" She saw him coldly eye the soldiers.

"I'll manage it somehow," she promised. "I must."

"When I come back, pretend to comment again on the horse. Get on him quickly and ride away. Don't wait for me." He turned from her and continued on his way around a building without apparent haste.

Nefrytatanen stood in the road trying to look as aimless as before, though she thought she must shine with excitement. Ankhneferu appeared and began talking to the others. He glanced at her, and, content with her behavior turned his attention to the guards. Nefrytatanen's heart pounded. If only Kheti would be fast enough! She had no idea how she might delay Ankhneferu if he insisted on going inside the building.

Finally Kheti came around the corner. This time he was riding his horse, and he held the reins of another horse which paced behind him. They plodded slowly toward Nefrytatanen. She hailed him again, as if to comment on the new horse, and Kheti stopped near her. She moved toward the second horse. She seemed to stroke his muzzle, but she was gathering the reins in her hand. She snatched them suddenly from Kheti's purposely loose fingers, leaped on the horse and, without waiting for Kheti or stopping to notice Ankhneferu's reaction, Nefrytatanen whipped the animal into a burst of speed that surprised even her.

Kheti was slightly behind her as they raced away. She could hear a commotion in the village, but she didn't look back. She bent low on the horse's neck and urged him to greater speed. She smiled at what Ankhneferu must be thinking. She laughed aloud then, getting some of the horse's mane in her mouth and not minding at all. Now neither Ankhneferu nor Sinuhe would know where she was. What turmoil it would cause! She laughed again.

Nefrytatanen let Kheti move ahead of her and followed him. Night was coming fast, and she hoped that, with the lead they had gotten, they would be lost to Ankhneferu. He would have to wait until morning to search for them, and their tracks would be hidden by the moving sands. It was a relief to recall that Kheti was used to desert travel. Nefrytatanen trusted his skill. He would save them.

Chapter Six

Although it was the middle of the night when Yazid came to awaken him, Amenemhet wasn't sleeping. Yazid held back his tears, leaving the task of telling Amenemhet to the unfortunate Meri. Amenemhet rose quickly, wondering what disaster had now befallen them. Yazid led him to the bedchamber of Mentuhotep and Meresank. Before the door was opened, a finger traced an icy path over Amenemhet's heart.

Mentuhotep lay sprawled on the floor; Meresank lay across the bed. Amenemhet could say nothing. For several moments he stared at them feeling nothing at all. This can't be so, he was thinking. It cannot be!

Beside him, Meri said, "Sire, I believe they've been poisoned, but the physician has not yet seen them." Meri knew of nothing more he could say to his new king, who stood as if he had been turned to stone.

Without moving, Amenemhet said softly, "Leave me." When he was alone, he stood in the same place for a long time. Pain had begun to creep into the numbness of his mind, growing slowly into an anguish threatening his sanity. He dragged his eyes from the bodies and struggled to gather his wits. Dulled by grief, Amenemhet looked around the room for traces of the killer. Whoever had done it had taken away the poisoned cups. Knowing his father, Amenemhet was sure the poison had taken instant effect. Otherwise the murderer, too, would lie there dead. Menthuhotep's position indicated that he might have made an effort to attack the traitor and failed. Imagining it, Amenemhet fought his tears.

Mentuhotep's body was still warm when Amenemhet lifted him up to lay him next to Meresank. Amenemhet swallowed the lump that grew in his throat as he arranged them in a more peaceful and dignified position. He didn't wish them to be gaped at by the servants who would come to bear them away.

Amenemhet sat on the edge of the bed and touched Meresank's soft hair. Her body seemed to nestle close to Mentuhotep's side, as she always had in life. Her generous smile, thought Amenemhet, would be seen no more by the living. An emptiness was left in the world by the loss of such a smile and the warmth behind it.

He looked at Mentuhotep but couldn't bear to touch him again. Mentuhotep looked as regal in his sudden death as he had in life. His closed eyes were like those of a hawk feigning sleep. Surely they would open and look at Amenemhet again any moment, and Mentuhotep would smile at him. Amenemhet recalled the night before the wedding when they had sat on the dais step talking about the kingdom, and Amenemhet had felt as if the spirits of other kings were present. Now his father would be among the invisible spirits who whispered in the chamber's drafts. He put his face in his hands and wept silently.

Finally Amenemhet wiped away his tears and stood up. He turned again to look at the bodies, gold fires rising in his eyes.

"You, my father, spoke of judgment for Nefrytatanen's kidnapping," Amenemhet said softly. "Whoever did this to you will pay as you promised." He was silent again as he thought of the penalty. It wasn't enough. He wished the murderer had more than one life and that each life could be taken from him one by one in the same way.

Amenemhet opened the door and left, closing it very softly behind him as if a noise would disturb his parents in their slumber. In the hall he turned to Yazid with a

look on his face that terrified the slave. Yazid felt that
Amenemhet was capable of wringing revenge from
him, and involuntarily he stepped back a little.

"First they take Nefrytatanen from me," said Amenemhet loudly. "Then they kill my father and mother.
What more can they do to me? What is left?" he ended
in despair.

Yazid saw the tear stains and was no longer afraid.
He said quietly, "Your own life, sire, and Tamera."

Amenemhet stared at Yazid, too submerged in grief
to swim to its surface until some moments had passed.
He turned without a word and went to his room, where
he took his dagger from the place he kept it and
buckled it at his side. He turned to Yazid and Korusko,
who had followed.

"They shall have neither my life nor Tamera. I swear
it," Amenemhet said. He thought a moment then
added softly, "No drop of liquid, no morsel of food
shall pass my lips until it has been tasted by another
first. Make this fact widely known. My chamber will be
guarded day and night. I'll go nowhere without an
armed guard who will have standing orders to kill at
the slightest hint of a threat against me. We've been
lax regarding such matters, but never before has such
a thing happened. My father and mother thought they
were loved—as well they deserved to be. Someone
doesn't love us, and I'll find out who it is. Korusko,
you'll chose my guards carefully, keeping it in mind
that should a traitor strike at me from among them,
your life hangs in the balance."

Korusko nodded and turned away. He didn't leave
the room but stood in the doorway, hand on his sword,
shouting orders into the hall. Sinuhe approached and
stared at Korusko, flinching slightly at the shouting.
Korusko didn't admit him but turned to glance at
Amenemhet for approval. Then Korusko stepped aside,
but he never fully took his attention from the priest.

Sinuhe stopped just inside the door, bowed, and

asked what the disturbance was. Amenemhet didn't answer but looked at him appraisingly a moment.

"Ask Meri," Amenemhet finally said and turned away. Sinuhe dared ask no more but left with Korusko still staring at him coldly.

Amenemhet stood looking out the window opening until the guards arrived. He watched them silently with hard eyes, as Korusko gave them their orders. Several were placed at the doors and another group was dispatched to stand outside the window openings. Several of them, apparently aware of the night's events, had watery eyes.

Korusko knew Amenemhet was angry that he needed such guards for this confirmed that he was hunted. He was also angry that he would have no more privacy in anything he did. When all were stationed in their respective places, Korusko carefully searched the rooms himself. At last he departed.

Amenemhet sank slowly to his bed, telling Yazid to quench the lamp and leave him. For long hours he lay awake, filled alternately with grief and emptiness.

While Mentuhotep and Meresank's bodies were being prepared for burial—a process that took many weeks—Amenemhet repeatedly thought of things he wished to tell them, and on his way to find them, he would realize they were no longer there. Then he would turn silently and go back to where he had started from. Amenemhet would often turn to speak to Mentuhotep or Meresank and find another standing there. Often he reflected on his childhood and the years he'd grown to manhood, and he was doubly grieved by the memories they had held.

Amenemhet remembered vividly only a few years ago when Mentuhotep had sent him on his first official mission with the honorary title of prime minister. Was it only a few years ago, Amenemhet wondered? Three years that seemed like three thousand years. Although he'd been expecting to be sent soon on some task or other, he had been proud to be sent to select the stones for his parents' sarcophagus covers. It was a serious responsibility and not an easy task, but he and the many men who had gone with him on the journey had finally found the stones and triumphantly brought them to Wast. Amenemhet had been proud that no man under his command had been lost or injured. He remembered Mentuhotep and Meresank listening happily when he had recounted his adventures. They had commented then that he would one day be a great king, and he had glowed with pride at their praise. They hadn't guessed how soon they would use the coffin lids.

Although Amenemhet had been officially crowned as a child upon the death of his brother, even as his brother had been crowned at birth—as was the custom with the first heir—now nobles and their wives trickled into Wast to visit the palace and renew their pledge of loyalty to Amenemhet. He wondered if one of them, overly ambitious in his province, were behind the crimes.

Amenemhet received his visitors with formal courtesy and spoke little, not trusting his voice. He would weep before none of them.

The nobles went away, remarking among themselves on the king's pallor and agreeing that he was a man of dignity grown to an imposing presence.

The ladies privately decided that their new king was a man of considerable personal magnetism, and they speculated on the extent of his grief for Nefrytatanen, wondering if it was possible to attract his favor. Such potential passion as they saw in him was, they thought, wasted on grief. Amenemhet had appeared unmoved by their charms, and they had left disappointed.

On the day of the funeral, as Amenemhet dressed, he realized he must watch the wrapped bodies placed in their coffins and lead the procession to the family tomb. He thought, too, of the intimate part he must play in the ritual. His blood ran cold.

Although he dressed in white to signify his joy for

his parents' entrance to the afterlife, there was no joy in his heart. He firmly believed in an afterlife, although unsure it was as the priests described it, but he felt smothered by grief.

When the dreaded hour came at last, the escort of soldiers closed around Amenemhet, and he straightened his back and lifted his head to perform this duty with dignity. He thought it disgraceful he should be accompanied by guards who carried weapons. He was filled with disgust that he must attend his parents' funeral train wearing his own sword and dagger.

In the tomb Amenemhet went through the necessary ritual, his mind a blur. When he finally left the ancient vault proclaiming Mentuhotep and Meresank "triumphant" and therefore at their happy destiny, he knew only that the tomb depressed him. Despite the treasures that filled it and the colorful paintings on the walls, he found the place oppressive beyond belief and shuddered to think that one day he would lie there. The ceremonies and his participation in them would be remembered later on many sleepless nights, but when he returned to the palace, his mind was mercifully empty.

Amenemhet spent the long evening alone in his chamber except for the guards posted outside. Yazid appeared regularly for no apparent reason. After several of these visits, Amenemhet wondered if the servant mistakenly feared he contemplated ending his own life. He did not. As great as was the pain that filled him, Amenemhet would live to find those guilty. He would find Nefrytatanen, too—alive or dead—before he died.

The next time Yazid entered the room, Amenemhet snapped, "Yazid, will you leave me in peace? Have you no compassion? May I not be left alone in my grief? Stay or leave as you will, but I'm weary with your creeping in and out."

Yazid left immediately. Amenemhet knew he was relieved after this outburst. Although Amenemhet knew there was no anger or resentment, and Yazid understood his meaning without explanation, Amenemhet was aware that this had been noticed by the guards, who didn't understand. He was disgusted that he would have no privacy until this all was over.

Nefrytatanen and Kheti rode swiftly until Kheti slowed their pace to save the horses. For some time they rode without speaking. Kheti asked no questions, and Nefrytatanen wondered how, without encouraging him too much, she might convince him she was worth all this bother. She kept her horse a little behind his, as befitted a slave, hoping to avoid conversation as long as possible.

At last Kheti slowed his pace to drop back and ride beside Nefrytatanen. The moonlight was pale, and they saw each other only as shadows. When he spoke it was as if the words came from a ghost.

"How did you escape the storm and the attack?" Kheti asked. She told him what she had done. "You're truly a marvel," he commented. "You still remember nothing?" he asked. She said she didn't. "Tell me what has happened to you since the storm." She told him briefly, not mentioning any name but Drankma's. "This priest or noble or whoever he was," said Kheti slowly, "didn't tell you who he was or where you were going, but you went with him?"

"I had no choice," she answered.

"And Drankma called you Lotus because of your eyes?" Kheti asked. Nefrytatanen said this was true. Kheti was silent for a time, as if wondering about Drankma's motives. She was sure now that Kheti thought she was Sira.

"Then I'll call you Lotus too," he finally said. "I really don't know your name, and you are a slave I captured in a task for which I was, I suspect, paid not nearly enough. I also think the attack in the desert was to assure I remained silent."

Nefrytatanen was surprised at Kheti's telling her this.

One didn't generally speak so intimately with slaves or servants.

"Tell me," Kheti asked, "why you turned to me for help. You weren't overly friendly the last time I saw you."

Nefrytatanen heard the smile behind his words and thought, if he took her that lightly, he might yet believe her. "I was more afraid of them than of you," she said after a moment.

Kheti laughed aloud at her answers. "You're honest," he replied, "but you've showed spirit ever since you first opened your eyes in my tent."

"The day the storm struck," she murmured dropping her head, "I was afraid of the storm and, as you seemed to trap me, I was afraid of you." She paused then added softly, "I may not remember my past, but there are some things one knows by instinct. I'm sure there's been no man—in my—life." Her voice faded at this. She was torn between revealing this or not. She didn't know if the knowledge might arouse some gentle feeling in him or only whet his appetite. She gambled on the former.

Kheti was silent for some time before he said, "That could be true of a person of your station." He seemed to deliberate then commented, "In that case, your fear —and you did look desperate—would be understandable. Perhaps a less forceful approach on my part would make you a more willing and far more satisfactory companion," he said softly.

Nefrytatanen didn't know how to answer. She needed Kheti's help but didn't want to encourage him. Finally she said meekly, "Perhaps. I cannot know." The silence following that was almost unendurable for her.

Suddenly Kheti laughed again. "Do you know?" he said. "Never have I treated a slave as I've treated you. I'm thinking of courting you as if you were a free lady, so I may win your favor." He chuckled in good humor. "But, though a slave, you're far from simple, and this new idea has its appeal." As he noted her continued silence, he became more sober. "You don't have to be afraid I'll leap off my horse and take you here, Lotus. I'm not really the beast you seem to think I am. I won't rape you. Besides, I have no wish to delay our journey. Your friends, no doubt, are searching for us. You'll have to wait for my attentions, which I promise will be less violent than you think." He sighed. "I have other matters to take care of now, although I am reluctant to leave you."

"Leave me?" Nefrytatanen was surprised.

"I have no intention of leaving you alone," he said quickly. "We're going to some friends of mine, who will take you to my house where you'll wait for me. Perhaps you'll spend your time relearning some of the manners of a proper slave, but I think you won't learn much." Kheti smiled again, and she felt more at ease with him. He didn't seem so evil to her now.

Kheti said nothing more as they continued riding through the night. Shortly before dawn they approached a camp. Kheti rode into the camp in the steadily growing light, appearing well-acquainted with its inhabitants. His arrival seemed to cause no comment.

When they had dismounted, Kheti led Nefrytatanen to a tent, and, without announcing himself, he went inside. There Nefrytatanen saw the man who had stared at her first when she had awakened in Kheti's tent in the desert.

"Ho, Kheti," Rakkor greeted them cheerfully. "What blossom have you brought to brighten this dreary place?"

Kheti smiled and sat down, motioning to Nefrytatanen to seat herself. He said softly, "I've brought her for you to take care of for me." Rakkor looked at Nefrytatanen with some interest, and Kheti, reading his friend's thoughts, added quickly, "Not the way you mean to take care of her, Rakkor. Lotus has again fallen into my hands, this time by her own choice, and I want you to take her to my house so she might await my coming when my business here is settled."

Rakkor was not surprised, but he was disappointed nonetheless. "I'll do as you say. She'll be in good hands."

"I want you to leave in the morning. She's being hunted," Kheti directed. He told Rakkor what Nefrytatanen had told him.

When a serving woman brought Rakkor his morning meal, he invited Kheti and Nefrytatanen to share the food. Nefrytatanen kept silent while the two men discussed her recent adventures because her thoughts had flown again to Amenemhet. She wondered what he now was doing, what he was thinking. She recalled the morning they'd stood on the terrace, and she almost forgot herself and smiled at the memory of Amenemhet looking through her nightdress in the sunlight.

Nefrytatanen's attention returned to Kheti and Rakkor when she heard them beginning to discuss business. She decided most of their business seemed to come very near the fringes of the law. Kheti's immediate concern was the replacement of men and equipment, for he, Rakkor, and herself had been the only survivors of the attack in the desert. While Kheti intended to continue hand-picking men, Rakkor was to escort those accompanying them to Kheti's house. They would wait there for Kheti and whoever else he brought with him.

Long after the sun had traveled high and the heat had grown intense, Kheti noticed Nefrytatanen discreetly squirming and fidgeting in Drankma's heavy and now filthy robe. He told Rakkor to have a servant find more suitable garments for her. Shortly after Rakkor's bellow, a woman came and took Nefrytatanen to another tent so she could wash herself and change.

Nefrytatanen was left alone for a time afterwards. She took advantage of her privacy and slept. They had ridden through the night, and she hadn't realized until now how tired she was.

When she was awakened by the same woman who had brought her to the tent, she realized the sun was almost gone. The woman took her to the tent where she had left Kheti and Rakkor.

When Nefrytatanen arrived, she noticed that Kheti's hair was again black and shining instead of dust-coated and that his eyes were alert and rested. In a tunic such as any man might wear during an evening at home, he looked no more menacing than the nobleman she met at court. He motioned her to sit down and have the evening meal with them.

Kheti inspected Nefrytatanen with open appreciation. She realized he had seen her clothed only in rags until now, and the cotton robe she wore was both sheer and feminine. Her hair hung loose in exactly the same simple way as when she'd first met Amenemhet.

Although Kheti's glances at Nefrytatanen throughout the evening were warm, he said little to her. Later, when she stood by the tent opening ready to leave, he stopped her a moment.

"I won't see you again until I return home," Kheti said softly. "I'll leave in the morning before you awaken." With his grey eyes still on her, he smiled, saying over his shoulder to Rakkor, "Remember, my friend, she's mine and in your keeping only. Treat her gently. Let the others know this also.

Beyond Kheti's shoulder, Nefrytatanen saw Rakkor roll his eyes in mock amazement at Kheti's attitude, but she made no comment.

Kheti said nothing more but before she turned to leave he bent as if by impulse and kissed her forehead lightly. She stared at him in surprise. It was a peculiar tender gesture, but Kheti said nothing and held the tent flap aside for her.

Chapter Seven

After several days of monotonous traveling, Nefrytatanen was glad to arrive at Kheti's house. It had seemed
to her as if the desert stretched to the four pillars of
heaven. She sighed with pleasure as a cool, watery-
scented breeze touched her face. She could see the
sparkle of water and realized they had journeyed to the
shores of the Narrow Sea, almost to the border of
Retenu.

As the travelers passed the gates and entered the
courtyard of Kheti's house, Nefrytatanen's eyes were
quietly appraising. The courtyard was large and cool
with a spring that fed a pond at its center. Graceful
palm trees swayed against the blue sky and acacias
whispered in the breeze. Flowers spilled over the
borders of neatly placed beds, and lotuses floated
serenely on the pond's shimmering surface.

Nefrytatanen continued to study her surroundings as
she docilely followed a servant into the house. It was
spacious and well-furnished, with an eye toward
beauty as well as comfort. Noting the number of servants and slaves passing through the rooms on their
various tasks, she concluded that Kheti's profession
was evidently profitable. His house was worthy of
a nobleman well favored by the king.

When she entered the room assigned to her, her
questions about Kheti's intentions were settled. She saw
at a glance that the room's furnishings were those of a

concubine's, being too costly for an ordinary servant, much less a slave. He must have a high opinion of her potential, she thought wryly, to give her so luxurious a room and not have her stay in his harem with the others. She wondered if he had a harem, after all. When the servant who had led her to her room smilingly opened a cabinet to reveal the new wardrobe Nefrytatanen acquired with the room, Nefrytatanen made no comment. But, glimpsing the garments, she noted that they would be cool, if somewhat less than modest.

On the evening of her first day at Kheti's house, Naomi, an older woman who served as Kheti's housekeeper, came to Nefrytatanen to introduce herself. As sometimes happens, an almost immediate rapport was established between them. In the days that followed, Naomi informed Nefrytatanen that she was to replace a girl named Yasmine. With raised eyebrows Naomi whispered that it was Yasmine who would teach her how to serve Kheti, and Yasmine was unlikely to be cooperative.

Nefrytatanen began her lessons with Yasmine and soon realized her lessons were made even more difficult by the return of her memory. It wasn't easy to set aside a lifetime of training for the throne while she pretended to be Lotus learning to be Kheti's concubine!

Yasmine proved petulant and tried to stir Nefrytatanen's temper every step of the way. Nefrytatanen found herself relying more and more on Naomi for, without Nefrytatanen's voicing her opinion, Naomi understood Nefrytatanen's distaste for what lay before her. Naomi's coaching was gentle and tactful.

Yasmine grudgingly taught Nefrytatanen to sing the songs Kheti most favored. When Yasmine began to teach Nefrytatanen to play the lyre, she smirked and hinted that the occasions on which he liked soothing music the most, preceded the occasions Nefrytatanen looked forward to least. Nefrytatanen, however, wouldn't give the girl the satisfaction of knowing her private feelings. She shrugged off Yasmine's remarks and learned to play her lyre in a simple, but satisfactory, fashion. She hid her lack of expertise at the instrument by singing while she played ánd carrying the melody with her voice.

Then one day while Nefrytatanen was conversing with Naomi, Yasmine entered the room announcing that Lotus had better begin to learn to dance. Naomi's eyes flashed a warning at this, but Nefrytatanen had already heard from others in the household that dancing was Yasmine's pride. She wouldn't teach her successor what she knew without giving trouble. Nefrytatanen never expected to learn the intricacies of such dancing by the time Kheti arrived, and she had already decided that, if she were really forced into a performance, it would have to be much simplified.

Yasmine began the lessons by demonstrating to Nefrytatanen what Nefrytatanen recognized immediately as being the most seductive and complicated dance possible. She stared at Yasmine in disbelief. The girl's movements were deliberately exaggerated to discourage Nefrytatanen, but Nefrytatanen was less worried about her lack of skill than Kheti's reaction to such a dance. If Kheti's interest had been awakened when she'd stood before him in dirty rags, even a simple version of such a dance would arouse him beyond her control. She herself had been unmoved by the most suggestive of dances in Tamehu, but such dances had been far more subtle. In Tamehu, provocative dances had been invitations. Yasmine's writhing simulated the act of love itself.

Nefrytatanen was not embarrassed by nakedness because her people were casual in dress, believing in comfort. But the little drifts of veiling and strings of moving beads made Yasmine's costume lewd. To wear such things and perform this dance to sensuous music would arouse a eunuch.

Naomi watched Nefrytatanen's expression as Yasmine danced, and her own face was sympathetic.

Finally Naomi stopped Yasmine and said sharply, "Lotus is not yet ready to learn such things, you little cow." Yasmine's green eyes filled with triumph. "She won't begin with this, and you know it," Naomi scolded. She turned to Nefrytatanen with her back to Yasmine, ignoring her. "Lotus, she starts you with the complicated steps when she knows you must begin with simple ones. She's a little viper who wishes to trouble you because she's envious."

Yasmine gave Naomi a cold glare but said nothing. She glided indignantly from the room, her movements like those of a serpent.

"Lotus," Naomi said softly, "I can see this appeals to you no more than it would to me, but you must try to learn some of it. It doesn't have to look the way she does it. If you can combine some of it with grace and imagination, you may give your dance more beauty than suggestion. She meant to make it very provocative to frighten you."

"Thank you, Naomi," Nefrytatanen whispered. "You give me hope."

"You weren't made for this kind of life," Naomi added softly. "Whoever you are and whatever your life was before, this is far below your station. I can tell it. Naboth, my husband, has also commented on this."

Nefrytatanen felt alarm rise in her at this, but Naomi laid her hand reassuringly on Nefrytatanen's arm.

"We speak of this only to each other," Naomi added quickly. "It isn't our business or our way to chatter with the rest of the household. We'll try to make what we can easier for you, but you'll have to accustom yourself to some things you won't enjoy. Perhaps I can show you some ways to alter this dance," Naomi offered. "My own people dance, and I haven't completely forgotten these things." Her dark eyes were sympathetic. "You may make whatever you wish of it in the end by your own way of doing it." As if she were speaking to herself more than to Nefrytatanen, she added, "I fear nothing will alter it enough. When

Lord Kheti sees you in one of those costumes, you won't need to dance at all."

She left Nefrytatanen alone then, and, as if to confirm Naomi's prediction, Nefrytatanen went to look doubtfully again at her wardrobe. One glance was sufficient.

"Oh, beloved," Nefrytatanen whispered, fingering the gauzy garments. "Where can you be? Can you have given me up for dead? Can you have forgotten?" She turned from the cabinet and stood in the middle of the room, her head drooping.

She knew she was wrong to ask such things. Amenemhet was searching for her yet. She raised her head to gaze through the window opening. Amenemhet was somewhere out there, she assured herself. He would find her. She sighed. She knew of no way she could escape Kheti's hands. She had nothing of value except her necklace so bribing her guards was impossible. Nefrytatanen would as soon have parted with her head as to give up Amenemhet's necklace. She turned from the window opening. She must wait for Amenemhet. It was in his hands to find her. But how? He had no way of guessing where she was. She lay across the bed, among the glittering beads and shimmering silks, weeping.

Never before had Nefrytatanen been so frightened. She thought of Sira and wondered if the servant yet survived, if she were being cruelly treated, if she were tortured. A chill ran over Nefrytatanen as she remembered Sira in her wedding gown. Kheti's men must have delivered her to Sinuhe, thinking Sira was herself. Perhaps Sinuhe had had Sira tortured, maybe mutilated beyond recognition, and sent her body to Amenemhet. Perhaps, even now, he mourned her own death. If so, both lands would be in mortal upheaval.

Nefrytatanen considered this possibility. That could have been Sinuhe's plan—to cause such confusion and turmoil that the Two Lands would fight each other. Then, Nefrytatanen wondered, would it be the priests or the Hyksos who would take over when Tamera's armies lay drenched in their own blood, too weak to resist?

She brushed aside her own worries about Kheti. They were unimportant in the face of this larger problem. She wondered if Mentuhotep and Amenemhet could resist such a struggle. She thought of her own army commander, Nessumontu, whose fierce temper would have terrifying results if he heard she was dead. She thought of Amenemhet lying in his own blood, or in chains, and she felt a depth of fear beyond any she'd known. She was suddenly cold, and she shivered in horror. Nefrytatanen sat up slowly and turned again to the window opening.

For some time Nefrytatanen sat in this state, staring at the hard, bright sky. She wished she hadn't left him. She would rather have died with him than have him alone, suffering and grieving.

In this place of unbelievers Nefrytatanen couldn't seek solace in a temple. She did not even have incense to light in prayer. What could she say, anyway? In the face of impending disaster, words were useless.

Rising slowly through Nefrytatanen's sorrow was another idea. There were some words that were more than words. These words had a special power. A new feeling came over her, stirring memories of times forgotten. Recalling her mother standing before the moonlit skies, Nefrytatanen saw again the small fires that sent away clouds, the colored sparks and vapors rising, and the results—the deed done, the illness healed, the arguer persuaded. Sharply the memories rushed in on her, insisting she heed them, commanding that she use her knowledge.

Nefrytatanen had done no magic for a long time, and she had seldom done so in the past. She preferred to rely on more conventional methods to accomplish her ends. Now she decided that if she had ever needed extraordinary methods, this was the time.

She wondered if she could obtain the items her mother had used or, at least, suitable substitutes. She wondered if she could manage to have privacy when Ra had sunk below the horizon and wasn't looking upon such things and when the spirits were free in the night darkness. She would try. She would do it that night.

Nefrytatanen thought of Naomi and hoped she was the friend she seemed. Nefrytatanen could think of no other way to get what she needed. She put her head out the door, and the guard looked at her coldly, impervious to her agitated state. She asked for Naomi before he closed the door. She sat down and waited while she planned.

It wasn't long before Naomi came. Nefrytatanen was more than half-surprised the guard had bothered to call her. Naomi said nothing. She merely looked expectantly at Nefrytatanen.

"Naomi," Nefrytatanen said softly, "I need your help."

"I've already told you it's yours," Naomi replied in a quiet voice. Her eyes were dark and filled with shadows. "What do you need?" she asked.

Nefrytatanen gave no explanation for what she requested. The articles were ordinary enough in themselves, but Naomi had a knowing expression on her face as she left.

It wasn't long until Naomi returned. She said nothing as she laid the things carefully on a low table. She left the room without a word, and Nefrytatanen heard her tell the guard to admit no one to Lotus' room but herself, explaining that Lotus was ill. Nefrytatanen wondered, despite Naomi's apparent trustworthiness, if she had set a trap.

When the evening meal came it was Naomi who brought it. It was as if Nefrytatanen had ordered the food herself. There was little she could eat before she began the ceremony, and Naomi had somehow known what was permitted.

When night had fallen and everyone was sleeping except the guards, Nefrytatanen lit a small lamp to see by, then drew aside the window hangings and allowed the night and its spirits admittance to her chamber.

Nefrytatanen took her robe off and loosened her hair. The night breeze touched it gently as if encouraging her to continue. She set down a bit of white silk, a silver dish, and a crystal cup with clear wine in it. She poured oil in the dish and lit it then blew out her lamp.

Lotus blossoms from the pond, papyrus pollen, and fresh mint were laid out before her, and Nefrytatanen mixed these things together carefully while she chanted in an ancient language. Then she cast a handful of the mixture on the fire, and blue sparks flared high, wafting a perfume into the night. She lifted the crystal cup in offering to the moonlight, which reflected from it sending shimmering white streaks through the blue and shadowy haze of the room. She chanted names. Then she drank the consecrated wine and spoke softly.

"Glory to thee, Aset, Queen of All Enchantments, I fall on my knees before thee." Nefrytatanen prostrated herself on the floor by the window, touching her forehead to the cool stone surface.

"I am but thy poor servant, Mistress of All Words of Power. From thine eyes emanates the silver light I look upon tonight, and in the circle of thy beauty, I beg thee for help."

Nefrytatanen straightened and gazed at the moon, holding out from her breast the lotus pendant. The moonlight struck the silver lotus to white fire, and the gem glowed in its core. "Here is Amenemhet's gift of love, oh Aset, most suitably chosen from the blue stars with a stone of rarest quality. The star this stone holds in its heart is Sept, and the blue is my one eye. My beloved has the other. Evils surround us both, Mistress of Enchantment, as thine own silver eyes have seen. Let this star be protection for us. Let this silver lotus, most excellently fashioned after thine own sacred flower, bind our fortunes to thee. Let these blue stones be thy eyes as well as mine. Aset, let me see with thine eyes. Aset, thy eyes are my eyes. Bring these eyes together once again so Amenemhet, son of Ra, may find me, thy daughter."

The walls of the room disappeared, and in their place Nefrytatanen saw a land of darkness and strange-looking forests, filled with shadows and twisted vines and trees. All kinds of strange and living beings came slowly in a long procession, drifting from the forest's depths toward immense silver doors carved with symbols Aset allowed Nefrytatanen to read. The perfume floated in layers of blue, drawing the beings from the darkness toward the sacred doors, which slowly opened. Following the beings were evil presences, but none of the procession faltered, nor did they hurry. Aset controlled the doors. All but the evil presences would enter them.

Nefrytatanen watched the sparkling blue fragrance entice the beings. They followed in the slow, rhythmic movement from which dreams are sometimes made. But this was no dream. Through the doors, Aset and Nefrytatanen's doors, they went. Nefrytatanen watched them all as they disappeared inside. When the last had entered, with the help of Aset, Nefrytatanen closed the doors, and the evil things were left without, dispersing into a vapor that disappeared.

Later Nefrytatanen lay awake in her bed thinking about what she had done, unable to sleep though she was exhausted. She knew, that if anyone—however uninformed—had entered the room tonight, no story could have saved her.

But no one had come. She had accomplished her purpose. Now she would wait with a more peaceful heart because, whatever else happened in her absence from Amenemhet, she was no longer helpless. She had set in motion forces no power could stop until her will was done.

Amenemhet was more restless than usual. The latest search party had just returned, once again without news. Now he sent them out each day mostly to show the people he hadn't lost hope. Though he was convinced they would find nothing, he couldn't help but hope they had news, and he knew fresh disappointment when they didn't.

Amenemhet had offered treasures as reward. He had offered pardon to those implicated in minor ways, who might come forth with information. He had questioned everyone and had drawn a wall of guards around the whole country. He knew some other way *must* be found, and he paced restlessly in the moonlit garden, wondering how he might next act.

The scent of flowers interfered with Amenemhet's concentration. They reminded him of that first evening when Nefrytatanen, resembling a night spirit, had stood on the terrace. He allowed himself to reflect upon that and other memories. Although he knew that grief would pierce him anew, he missed Nefrytatanen too much this night to resist thinking of her.

It seemed to him that Nefrytatanen had been even more sharply on his mind since his lonely evening meal. It was impossible for him to concentrate. He was driven almost to madness thinking of her. He thought he could see her eyes before him, and he remembered too well the touch of her lips.

Amenemhet gazed up at the full moon, which was filling the garden with soft silver, and he stopped walking. He felt more peaceful as he watched it, as though it reassured him somehow. He touched his pendant and thought of how like Nefrytatanen's eyes the stone was. The gem grew dark and shadowy in the night just as her eyes did.

Sighing Amenemhet glanced up at his chamber. He saw Yazid's shadow as the servant prepared the room for the night.

A soft, metallic sound drew Amenemhet's attention to the nearby guards and reminded him again of his own danger. He felt at his hip the dagger's weight. Still the moon's pale light seemed to soothe him, as did the swishing of the palm fronds in the slight breeze.

It came to Amenemhet that he hadn't yet returned to the tomb to give his mortuary offering and pray for Mentuhotep and Meresank. He hadn't been able to face those massive doors since the funeral, and each time he had thought of it, he had turned to something else for distraction. Now he felt a strong desire, almost a compulsion, to visit their House of Silence, and he suddenly decided to go this very night.

Amenemhet called for Yazid and told the servant his wishes. Yazid was surprised. It wasn't the practice to visit tombs in the middle of the night when spirits walked. Yazid said nothing but hurried to arrange for guards to accompany them.

They approached the mountain out of which the vaults had been hewn. Amenemhet was surprised because the place no longer seemed oppressive. He felt no hint of the dread which had hung over him since the funeral. He was peculiarly eager to enter the tomb, and he dismounted before the rest of them. He had almost reached the doors when Commander Korusko caught up with him.

"Sire," Korusko said, "we must go with you."

"If someone must come," declared Amenemhet firmly, "I'll have only Yazid." And he wondered why he felt so strong a desire to be alone.

Korusko's face was solemn. He knew Amenemhet's mind was set. One didn't debate with the king. Korusko said, "Then let some of the guards enter first to make sure it's safe before you go in." Korusko was relieved at Amenemhet's nod of agreement, but he knew Amenemhet was still unable to smother his resentment at having to fear for his life.

As Amenemhet watched the soldiers hesitantly enter the tomb—because they weren't anxious to meet royal spirits in their burial places at night—he was disgusted anew. The very tomb of his family might not be safe from assassins. Shortly afterward the soldiers emerged, pale and relieved, to confirm that none but the dead occupied the place.

Followed by Yazid, Amenemhet went into the chamber where his parents' coffins lay. The flickering light was a small island in the immense darkness.

"An offering which the king gives . . . " Amenemhet began the traditional prayer. He placed his gifts on the table and offered his prayers, and he felt comforted.

As he stood silently before leaving, he felt an impulse to follow the passage to the older section of the tomb, long unvisited by any living being. He told Yazid and instructed him to wait. Yazid protested, hoping Amenemhet would change his mind. Thinking of the dark, ancient chambers lying deep within the mountain made his scalp prickle. "There may be danger."

"No one would go there, and I have something I must do before I leave," Amenemhet answered, wondering himself what it was he felt he must do. "You stay here unless you hear or see something that alarms you."

He crept a short distance down the old passage, made two turns, and suddenly felt as far removed from Yazid as if the Great Green Sea stood between them. As he had once before, in the throne room, he felt again the powerful presence of those who had ruled before him. In this place the feeling wasn't comforting.

Amenemhet moved quietly through the heavy gloom, the dust of centuries. He didn't wish to make a sound and disturb those who lay there. Massive paintings hung peeling from walls patterned with the greying pathways of long dead spiders and other crawling things. Black tunnels beckoned, but he ignored them feeling that something directed his steps. Oppressive silence penetrated his being with increasing clouds of dark and fearful dread. Purple shadows gathered in the distant corners as the faint light of his torch wavered against the rock ceiling high over head.

Pausing to peer into a drafty black tunnel, Amenemhet fancied he saw light in the distance. He stepped into the passage, knowing this was the one he must explore. An icy finger traced a path across his soul. Was his tortured imaginations conjuring up visions or was that Nefrytatanen he saw ahead? Without thinking further, he raced forward into the darkness.

"Nefrytatanen, wait!" Amenemhet shouted.

She seemed not to see him; and he hurried blindly on, the fire of his torch nearly snuffed out. The figure ahead seemed to recede and dwindle like the struggling flame he held. Surrounding her in wavering streaks of blue light were strange shapes—surely beings cursed by the gods. He shivered for they seemed to be leering at him. He stared at the accursed creatures and almost recognized a familiar face in one of them when, like a flame suddenly snuffed out, Nefrytatanen and the creatures disappeared.

Amenemhet tripped and sprawled over the rough stone floor and felt himself sliding on a slight slant downward. He felt his chest brush over the edge of an open space, and he grasped frantically for the edge, briefly holding himself. But the slope was smooth and worn with age, and, slowly, his muscles straining, he slipped off the ledge. He hurtled into black emptiness.

"Beloved!" He cried out, then hit the bottom with a force that knocked the breath from him. Amenemhet lay still a moment, dazed and gasping. The slightest movement made his head reel. His vision had grown dark and clouded. Dizzily looking upward, he saw he had fallen from the open side of a flight of stairs. He closed his eyes for a moment to clear his spinning head and then opened them. The room was still cloudy.

When Amenemhet dragged himself to his feet, he realized he was trembling not only with the fear and shock of his fall, but also because of the strange, slowly growing blue light. Amenemhet wondered if his fall had affected his sight—or his mind.

It was, he observed, a very old section of the ancient tombs, and he stared as the light steadily grew until the vaults was clearly lit by its eerie glow.

Again Nefrytatanen appeared.

"Beloved?" Amenemhet's call was but a hoarse echoing whisper.

Nefrytatanen said nothing, only smiled slightly at him, her eyes glowing as they had that night on the path to the temple. They were the same color as the glow filling the room, as if the light came from them. He felt his love for her swelling his heart, and he was terrified that what he saw was her spirit, and that she was dead. Her hand reached slowly toward the lotus pendant he'd given her, and as her fingers touched it the stone began to glow with the same blue light. He glanced at his pendant. It, too, was glowing.

Gathering near Nefrytatanen, clearer and clearer, were the strange shapes Amenemhet had seen before. He felt cold and helpless as he watched them surround Nefrytatanen with their shadowy, grimacing faces. But she seemed undisturbed by them. Amenemhet now saw the face of one of them clearly, its evil mouth sneering. Its cavernous eyes filled with terror when it looked upon her. It reminded Amenemhet of something, but he could not quite remember what it was.

Nefrytatanen smiled at Amenemhet, unconcerned with the monstrous creatures. With a wave of her hands, the blue light rose in clouds, carrying her beloved scent. The evil creatures began to fade, leaving Nefrytatanen alone looking at Amenemhet with profound loneliness. She held out her arms to him. Her smile soared through his heart, and the blood flowed singing again in his veins.

The blue light and Nefrytatanen faded, but her fragrance still clung faintly to the air. Amenemhet was reassured and even happy, and he wondered why.

Still a little dizzy, he slowly climbed the stairs and met Yazid coming fearfully in search of him Amenemhet assured Yazid that the noises he had heard had been his fall from the ledge, and they left quickly. Yazid casting frightened glances over his shoulder.

Chapter Eight

As Amenemhet lay weary but sleepless, he thought of the strange and evil beings he had seen with his beloved in the tomb. He shuddered. He wondered if he had dreamed them as he lay unconscious after his fall, but he rejected that. He could remember too well the scent that clung to his clothing even on his ride back to the palace. He remembered her unfaltering eyes, her untroubled smile. And he knew she was alive.

"Nefrytatanen," Amenemhet whispered to the shadows and the moonlight, "I have searched for you by the river among the bodies of the dead. I have looked into every hut in every village. I have looked upon the fields and the roads. I have begged all the divine beings of the firmament. My love searches for you to the uttermost parts of heaven, even as flowers seek the sun. Where *are* you, Nefrytatanen? Where?"

Amenemhet prayed once again to Aset to bring his beloved to him, even as she had searched for Asar and restored him to life.

The evil beings Amenemhet had seen in the burial place still haunted him, and he couldn't sleep until tears of despair had exhausted him.

In the days following their visit to the tomb, Yazid became aware of a subtle change in Amenemhet. Although Amenemhet had been bitterly aware of his guards, now he no longer acknowledged their presence.

131

Amenemhet seemed to have his eyes turned inward. He neither avoided nor confronted anything. But during the rare times when Amenemhet's eyes lit momentarily with the glow of angry inner fires, Yazid rejoiced. He had begun to fear that Amenemhet was losing heart.

One day while Amenemhet sat silently staring at nothing, as he often did, a commotion in the hall brought him to sudden alertness. He rose quickly, but before he could move, Ankhneferu burst into the room and threw himself at Amenemhet's feet. A guard on the priest's heels held his sword's point a finger's length from the nape of Ankhneferu's neck as he lay prostrate before Amenemhet. Amenemhet held up his hand to the guard.

"A word, sire, in private—I beg you!" Ankhneferu gasped.

Amenemhet studied the priest's garments, which were badly travel-stained.

"Clear the room," Amenemhet ordered the soldiers who were watching.

The guard standing over Ankhneferu put his sword away and, looking doubtfully at Amenemhet, joined the others as they filed out. When the door had closed, Amenemhet—his hand on his dagger—stepped a little away from Ankhneferu. The priest remained on the floor, afraid to move.

"Rise and speak," Amenemhet commanded. "Why have you come to me this way?"

"Sire, I have seen the queen," Ankhneferu gasped, dragging himself to his feet. Amenemhet's mouth had fallen open. "Sire, she's alive. She was being held by a man named Drankma. Hathorbes received a message from Drankma who claimed that Sinuhe had paid him to hold her after she had dragged herself half-dead out of the desert and to his camp. She had no memory of her past and did not know who she was. Drankma was afraid of Sinuhe and said he only suspected it was the queen, for Sinuhe had never spoken her name."

Ankhneferu hesitated, then paused. Amenemhet's

rising fury was terrifying. The priest took a deep breath then continued haltingly.

"Drankma wanted no more to do with the matter. Hathorbes sent me to find her and charged me to say nothing until I delivered her to him. I went to Drankma's camp, and it was as he'd said. The queen appeared to have no memory. They called her Lotus and had told her she was a slave. It was a terrible thing to see her in those surroundings." Ankhneferu shook his head slowly. "I paid Drankma and took her with me. But when we came to a small village in an oasis, she tricked us and escaped with a man called Kheti. I suspect she fooled us all about her loss of memory, and likely thought I was part of the plot, doubtless deciding by that time to trust no one. Where she now is, I cannot say, but she was surely well when last I saw her." Ankhneferu paused to catch his breath. "Sire, I don't know what Hathorbes planned. It seemed peculiar to me that he wished to keep this news from you. I beg you, sire, whatever *his* intentions, *I* am blameless in this thing!"

Amenemhet turned away closing his eyes while he allowed joy to wash over him and this news to enter his incredulous mind. But realizing Sinuhe's treachery, he turned abruptly to Ankhneferu with eyes of ice.

"You have my deepest gratitude, Ankhneferu, and you will be rewarded accordingly. You will next go to Hathorbes and tell him how she escaped you. Say nothing of coming here or speaking to me. Keep your eyes and ears open and report to me, or to Korusko if I'm unavailable. Trust no one else."

"I'll gladly do what you ask, sire," Ankhneferu replied promptly.

"Go. Rest and refresh yourself. Leave Wast as soon as you're ready." Amenemhet paused then added, "Remember, trust no one. Your life as well as hers depends on you."

Ankhneferu left immediately, and Amenemhet called one of the guards, instructing him to send Yazid and

Korusko. While Amenemhet waited, he thought again of Nefrytatanen's possible safety. He might have laughed aloud with joy but for his fury with Sinuhe. Now he knew how this had been so excellently carried out and so well paid for.

Amenemhet was certain, if he could locate Kheti, he would find Nefrytatanen as well. He considered ways he might accomplish this. Sinuhe mustn't suspect that his king knew anything. Amenemhet didn't know what connection Kheti had with the traitorous priest. That Nefrytatanen had chosen to escape Ankhneferu with Kheti was encouraging.

When Korusko and Yazid arrived, Amenemhet sent Korusko immediately to seize the soldiers who had traveled with Ankhneferu and to substitute their own in place of Hathorbes's guards. Korusko took only moments to accomplish this task, and Amenemhet waited silently with Yazid until his return. Yazid studied his master intently. He knew something had greatly excited Amenemhet, and he couldn't tell whether it was anger or happiness he saw.

At last, without hesitation, Amenemhet told them the story. Yazid was speechless. Korusko, hand on his sword and knuckles whitened with his grip, swore vengeance in a voice that would make any man's blood run cold. Korusko had seen and learned much about pain and death during his career, and his threats were not empty.

"Although we know who the enemy is," Amenemhet said, "we can risk nothing until Nefrytatanen is safe. I don't know who this man Kheti is or whether he has any connection with Sinuhe." Amenemhet's gaze traveled to the window and the garden outside as he talked. "Kheti holds her unless she has since escaped him or has been passed to others."

Yazid had been silent, thoughtful expressions playing on his face. Now he rubbed his chin and mumbled, "I have heard something of Kheti."

"Speak then!" Korusko exclaimed, his dark eyes flashing. "Why do you hold your tongue?"

Yazid was insulted. "I don't know how true the stories are. Perhaps they are false and would only mislead us."

"I will hear them and judge for myself," Amenemhet said firmly.

Yazid looked resigned as he related what he knew. "Kheti is a wanderer with a large band of men who follow him. It's said that somewhere—perhaps near Retenú—he has a house or headquarters of some size. The place is known to no one but his own men and household. The secret is well-guarded for his men are loyal and closemouthed. It's said they've grown prosperous selling their swords for a high price without many questions. It's also said their skill is worth the cost. I've heard that Kheti is a son of Tamera and possibly of noble blood. That could be. It may also be that he's merely a common thief."

Amenemhet turned this information over in his mind, examined it, then remarked, "Kheti sounds like a romantic figure."

"So do some regard him," answered Yazid.

Amenemhet turned again to the window opening, gazed at the river awhile, then said over his shoulder, "He would seem to be a cut about the common thief if he can kidnap the queen. He cannot be stupid. Say what you will, thieves are generally stupid, though a few may be clever." Amenemhet turned to them again, and from his manner they could see that he had made his decision.

"Yazid," Amenemhet began, "you and I are going to join Kheti's gang." Yazid's mouth fell open. "We'll dress as wanderers and go into the desert to search for him. He probably travels the general caravan routes, and he must surely visit watering places from time to time. Perhaps we can linger in these possible areas and meet him. When we do find him, we'll learn some way to get him to lead us to the queen."

"Sire!" Korusko exclaimed. "There would be great personal danger to you in such an undertaking. And while you were gone, who would rule? Who would deal with Sinuhe?"

"Sinuhe must wait," muttered Amenemhet angrily. "I can do nothing about him until I'm assured of her safety. As for my own safety, I've been well trained in self-defense. Anyway it would seem the palace isn't the safest of all places for me. The kingdom will run for awhile on its own well-greased wheels. The story will be spread that, in my trials and sorrow, I have gone into seclusion for a time. Korusko, you'll pretend to be my contact. No one else will be admitted to my chambers under any cirumstances. Each night while I'm gone, you'll visit and pretend to consult with me. It will be announced that only Yazid attends me. The officials can manage their duties, but if they press to see me, tell them I trust their decisions if it's a matter you cannot decide with your own good sense. I think Meri will be able to handle most of it anyway. I will, in any case, leave you some instructions. Sinuhe will no doubt attempt to see me to offer spiritual consolation. It won't be easy for you, but make sure he suspects nothing. Tell him I wish time alone, to meditate."

"But, sire, what if he suspects and acts on his suspicions?"

"Do what you must, Korusko. Wait until the last possible moment to make any major move of your own. Let them say what they will, and grind your teeth if you must, but keep your silence. I'm putting it all in your hands until I return. After I come back, I'll untangle anything needing it."

Korusko was pale, contemplating the responsibility he would hold, but he was also proud of the king's trust in him.

"Don't be so agitated, Korusko," Amenemhet said, smiling bitterly. "I have such matters in my hands every day."

"But you cannot do this thing!" Korusko gasped.

Amenemhet gave him a cold stare. "I am king, he said. "I do what I wish. Go now, Korusko, and plan for our leaving. We'll need supplies and horses. Get the best animals you can buy—or steal them if you must! No one must know whom they're for. None from my stables may be used, for we must not give a hint of anything to do with the royal house." Amenemhet considered this for a moment then said, "Perhaps stealing them *is* a good idea. It would further enhance our new identities. Steal them, Korusko. I've decided. We'll leave tonight. Remember, everything must be accomplished with absolute secrecy." Amenemhet finished, "I trust you to devise whatever means you must."

Korusko saluted Amenemhet when he left, rather than giving his usual bow. It was a special tribute from one soldier to another. Amenemhet understood his meaning. It warmed him.

"Now, Yazid," Amenemhet said, sitting down at his writing table, "I must compile a list of instructions for Korusko regarding matters which are yet undecided. I can foresee some of them, so he'll have some basis for making his interviews with me convincing. In the meantime, you'll obtain suitable garments for our travels."

Yazid bowed his way out then muttering in his native tongue, that of the sand-dwellers, went down the hall. He could see no way to get such garments unless he stole them from the women who did the laundry. He didn't look forward to stealing from them. There were forbidding women with whom he had already had unhappy experiences.

That night, long after the household was sleeping and as many of the lights as possible had been extinguished, Korusko managed to place a very large and venomous serpent in the garden near enough to Amenemhet's window openings to attract the guards that stood there, but far enough away that Amenemhet and Yazid could slip out of the palace while the soldiers captured the snake. They couldn't chance its gaining entrance to the palace.

Beyond a small side gate in the palace wall, the horses waited in the darkness, equipped with supplies. When Amenemhet and Yazid were mounted, Korusko stood silently looking up at them, still wishing the king would change his mind.

Amenemhet laid his hand on Korusko's arm and whispered, "May Tehuti and his wisdom guide you and may Heru come to your aid."

Korusko was thinking that he'd need them both and more besides. He whispered, "May Ra himself guide your every step. May you accomplish your purpose safely and swiftly." Especially *swiftly,* he added silently.

Amenemhet and Yazid walked the horses into the darkness. When they were far enough away so that no sound of hoof beats would carry back to the palace, they galloped toward the desert.

Korusko stood alone looking after them into the night.

The desert, reflected Amenemhet, was a terrible and beautiful place, filled with Sekhmet's power of destruction at the same time that Ra, giver of life, shone so abundantly upon it. As dawn approached, gradually turning the sky into a bright display so magnificent that even the richest of Tamera's tapestries couldn't compare with it, Amenemhet watched the desert become patterns of violet shadows. The sand would soon become a steady, eye-blinding glare, and it would sear their skin with fiery pain. The only noises were the soft sound of the horses' hooves and the occasional clinking of the metal parts of their equipment.

Although Yazid's blood was that of the desert people, he had been a household slave a long time, and he didn't for a moment appreciate the desert's stark beauty. He was convinced that prolonged riding in this place was a torment. Although he said nothing, his opinion was clear to Amenemhet, who knew Yazid's mind almost as well as his own.

Amenemhet rapidly tired of the endless riding. Although the garments Yazid had obtained were suitable for desert travel as well as for their new identities, Amenemhet found the heavy, coarse robe and cloak cumbersome. Accustomed to sandals and often barefoot, his feet were extremely hot and uncomfortable in boots.

After a single day on the desert, he had yearned for the baths he took for granted in the palace. After a week, his skin itched and felt ready to crawl off his body. He also longed for his comfortable bed, as the sand became increasingly unyielding each night.

Yazid's preparation of their meals left much to be desired, and it wasn't long before Amenemhet had become leaner. He knew his physical condition had never been better because he moved and walked with the alert grace of a cat. However, he was becoming tired and wondered if they would ever find Kheti.

This immensity of sand seemed to have swallowed forever any sign of life, and when Amenemhet thought of Nefrytatanen struggling through the desert alone and on foot, he shook his head in renewed wonder that she had survived.

Both Amenemhet and Yazid had become as dark from the sun as if they had been desert dwellers all their lives, and Amenemhet thought they must certainly look the parts they played. He sighed. No one would guess who they were by smelling them, either. His nose wrinkled in distaste whenever a breeze blew the wrong way.

Eventually they found a small oasis with a minuscule pool of warm and still water. It seemed a miracle to them. They bathed with as much enthusiasm as if it had been a cool, perfumed pool with lotuses floating on it.

When they left the water. Yazid commented that it was hopeless to try to find Kheti in this manner. When Amenemhet questioned him. Yazid replied that it was his opinion the whole army should be sent to search.

Amenemhet considered this carefully as they dressed then said, "Force isn't always the fastest or the best way, Yazid. A herd of oxen hauling sand would make no lasting mark on this desert. Observe the gentleness of the wind, and yet it unceasingly changes the face of the sand. Sometimes, Yazid, a feather's touch may bring better results than the beating of a fist."

Yazid shook his head, unconvinced.

Amenemhet looked at him sternly, adding, "We must work carefully to see where Kheti's loyalty lies before we can act openly."

One day Yazid pointed toward the hard, blue arch of sky, and Amenemhet, narrowing his eyes against the glare, observed the ominous circling of vultures.

"It doesn't look far, sire," Yazid remarked.

"Perhaps it's the result of some of Kheti's work, and we may find a trail to follow," Amenemhet exclaimed. "Besides, if the birds still circle, whatever is there may not yet be dead." He turned his horse in their direction and urged the powerful animal up the hill that stood before them.

The horse slithered in the sand that shifted with his every step, and Amenemhet leaned forward, low on the animal's glistening black neck, murmuring soft encouragement. Twice, the horse's hindquarters dropped in the slippery, shifting grains, and he floundered, but his strong legs coiled under him to lift and send him struggling forward.

Amenemhet was too busy to look back at Yazid's progress. He only hoped a wrong move wouldn't cause an accident. On the desert a minor injury could mean disaster. Amenemhet felt the horse's powerful muscles straining as it struggled over the crest of the hill. He paused at the top to look at Yazid, whose animal appeared at the limit of its strength. The faint sounds of clashing weapons came to Amenemhet and he turned in their direction.

He saw below the remnants of a camp. What had been the tents of its inhabitants had been burned.

Bodies were strewn over the sand. The struggle came from a small group of men fighting off a large group of soldiers.

Amenemhet stared at them incredulously. The soldiers wore the uniform of his own Tashemau. He saw other soldiers driving away the animals of the camp. The fight of the survivors was desperate, and Amenemhet could see that the soldiers meant to kill them all, and not to take prisoners. Finally Amenemhet realized that, although the attackers were clad in the uniform of his army, they followed no orders he or Korusko had ever given. He was furious at these men who masqueraded as his soldiers while they committed murder.

"Yazid!" Amenemhet shouted. "Hurry!"

He could see the fight was almost over, for the defenders of the camp had dwindled to three. And as his horse plunged down the hill through the sand toward them, Amenemhet saw one of them fall. He lifted his lance and, aiming, sent it in a shining arc to impale one of the soldiers.

Amenemhet came at them like a messenger of Sekhmet, his naked sword flashing in the sun. A surprised face turned toward him, only to be slashed. Amenemhet slipped his sword cunningly past a shield and tore into the vitals of another soldier before becoming aware that Yazid had caught up and was beside him.

The fierce and sudden onslaught of the two strangers caused the soldiers to hurriedly finish off the remaining two defenders and turn their attentions fully to Amenemhet and Yazid.

Yazid reined his horse's hindquarters beside Amenemhet's horse's shoulder, so that each covered the other's back while they fought. They were outmatched in number, but not in skill or vigor. And they had one strategic advantage. In their close position, they could limit their opponents, there being no room in which more could approach them.

For each man they sent sprawling, however, another replaced him. To dream of holding out against them all, Amenemhet began to realize, was fantasy. He was so desperately engrossed with the flashing blades around him that he didnt' notice a group of horsemen watching from a nearby hilltop.

For a moment the group didn't move, but merely watched the battle. Then they suddenly came racing down the hill, the sun reflecting from their drawn weapons.

When the soldiers saw the wave of riders rushing toward them, they quickly backed away. Amenemhet had a chance only to slice through the shield of one of them, sending him from his horse with a crash, before the rest escaped.

Bloodstained and panting, Amenemhet and Yazid dismounted to watch their approaching rescuers. Amenemhet shielded his eyes from the sun until the riders stopped before them. They were well-armed and numerous. Their leader dismounted and, looking around with disgust, turned to Amenemhet.

"Who are you?" It was a demand, not a question. "What happened here?"

Amenemhet silenced Yazid with a look. He turned his golden stare on the man.

"You can see for yourself what happened," he said coolly. "Why it did, I don't know. We saw the circling vultures from a distance and came to find the soldiers finishing off the last of these people. I'm Nakht. Who are you?"

"I'm Kheti," the man said glancing at the wreckage again.

Amenemhet's heart leaped, but his expression remained unchanged.

Kheti looked at Amenemhet again, meeting his steady eyes as if in appraisal. "You fought well," he commented.

Amenemhet saw respect in Kheti's eyes. "If you hadn't come," Amenemhet said, "the fight might well have been over soon. Do you know who these people are?"

Kheti shrugged and turned to look at one of the bodies. He walked to the next. Amenemhet walked with him, inspecting the havoc. It was obvious the camp had been fairly large but hadn't been well-defended. Amenemhet's eyes took in the few weapons and the evidence that most of the people had been struck down while fleeing or begging for mercy.

Anger grew in Amenemhet as they walked among the dead. These people had been, despite their helplessness, slashed and hacked without mercy.

Eyes wide with horror, Yazid whispered, "This work reminds me of the attack on the queen's ship."

Amenemhet made no reply. His face was grim. He stepped over a bloody, dismembered body, feeling his throat tighten, and commented, "I wonder who they were and why this was done to them. The soldiers were as savage as beasts."

Kheti threw him a black look but said nothing.

One of Kheti's men, who had been walking among the bodies and turning them over, shouted to them. Kheti went to him quickly and Amenemhet followed.

"Drankma?" Kheti stared at a body that consisted only of a head and trunk.

"You know him?" Amenemhet asked looking distastefully at the mutilated remains of the man he knew had saved Nefrytatanen then had eagerly sold her.

"Only a little," Kheti answered. "Although Drankma has been known to associate with some shadowy company, I cannot understand why this was done to him." Kheti stared at the corpse fixedly. "That he might do anything to deserve this treatment is surprising to me," he muttered.

Yazid shouted from a little distance away, and they hurried to where he knelt beside the body of a woman.

When they stood over her, they saw she was barely alive. Kheti knelt, took her head on his arm, and whispered gently to her. He sprinkled water on a cloth and squeezed some of it on her lips so she could speak. She was, Amenemhet judged, resigned to her death. When she could speak, her voice was a whisper only Kheti could hear. He answered her softly and wiped her face with the cloth as she panted. Then she spoke again, and he bent to hear her. Finally he looked up at them, his eyes angry. He still held the woman, but her head had fallen back, hanging lifelessly.

"She's dead," Kheti said. "She had little to say."

"What did she say?" Amenemhet pressed.

"The attackers came as friends to their camp," Kheti answered. "They had been here before, visiting Drankma. Drankma came out of his tent to talk with them, and they didn't dismount but stood talking from their horses until all of them were in camp. Then they struck. It didn't take long."

"Did she give no hint who they were?" Amenemhet asked.

Kheti looked up at him, his grey eyes like granite. "You saw the uniforms they wore. The last she said was a curse on the priests of the white crown."

Amenemhet was silent and thoughtful a moment. Yazid stood helplessly back, looking angry.

"Just like me," Kheti said as if to himself.

Amenemhet inquired as to his meaning.

Kheti replied, "The jackal behind this did such a thing to me, almost costing my life and killing most of my men. I know who lies behind this, or I suspect I do. I just don't understand why they did this to Drankma. He must have been used by them in some way. When they attacked me, they would even have killed Lotus."

Amenemhet's heart leaped suddenly to his throat, and he found it difficult to sound casual when he asked who Lotus was.

"A slave girl I have now safe in my house, no thanks to them." Kheti stood up.

Amenemhet asked Kheti who he suspected of these crimes.

"Never did I know his true name, but his men bore

the royal insignia of the White House, so I can well imagine who sent them. I only shudder thinking of the identity of a lady we delivered into his bloody hands." Kheti did shiver. "How might a husband, royal or not, have the evil to do such a thing to his bride?" Kheti stared at the body of the woman before him. "Had I known from the beginning the web I was being wound in, I would never have done the job. Now I can do nothing."

Amenemhet absorbed this for a moment then suggested quietly, "Perhaps it wasn't the king. Maybe it was someone else, someone hungry for power who needs something of value for a weapon."

Kheti considered this then said with sudden passion, "If I were her husband, she wouldn't have been carried away while I sat hidden in my palace. I would be after her!"

Amenemhet hid his bitter smile and commented dryly, "Perhaps he is. From what I've heard, no one seems sure he's there at all. Don't forget, someone also struck down his father and mother—with whom *he* had no quarrel."

Kheti said promptly, "They're two more reasons for him to act. If he hasn't been killed, which I doubt, why does he not move? If it were me, they'd well know where I was because I'd be at their necks with the blade of my sword!"

"A serpent isn't always so easily found," said Amenemhet.

Kheti looked at him a moment then gave his men orders to bury the dead as best they could. Amenemhet walked away a few steps, and Kheti followed him, a thoughtful look on his face.

"Why do you travel with your friend, alone in the desert?" Kheti inquired.

Amenemhet's eyes narrowed as he turned to Kheti. "No doubt for the same reason you do. Towns are sometimes not best for my health. I've heard of you."

Kheti laughed softly without humor. "I guessed as

much. I could use more men. Would you be interested
in joining us for awhile? Perhaps you might even join us
permanently," he added, "or at least as permanently as
our business allows."

Amenemhet wondered if he had somehow given himself away because Kheti's sharp eyes watched him intently. He pretended to consider the idea of a moment
then answered slowly, "Maybe that's an idea of some
worth. If attacks like this happen frequently on the
desert, I'm not sure I wish to travel with only Ahmed
beside me." He waved a hand at the carnage around
them.

As they rode, Amenemhet became certain that Kheti
didn't suspect his real identity but was being cautious
with a stranger—as was surely to be expected. Amenemhet found it difficult to restrain himself from asking
more qeustions about Lotus, but he could think of no
way to bring her casually into the conversation.

They made their camp as night was falling, and as
they were settling down to their evening meal, Kheti
remarked that they were traveling to his house near
the Narrow Sea. He said he wished they had already
gotten there so they could eat and sleep in comfort.

Amenemhet asked Kheti about his house, and Kheti
willingly described it, briefly, but with pride. Amenemhet led Kheti's conversation carefully, asking about his
family and finding he had none. Kheti seemed not to
want to talk about this subject. He seemed to hide
bitterness.

It surprised Amenemhet when Kheti mentioned
Lotus of his own accord. It seemed he thought often of
her in his silences, which made Amenemhet uneasy.

"Ah," Kheti sighed, "to have Lotus here with me
would comfort me greatly on this chilly night."

"She's pretty?" Amenemhet asked slowly. He could
almost see Yazid's ears growing.

Kheti smiled serenely. "That's a pale description for
one such as she. She's the luckier of the two women,

although she has lost her memory. To think of the fate of that lady I delivered to those others makes my hair stand on end."

Thinking of gentle Sira in Sinuhe's hands, Amenemhet felt the same. Finally he said casually, "Tell me of this slave girl. It's been long since I've had a woman, and it would be pleasant to hear of one, especially if she's as beautiful as it would seem."

"She's more beautiful than I have wit to describe," Kheti said simply. "You'll see her at my house. I'm having my servants teach her again the duties and manners she forgot, and Yasmine is teaching her some things she may never have known." He grinned, and Amenemhet clenched his fist, hoping his expression remained unchanged. Kheti went on more seriously, not noticing Amenemhet's tension. "She's different from any others I've seen and, though a slave, not to be told light tales of. How she managed to survive a walk through the desert, I don't know. It was Drankma who found and saved her, in fact." Kheti's eyes clouded again with anger as he remembered the slaughter in Drankma's camp. After a moment, he said more lightly, "I hope they've taught Lotus not to talk back so much." He grinned. "She does argue, and, though some spirit can be interesting, too much impudence is tiresome in a woman."

"That can be true," Amenemhet observed, wondering what might have caused Nefrytatanen's arguing. He forced himself to smile and commented, "Impudent or not, a fair woman would be welcome on this night to distract my dreams from what I've seen today."

Kheti smiled amiably. "When we arrived at my house, perhaps some distraction can be found for you. Comfortable surroundings and congenial companions can do much to turn a man's mind from his burdens." Kheti fell silent again and Amenemhet dared ask no more.

The men talked quietly until they drifted away one by one to roll out in their blankets on the sand.

Finally Kheti bid Amenemhet and Yazid good night and went a little away from the others to sleep. Amenemhet knew Yazid wished to speak to him, but he thought it unwise in the silence and signaled this. Yazid nodded and lay down not far away.

Amenemhet lay awake thinking of Nefrytatanen, trying to imagine what she was doing now. Did she sleep or lie awake as troubled as he was? The thought of her impudence to Kheti made Amenemhet smile, but thinking of the possible reasons she had been impudent wiped the smile away. He wondered if Kheti was a man to force himself upon a woman and concluded he seemed not to be. Amenemhet's thoughts stirred around in his mind like a stick in river mud until his brain felt as cloudy. He decided, finally, that he was grateful she was alive. And he put aside jealousy for the time.

Amenemhet closed his eyes and tried to sleep, but sleep was not so easy in coming. He couldn't help continuing to wonder what Kheti had done with Nefrytatanen. He lay a while longer, eyes still closed. But as he was beginning to drift into slumber, he slowly became aware of the feeling that someone was standing over him watching. He opened his eyes to slits, concealing their shine by his lashes, to see the gleam of a knife blade plunging silently toward him.

Instinctively Amenemhet rolled to the side—the dull thud of the blade striking his blanket and the sand beneath. As he leaped to his feet, he briefly caught the ankle of his assailant and, with a quick turn of his wrist, flipped the man off balance.

As Amenemhet gained his feet, he was ready to leap on his attacker but stopped his assault at the last instant for the man's legs were bunched against his chest, anticipating him. Amenemhet realized his attacker was very nearly as quick as he was himself, and so he waited for the moment the man sprang to his feet.

This time the man came with his blade held low, and as he lunged forward, Amenemhet seemed to step into the path of the knife. Instead Amenemhet reached out to grasp the wrist of the hand that held it. Using the momentum of the man's thrust, Amenemhet put out his nearest foot and jerked the man past him, plunging him headlong to the ground. Taking no further chances, Amenemhet immediately leaped on the man, and his blade found its place. The man screamed once, then was silent.

His cry awakened the others, and they came running from their various sleeping places holding whatever weapons had been nearest. Yazid waved a sword as he reached Amenemhet's side. Kheti raced to him at the same time.

Amenemhet said angrily, "Who is this man that attacks me in my sleep? Get out of the way so I may see his face in the firelight." He bent over the still body.

Kheti exclaimed, "It's Nekhen! He's one of my latest recruits. Why should he attack you? Did you have to kill him?"

"Of course I had to kill him," Amenemhet muttered thinking of the only reason Nekhen might have tried to murder him in his sleep. He had recognized Amenemhet.

Yazid interrupted. "Nakht, is this not the one we saw in Wast walking with the high priest?"

Amenemhet immediately understood Yazid's thinking and, silently thanking Yazid for his quick and crafty brain, said, "Yes, Ahmed, it is." He looked at Kheti. "I think we've caught a spy for you, Kheti." Kheti stared at him but said nothing. Amenemhet went on, "He must have realized we'd recognize him eventually and was taking no chances. Once he'd quietly slit my and Ahmed's throats, he could tell you any tale for his reason. He must have been in the high priest's pay, perhaps to report your direction and strength so they might attack again—as they did in the storm."

Kheti's face paled at the memory of the slaughter of his men, blinded by the sand and helpless, and he cursed softly.

Amenemhet said, "He was a new man? I advise you to choose them with great care, for your enemy is most determined."

Kheti's hand pressed Amenemhet's shoulder. "His greedy fingers reach far. I'm grateful to you, Nakht." He motioned to some of the men standing around to carry away the body. "Dig a hole in the sand for Nekhen," he instructed. "Don't bother to mark it. Traitors deserve no marker."

"My own thought exactly," Amenemhet muttered.

Two men carried the body into the shadows, and the rest of them gradually dispersed, mumbling as they went back to their blankets.

Kheti guided Amenemhet and Yazid toward the fire. "Have a little wine with me," he invited. "It may make going to sleep easier."

When they had drunk the wine silently and were walking back to their blankets. Kheti took Amenemhet's arm, saying, "It's well you sleep so lightly, Nakht. Nekhen might easily have decided to kill me instead of you and blame it on you. Who, then, would have taken the time to hear your story before they killed you both?"

Amenemhet thought about that then chuckled softly. "He might have done that, but if he had the head to think that deviously, then he—not the priest—would be the plotter behind all this."

Kheti laughed at the subtle compliment. "Sleep lightly, my friends," he said when he bid them good night. "If we have more than one spy among us, I'll be glad for your protection."

As they traveled, Amenemhet often wondered what was happening in Wast and Noph. If some open move was made to take the throne, he was glad that at least Korusko knew he was alive. He only hoped he might return in time to avoid more bloodshed and a further weakening of his power.

Amenemhet observed Kheti closely, judging much of

his character and ability in the way Kheti handled his men. Amenemhet decided he might yet make an ally of this man, for Kheti was an able leader, intelligent, and in his own way, a man of honor.

With less than a day's journey still before them, Kheti dispatched a messenger to his house to enable the servants to prepare for his arrival. Kheti was now so at ease with Amenemhet he spoke unguardedly to him. The men's mood had also become lighter in anticipation of the journey's end.

Kheti promised Amenemhet his own favorite slave, Yasmine. He assured Amenemhet she was a beauty and would—without a doubt—make him forget his troubles. Kheti's generosity with Yasmine was due to his plans to replace her with Lotus. Amenemhet knew this, and he felt a stab of jealousy even while he knew that somehow he would prevent it.

Kheti remarked that Yasmine was teaching Lotus to dance in the manner of the sand-dwellers and that they would be treated to this entertainment at the evening meal. This he had arranged through his messenger.

Amenemhet was well-acquainted with the dances Kheti meant, and his heart missed a beat at the thought of Nefrytatanen's performing such a dance. He was filled with wonder that she should do it at all. He was not anxious to have other eyes witness it, but at this time he could see no way to prevent it. With the thought of seeing her again, his heart felt lighter, and he decided that, come what may, he was much happier.

Even Yazid became almost merry, for Kheti had promised him, too, a beautiful slave girl.

Amenemhet wondered about Kheti's household, which seemed so well supplied with beautiful and willing women. He wondered if Kheti's life was, perhaps, preferable to his.

When Kheti's messenger arrived, the house was thrown into a turmoil of preparation. Nefrytatanen was told she would make her appearance at the evening meal as amusement for Kheti and his guests, but she knew his intention was not that of entertaining his men. She had become so resigned to his return and to the life that had been thrust upon her that she merely shrugged her shoulders.

When Kheti and his men arrived, Nefrytatanen saw none of them because she was kept occupied in the preparations for her dance. These preparations weren't of her own choosing but of Yasmine's.

Nefrytatanen's heart fell when she saw the garments she would wear. Yasmine—knowing her reluctance— had chosen a costume calculated to make her even more embarrassed for Yasmine hoped she would be clumsy with self-consciousness. Nefrytatanen knew that when Kheti saw her so attired, he would be more anxious than ever for her. She hoped his guests would keep him occupied. She also hoped he hadn't forgotten what he had said to her on the desert.

Nefrytatanen stared at her image in a mirror and shook her head silently. The fine gold chains and beads barely covered her breasts, and the smallest of golden girdles around her hips made an invitation of even the most careful walk. When she turned, the long and filmy skirt swirled like an unfolding scarlet flower. More gold beads draped on her forehead accented the slight slant of her eyes and drew attention to them. She stared at her glittering image and was afraid to leave her room.

Nefrytatanen had no choice. She was firmly escorted out by a burly guard and thrust onto the darkened stage-like area in the room where the men had finished eating and now were sipping wine. The floor was cold under her bare feet but felt no colder than her heart. The space outside the area in which she stood was dark, and she could see nothing but shadowy shapes.

A single reed flute began to play, and as Nefrytatanen stood poised with arms upraised in the beginning posture of the dance, the lamps around her were silently lit by unseen servants. As they more clearly revealed her form, she heard the quick intake of someone's breath in the darkness beyond the flickering light.

She recognized Kheti's whisper, "That is Lotus, Nakht. Is she not all I said and more?" There was no answering comment.

To the music of the flute was added the soft drumming of the timbrels in a throbbing beat designed to excite a man's senses. It was accented at intervals with the soft clinking of small finger cymbals. Nefrytatanen began, as she had been taught, a slow rhythmic movement of open invitation. Her face was impassive, impossible to read, and a fire flared within Amenemhet that, despite the situation, slowly drained him of reason and consumed him with so powerful a desire that he trembled.

Slowly and subtly, the tone of the dance changed. Amenemhet's reeling mind began to perceive that she now made of the flute's song a poignant voice, and of the timbrels' throb, another emotion. The soft sounds of her golden chains became her own whisper.

Nefrytatanen kept time to the music, writhing like a serpent, but it was no sand-dweller's dance now. It was her own Tamehu singing, rich with pride. It was Nefrytatanen's own spirit that took the dance and made of it herself. There was nothing here of a slave or a concubine. She was Aset waiting in loneliness for her beloved Asar. Here was her promise of delight. The promise held much because her face was no longer the implacable emptiness of before. It was filled with an emotion each man recognized; however hardened, each of them was shaken by it. Everyone of them watching wished he were the one she dreamed of and spoke to. And one knew he was.

The tempo changed, and Nefrytatanen's dance changed with it. Here was the queen who demanded release. Amenemhet saw the lift of her chin in defiance. The flower flame of her skirt unfolding revealed the clean line of a long and curving leg as she turned sharply. Amenemhet longed to leap to the stage and shield her from those other watching eyes.

Almost imperceptibly, the music grew faster, and somehow she made of it her plea to him, heightened with the music's pace. Abruptly the music ended, and she sank slowly to the floor, face down, her hair spreading in a river of black that cascaded toward him so closely he could almost touch it. He stood up without knowing it.

While the lamps were being lit Nefrytatanen lay panting, wondering what the rest of the night held for her. Finally she raised her head, and her eyes rested on Amenemhet.

Nefrytatanen rose slowly, shocked, incredulous with joy. Amenemhet stood motionless, looking at her.

She felt as if she had been dead and had now returned to life. Had she died during the dance and awakened in Tuat? She searched for words and found none. She only stared at him and he at her. Dimly she saw Kheti rise and look silently at both of them.

Amenemhet walked toward her, and she couldn't move. She thought she would faint. He stood before her, and her reeling mind couldn't believe he was there. She remained silent though the singing of her heart surely filled the room.

Amenemhet must know. Whatever Kheti had told him, he must know that, in truth, she remembered everything.

Finally Amenemhet—without taking his eyes from Nefrytatanen—spoke over his shoulder to Kheti, who now stood just behind him watching the radiance of her face. "Kheti, let the three of us speak together alone." Kheti, surprisingly, asked no questions but turned to lead them into the hall.

As they walked the short way, Amenemhet's nearness set the hair on Nefrytatanen's neck standing, and she was bursting with wonder. She could barely walk. At the same time, she wanted to run—to fly. They were silent until they entered a small room, and Kheti closed the door behind them. Then he regarded them with much curiosity—and some fear.

Amenemhet turned to Kheti, taking Nefrytatanen's arm so she stood at his side. "Kheti," he said, "I'm not Nakht, and she's not Lotus. You see before you your king and queen."

Kheti's mouth fell open, and he stared.

Nefrytatanen's eyes also widened. King and queen? She was thinking of Mentuhotep and Meresank. Her emotions were scattered like dry leaves before the wind. Then Amenemhet turned to her.

"My father and mother were poisoned by Sinuhe," he said softly.

Tears filled her eyes, and pain flashed through her.

Amenemhet turned and resumed speaking to Kheti. "You've been a friend since I met you, but what you did before that has caused grievous pain. You took the queen from me and greatly endangered her life—and you handed her servant, who was also her dear friend, to Sinuhe, who has probably killed her." Amenemhet's voice was quiet but angry. "I offer you a chance to repay us by helping clean out this nest of vipers in our land."

Nefrytatanen felt pity for Kheti. His expression had gradually changed from shock to disbelief and finally to belief, as he realized Nakht was, indeed, his king. He looked paralyzed, as if he didn't know whether to call his men or prostrate himself on the floor.

"Beloved," Nefrytatanen said quietly, "Kheti hasn't treated me too badly, considering all things." She couldn't help but smile faintly at this. "He thought me a slave for, on the ship, Sira had put on my gown to amuse me. I don't know what happened after that because I was unconscious. When I awoke, I remembered nothing. I can forgive Kheti. I'm sure he didn't know whose ship it was." She looked up at Amenemhet, her eyes again filling with tears. "What can I say of your father and mother? For myself, I think there's nothing to do but to avenge them with Sinuhe's life."

She paused a moment then asked, "Is Hathorbes involved as well?"

"I'm not sure," Amenemhet answered. "It looks suspicious, and I have Ankhneferu watching him." He smiled faintly. "Ankhneferu would have taken you to me, by the way."

Nefrytatanen stared at Amenemhet, but, before she was able to reply, Kheti stepped forward.

He said, "The Two Lands are in confusion with both of you disappeared and King Mentuhotep and Queen Meresank dead. The armies are ready, and Sinuhe hopes to win the throne." He paced the floor, now more interested in these events than his own fate. "I would not wish it to end this way," he muttered as if to himself. He stopped pacing and looked at them. "What can I say to so generous an offer as you have made? I beg you to believe that we didn't come to the ship to kill. I had been away from Tamera for a time and only recently had returned to Wast. Although I'd heard of the marriage, I knew nothing of Queen Nefrytatanen's proposed journey to Noph—not until afterwards. I had never seen you to recognize you. Sinuhe's messenger said only that a noble lady was traveling north on a ship to escape her husband. I was to capture her and return her to him. We killed no one."

Kheti paused and took a deep breath. "I think, later, Sinuhe must have sent men to murder those on the ship —as he sent them to kill me on the desert and as he sent them to silence Drankma. He takes no chances that anyone will talk." Kheti looked at Amenemhet with steady eyes. "He knew I wouldn't have done what I did had I known the truth. Still, it was my hand that stopped the ship and made the rest possible." He looked at the floor, his distress obvious. "I did not know!" he finished.

Amenemhet looked at Kheti coldly. "I would ask if it was part of your reward to take the noble lady's attendant for yourself except, if you hadn't taken her, my queen would have lain with the other serving women—hacked and burned. I cannot fully blame you for what happened," Amenemhet conceded. "You were taken in by Sinuhe's lies. Neither can I blame you for wanting Nefrytatanen. In truth, your desire saved her life, and you didn't know who she was."

Kheti's tanned face, which had grown pale, now became as scarlet as Nefrytatanen's skirts. He said nothing for a time, staring shamefacedly at the floor. Finally he whispered, "My life and men are yours."

Amenemhet's eyes were no warmer as he said, "Prepare your men, and we'll leave when they're ready. No time can be wasted. We'll ride to Noph for ships and sail to Wast from there." He put his arm around Nefrytatanen and held her tightly to his side. "You will come with us," he said looking down into her eyes. "I cannot let you be separated from me again."

She said, "If you told me to stay, I would not, beloved, I could not."

Amenemhet finally smiled at her, but when he turned again to Kheti, his smile faded. Sharply he said, "We can delay no longer. Get the men ready."

"I can have them and the supplies ready to leave tomorrow night," Kheti answered quickly. He bowed low and backed hurriedly out.

Amenemhet turned to Nefrytatanen, saying nothing. He took her in his arms and held her tightly, and they were content in the embrace, neither talking nor kissing, not wanting to separate after so long a time apart.

Finally they moved away from one another, and she whispered, "Soon, beloved, we will win everything."

As Naomi sat quietly with her husband, her mind dwelt on Lotus's dance, which she guessed must now be finished. However unenthusiastic Lotus's attitude had been, she had learned quickly, and Naomi knew her natural grace would further enhance the dancing.

Naomi wondered at Kheti's pursuit of Lotus. That she was unwilling was apparent, and it had never been Kheti's way to force such matters. Naomi shook her head as she mused. She could only conclude that the girl's exceptional beauty must be causing his strange behavior. Naomi was saddened. She had grown fond of Lotus and disliked to think of the girl unhappy.

Lotus was different from the others. Naomi had seen it from the first. Had she been a gambler, Naomi would have bet Lotus was not and had never been a slave. Naomi had some idea of what Lotus had been doing the night she had brought her the peculiar articles. Naomi had heard of such things among her own people. That Lotus should know of magic was additional evidence she was no slave. She would never have fallen into slavery if she possessed such knowledge. Naomi decided Lotus had fallen into Kheti's hands only because of her memory loss.

Naomi was sure Lotus's memory was partially if not fully restored; otherwise, Naomi reasoned, Lotus would not have been able to do what Naomi suspected she'd done that night. Naomi told no one at all of her suspicions. Although she had no quarrel with Kheti, she was burning with curiosity to see what would happen next.

Naboth was hard at work weighing Kheti's gold and entering his figures in his accounts. He wasn't seriously concerned with the matters Naomi dwelt upon. Although he could appreciate Lotus's position, he also knew his own. Keeping Kheti's accounts was his job, and it was an unusually exalted one for a slave. His clever management had won and held his position, and he made certain of it with continuing excellence. He only hoped Naomi's sympathy for Lotus wouldn't cause them trouble.

Suddenly Yasmine burst through the door, her red hair flying loose and her face slightly flushed, as if from running. Closing the door securely behind her, she turned to them with wide eyes and a pale face, hesitating while she caught her breath.

"What's wrong, Yasmine?" Naomi rose quickly. Naboth had looked up from his work and stared at her, finally distracted.

"Kheti has brought the king here!" the girl panted.

"Yasmine has been drinking," Naboth said serenely, "or she has gone mad."

"If you think me drunk or mad, see what you decide when you hear the rest of my story." Yasmine's hands were on her hips, her green eyes glittering.

Naboth watched her with little interest. "Well, well, Yasmine, out with it," he sighed. "Tell us what you've dreamed."

"I didn't dream it. I saw it. I peeked at Lotus's dance to see how she'd manage." Yasmine looked a little dejected for a moment at the memory of the dance. "She did it well," she admitted. "When it was over and the lamps lit, as she arose from the floor, a man named Nakht stood up and went to her. They stared at each other as if they looked at ghosts! They said nothing— but the looks! It made my blood run hot and cold at one time! Kheti went to them, puzzled, and Nakht said they must talk privately. Kheti, too, was struck by their expressions and took them away without a word. I followed and hid myself and saw and heard everything." She stared at them and the awe in her face was unmistakable. "Nakht said he was King Amenemhet, and Lotus is the missing Queen Nefrytatanen." Yasmine waited smugly for their reaction.

Naboth stood up suddenly, and a cloud of gold dust rose shimmering on the air. He ignored it. Naomi sat with a pale face, biting her lips.

"He said," Yasmine continued, "he would grant Kheti pardon if Kheti will help him and the queen fight Sinuhe, the high priest in the south, who is the plotter."

"By the gods' mercy, girl, did Kheti believe this?" Naomi finally gasped.

"He did," Yasmine declared. She sat down. "If you saw them together, you'd know it, too. The queen remembers everything. She was playing a part to see how she might escape. Ah, yes, they're who they say they are. To see them together is to know it." Yasmine was quiet then, as they all were while they absorbed the astounding news, and then Yasmine jumped up and shook Naomi's shoulders.

"Naomi, they'll leave tomorrow night and spend tonight here!" Naomi stared at her without comprehension. "Naomi, here! Under this roof will the king and queen celebrate their lost wedding night!"

"That's true," Naomi said slowly. "We must prepare the room." She remembered the Lotus she had known and suddenly smiled. "What joy for them!" she exclaimed. "To find each other at last after such pain. Yasmine, you must help me. We must do the best we can to make the room beautiful. Get others to help you. Gather many flowers. I'll go to the queen's room and see what can be done." Smiling widely, she went out the door.

Amenemhet kept his arm around Nefrytatanen as they walked to her chamber later that evening. After Kheti had left, they had spent some time in the room, catching up on each other's adventures and filling in blank places with scraps of information. Now Amenemhet touched a strand of her hair thoughtfully. His fingertips touched her cheek. They stood in the corridor looking into each other's eyes until Naomi, hurrying down the hall, turned a corner quickly and almost collided with them. She stopped, staring at Amenemhet, then bowed deeply.

"I beg your forgiveness," she whispered backing away.

"Naomi, will you help me?" Nefrytatanen asked softly. "I wish to prepare myself for my wedding night."

Amenemhet looked at Nefrytatanen in surprise, becoming joyful, while Naomi stood like a statue. He kissed Nefrytatanen gently for the first time since the night her ship had sailed from him, leaving him standing in the darkness of the lost moon. When he released her, she smiled and turned to enter her chamber with

Amenemhet's golden eyes following, dreaming of the night they'd share at last.

Naomi closed the door softly before Amenemhet, and he smiled at himself then followed a waiting servant to another room to bathe.

Amenemhet stood in his robe, knowing he had hurried but unable to slow his pace. He had imagined how Nefrytatanen had bathed, seeing in his mind's eye how Naomi had dried her body and perfumed her skin —and how she slid the comb through her black hair.

Finally Amenemhet thought he'd go mad with his imaginings and didn't care if he did. He stepped onto the terrace, and, gazing at the sky, he saw Nefrytatanen's eyes in the gleam of the stars. Although he was a reasonably patient man, he began to wonder how long he must wait. He started to pace the room, wondering if he might march into her chamber now, and he felt foolish for the idea. He stopped pacing and stood, by chance, near the door. Naomi opened it and faced him. Surprised by his closeness, she backed away a step.

"Sire," Naomi said softly, inclining her head, "the queen is ready." A barely concealed smile tilted the corners of her mouth. She turned, and Amenemhet followed her to Nefrytatanen's door.

The chamber had been transformed by white silken hangings and flowers. A golden lamp cast its glow upon a bed strewn with silk pillows. Nefrytatanen's scent was a living thing in the room.

Yasmine led Nefrytatanen into the room from between a fall of filmy draperies and bowed deeply, staring all the time in awe at Amenemhet. She and Naomi left silently.

Nefrytatanen stood alone facing Amenemhet. In this silver room, she was the gem in the lotus. Her hair was a shining black stream of silk falling to her hips. Her gown, a veil of blue, was the color of the sky after the sun was gone and before the black of night. Beneath gossamer folds of her gown, the soft curves of her body

were a promise. Her eyes glowed the smoky dark blue
he remembered so well.

Seeing the golden light in Amenemhet's eyes, Nefrytatanen felt herself beginning to tremble.

"Beloved," he heard her whisper as he came slowly
toward her, walking as if dreaming, not believing this
moment was real.

Then he had her folded in his arms, her soft body
clinging eagerly to him, her perfume drowning him, her
mouth the very essence of life against his. His touch
made a trembling leaf of her, and he trembled, too,
with wonder. The gold of his eyes warmed, turning to
fire, and he ached from the touch of her. In her kiss he
lost himself completely. He took her in his arms and
laid her gently on the bed. He drew away her gown,
and was filled with elation as he beheld this most
beautiful of all women.

"Beloved, mine," Nefrytatanen whispered close to
his ear, and Amenemhet shivered. Then he allowed his
senses to rise to the ecstasy her lips gave him, the
warmth of her.

They gave themselves gifts of one another, gladly,
eagerly, and with pride, and while they seemed to sink,
whirling, they presently rose together to become a
shattering sunburst of light that sent them spinning.

Amenemhet knew, as they lay serene, that she was
truly his at last. He smiled. He was surely hers.

All through the night they held each other close,
awakening to know again their desire, to share love, to
fall asleep again, smiling and murmuring love words.

When the first light of dawn touched the sky, they
stood naked at the window opening, folded in each
other's arms, and watched Ra's first golden rays enter
the sanctuary they had made of this room. Amenemhet
pointed to the morning star that glowed low on the
horizon. "Look," he whispered, "Sept brings for Tamera a new year, and a new life begins for us with it."
Nefrytatanen smiled up at him while she drew a little

closer to his side. "Today," he added softly, "the flood begins, and the Nile brings fruitfulness."

After a time of silence, Nefrytatanen sighed and said, "Beloved, Ra gives us a new day, but let us go back and enjoy our solitude before the world interferes with it once more."

He took her hand, laughing, and led her again to their silken place to love, and then to sleep again.

Naomi's soft voice awoke them for the morning meal. They ate in bed, smiling into each other's eyes, lingering, reluctant to move from their place, hip to hip, leg to leg, finding ways to remain close.

When the food was carried away, they released the servants and bathed alone together, washing each other and laughing with the abandon of children—until they knew love again.

Finally, knowing they could no longer hold the world away from them, they admitted the servants to help them dress. They watched each other, still wanting solitude, knowing each other at last, and longing for endless nights to come.

Chapter Nine

By the time the caravan of Kheti's men had reached
the gates of Noph, word of their arrival had spread
from the watching countryside, and the streets of the
city were filled with people who stared openmouthed
at the king and queen they'd thought dead.

Nefrytatanen's happiness at seeing her familiar home
was dampened by their strange reception. Amenemhet,
considering the faces of the silent crowd, realized that
they were not only astonished at their king and queen
plodding dusty and disheveled through the streets, but
that Kheti's men confused them. They weren't sure
whether Amenemhet and Nefrytatanen arrived in
triumph or as prisoners.

Finally Amenemhet drew his horse to a stop, halting
the column. Kheti rode to his side. "They don't know
what to think of our arrival," Amenemhet said. "They
don't know you, Kheti, and I can well imagine the wild
stories that have spread since we both disappeared."

Nefrytatanen breathed in relief. "That must be the
reason for their queer silence. We must make some
announcement to put them at ease."

"Yes," he answered promptly. "And let us do it now,
informally, from our horses. We have no time to spare
for ceremony."

Kheti signaled the men to be at ease because they,
too, were disconcerted by the quiet, staring faces.

Amenemhet leaned from his saddle and addressed

a man. "What stories have you heard that you greet your rulers with silence?"

The man stared at Amenemhet, too amazed at being personally addressed by his king to speak.

"Let me say a word to them, beloved," said Nefrytatanen. "They still don't know you and may be suspicious of my silence."

She put her hand affectionately on his arm—so the people could see her gesture—and raised her other hand to drop the hood of her cloak—so her face would be clearly recognized.

"Greetings, our people," she began. "Well may you be confused at the sight of our coming with these armed strangers. I know you've heard stories of treachery in the south, and treachery there has been. The king rescued me, and we have found friends among those who travel with us. Be at ease with them because they'll accompany us to Wast and help us put right the evil."

Faces in the throng started to smile, and, as the people began to understand the importance of what they had been told, the smiles burst into a cheer, the roar of it striking the travelers in waves that almost deafened them. Kheti grinned at Nefrytatanen because his men had now become heroes. Amenemhet also smiled, very pleased with her.

Nefrytatanen raised a hand to silence the crowd. "I must tell you," she said, suddenly stern. "You will accept King Amenemhet as his people accept me. This is one land—Tamera—and we are now one people. King Amenemhet and I rule together." Amenemhet raised his eyebrows slightly at the threat in her voice as she finished, "I will not say this again." She turned to Amenemhet with a sweet smile on her lips, and mischief in her eyes. She said softly, "It's your turn, sire."

He smiled at her then restrained his smile when he addressed the crowd. "Queen Nefrytatanen speaks plainly, which I will also do. As soon as we can be ready, we will sail up the Nile with as much speed as possible. In the meantime we'll stay at the palace here.

We've all seen too much bloodshed and suffering. This time of treachery will be ended soon, and we'll have peace once again."

The air again rang with relieved and happy voices. As the caravan resumed its march through the streets, flower petals flew over their heads and into their path. Kheti's men smiled at pretty faces looking with friendliness and curiosity at these strange, new heroes. Kheti observed silently that he might well enjoy a return to Noph, when matters were settled at Wast.

Amenemhet didn't miss the inviting looks, and he smiled back at them. Nefrytatanen, riding slightly behind him and out of his vision, said nothing. But she occasionally withered a pretty smile with a cold stare.

When the gates of the palace opened, Ankhneferu stood with Seti, Nefrytatanen's prime minister, to greet them. Hathorbes was nowhere in evidence. They dismounted. Kheti and his men were shown to a place to rest and refresh themselves. Amenemhet and Nefrytatanen were stopped by Ankhneferu before they entered the palace doors.

"Sire," Ankhneferu said, "I must relate unhappy news." His face was a reflection of his distress.

"What is it?" Amenemhet asked.

"Two days ago I received news from the south that Commander Korusko is dead. I strongly suspect Sinuhe had him killed. I fear that, in order to stir more strife between the people of the two kingdoms, he's blamed spies from Noph for the commander's death."

"Then Sinuhe has discovered your disappearance also," Nefrytatanen observed.

"And now I have also lost Korusko, who was a friend," Amenemhet said in disgust, remembering Korusko standing alone in the darkness watching them leave. He turned abruptly and went into the palace.

Nefrytatanen led Amenemhet to the throne room and, dusty and travel-stained as she was, immediately sat in her place. Amenemhet sat beside her, looking angry.

"Where is Hathorbes?" Nefrytatanen commanded, her eyes glimmering blue ice.

"I am here," came a voice from the entrance. Hathorbes stood looking at them.

"Enter, Hathorbes," said Amenemhet studying the high priest of the north kingdom. Hathorbes walked slowly forward and knelt quietly before them. Amenemhet spoke softly, but his voice carried accusation. "Hathorbes, you give your rulers no congratulations or even greetings to your queen?" he asked. "You almost seem disappointed to see us. Are you not filled with happiness at the sight of your beloved queen's safe return?"

Hathorbes's eyes met Amenemhet's. "I'm glad you both are well and have returned." His eyes were blank, and his voice was flat and expressionless.

"Tell us what happened since I left," said Nefrytatanen. Her voice was cordial, but her eyes remained cold and suspicious. "Tell us the news. I haven't seen Commander Nessumontu. Has he gone somewhere?"

Since you disappeared and I suspected treachery from the Upper Kingdom, all kinds of reports have come in from every direction. When Drankma's messenger said he had you I, fearing more treachery from the south—," he glanced at Amenemhet— "decided to have you brought secretly here while you had no memory. With the news of your disappearance and the king's seclusion and subsequent disappearance, I was confused. To safeguard Tamehu, I sent Nessumontu with the army to watch Wast so they might not surprise us with an attack."

Hathorbes answered well enough, thought Amenemhet, but he had certainly overstepped his authority. His lack of formal address to them was more than impudent. And his story sounded rehearsed.

Nefrytatanen glanced at Amenemhet, and their thoughts were transferred in that look. She said, "Hathorbes, since when do you make such decisions and even give the military commander orders when we're not present? Is it not your proper position to attend to religious matters only?"

"I didn't know what to do," he answered. "No one else seemed ready to act, and there was great confusion. The people were angry and fearful. I was afraid of attack from Tashemau. Seti did nothing. He wished to wait. I thought waiting would leave us helpless so I gave the order."

"How diligent you are," commented Amenemhet, "and how ready to give orders. Did you, perhaps, stir the people's fear and anger a bit? Possibly the same way in which you stirred them before by talking against our marriage?"

"It's Seti's place to make decisions when we're absent," Nefrytatanen said firmly. She was thinking of Hathorbes's plan to keep her from Amenemhet.

Amenemhet turned his attention from Hathorbes. "Ankhneferu, tell us. Did Nessumontu think the danger great enough to march against Wast?"

Ankhneferu, who had been silent all through this, looked uncomfortably at Hathorbes, his superior, then answered, "Nessumontu was reluctant."

Amenemhet rose. "Hathorbes, you'll be placed under guard in your quarters until these questions are settled. We haven't decided your guilt, but your explanation doesn't prove innocence. While we're gone, Ankhneferu, you and Prime Minister Seti will be in charge."

Ankhneferu silently inclined his head in assent then left. Hathorbes looked coldly at Nefrytatanen, who nodded her agreement with Amenemhet's decision. Without a word Hathorbes left with the guard.

Nefrytatanen addressed Seti. "See that a messenger is sent immediately to Nessumontu. Inform him we're coming with more help. No attack is to be made or provoked. All efforts must be made to avoid combat, unless it becomes necessary to defend themselves."

Seti backed out the door to hurry to his task. Kheti then arrived to inform them that he was making arrangements to have twenty cedar ships equipped and ready to sail that evening. Amenemhet congratulated Kheti on his speed then sighed with weariness. Nefrytatanen's smile was as tired.

"We must rest today," Amenemhet said to Nefrytatanen then turned to Kheti adding, "Arrange that your men are comfortable and content in every way—as long as they're ready to leave tonight."

"We can use my chambers today," Nefrytatanen told Amenemhet. A shadow passed her eyes at the thought of her familiar room without Sira's presence. Amenemhet noted her expression and took her arm gently.

"We'll learn what happened to Sira," he promised. "If she has been badly treated or is dead, those who are guilty will be punished." Nefrytatanen looked at him gratefully but said nothing.

Yazid plodded slowly behind them down the hall as they walked to Nefrytatanen's chamber. They were followed by a servant girl named Bekhet.

At the door Amenemhet turned. "Yazid," he said quietly, "you're as tired as we are for you've faithfully followed us all the way. Go to your quarters and tend to yourself. Rest and don't be concerned with us. Bekhet can give any help we need."

Yazid gave Amenemhet a smile of gratitude, bowed slightly, and left them.

"Yazid is to you as Sira always was to me," Nefrytatanen commented.

Amenemhet found Nefrytatanen's apartments cool and refreshing after the dusty desert. Glancing around, Amenemhet remembered how he had had his apartment at Wast refurnished for her arrival. It seemed as if that had happened in another lifetime.

Nefrytatanen went alone to her bath, and when she returned, Amenemhet went. When he came back, she was lying on her bed, her eyes closed. He joined her, kissing her lightly and taking her hand. Sinking into the bed, he felt as if his bones had been crushed during the hard, fast ride from Kheti's house.

A fountain in the courtyard outside the window

openings whispered softly, and a cool breeze ruffled the floating curtains as Amenemhet and Nefrytatanen slept lightly. Gradually they became aware of noises outside the palace walls. They sat up and drowsily listened. The sounds seemed to be marching feet, and rumbling carts and animals, moving in sizable numbers. They looked at each other in alarm.

Amenemhet got up and, pulling a robe around him, put his head out the doorway to ask what the commotion was. The smiling guard spoke softly. Amenemhet came back to the bed, also smiling. He shook his head, amazed.

"What is it?" Nefrytatanen asked.

"The citizens of Noph have already decided that we'll overcome the evil at Wast, set Tamera in order, and have a great celebration afterwards! They don't wish to miss this joyous event, and everyone is traveling to Wast." He laughed delightedly.

Nefrytatanen smiled. "But they'll arrive before us!"

"They might," Amenemhet said thoughtfully. "I wonder what Sinuhe will think if that great crowd suddenly enters Wast's gates in a holiday mood, when the city is almost under siege."

Nefrytatanen frowned. "Do you think he'd attack them?"

Amenemhet considered this a moment then answered, "I think they'll confuse him, but I don't think he'll be panicked into attack. Whatever else Sinuhe is, he's no fool. If he hopes to rule the people eventually, he can't begin by slaughtering them. They won't seem a threat anyway."

Amenemhet and Nefrytatanen sat together awhile, still holding hands, thinking about what lay before them. Finally Amenemhet pressed her shoulders back to the pillows.

Kissing her cheek gently, he smiled and whispered, "Rest, beloved, and stop worrying about it. Noph's people are confident enough of us to walk into Sinuhe's hands and wait for our triumph. Go to sleep so we can later enjoy the celebration."

When this is over," she murmured. "I won't care to attend any parties. I want to be alone with you for a very long time."

He smiled and lay back beside her, thinking that her wishes echoed his own, and he resolved to make sure they came true.

Their evening meal was a simple and hasty one for it was necessary to leave quickly. Nefrytatanen watched Amenemhet finish dressing, looking a little alarmed at his weapons.

"When I went into the desert with Yazid," Amenemhet remarked, "I had less protection than this." He put his arms around her. "Prince or not," he said quietly, "I was trained like any soldier, and I know how to use these grim instruments. I'll be safe." His gold eyes looked solemnly into hers. "I know what you're thinking, beloved. You'll get nowhere near the battle, if there is one. Your Commander Nessumontu will recognize my blue war crown and obey me. I won't chance your being wounded, and I won't argue with you," he finished, putting his fingers lightly over her mouth, knowing she had been ready to protest. He replaced his fingers with his lips in a kiss which began in affection, lingered, and turned to fire. He drew away and smiled.

"If we had more time, I'd enjoy what those lips promise," he said softly. "We'll have no parties in Wast when this is over—except our own, very private, party."

When they met the others, who had been waiting, Amenemhet instructed Yazid and Rakkor to remain on the ship with Nefrytatanen and a few guards. Although Rakkor felt honored to be selected as the queen's protector, he would have preferred the battle for he felt he should be with Kheti. Yazid said nothing, but he, too, wished he might fight at Amenemhet's side.

When the twenty ships finally moved up the river, their great red and gold sails glinting in the moonlight,

Kheti paused from his duties, thinking how impressive they must seem to the surrounding countryside.

He stood in the shadows of the deck and saw Amenemhet and Nefrytatanen appear and stand by the rail. Kheti hesitated to leave, having something to report to Amenemhet, but he didn't like to come forward either. Their moment was obviously a private one. He wondered, as he thought of the adventures they had all experienced since their first meeting, about the emotions they felt. Kheti couldn't imagine how he would feel in their situation, but he was sure he would be afraid of losing all they stood to lose.

Kheti's musing kept him standing motionless so long that Nefrytatanen moved a little, and Amenemhet now faced him. Kheti was about to step forward when he realized that Amenemhet was occupied solely with her and that he did not notice Kheti at all. Amenemhet bent and kissed Nefrytatanen.

Now Kheti dared not move. To observe such a thing was embarrassing, but to reveal his observation of this intimate moment was unquestionably worse. He had no choice but to remain in the shadows, trying to be invisible, fervently wishing he were elsewhere.

"I would stay with you forever on this ship, in your house, my house, a tent, anywhere," Nefrytatanen said clearly. She was looking into Amenemhet's eyes, which Kheti could see easily in the bright moonlight. He wondered if a man had ever loved a woman more.

Nefrytatanen trembled slightly in Amenemhet's arms and whispered, "Beloved, you are a mysterious man."

"How can I now be mysterious to you?" Amenemhet smiled.

"I cannot really say," she murmured. "I look into your eyes and sometimes find them as open and merry as a child's, but sometimes they're as deep and old as all of time. There are moments they're filled with such strength that I am awed."

Amenemhet turned to look out over the water. "And yours are sometimes warm and clear as the summer

sky, but now they're as full of shadows as the night."
He turned again to look at her. "I could never tire of
you because you're a mystery to me also. The first time
I saw you, I wondered if you were a spell-caster who
had put an enchantment on me, so strange were the
feelings you gave me. I decided, later, that I didn't care
if you were."

"And if I admitted I can do magic," she asked slowly,
"what would you think?"

"I wouldn't care," he replied. "Cast your spells, if you
will. You are too beautiful to resist."

"Beloved," she whispered, "I feel as if we have a
whole new world to discover."

"We'll explore it together," Amenemhet promised,
putting his arm around her waist. "When this is over
and the land is at peace, we'll explore all the world and
all of time and all the love we'll fill it with."

"And if we don't succeed?" Nefrytatanen asked.
"What will we then do?"

"If we don't win, I'll be dead," he said grimly. "Then
you must flee."

"I won't leave you," she said firmly. "If you die, I
will also. If I see you fall, I'll go into the battle alone.
No one will stop me. I'll go to your side, even then,
wishing for an end to my own life, for without you I'd
be merely an empty body. My soul would be with
yours."

Kheti could see that Amenemhet was deeply moved
by her words because he took a moment to answer.

"Beloved, to know you await me will strengthen my
arm. I won't be struck down. Your love will protect
me as a wall of soldiers couldn't. Don't speak of death
or longing to die. Wait for me with confidence. Prepare
for my return so I may think of you that way, perfumed
and waiting as at Kheti's house. In a few days we'll be
in our palace at Wast."

Amenemhet kissed Nefrytatanen again and Kheti
watched them enviously, wondering if he'd ever find
such love.

The sweet smell of the ship's cedar mingled with Nefrytatanen's perfume and drifted to where Kheti silently stood. Seeing that they were lost in each other and oblivious to the rest of the world, Kheti slipped away. They shouldn't be interrupted by him and his questions about war, he decided. Let them have what they might now. King or not, Kheti reflected, Amenemhet could be killed as easily as anyone else, and if he were, then Nefrytatanen would be lost.

It was mid-morning when the ship sailed around the last bend in the widening river, and those who stood on deck saw the two armies before the gates of Wast. The army carrying Amenemhet's white banner was moving forward.

Amenemhet observed that Sinuhe took no chances because he hadn't bothered with foot soldiers or even archers on foot. All were mounted, as they began their sweep toward Nessumontu's more conventionally lined forces, evidently hoping to panic and ride down the soldiers on foot.

"So Sinuhe gave the order," Amenemhet said softly.

"I would have guessed so, if only from the formation he uses," Kheti replied sarcastically.

"Nessumontu holds and waits," cried Nefrytatanen, "but not for long. See what he will yet do!"

Amenemhet watched by the rail as the ship pulled closer to shore. He was anxious to be off and away. Nessumontu's men surely didn't panic, he noted. They began to move with discipline. The ranks of Nesssumontu's foot soldiers and archers split, allowing the attacking mounted men to burst through them. The archers and foot soldiers then reformed into two flanking forces in a maneuver Amenemhet admired. The archers quickly rained a shower of arrows on the riders, taking advantage of their lethal power before their own mounted men got in the way. Many of Amenemhet's soldiers fell, and he cursed as he watched. Still the southern army pressed forward in waves of white and gold.

When the ship drew to the river bank, Amenemhet immediately mounted his horse. "Kheti," he commanded, "send a guard to the city to take Sinuhe. He probably won't be in the battle but in the palace."

Amenemhet bent to kiss Nefrytatanen, and she reached up to touch his face. They said nothing.

She watched him urge his horse off the ship and onto the ramp with a clatter, then race away. She was thinking of the many ways, and how easily, men could die and of how little anything would mean to her without him.

Amenemhet gathered speed as he and his men rode swiftly toward the conflict. The wind rushing past him closed his eyes to slits and tangled his cloak. With a free hand, he undid its fastening and let it fall to the dust behind.

The fighting churned around their little band of men like a river around rocks. Amenemhet used his sword vigorously, trying to strike with its flat side, rather than kill. All these soldiers were Tamera's men, and he wanted as many as possible to survive. More than one startled face stared at him and turned aside a weapon in confusion. The clamor of clashing weapons, the screaming of the horses, and the struggle of the men made it impossible for Amenemhet to be heard. He didn't try to shout above the din but, swinging his sword to clear a path, headed for the soldier with the signal horn.

The soldier stared at him in disbelief as Amenemhet ordered him to blow the signal for withdrawal. Finally Amenemhet wrenched the horn out of his hands and, standing in his stirrups, blew the signal himself.

The sound didn't stop Nefrytatanen's soldiers, and it threw Amenemhet's army into confusion, so there was only a slight pause in the combat. Amenemhet handed the horn back to its owner, ordering him to continue the signal. Then Amenemhet struck a helmet near him with the handle of his sword, sending the

man under it reeling and helpless, while he rode on to
the next.

Nefrytatanen could see Amenemhet's course and
knew he would try to reach Nessumontu now. She was
sure Nessumontu wouldn't order a halt unless she appeared because he would suspect more treachery. She
could endure watching no longer. She climbed onto a
horse. Rakkor shouted at her to get down.

"I must go," she shouted back. "If I don't, Nessumontu may not stop. He may think this is a trap."

"She could be right," Rakkor said helplessly to
Yazid.

"Then I'll also go!" Yazid exclaimed. "The king will
never forgive me if she's killed. If the queen insists on
suicide, I must be with her to die also." He, too,
mounted a horse. Rakkor wanted to be in the battle
with Kheti, but he wasn't happy to take the queen with
him. Yet he couldn't refuse her. They all clattered off
the ship and raced toward the struggle together.

Nefrytatanen caught her breath as they came closer,
observing details that horrified her. But she didn't
slow or stop. She urged her horse around a man who
lay dying only to hear the horses behind her trample
him. A soldier clutched blindly at her reins, trying to
stop her as he bled from a mortal wound in his skull.
She saw Yazid's sword flash in the sunlight, and she
looked away. Shuddering, she urged her horse on,
thinking angrily that it was for Sinuhe so many died.
She saw Rakkor ride ahead and strike down a man
aiming a spear at her.

Nefrytatanen finally saw an open space. Knowing
her horse wouldn't get through, she dismounted and,
racing around Rakkor, ran toward Nessumontu.

Meanwhile Amenemhet, seeing himself near Nessumontu, shouted to him to stop his men. Nessumontu,
in his surprise, almost slipped from his rearing horse.
His slanted eyes widened and stared at Amenemhet,
while Amenemhet again shouted his order. Then Nessumontu turned to his own horn bearer and signaled.

Amenemhet suddenly paled. Nefrytatanen, hair flying behind her, was running to him. Nessumontu saw her at the same moment, and they both rushed toward her. Meanwhile Kheti, some distance away, saw Nefrytatanen and, with one arm handing bloody and useless, began to fight his way to her.

Both signal horns were blowing. Finally the tumult began to slow. The soldiers and Kheti's men were all confused by the conflicting blasts. Eventually they paused, milling about, looking perplexed at each other, while the moans and screams of men and animals became apparent in the gathering quiet.

Amenemhet looked down at Nefrytatanen, confirming her safety. There was fear as well as anger in his eyes, but he said nothing.

"I was afraid for you," she said simply. He shook his head, still silent. Then he lifted his eyes to gaze, shocked, at the wreckage.

Kheti, his arm still bleeding, reached their side, while Yazid sat staring speechlessly at the dying and wounded.

Nessumontu began to apologize for his delay in obeying Amenemhet's order, but Amenemhet waved his apologies away. He said simply, "Commander Nessumontu, see that the wounded are cared for and the dead gathered up. Then take both armies back to Wast. Sinuhe's war is over."

Amenemhet turned to Nefrytatanen who was staring at the battlefield, eyes wide in horror and shock. He reached down to her and pulled her up behind him. She put her head against his back and, closing her eyes to the scene, clung to him. He signaled the others, and they began the ride back to the palace.

Amenemhet didn't hurry. He knew Sinuhe was being held by Kheti's men. He felt more pensive than anxious. He thought of the men who had just died for nothing. He thought of Korusko. He remembered his father and mother. He felt the quiet anger in him rising into fury even as he felt Nefrytatanen's warm tears on his back.

His anger continued to grow with every step his horse took.

When they rode through the palace gates, Nefryta-tanen was only dimly aware of the guards noisily welcoming them. Clinging to Amenemhet, she struggled to stop weeping. When Amenemhet dismounted, he reached up to her, and she slid into his arms. As she stepped away from him, she saw his look of triumphant fury, and it terrified her.

When they stood before the palace doors, Nefryta-tanen saw Amenemhet's fury rise even higher, and she knew that it was because they entered his home as conquerors, and not as its rightful owners. Amenemhet strode down the hall ahead of her, almost as if he'd forgotten her. He marched into the throne room and through its length to the distant thrones. He stepped up to the dais and stood before the throne, refusing to sit. Nefrytatanen followed his example and remained standing.

With his bloodstained garments and his angry eyes, Amenemhet made a frightening figure. He demanded, "Where is he who soils the palace with his presence?"

Several of Kheti's men immediately appeared in the entrance of the throne room and between them stood Sinuhe. The high priest hesitated at the threshhold, saw Amenemhet's expression, composed himself, and walked without faltering across the immense room.

Amenemhet was silent, thinking of the times Sinuhe had approached Mentuhotep, honored and welcome, and Amenemhet's eyes became glittering triangles of gold ice. Sinuhe stopped at the foot of the thrones, waiting.

Nefrytatanen had been watching Amenemhet, awed and fascinated by this new and terrible side of him, unable to take her gaze from him.

When Amenemhet spoke, his voice was as soft as when he caressed her, but Sinuhe couldn't conceal the terror in his eyes.

"Jackals gather after a battle to tear the flesh of the

men and animals left helpless," Amenemhet said quietly. "My high priest circles the field of battle like the scavengers, until all are helpless and drenched in blood, before he dares step forward to claim his victim, the double crown."

Amenemhet paused, not taking his eyes from Sinuhe, who seemed unable to look away from his king.

"You are without words, my trusted high priest? Defend yourself now, if you have a defense, for you'll have no other chance." Amenemhet fell silent again, his hands at his sides, as he stared at the priest.

Nefrytatanen thought that except for his eyes Amenemhet looked as relaxed as if he waited for a grain report.

"You have no words, Sinuhe?" Amenemhet demanded. "You dare have none? No lies?" Amenemhet paused a moment then asked, "Then tell me where is the serving woman, Sira? What did you do with her? Did you add her death to your list of crimes?" His tone grew even softer but was no less menacing. "Tell me, Sinuhe, for the life of one slave will add nothing to your penalty."

Sinuhe slowly turned his gaze to Nefrytatanen, who watched him intently now. The look of hatred he gave her was almost a physical blow.

"She's where she's been all through this, in the cellar of the temple. The entrance is behind the altar in the sanctuary." Sinuhe's eyes held a strange light.

Nefrytatanen inwardly shivered at his look, but she asked quietly, "Is she alive?"

Sinuhe shrugged. "Go to her and see," he answered. Then he was silent, and they knew he would say no more.

Still looking at Sinuhe, no hint of mercy in his bearing, Amenemhet commanded the guards, "Take him from my sight." Turning from Sinuhe as if dismissing the matter, he added, "Now, I may rightfully sit in my father's place."

Amenemhet sat down, motioning for Nefrytatanen to

do the same. She felt she had no strength left for standing, and she sank weakly into Meresank's place. Amenemhet smiled coldly, looking at no one. He sensed again the presence of the dead kings and their solemn approval of him.

"Beloved," Nefrytatanen whispered after a moment, "I must now go to the temple and find Sira."

"No," he said firmly. "I'll send someone." He was afraid of what she might find.

Nefrytatanen shook her head, adamant. "I must go," she said slowly. "If Sira's alive, she must see me come to her. If she's dying, it must be in my own arms."

Amenemhet understood this but, dreading what they'd find, rose and signaled Kheti and Yazid to follow them. When Nefrytatanen stood up, Amenemhet put his arm around her waist. She was shivering and seemed faint. Concerned, he hesitated, but she urged him forward. When they began to walk, she trembled only a little, and Amenemhet alone knew how weak she was.

When the temple doors stood open before them, both their minds leaped to the memory of their joyful wedding day, a strong contrast to their present bitter torment. They walked through the colonnaded court where they had been married, to the small hall beyond, their boots clattering noisily on the granite floor and echoing through the immense rooms. In the chamber of the sacred barge, Nefrytatanen paused, fearful of entering the inner sanctuary which was forbidden to all but the high priest.

"Come, beloved," Amenemhet whispered. "This place is, I think, less holy after Sinuhe's presence."

They went slowly through the entrance and up two low steps. The columns here were not as high as in the other rooms, for the ceiling was lower. Slits in the roof sent transparent pillars of sunlight to touch the statues of Asar and Aset, which were made of purest gold. A gem in Aset's hand sent rays of broken rainbows over the onyx walls. They stood, gazing at the room in silent awe, for, of course, none of them had ever seen the inner sanctuary. They stood close together, turning slowly, taking in the beauty of the golden statues and ornaments, the gleaming black onyx lotus-and-papyrus-shaped columns.

Nefrytatanen slowly walked a few steps forward, pausing at the statue of Aset, and looked up into the face of the goddess. She could hear again, in an echo, Sira's words before the marriage, wishing them love to compare with that of Asar and Aset. It was as if Sira whispered to her again, but this time from the afterlife. Nefrytatanen turned her eyes from the goddess and moved silently away.

Yazid lit a torch, and they began walking down the stone steps into the cellar's darkness. Yazid went first and lit the way for them. Kheti followed him, then Amenemhet who still held onto Nefrytatanen, hoping to shield her from whatever they might find. When they reached the stone floor, it seemed the room was empty.

Slowly Yazid lifted the torch higher to light the place, and its wavering yellow flame cast a pale and sickly color in the room. Looking around the room, they stood in a small, uncertain group at the foot of the stairs. Amenemhet's grip on Nefrytatanen's arm loosened; it seemed that Sinuhe had lied again.

Yazid held the torch as high as he could. Suddenly Nefrytatanen, with a choking sob, broke away from Amenemhet and ran to a far corner. Amenemhet saw, in the shadows on the floor, a small pile of what seemed to be silvery rags. Then he realized that it was what remained of Nefrytatanen's wedding dress, torn and bloodstained.

The dress wasn't empty. A long coil of black hair lay against its stained and ragged folds. Amenemhet ran to Nefrytatanen who knelt on the rocky floor unconcerned with the sharp edges of the stones that cut and bruised her knees. She stared for a long moment then fell over the bundle, throwing her arms around it, her face

against it, her hair flowing over it, hiding from them
what she held and sobbed over.

Amenemhet bent to stop her, changed his mind, and
stepped back, holding the others away. For a moment
they stood helpless, merely looking at her. Then they
turned away to afford Nefrytatanen some privacy, although, in her grief, she was unaware of them.

When her sobs began to subside, and she seemed a
little calmer, Amenemhet loosened her grasp on the
body and pulled her up into his arms. She trembled
against his chest, her face pressed to his neck, and
continued weeping. Amenemhet looked over her shoulder and was horrified at what she'd held so close to her.

Hardened as he had become by terrible sights, Kheti
felt sick when he saw Sira. Yazid, coming closer, recognized only too well the gentle brown eyes as they now
stared lifelessly at him. Sinuhe's men had used Sira for
amusement once they had realized their mistake and
knew she wasn't the queen. It was obvious that she had
died very slowly from delicate torture.

Kheti unfastened his cloak, struggling because of his
one good arm, until Yazid remembered his wound
and helped him. They wrapped the body very gently.
As he touched Sira, Yazid's eyes went up in surprise
to meet Kheti's, and Kheti silently shook his head. He
didn't wish to have Nefrytatanen told, in case she
hadn't realized it, that the body was still warm. Sira had
evidently lain suffering a long time and had just recently died. Yazid picked Sira up, thinking how piti-
fully small and light she was, and carried her out.
Kheti followed Yazid, holding the torch so that Amenemhet and Nefrytatanen could see their way up the
stairs.

Walking through the temple's chambers, Nefrytatanen never lifted her head, and Amenemhet kept his
arm around her, watching her closely. Leaving the
temple was a relief, and the cool wind of the coming
night was a touch of mercy. When they reached the
palace, Amenemhet picked Nefrytatanen up like a child,

for he realized that she was ready to faint. Before he took her to their room, he turned to Kheti and Yazid.

"Ankhneferu will soon arrive," he said. "Bring Sira's body to him. Tell him she's to be prepared for burial in the manner of a queen. This whole temple is stained with evil. I'll have it torn down and another built. Until this can be accomplished, take the statues and the holy articles away and have Ankhneferu set them up elsewhere. Seal the doors to this place. Let no one near it again."

"I couldn't even give her comfort in her dying," Nefrytatanen mumbled and closed her eyes.

Amenemhet carried Nefrytatanen up to their chambers and laid her carefully on the nearest couch. Her eyes were still closed when he sat beside her, holding her hand. He thought she was unconscious until he saw tears trickle from the corners of her eyes and run silently down her face. He held her hand, saying nothing.

Finally Nefrytatanen stopped weeping and sat up slowly. She moved to the edge of the couch and sat next to him, leaning her head on his shoulder. He smoothed her hair gently and her trembling finally ceased.

"Beloved," Amenemhet whispered, "we must decide now. It must be done as quickly as possible so the country sees that the turmoil has ended. If you cannot do this, I'll make the judgments myself. I'll try to do as you would wish," he offered.

"I know, beloved," she murmured. "It's not a pleasant task, and I'd like to help you with it. I should do it, and I have the strength now, I think. Let us get it over with. We can then rest all the sooner. Tomorrow, after this is finished, we'll have all the rest of our lives." She looked up at him and smiled faintly. "We have all of time and all the love we'll fill it with to explore—remember?"

Amenemhet smiled. Then he stood up and walked to a table. He took a goblet and poured water into it.

He offered it to her, and she sipped a little. He drank. He dampened a cloth from the tray and gently wiped her face with it. The coolness eased her aching head and helped clear her thoughts. She leaned closer.

"It helps, does it not?" he asked softly.

"Yes." She sighed.

"There have been other nights I needed to think, and the cold water helped. Yazid always remembers to leave it for me." He poured more water on the cloth as he spoke and wiped his face, holding the linen over his eyes a moment. "I wish to do more than pardon Kheti," Amenemhet said finally. "He did much for us. I've been thinking of rewarding him by giving him a province to govern. We have a couple provinces without governors now."

Nefrytatanen looked at Amenemhet, a little startled. Then she realized his implication.

"And assure us of having at least one loyal governor?" she asked, smiling wanly.

"Exactly," he answered. "Too many of the nobles think too highly of themselves and pull, like untrained horses, all in different directions. One of our biggest tasks will be to get them to pull together."

"Such was my thinking before all this happened," she admitted, "but, alone, I hadn't the strength—not with all my other troubles."

They sat at the table in the circle of light from the lamp and made their decisions, taking each case individually. The lamp burned nearly to the end of its oil as they talked. Finally they finished the last of it and went back to the couch and lay down together. They were too tired to go to bed or to undress themselves or even to call the servants to do it.

When Amenemhet felt on his shoulder the soft, even breath of Nefrytatanen's slumber, he thought again of the many nights he had spent wondering if she were alive. He couldn't believe that the nightmare was finished at last. He was filled with pride by how quickly her thoughts had followed his own, and he was pleased at how well their minds worked together. When, at last, he slept for the few hours left to him, he lay smiling in his sleep.

When Bekhet, accompanied by Yazid, tapped gently on the door in the morning, there was no answer. She looked at him, and he at her, wondering if they might enter. Yazid pressed his ear to the door.

"I hear nothing," he said. "Let us go in. They won't thank us if they oversleep."

Bekhet was thinking that the king and queen also wouldn't thank them if they were interrupted in a private moment. Before she could mention this, Yazid had opened the door a little. After a moment's hesitation, he stepped inside. Bekhet followed him cautiously. Seeing their king and queen laying on the couch wearing yesterday's bloodied and wrinkled garments made them frown.

"So," said Yazid, "they still sleep."

"Shush," whispered Bekhet. "You old crocodile, they've been through much, and what they face today isn't pleasant either."

She rolled up the window hangings to let in the sun. Yazid crept to the cabinet and brought out two robes.

"You needn't sneak around, you old crocodile," came Amenemhet's voice. "We're awake." He sat up, smiling at Yazid.

Nefrytatanen yawned and stretched like a cat, but her eyes still held the ghost of yesterday's weeping. "We've been awake almost all night planning for today," she said slowly. "Bekhet, come and help me out of these rags so I can bathe."

Bekhet took the robe from Yazid, motioning to him to avert his eyes. He turned discreetly to help Amenemhet, whose own eyes watched Nefrytatanen as she changed. Yazid could see the sorrow that lingered in his king's face, and he went about his task solemnly.

Today there was nothing of the playfulness of that morning at Kheti's house; little time was lost in preparations. At the morning meal, Amenemhet gave crisp orders for the day's procedure, and it wasn't long before they were ready.

Kheti stood with Rakkor by the doors in the palace hall. He was silent and stared dejectedly at his feet. They were waiting for their turn to walk onto the Platform of Appearances where announcements would be made by Amenemhet and Nefrytatanen. Kheti, glancing down the hall to where the king and queen stood waiting, observed Amenemhet's tender expression as he gazed at his beloved. Seeing that Nefrytatanen's eyes were yet shadowed from sleeplessness, Kheti was filled anew with disgust at himself for his attack on the ship, telling himself once again that, but for him, it all might not have happened. Thinking of Nefrytatanen holding Sira's corpse, Kheti was doubly angry with himself.

"Why are you so dreary?" Rakkor, observing Kheti, asked. "Today we'll be pardoned for our colorful past, and we can be respected citizens once more."

"Don't be so sure of that," Kheti said grimly, adjusting his bandaged arm more comfortably and wincing.

"Why not?" asked Rakkor. "The king promised it."

"The king also didn't know at the time all that had passed between the queen and us when we thought her a slave." Kheti paled at this memory. "He wouldn't be happy to learn we looked upon her naked after I tore away her robe—or to hear of another incident I remember only too well." Kheti looked at the royal couple again. "Rakkor, remember, he isn't Nakht. Amenemhet is king, and he can do anything he wishes, promise or not."

Rakkor was undisturbed. "I don't think the queen will even mention such things to him. She has other things on her mind now, and we didn't harm her."

Kheti smiled without humor. "Yes, she's no doubt thinking of how Sira died. We handed Sira to Sinuhe. Remember, old friend?"

"We didn't know what we were doing," Rakkor insisted. He was quiet a moment. Then he added in a cheerful tone, "I think we'll be rewarded. After all, we risked our lives."

"Rakkor! You expect not only pardon, but reward? Are you mad? The king could easily decide that our lives—which up to now haven't been exactly shining— aren't worth the value we place on them."

"I think not," Rakkor said serenely. "He doesn't seem so. After all, he's gotten everything he wanted. He has the queen, he has the kingdom, he has the traitors. He should be happy and in a generous mood. Whatever we did before this, we still helped him accomplish those things. Without us he might have done nothing at all."

Kheti looked at Amenemhet, whose eyes were still on Nefrytatanen. "Maybe," Kheti said slowly, "but I think, with or without us, with or without the whole world, he would have found her. And I know that what happened has given them many sad memories and has meant the deaths of many they loved," he reminded.

"You're too grim," Rakkor said impatiently as they moved to their places. But he began to wonder. Disgusted, he shrugged off his doubts. He wouldn't allow himself to be so easily discouraged but instead clung stubbornly to his hopes.

Nefrytatanen wasn't thinking of Sira. She had deliberately turned her thoughts from her. She had dreamed terrible things during the night about Sira's death and had awakened twice shivering against Amenemhet's side. She had wished she could awaken him to comfort her, but, knowing how tired he was, she had not. Feeling the warmth of his nearness had been her comfort. When morning had come, she had resolved to put the shadows aside.

As she stood beside Amenemhet, she thought of the time she had stood with him for the inundation ceremony. She remembered how little she had known of him then. She thought how much about him she had learned since. Her mind was more peaceful when she concentrated on Amenemhet. His was the only power

strong enough to hold off her nightmares. She recalled
how she had looked at him the afternoon they had met
and how she decided that, whatever else he might be,
he was a man. Only now she knew fully what that
meant. She remembered how gentle and wise he had
been with her, how tender. She thought of how he had
gone into the battle unafraid and of the look on his
face when confronting Sinuhe. His strength was hers,
and she marveled at this. She began to think of the love
they had shared at Kheti's house, and at the memory of
it, she felt so strong a desire that she was almost
staggered.

Nefrytatanen looked up at Amenemhet, who looked
straight ahead. She wondered where those eyes were focused. She thought of the plans Amenemhet had made
for the future. Yes, she was sure he was the Ameni of
Neferu's prophecy. She knew he could accomplish his
goals. She was convinced he could do anything. She
would share it all with him. To think of their future was
so exciting she couldn't quite believe it was possible.
She let happiness flood over her, feeling so alive and
free that her joy was almost painful.

Amenemhet stood quietly beside Nefrytatanen. As he
waited for the procession to begin, he looked at her
proudly. She was beautiful. Today her hair was hidden beneath the golden wrappings upon which she
wore the ornate crown of Aset. Beneath it, her face was
a small, golden oval. Her eyelashes were like a fan of
delicate, black feathers, only partly hiding the blue
gleam of her eyes. He looked lingeringly at her full
lips, which had a serious, but serene, expression. Her
gown covered her from neck to ankles, but the clinging
material hid little.

Idly, Amenemhet watched the others placing themselves in line, thinking of how many more processions
he would watch in future days and years. This occasion
had been relatively unplanned and far less elaborate
than others would be.

He grew impatient to begin, then decided that if he

could look at Nefrytatanen each time he waited for a
procession, he might distract himself pleasantly enough
to have patience. He heard the heralding trumpets, and
the line began to move.

First the scribes disappeared through the doors. Then
went Meri and Seti and a group of officials, followed by
Ankhneferu and other priests, and a contingent of
nobles and their ladies and servants. A guard of soldiers
moved in behind them, and Amenemhet and Nefrytatanen followed, with Yazid and Bekhet a pace or two
behind. Nessumontu followed with two more guards.

Those awaiting judgment were already in their places.
Sinuhe and as many of his accomplices as had been
found and brought back alive were under heavy guard.

When Amenemhet and Nefrytatanen stepped into
the sunshine, the crowd—which had been silent—rippled with whispers. When Amenemhet and Nefrytatanen were seated in the shade, the trumpets gave a
last chorus; and the people grew quiet and solemn.

The prisoners' faces held a common look of fear.
Only Hathorbes's expression betrayed nothing of his
inner thoughts. Kheti and Rakkor sat together. Amenemhet thought Kheti looked disturbed, as if unsure of
his fate. Amenemhet concealed his smile.

He gave the signal, and Ankhneferu stepped forward
to offer a short prayer of thanksgiving and a plea that
all wrong be turned out and that order and justice again
prevail. At this pronouncement, Amenemhet recalled
Nefrytatanen's quoting Neferu, and he wondered at the
prophecy. When the prayer was finished, he allowed a
moment of silence so its message might be absorbed.
Then Amenemhet gave the second signal.

Meri stepped out near the edge of the platform and
unrolled his scroll with a flourish. Facing the throne he
began in his clear and well-trained voice, "People of
Tamera . . ."

The crowd was silent, curious at this first official
joint decision by their new rulers.

"King of Upper and Lower Tamera, son of Ra,

Amenemhet, living forever and ever, and queen of Upper and Lower Tamera, daughter of Ra, Nefrytatanen, living forever and ever, have summoned you so you may witness yourselves the judgments. Scrolls bearing the royal seal of the double crown relating all that follows will be carried to every corner of the land by messengers so all may know the justice of our king and queen. King Amenemhet and Queen Nefrytatanen have already, in private, decided the fates of those involved in the recent events, but here shall the truth be heard from their own lips, and here will they pronounce the judgments."

Meri rolled his scroll and backed away, bowing very low, as Amenemhet led Nefrytatanen forward.

Amenemhet and Nefrytatanen walked forward with triumph clearly written on their faces and in each move they made. As the sun struck their robes, which were woven of gold threads, the crowd squinted in the glare, whispering in awe among themselves that their king and queen truly looked as if they were descended from Ra.

Amenemhet, head flung high, his eyes as gold as the robe he wore, spoke in a quiet voice that carried to even the farthest ear; the listeners were as silent as the footfalls of the ibis.

"Many of those involved are no longer living and to them who deserve it will be afforded every honor. Their families will be awarded gold in compensation for their loss. Although gold is small comfort for the loss of loved ones, it's all we can give."

He paused, and the tension of those awaiting sentence grew. The crowd seemed to hold its breath. Amenemhet smiled slightly, having a few pleasant matters to announce first.

"Yazid, my slave, you've been faithful to me since I was a child. You have followed me through all this evil, risking your life without hesitation. I free you. You are, as of this day, a free citizen of Tamera. If you wish yet to serve me, I will be glad, but it will now be as a member of the court."

Yazid's mouth fell open in surprise. He had never expected reward of any kind.

Amenemhet smiled at Yazid's expression and continued, "Kheti, you risked everything to help the queen and me regain our rightful place. From this day you are pardoned for your past misdeeds, whatever they were, and you will henceforth be known as Khnumhotep, count of the city of Menet Khufu, and lord of Orynx Province. Rakkor, you also did much to help us, and we give you pardon as well. From this day you'll be lord of Hare Province."

At this, Rakkor smiled broadly and looked meaningfully at Kheti, who stared at Amenemhet. Rakkor squeezed Kheti's knee; as Kheti glanced at him, Rakkor gave him a triumphant look.

Amenemhet, seeing these reactions, smiled as he continued, "Nessumontu, leader of the army of Tamehu, today you become commander of all of Tamera's army. Having seen you fight yesterday. I greatly admire your skill and am certain that no man is more deserving of the title than you."

Nessumontu, more than half-expecting this promotion after Korusko's death, was still proud to hear it, and his slanted eyes gleamed with pleasure.

Amenemhet went on, "Those of both armies and Kheti's men, who were noted for special courage or service, will also be rewarded. The list is too long to relate their names one by one, but their names are inscribed on the proclamations you will shortly see.

"Ankhneferu, who remained loyal despite great temptation, who acted as a spy and risked his life, to you we give the honor of the office of high priest of all Tamera. May you bring to this position the honor it deserves and wipe away the blot that has been placed upon it."

Amenemhet took a deep breath. "We will not go through the necessary rituals to install all of you in

your new places now. Notice will be given later as to
when the ceremonies will take place."

Throughout the ceremony, Ankhneferu stood with
his head bowed. He was confused. He was grateful and
happy about his elevated status, but saddened by the
stain left by Sinuhe on all the priesthood. He wondered what the judgment for Hathorbes would now be,
for the high priest of the north would have been more
eligible for the place he'd just been given.

Amenemhet looked at Hathorbes, who sat quietly
staring at Nefrytatanen. Having heard Ankhneferu pro-
moted over him, he knew his fate was fearful. He
looked at Nefrytatanen with hatred in his eyes. Observing Hathorbes's expression, Amenemhet decided it
was well they had decided for him as they had. As
Amenemhet addressed Hathorbes, his voice was cold.
"Hathorbes, we know only that your motives were
questionable. You spoke against your queen from the
first, when she needed your support in the north. And
we don't yet know what you intended when you had
her taken from Drankma. When the golden eye of Ra
rises tomorrow, you will be escorted from Tamera's
borders, and if ever you are seen in the Two Lands
again, you will risk the penalty of death."

As Amenemhet turned his attention to Sinuhe, his
eyes grew black with anger. "Sinuhe," he said softly,
"high priest of Tashemau, we trusted and honored you.
You performed our marriage, and that very night,
under your orders, those on the queen's ship were slain
and the queen carried away. On your orders—if not by
your own hand, which I strongly suspect—were King
Mentuhotep and Queen Meresank poisoned. On your
head is the blood of Commander Korusko, that of Sira,
Drankma, Drankma's people, Kheti's men, and many
others yet uncounted. You plotted to gain the throne
for yourself. Each of these crimes is, in itself, punish-
able by death."

Amenemhet paused to regard Sinuhe a moment.
There was no mercy in his eyes. "Such is your evil,

Sinuhe, that no mercy can be shown. So all may remember the fate of a traitor and tremble at it, your name will be struck from each place it has been written. Neither will any child again be called by your name. Those who have the same name as you will change it. To merely speak your name is forbidden. Your name is here stricken from all memory, and no prayers will be offered for you. Your soul will be weighed and judged only by Asar, but so the grief you caused may be avenged in some small fashion, you will suffer the penalty of living death. Those who acted under your orders and are still living will be executed in the usual way."

The crowd shuddered at the horror Sinuhe faced—live burial in an unmarked and lonely grave and banishment for eternity, with none to pray for his soul. But they concurred with his sentence. The weight of his crimes justified the terrible price he would pay.

Amenemhet, eyes black with fury, watched Sinuhe, who had grown paler and paler as he had heard Amenemhet's words. Now he collapsed, and guards carried him away.

Nefrytatanen watched them leave, and when they disappeared she turned her gaze to the crowd and said clearly, "We have endured our suffering together, and we face the future together. We are now truly one people and one land." She looked up at Amenemhet's face and saw his anger fading slowly at her gaze. "May the love shared by your rulers reach your hearts and warm you," she said. "Be happy Tamera is united at last, so the One Alone will favor Tamera with maet." She took Amenemhet's arm as she finished.

Amenemhet's eyes had softened as he watched and listened to Nefrytatanen. She was right, he decided, to look ahead instead of behind. As he took her hand to lead her from the Platform of Appearances, he saw that many in the crowd were weeping openly with relief and happiness. The royal guards cleared the way to the palace door. As Amenemhet and Nefrytatanen entered the cool and peaceful hall, they could hear the sound of singing. The people were celebrating.

Although the guards kept their eyes straight ahead, they could sense the growing happiness of their king. They also found, gradually, that the conversation between Amenemhet and Nefrytatanen became too intimate for their ears.

"The people are much relieved there will be no more fighting," Amenemhet remarked quietly. Thinking again of the future, he smiled and said, "When the flood recedes, I think I'll have the land remeasured and the boundaries reset."

"Already the prophecy begins to come true." Nefrytatanen observed softly. After a moment she added, "In any case, that's a good idea. I noticed when we sailed from Noph that the inundation is beginning well."

"Yes," he replied, "and if it continues, the crops will be abundant next year."

"All of them should be," Nefrytatanen murmured in a meaningful tone.

"What do you mean, beloved?" Amenemhet stopped walking to face her. Her tone confused him. The guards came to a halt.

"When we sing the spring song, it will be with true joy, I think," she replied smiling.

"The spring song?"

Nefrytatanen began walking, and the others resumed their pace. She smiled wider as she recited the ritual planting song: "The earth god has implanted his beauty in every body. The Creator has done this with His two hands as balm to His heart. The channels are filled anew with water, and the land is flooded with His love." She added softly, "If it has not already been done, I think we'll soon assure it."

"I don't understand your meaning," Amenemhet said faintly, though he was less uncertain of it now. She made no comment but continued looking ahead. He was quiet for a moment, thinking.

As they stopped at their chamber door, he asked, "Nefrytatanen, can you really do magic?"

"As my mother and my grandmother and all before them," she replied.

Amenemhet's lips curved in a smile. "Do you still remember that dance Yasmine taught you?"

"What I did was my own dance," she answered slowly. She looked up at him. "I remember it very well. I remember Yasmine's dance too—and many more interesting things."

Amenemhet turned abruptly to the guards. "Let no one pass these doors but those servants we request," he ordered. Looking at Nefrytatanen again, his eyes gleaming with golden lights, he said softly, "It may be next spring before we leave this room."

Nefrytatanen smiled faintly, her eyes becoming a dark and smoky sapphire. "It may be," she agreed.

They closed their door softly behind them, and it was indeed a long time before they were seen again.

PART II

Chapter Ten

As the sun rose above the golden curve of the desert, Kheti could see the double walls of Ithtawe growing clearer with the light. In the stillness of early morning, he stared as if the awesome sight were new to him, although he had seen it during several stages in its construction. Now the new capital of the Two Lands appeared almost finished, and the palace-fortress promised to be extraordinarily beautiful.

Sometime ago, Queen Nefrytatanen had announced the coming of the heir to the crown. King Amenemhet had made it known that he wished the child to be born within Ithtawe's walls, and the workers seemed no less anxious than the king to see this come to pass. They labored willingly from sunrise to dark.

Kheti reflected on the meaning of the name given the capital—Ithtawe. To call this place "captor of the Two Lands" wasn't really fitting unless, by "captor," it was meant "he who held the gladly surrendered hearts of his people." The story of Amenemhet from the Upper Kingdom and Neyfrytatanen from the Lower Kingdom had become legend. The story appealed to the romantically-inclined people.

As he approached Ithtawe, he stared in fresh delight and wonder at the soaring beauty of the white limestone walls. Sadly, he then reflected on the blood spilled before all this had come to be.

Since Amenemhet's return to reclaim Wast from

Sinuhe and the subsequent sealing of the union of the
kingdoms, much had been done to build the future.
Amenemhet and Nefrytatanen had wasted no time in
beating the Hyksos from their northern border. And
Kheti and his friend Rakkor had made it known to
their former lawless comrades that they were solidly
on the king and queen's side. The result had been that
many roving outlaw gangs had suddenly disappeared,
and those unwise enough to stay had been persistently
pursued by Kheti and his men. Kheti reflected that,
before now, no person of rank would have dared ride
alone. His grey eyes were as cold as night shadows as
he reflected on these matters.

Kheti came to Ithtawe to offer Amenemhet news of
the latest movements of some of the nobles who were
still greedily trying to hold their provinces, thinking
themselves above the king.

Kheti also came to tell Amenemhet, as a friend, of
his plans to marry. He smiled faintly as he thought
that this news would finally lay to rest the rumors of his
infatuation with Nefrytatanen. There were still those
who whispered of how he'd kidnapped and carried her
off to his house, not knowing her identity. Kheti
couldn't have, in his own conscience, truthfully dis-
claimed feelings for her. He had come very near to
loving her when he had thought her a slave. Although
her love for Amenemhet had never faltered, Kheti had
felt then, and still felt, a special warmth for his queen.
Now he could bring to her and the king the joyous
news of his own forthcoming marriage. Kheti only
hoped he might share with his bride some fraction of
the happiness that Amenemhet and Nefrytatanen had
found.

Never had Kheti seen the same depth of emotion between Amenemhet and Nefrytatanen in any other
couple. Although they never displayed their private
feelings, it was as if the radiance between them touched
everyone in their presence, and Kheti was happy for

them, looking forward to the birth of their heir as if the child were his own.

The sentries at the entrance gates began to shout to Kheti to stop. Then, recognizing him, they smiled widely and saluted, bidding him pass.

Dismounting, Kheti gave his reins to a guard and greeted him, then turned and ran lightly up the steps to the copper doors of the royal courtyard. These doors were also immediately opened to him, and, he paused on the threshhold, staring at the many gardeners at work and amazed at the progress being made.

In the distance Kheti saw Yazid's familiar figure hurrying beneath an aisle of feathery, young olive trees, toward the entrance of the royal living quarters. Kheti called out a greeting, and Yazid stopped, looked his way, then waved and waited. Yazid, although now a free citizen, had chosen to continue serving Amenemhet.

"We didn't expect you for another decan," exclaimed Yazid as Kheti approached. "Has something extraordinary happened that you came sooner?" The servant's face, seldom jovial, was knitted in even a deeper frown than it usually was.

"Yes, Yazid," Kheti answered, "something very extraordinary. Are the king and queen here? Would I be able to see them? I have something important to tell them."

Yazid nodded, and they entered the palace together. Kheti whistled softly, in wonder. The walls were paneled in lapis lazuli flecked with gold, broken at regular intervals by lines of lotus-patterned columns covered with gold leaf.

"I thought the plans were beautiful, but the promise was nothing beside the reality," Kheti said softly.

"It isn't finished. There's much to be done yet. What news is this you bring?" Yazid asked, his eyebrows raised in curiosity.

"I'll tell all of you at one time, if the king and queen are able to see me."

"Give them a few minutes alone without plans to study or problems to solve," said Yazid, permitting himself a small smile, "and they quickly occupy themselves." Kheti said nothing, but grinned. Yazid went on grumbling happily, "It isn't recommended to open doors without warning or walk too quietly around here these days."

Kheti laughed aloud and shook his head.

"Who's laughing out there?" Amenemhet's puzzled face appeared from around a doorway. Seeing Kheti, he grinned and strode into the hall. "We didn't expect to see you for awhile," Amenemhet said. "What brings you early and in so merry a mood?" His golden eyes were warm with welcome.

"Good news, which may shake no one's world but my own."

"Come and tell us," Amenemhet invited, leading him into the room from which he'd emerged. Kheti stopped again and stared in genuine admiration. Amenemhet proudly watched his reaction, saying nothing.

The chamber was a semicircular sitting room, and the curving wall opposite the door was really a series of floor-to-ceiling open doorways. Kheti could see the unfinished garden beyond, where Nefrytatanen stood, her face upturned to the morning sun, eyes closed, hair hanging straight and unbound. The walls of the room were sheathed with green jasper carved with scenes of their past adventures. Couches of ebony inlaid with ivory and amber and trimmed with gold were heaped with green and gold pillows. Cases of piled scrolls lay on a papyrus-patterned ebony table.

"From the little I've seen of Ithtawe," breathed Kheti, "I can truly say it's magnificent."

Amenemhet smiled widely. "It's beginning to look as we'd planned, but there's much to be done. This is one of the finished rooms—there are many not yet begun."

Nefrytatanen had come through the door and hesitated a moment while her eyes adjusted to the shade of the room. She walked toward them, smiling. She was just beginning to show her pregnancy, and her cotton robe was a little fuller than the slim ones Kheti had seen her wear before.

"Kheti, you've come to us early," she smiled. "You look happy, so you must bring us good news."

"It isn't *all* good," Kheti admitted, "but the bad could be worse."

They relaxed on the couches, and Kheti was silently grateful for the comfort, having ridden through the night.

Amenemhet commented, "We've already seen the results of your eliminating the roving thieves. You seem to have effective methods."

Kheti smiled humorlessly. "It was unnecessary to eliminate some. A few decided to find other, safer occupations or to seek other lands."

"You've been busy, however you accomplished it," Nefrytatanen declared. After a moment she said proudly, "When Ithtawe is finished, Amenemhet will have the workers begin on the new irrigation system he's planned."

"I've done only a little thinking about it so far," Amenemhet said. "A more pressing problem is the measuring and marking of the straggling borders. In the hope of distracting me from their own power struggles, many of the governors continue to quarrel over the new surveying lines.

Kheti sighed. "They're like geese, each racing to pick up as many kernels of grain as they can before someone else does."

Amenemhet's voice was soft, but his golden eyes held anger as he said, "Some of them are getting their bills so full they'd better take care before they lose it all."

"Lord Hunefer is one I'd keep an eye on," Kheti cautioned. "He's a greedy man and thinks he's far enough away that he can escape supervision."

"I've been watching him," Amenemhet said quietly,

"and he may be the first goose to lose what he's collected. When I was in Noph a few days ago, I gave him a discreet warning. If he doesn't heed that warning, he won't get another."

"I doubt that he'll stop," Nefrytatanen observed in a thoughtful tone.

"He'd better," Amenemhet murmured.

"I didn't know you were in Noph," Kheti said leaning forward. "I was there also. In fact that leads me to the reason I'm here early."

As if he had stepped out of a wall, Yazid was suddenly back in the room, and he muttered, "Tell us and keep me waiting no longer. I have chores to do in other places."

They laughed at this, but Yazid allowed only a faint smile to cross his face.

"I've found a wife—at least she will be my wife before very long." Kheti, enjoying the surprise on their faces, sat back on the couch.

"Who is she?" Nefrytatanen asked quickly. "This is sudden."

"It may seem so. However, we've decided," Kheti replied.

"We must meet her," Amenemhet declared. "When will you bring her to us?"

Kheti smiled. "I thought you'd ask that, so she's already on her way. She'll arrive the day after tomorrow."

"How wonderful this is!" Nefrytatanen's sapphire eyes sparkled with pleasure. "I'm glad to hear this happy news. We've had enough of the other kind."

"Yes, we have at that," Amenemhet remarked. His eyes were still shadowed by the grief of the not-so-distant past.

Kheti, seeing his look, changed the subject. Turning to Nefrytatanen, he said, "Ithtawe must be the most beautiful palace ever built."

"Although it's far from complete, we can't resist stopping from time to time to inspect it," Nefrytatanen replied, and then added promptly, "but the credit must

go to Amenemhet for he confessed that he began to
plan Ithtawe the day we met."

"If I planned a hundred years, I couldn't design such
a place," Kheti said with genuine admiration. He smiled
at her. "You're his inspiration, you know. You're feeling well? You're more beautiful than ever."

"Yes, I'm well, though my robes don't fit as they
did," she answered. She felt self-conscious about her
condition and was having to accustom herself slowly
to each new stage. With her figure beginning to change,
she was anxious that Amenemhet not think her ugly
and turn his eyes elsewhere. It was ever in her mind
that their marriage contract permitted him other wom-
en.

Nefrytatanen smiled and said, "Come often, Kheti,
and give me more such compliments. Keep my confidence high, that Amenemhet will look at no other
when I attain the shape of a giant melon."

Amenemhet smiled faintly, knowing her mind, but
said nothing.

Kheti said, "Surely you joke. From the look in his
eyes, I think you've no reason to worry." More softly
he added, "I've seldom seen any man look in such a
way at his wife so far after their wedding day."

Amenemhet chuckled. "That day was but a door to
treasures which have increased each day."

Nefrytatanen met Amenemhet's eyes and, seeing how
they glowed on her, smiled and looked away quickly.
His expression was so distracting that she forgot what
she was about to say. But she was reassured.

The day was passed in showing Kheti the changes
in the palace, and the evening meal was leisurely, not
given to serious discussions but made light with rem-
iniscing. Later, when the last goblet of wine had been
drunk, Kheti bid them good night and went to his room
alone.

In their private chamber, lit now only by the moon,
Amenemhet drew Nefrytatanen close to demonstrate
again, with great tenderness, his feelings for her. The

fire which was aroused each time they touched, flared again to brilliance.

When Nefrytatanen lay warmly in Amenemhet's arms before sleeping, she smiled. If their feelings always rose to this brightness, she had no need of pretty compliments from others—pleasant though they might be. If Amenemhet's feelings were comparable to hers, then he would never look for another woman.

Chapter Eleven

While Amenardis waited in the hall, she thought of the many stories she had heard of the king and queen, and she speculated on the possible extent of their exaggeration. When she saw the great copper doors swing slowly open before her, she suddenly felt nervous, and she took Kheti's arm.

As they walked forward, Amenardis studied the king curiously. He was dressed informally, in a short tunic of creamy linen bordered with gold, and his thick, black hair was uncovered. He was tall and as broad-shouldered as she had heard he was, with a lean waist and flat hips. In the flesh, he had an almost animallike awareness of his physical being, and she could easily see how the queen had been so strongly attracted to him. Here, she thought, was power—power so absolute he needed no crown to demonstrate it. The light in his tilted golden eyes reflected this knowledge, and his posture and the way he held his head revealed that power was as natural to him as was the beating of his heart.

Pausing before Amenemhet, Amenardis bowed low only to feel his hands grasp her shoulders, gently raising her to face him. Looking up at him, she was surprised by his open and friendly smile.

"Kheti's bride-to-be is welcome here," Amenemhet said softly.

Amenardis was at a loss to reply. She stared into

those warm eyes feeling foolish for her lack of words, but the queen rescued her.

"We're very happy to meet you," Nefrytatanen said in a friendly, but slightly reserved, tone.

Amenardis turned to Nefrytatanen, prepared for the blue eyes which were already a legend, but unprepared for the look in them. They seemed to penetrate her very soul, and she wondered, uneasily, what thoughts lay behind them.

"Amenardis is unusually quiet and, so, must be impressed, because she's not shy by nature," Kheti remarked.

Amenardis glanced up to see that Kheti was smiling down on her. "Forgive my rudeness," she apologized. What did one say to one's king and queen when they, like ordinary people, expected to engage you in conversation? Without thinking, she blurted, "I was deciding that all the descriptions I'd heard of you were accurate, after all."

Amenemhet smiled faintly at this, but Nefrytatanen's full lips remained serious. Amenardis realized that such bluntness was not appropriate, and she flushed.

"I mean—," Amenardis stammered, "such stories change from mouth to mouth and—" She stopped, not knowing what to say. She was only making it worse.

Amenemhet laughed softly. "I cannot blame you for being curious. We understand," he said easily. Nefrytatanen smiled slightly but said nothing.

Still blushing, Amenardis looked at her feet. "You're very kind to a blundering girl who is unused to meeting nobles, much less her king and queen."

Amenemhet glanced around the room then said quietly, "I'll call Dedjet to serve us wine. This is a happy occasion."

"Don't bother Dedjet," Nefrytatanen suddenly said. "She's busy at another task. I'll pour the wine. There's a container here." She nodded toward a small cabinet in a corner of the room.

"Don't trouble yourself," Amenardis said quickly.

"Let me do it." She went to the cabinet Nefrytatanen had indicated and busied herself immediately.

While they waited, Amenemhet studied the girl. There was something familiar in the set of her dark eyes, but he couldn't decide what it was. He observed Kheti had good taste in women—Amenardis was both pretty and graceful—and if her manners lacked polish, it was probably just that she was nervous meeting them.

"Kheti, where did you and Amenardis meet?" Amenemhet asked. "She seems familiar to me."

"In Noph," Kheti answered. "Amenardis lives there with friends, for she's an orphan." Kheti paused a moment then added softly. "Now I'm wondering where the wedding banquet will be held. My house is too far in the desert, and our new one isn't finished. The friends in whose house she lives do not seem eager for the trouble involved."

"Why don't you be married at Ithtawe's temple?" Amenemhet suggested. "The palace will be finished before too long, and it would be a happy event to begin our lives with here."

Kheti looked questioningly at Nefrytatanen who said, "If this would be to your and Amenardis's liking, please don't hesitate to agree."

Kheti was silent a moment watching Amenardis pass them their goblets. "What do you think?" he asked.

"What can I say?" Amenardis replied quickly. "To be married in the king's temple and enjoy the banquet in the palace would be a great honor."

"Say only yes," Amenemhet urged raising his goblet.

"Yes, yes!" Amenardis promptly replied.

Amenemhet chuckled. "Then it's settled," he said. "May you be as happy as Nefrytatanen and I are."

They took a sip of wine. Then Nefrytatanen began to tell Kheti and Amenardis a light story which brought a smile to Amenardis's face, though she still seemed tense.

Amenemhet listened in silence, but after a moment he began to feel oddly uncomfortable. It seemed as if his throat were swelling, and he became dizzy. Then he remembered something from his childhood, and he shivered in horror. A sudden coldness swept through him. Incredulous, he didn't know what to say, but fear spoke for him, and he put his goblet down.

Hoping he wasn't too late, he said loudly, "Beloved, drink no more!"

Nefrytatanen startled by his tone, looked up quickly.

"There's a plant to which I have a strange reaction," he whispered. The look in his eyes sent a chill through Nefrytatanen. "Its blossoms are beautiful, but the slightest touch of them against my skin causes my throat to close and gives me a weakness. From these blossoms a poison can be made. . . ." He looked at Amenardis, his face growing pale. "Amenardis, have you poisoned us?" he asked. Now he was perspiring and shivering at one time.

Nefrytatanen stared at Amenemhet, unable to move. Her heart was a stone in her breast. Kheti dropped his goblet and quickly took Nefrytatanen's from her numb fingers.

Amenemhet wavered where he stood. Then, with a look of bewilderment, he began to sink slowly to the couch behind him. Nefrytatanen leaped to his side and prevented him from toppling to the floor. She dragged him to the couch, and held his head in her lap.

"Yazid! Yazid!" Nefrytatanen screamed. Yazid's face appeared around the door. "Get Horemheb!" she cried. Yazid glanced at Amenemhet and, paling, disappeared. She could hear him running down the hall calling for the physician. Nefrytatanen cradled Amenemhet's head and put her cheek against his. Slowly she raised her head to look at him.

Amenemhet thought of all the things he wanted to say before he died. With an effort, he whispered, "I've always loved you and—" He tried to finish, his lips moved, but his voice had gone, and he looked at her helplessly.

She was too filled with horror to speak. She raised

here eyes to stare at Kheti. Kheti was holding Amenardis's arm so tightly that Nefrytatanen could see the bruises his fingers made.

"What did you give the king?" he demanded. "Have you poisoned us all?"

"Nothing, I gave him nothing!" Amenardis struggled to free herself from his grasp.

"If there's only wine in this cup then drink it," Kheti ordered, holding Amenemhet's goblet close to her face. She shrank from it. "Prove your innocence," Kheti's words were ice crystals hanging in the air. At her silence, he shook her until her dark hair tumbled loose. Then he held her face close to his and said quietly, "You poured the wine we all drank from the same container. If you added nothing to his, nothing will happen to you. Drink from the king's goblet. To share his cup is an honor!" He put the goblet to her mouth and glared unmercifully into her terrified face.

Nefrytatanen looked again into the golden eyes that stared helplessly up at her. Anger charged through grief to flood her with fire.

"Drink it," Nefrytatanen commanded.

Amenardis stared at her, startled by her tone. Then, seeming to find a new strength, Amenardis took the goblet and finished the wine in several large swallows.

"The king will die," she spat. "I will also die. But I'll die more happily, for I have avenged Sinuhe, my father." Seeing Kheti's shock, she laughed harshly. "You thought I loved you, when all the while I used you to lead me to the king," she said contemptuously. "My father hid his child, but had he won the throne as he'd planned, I'd be princess."

Amenardis wavered, and Kheti stepped away as if repelled by the touch of some loathesome insect. She staggered slightly as she turned to Nefrytatanen, who still sat with Amenemhet's head in her lap. The queen's eyes held the expression of a striking cobra's.

"I'll kill you myself if you come nearer," Nefrytatanen said.

The venom of her words stopped Amenardis, and she stood, unsteadily. Nefrytatanen could see that Amenardis held a small dagger, but before she took a step closer her eyes rolled upward. Amenardis fell at Nefrytatanen's feet.

Yazid rushed in with Horemheb, and several guards following him. The physician immediately went to Amenemhet. Kheti looked at the guards staring at their fallen king.

"Carry the carcass of this dead thing from the presence of your king and queen," Kheti said hoarsely.

The soldiers looked to Nefrytatanen, who nodded. One of them easily picked up Amenardis's small frame and hurried from the room. Kheti turned to Nefrytatanen, who was now standing, watching Horemheb bent over Amenemhet.

"I brought her here," Kheti muttered.

Nefrytatanen turned to look at him through her tears. "And you killed her," she finished. "Don't go, Kheti. I need you here." He looked at her a moment, then, enveloped in self-hatred, angrily threw himself into the nearest chair.

Nefrytatanen knelt on the floor beside the couch, still holding Amenemhet's hand, which had become oddly cold and moist. She saw that his eyes stilled watched her. "I love you," she whispered. Tears from her face fell on his. "You won't die. I won't let you die. I love you," she murmured.

Amenemhet's sad eyes closed.

Nefrytatanen stared at him, unable to speak, unable to move.

Horemheb turned to her, hesitated, swallowed, and said nothing. His face was pale and grim.

"Horemheb!" Nefrytatanen finally cried out. "Is he dead?" Horemheb shook his head. "What can be done?" she begged. The physician shook his head a second time. "Please speak," she urged. "Tell me what you can."

Slowly Horemheb's eyes met Nefrytatanen's, and

they were filled with dread. "My queen," he whispered, "I can do nothing. I have no drug to reverse this poison. It's already in his blood, and there's no way now to remove or dilute it," he said helplessly. "Only his sensitivity to the plant, which warned him from drinking more, has kept him from immediate death." Horemheb's eyes were filled with sorrow. "Now, it seems, he dies slowly. I cannot say how long it will take. It depends on the quantity he drank, his health, and his desire to live. I think it will take a long time because he's strong and has much to live for."

"Days? Months?" Nefrytatanen asked quietly.

"I cannot say," Horemheb answered. "I can do nothing, and I know of no one who can."

Horemheb had been watching Nefrytatanen intently while they talked, trying to measure her reaction. She seemed controlled enough, despite the tears that continued soundlessly. She turned to stare at Amenemhet for some time, as if in a stupor. Horemheb began to wonder if she had become frozen with shock. Finally, seeming to arouse herself, Nefrytatanen looked up at the two remaining guards.

"Bring him to our chamber," she whispered. She watched them carry Amenemhet past her, then turned to Yazid who had been waiting silently. "Send messengers immediately to call the governors to Ithtawe. I'll hold formal court in two days. Let it be known everywhere what has happened. If anyone knows of a cure, whatever it may be, let him come forward. If it works, I'll shower him with gold. If anyone knows of a plot or even the hint of one, let me hear this also."

Yazid backed out of the door, still so shocked he was speechless. When he had left, Nefrytatanen turned to Kheti.

"Your grief is not unlike mine because you loved the woman you thought she was. Now she's dead, and, surely, you must grieve. Don't burden yourself with guilt because she fooled you, Kheti, and please don't leave Ithtawe. I need you here," Nefrytatanen whispered.

During the next two days, Nefrytatanen and Kheti stayed in their respective apartments, seeing no one but their attendants, though the noblemen arrived one by one. Prime Minister Meri alone unsmilingly greeted the lords on their arrival and, after sending them to their chambers, ignored them. The nobles were quiet, hesitant to speak even among themselves.

Finally Nefrytatanen had them sent to the partly finished throne room. While they waited for her, they stared in awe at the soaring walls and ceilings solidly inlaid with deep blue lapis lazuli. Everywhere they turned they saw the sparkle of gold. With open mouths they looked at the lotus-bundle pillars, distracted by this splendor from the impending death of the man who had designed it.

Unannounced, Nefrytatanen walked in quietly through a side door. The nobles were startled by her unpretentious entrance and watched curiously as she stepped up into the dais and sat on her golden throne. She was a small and lonely figure in purple robes, her head high, bearing proudly the weight of the formal double crown.

Glancing at the empty place beside her, Nefrytatanen's eyes filled with tears, and she blinked, forcing them back, determined not to weep before the court. Then she leveled eyes, the color of the walls, on the silent group.

"The king still lives, but no one has come forth with a suggestion to save him," Nefrytatanen said bluntly. She rose from her seat and stared at them, her eyes sweeping slowly over their faces, seeming to meet each of theirs as she continued, "If anyone of you knows any scrap of information, anything that now seems out of place or suspicious, say so. If you hope the king dies so that you may gain power over a mere woman, you will be disappointed. I have seen much evil since ruling Tamehu and have learned from my experience," Nefrytatanen said in a voice stiff with anger. "If the king dies, I will rule alone, and under my rule you'll find little compassion. I've had enough of fear and grief. I shall turn Tamera into a land of army patrols and chains, if need be. I shall turn my face from all requests for mercy. You'll swear Sekhmet is your queen."

She was silent, waiting, scanning the room, again meetng each pair of eyes. When her gaze swept over them, many secretly cringed in fear because their loyalty had been less than complete. In the blue fire of her eyes, it seemed as if the avenging goddess did reign.

Finally one nobleman came forward and knelt before speaking to Nefrytatanen. She lifted the scepter of magic knots and looked for a moment as if she would strike him. But she merely brushed his back impatiently with it and said, "Rise and speak, Semerkhet, lord of Uto Province."

Semerkhet looked at her steadily enough, she observed. His black eyes seemed not to hold the fear of guilt.

"I would have Lord Nectanebes speak," Semerkhet said, continuing to look calmly at her. "I think he may know something that would be of interest to you."

"Nectanebes, lord of Tekhi Province," Meri summoned. The room was silent. Looking over the faces, Meri turned to Nefrytatanen and said, "He's not here. I don't remember his arrival. His province is far away and I think he's still on his way."

"Is he one of those who would not mourn Amenemhet's death?" Nefrytatanen asked accusingly. "Is he not one of those who has tried to rule as the king when he's but a governor?"

Meri replied, "He's given us some trouble."

"If he doesn't come in a reasonable time," she said, less softly, "we'll send soldiers for him. In the meanwhile, tell me, Lord Semerkhet, what you know." She was being purposely sarcastic in order to observe Semerkhet's reaction.

He flushed slightly at her sharp tone but answered

in a quiet voice, "I dislike carrying tales. I heard only a rumor, and if I repeat it incorrectly as fact I might lay blame on the innocent.

"It would be investigated," she said coldly. "The guilty will pay highly, but only the guilty."

"I've heard that Lord Nectanebes, has reason to believe that Hathorbes is in Tamera."

Nefrytatanen remembered only too well her high priest's look of hatred when he had heard his sentence of exile. "Tell me all of it, Semerkhet," she said. "Why has no one informed us of this?"

"It was but a rumor," Semerkhet replied. "We're some distance from Ithtawe, and if the soldiers had traveled all that way and we were wrong, we'd look like fools."

"Look like fools? You are fools! Shall I escort you to the king's pallet so you may see how he looks?" Nefrytatanen was so furious her voice shook. "Didn't we send Hathorbes away? Do we lightly banish people? It isn't your place to question such matters. The next man who comes to pass judgment on such important matters will find himself the next to be judged." She had raised her eyes from Semerkhet to include them all. Now she again turned her full attention on him. "What else have you heard, Semerkhet? What other bits of unimportant gossip have drifted your way?"

Semerkhet could almost feel his skin shrivel from the fires that burned behind her eyes. He said, "Nectanebes said that Hunefer—whose province borders his—is rumored to have seen Hathorbes."

At the mention of Hunefer's name, Nefrytatanen paled.

"Hathorbes may have sought his revenge by plotting with Hunefer and Amenardis," Kheti suggested.

"Who but Sinuhe's daughter would be more willing to act as poisoner?" Meri observed.

"Rakkor," Nefrytatanen said, "go to Ibex Province to investigate this story and return as quickly as possible."

"Take plenty of men and arm them well is my advice, Rakkor," cautioned Semerkhet.

Rakkor said nothing. He marched grimly from the room, his hand already on his sword.

"The rest of you will stay at Ithtawe until his return," Nefrytatanen ordered. She glanced at Commander Nessumontu, who stood quietly in the corner of the room and said slyly, "You all have heard rumors about the commander of Tamera's military forces? He stands by the door." The noblemen turned to look uneasily at Nessumontu. He didn't appear particularly formidable, being only a few years older than their queen and of slight physique, but they had heard of his ferocity in battle. Nefrytatanen said, "All the rumors you've heard are true." Nessumontu smiled coldly at them, as if he enjoyed their fear, and his narrow eyes were sharply alert.

Nefrytatanen continued, "Nessumontu is here with a number—a large number—of his men. He has orders that you will leave Ithtawe only when I allow it. If any of you still have an interest in higher ranks, you should consider his presence carefully." She turned abruptly and walked from the dais.

Nessumontu had moved to open the door for her, and he smiled slightly as she paused by him. "I'll watch them carefully," he said softly, "but I don't think there's much danger they'll disobey. You've made them too afraid to leave their rooms. But I'll be no less alert."

Nefrytatanen thanked him and left the throne room. When the other doors were opened to allow the nobles to leave, they weren't comforted by the sight of armed guards placed generously throughout the halls.

On the next day, Nectanebes arrived and came to her quickly. With a face stiff from fear, he confirmed what Semerkhet had said. After violently pointing out to him the error of his silence, Nefrytatanen dismissed him to his room.

While Nefrytatanen waited for Rakkor's return, she

sat by Amenemhet's side day and night, sleeping only
when exhaustion defeated her. Often she spoke to
Amenemhet, trying to rouse some spark of conscious-
ness. Hours passed while she held his cool hand and
told his unhearing ears about their bright future, about
the coming child, and about past events. He showed
no response.

Bekhet placed trays of food before Nefrytatanen and
scolded her until she ate. Yazid tried lamely to cheer
Nefrytatanen, but she ignored him.

Sometimes Nefrytatanen wondered what her life
would be like without Amenemhet, and this thought
either sent her again to his side in renewed effort to
rouse him or sent her rushing to another room, overcome
by bitter weeping.

On the afternoon of the sixth day, word came that
Rakkor had returned, and Nefrytatanen hurried to the
throne room to see him. A few of the noblemen were already gathered there when she arrived. As they waited
for Rakkor, others came slowly.

The governors seemed to have changed their attitude
because there was now an air of shame about them,
rather than of fear. Lord Semerkhet asked Meri if he
might speak to Nefrytatanen a moment. When she
agreed, Semerkhet apologized humbly for his past silence, telling her he had begged Tehuti for Amenemhet's recovery. He said he spoke for many of the others
who wished to express sorrow. Some of them had sent
generous offerings to the high priest, Ankhneferu, be-
seeching the help of Heru and Anpu alike. Nefrytatanen thanked him graciously and pondered on the
change in them.

Finally, still dusty from his ride, Rakkor marched
into the room. Anger made his eyes seem blacker than
ever, and they were red-rimmed from lack of sleep. He
looked even more formidable than the first time she
had laid eyes on him, Nefrytatanen observed, and she
was thankful he was loyal. Humbly he knelt before her,
his eyes downcast.

"Rise, Rakkor," Nefrytatanen said quickly. "Speak plainly as the friend you are. I'm tired of formalities." She laid her hand on his shoulder as he rose. Meeting the anger in his eyes, Nefrytatanen was shaken. "Rakkor," she said softly, "what did you find?"

Kheti, Meri, and Semerkhet came closer. Nessumontu slipped into the room and stood again quietly listening by the door, his hand on his sword.

"I went to Hunefer and found that he'd killed himself rather than face disgrace. Hathorbes had been there, but he'd fled. The servants said a girl of Amenardis's description had been there many times talking with them in a furtive manner. The servants were very cooperative."

"Why were they so willing to help, I wonder," Meri commented.

"Most of them are slaves and had been badly used." Rakkor turned to him. "Hunefer didn't believe in observing the ancient law about treating slaves well, but he answers to Asar for that now."

"So we have a province without a governor at the worst possible time." Nefrytatanen turnd to look at the gathering of nobles. She bit her lip a moment then turned to Seti, who had served as her prime minister in Tamehu before her marriage. He had been silent all through this.

"Seti, since the joining of the Two Lands, Meri has been prime minister. Although you've been of great service in many ways, no title or office has been given you." Nefrytatanen said clearly. "I choose you, therefore, to succeed Hunefer as lord of Ibex Province."

Seti's mouth dropped open. "My queen, what can I say to express my gratitude?" Ibex Province was very prosperous and most desirable.

"Say nothing, Seti," Nefrytatanen replied. She suddenly felt tired. As she looked at Seti, her weariness showed clearly on her face. "Be a good governor," she said. "That's all I ask. Send me no assassins, kidnap no one, harm none but my enemies. Oh, Seti, be as good a governor as you were Tamehu's prime minister, and I ask no more! I'll be more grateful than you can guess." She turned quickly and walked from the room, her purple robe billowing with her step. They stared silently after her.

When the door closed behind her, Nefrytatanen leaned her back against the wall, and, covering her face with her hands, she began to weep. Bekhet hurried to her side.

Wondering for a moment what to do for her mistress, Bekhet finally decided to treat the queen like a woman, and she put her arm comfortingly around Nefrytatanen's shoulder. Nefrytatanen was unprotesting as Bekhet led her to the couch in her private dressing room. There Bekhet sat with her and allowed her to cry without restraint.

When Nefrytatanen's sobbing began to subside, Bekhet brought her a goblet of wine. Wiping her queen's tears gently away, Bekhet said nothing. But she wished with all her heart to know what she might say or do.

"Thank you, Bekhet," Nefrytatanen whispered at last. She sipped her wine slowly, suddenly calm, seeming deep in thought. Abruptly she stood up and gave Bekhet the goblet. "Thank you, Bekhet," she said more purposefully. "Please leave me now. Don't bring the evening meal to me. I won't want it, baby or not. Tell the guard to allow no one to disturb the king and me. Tell him I command that no one enter these apartments until I request it."

"Yes, my lady," Bekhet answered. Giving Nefrytatanen a curious glance, she left.

Nefrytatanen knew Bekhet was alarmed and confused at her abruptness, but she heard her servant relay the orders to the guard, word for word.

Chapter Twelve

Nefrytatanen spent the rest of the afternoon watching Amenemhet's motionless figure, wondering what he dreamed all this time—or whether he was even able to dream.

The sun sank slowly beyond the terrace, and she watched darkness reach into the silent garden. When the moon glowed over the trees, drenching the room in light, she still sat unmoving.

She looked at Amenemhet through the silvery glow and thought of his strength, his tenderness, his passion. His stillness was doubly awful because it was so unlike him. To think that he might never rise again, that those golden eyes might be forever closed, that she might never again hear his voice or know his touch was agony.

Nefrytatanen was disgusted as well. Amenemhet, who had planned to accomplish so much, lay helpless, the victim of undeserved revenge. Nefrytatanen reflected on the many times when he had kept patient though she could not.

She remembered him courageously struggling to tell her of his love before he had dropped into this mysterious sleep. She shivered. Whatever he had wanted to tell her was unnecessary. He had shown her in ways she couldn't count how deep and unfailing was his love. She was ashamed, remembering that she had thought he might look for another when she grew heavy with the

child. She remembered everything, and her soul was
wrenched with grief.

Nefrytatanen glanced down at Amenemhet and was
startled to see the golden eyes again alert and watching
her. She stared incredulously at him a moment. Then
she remembered what she had planned to do and knew
she must explain it to him, now that he was conscious.

"Beloved," she whispered, "can you speak or move?"
There was no response. "Can you hear and understand
me? If you can, close your eyes to answer yes."

Amenemhet's eyes closed and opened. Even this
small movement filled Nefrytatanen with joy. She
grasped his hands and kissed them.

"Beloved," she whispered, hating to ask this, "do
you know what Horemheb said about your condition?"

He closed his eyes and opened them. Their expression spoke for him.

"Do you have any sensation?" she asked. He blinked
promptly, and she put one of his hands against her
abdomen because the child was moving. "Can you feel
your son?"

Amenemhet blinked while a tear squeezed from his
eye.

"You'll see him, beloved," she promised. "Together
we'll watch him grow to manhood. And there will be
other children." Her eyes were shining with hope. "I
won't let you die," she promised. "I'll call Issella—my
mother. I must get her help tonight while the moon is
shining full. Beloved, do you understand what I mean?"

Amenemhet stared at Nefrytatanen. She could see he
understood. She didn't know what to say next because
she didn't know how he felt about this.

"It will have to be here, beloved, before your eyes."
Her voice was very gentle. "You'll see what I do. It will
be strange to you, but I'll be in control of what happens.
Don't be afraid for me, for yourself, or for the child.
Do you understand this?"

Amenemhet blinked, his eyes unafraid and curious.

"Later, beloved, when you're well, remember that

what you'll see here tonight must never be repeated to others," she warned. She leaned over him and kissed his cheek. "I must do it. It's the only thing I can think of. You are my very life," she whispered.

Nefrytatanen turned away and searched through a cabinet. When she came back, she carried a lamp, a silver dish, oil, and a container of powder. She unbound her hair, shook it loose and then slipped out of her robe. She threw open the terrace doors and stood naked, glowing ivory like a statue, in the moonlight.

Amenemhet's mind was very clear. Watching her, he thought that if his will were strong enough to overcome the poison, he would now rise from the pallet.

Nefrytatanen stood quietly, head down, as if deep in thought. Then, seeming to rouse herself, she poured oil into the silver dish, lit it, and blew out the lamp.

Standing before the window opening, in a cool draft from the garden, Nefrytatanen slowly raised her arms to the sky and spoke, in a firm, clear tone, words Amenemhet could not understand. She lowered her arms and tossed powder onto the fire. The darkness was filled with her perfume. Blue sparks, like stars, rose from the flame and scattered through the silvery air. She repeated the strange words, and her tone made Amenemhet think she made a pledge or a declaration. The room seemed to whisper from its shadows, as if the spirits she invoked talked to her. Then she sat on the floor before the fiery dish. Amenemhet wondered what strange sights he would see now. He felt his soul shudder.

"Homage to thee, O Asar, Lord of Eternity," Nefrytatanen cried, "I have used the words of power. Hail, Tehuti, who made the word of Asar to be true against his enemies, I have called the secret names. Praise to thee, O Anpu, messenger of Asar, bring my petition to him." Now her tone changed into one of pleading. "Behold, O Aset, Lady of Light, Mistress of Enchantment, your servant, whose name you know, lamenting for my Amenemhet as once you lamented for Asar. For a time, release from Tuat my mother, Issella. Let her come forth to help me, even as Tehuti came to you." Nefrytatanen alternately commanded and pleaded with the powers whose help she sought.

Amenemhet watched and listened, fascinated. The blue glow reflected on Nefrytatanen's skin and made her seem a spirit, something other than mortal.

The blue sparkles that had floated at random seemed to take direction and gather in one place. A form slowly took shape. Before Amenemhet's amazed eyes, a woman gradually became clear. He knew it was Issella. She looked like her daughter.

The soft, whispering voice was barely distinguishable from the night breezes, "My daughter, such evils plague you that Asar has released me, and Aset sends you this message—your Amenemhet can be saved."

"Mother," Nefrytatanen cried. "How?"

"You must travel to Atalan. Have built for your voyage a ship of papyrus as are shown on the walls of the tombs. Sail to the Great Green Sea and west, even beyond the gateway to the ocean. Go south following the coast until you reach the current to take you west into the open ocean. It will bring you to Atalan." She paused then added gently, "My child, waste no time. Only in Atalan is there knowledge to save him." As she began, slowly, to fade into a blue glow, she whispered, "If you need me again, call me, for Aset knows you well and will let me come to you." Her eyes, glowing silver as the moonlight, turned to Amenemhet. "Amenemhet," she said, "you are much in the favor of the divine beings." Then she disappeared.

Nefrytatanen sat quietly a moment before putting out the fire. Then she came to Amenemhet through the blue smoke which yet drifted in the room, and she put her arms around his shoulders.

"Beloved, we can do it. We can save you! If I had had to bargain with Sutekh, I wouldn't have let you die. Aset knows my pain too well to turn from us." She began to shiver with relief, and she put her face against his chest. He wanted to put his arms around her. He would have leaped from the couch and held her and laughed with her, for he could hardly believe this news. His heart was pounding, but he remained motionless and silent, the glow of his eyes alone expressing his happiness. Nefrytatanen couldn't see this. She lay exhausted and trembling against him.

Dedjet plodded forlornly in the moonlight in the garden. She paused in the shadows near the palace and sat on a flat stone by a bush to contemplate her misery.

It wasn't that she was ugly. Other men surely admired her when she passed, and Nekhen had looked at her with a smile the first time they had met. What had she done wrong? She had been pleasant, careful not to complain or scold, as other women often did. She hadn't flirted to make him jealous or deceived him in any way. She sighed.

Before tonight he had used sweet and tender words with her, and he had touched her face and hair in a loving way. They had laughed merrily together. With his smiling eyes and quiet words, he had made her fall in love with him, and with all the intensity of the innocent, she had gone to him in the night. She had tried to please him, and he had seemed pleased. Why had he then told her to go away?

Dedjet sat with hanging head. She had given him herself, which was all she had to give, and now he turned from her. Recalling his words, she felt anger. She felt disgust with herself for not realizing that he'd only sought a conquest. Her innocence had made her a choice target. Now that could never be again. She sat in the night, her humiliation haunting her.

Dedjet heard behind her the sound of an opening door. Realizing it belonged to the royal bedchamber, she quickly turned to squeeze farther into the shadows. She knew she wasn't supposed to be here at this hour. Fearfully she peered through the leaves expecting a scolding voice. There was none.

A peculiar blue light came from the room, and the scent of the queen's perfume drifted into the garden. Dedjet's scalp prickled. A shiver ran down her spine as she saw Nefrytatanen standing naked before the window opening, her eyes shining through the darkness like a wild creature's. Dedjet hardly dared breathe, and her heart thundered with fear. The queen's arms raised as if in supplication, and she spoke a language Dedjet couldn't understand. Dedjet remembered rumors she had heard about the queen, and her body stiffened even more with terror. When Dedjet heard Nefrytatanen invoking Asar and Aset, she knew the stories were true.

Round-eyed, Dedjet watched the blue sparkles that filled the room. She dared not move a muscle. When Issella's spirit appeared, Dedjet almost fainted. She was certain the divine beings would know where she hid and reveal this to Nefrytatanen. Though she couldn't stop trembling, she watched and listened to it all.

Long after it was over, Dedjet crouched in the dark, afraid to move. But when she saw that nothing was going to happen to her, she began to wonder at what she had seen. An idea took shape in her mind.

If she went to Nekhen with this news, would he not speak to her? It wasn't everyone who could say he had witnessed his queen casting a spell, summoning spirits, and conversing with the dead. It would give Dedjet a reason to see him again; and, perhaps, while she asked his advice about this, she might also learn how she had angered him. She could then convince herself that she hadn't been only a new adventure for him. Perhaps, seeing her afraid and trembling, he might even comfort her. In any case, she decided, who else could she tell this thing to?

Dedjet rose slowly, keeping herself from trembling. Glancing fearfully at the now silent, darkened room, she tiptoed cautiously away. Once she reached the other side of the garden, she surrendered to vivid terror, and ran.

Chapter Thirteen

The morning sun felt pleasant to Bekhet as she walked briskly toward the royal apartments to awaken the queen. Bekhet didn't feel as efficient as her steps sounded because her night had been spent in sleeplessness. She resolved she wouldn't depress her mistress with her own long face, although she felt anything but cheerful.

As she passed a doorway, she heard the sound of whispering. To Bekhet whispers meant secrets, and secrets usually meant gossip. Bekhet abhorred gossiping among the servants, and she interfered whenever possible. She stopped, and like a cat she crept silently back. Arranging herself so that not even her shadow fell across the doorway, she stood motionless and listened.

"You saw this?" asked a shocked male voice.

"I couldn't find you last night, or I would have told you then. I was so frightened I didn't know what to do! She can do magic just as those old stories said."

Bekhet recognized Dedjet's voice and waited while the girl repeated the story to an apparently incredulous listener. Bekhet's eyes grew wide at what she heard, and many thoughts flew through her mind in rapid succession. She had also heard such rumors, but she had sneered at them. Now Bekhet heard them confirmed as Dedjet related in detail what had happened.

At first Bekhet felt fear chill her. Then she decided

that, even if Nefrytatanen had this awesome power, she knew Nefrytatanen too well to become afraid of her now. Her loyalty stood as solidly unshaken as the pyramids in the north.

When Bekhet heard a derisive laugh and the sound of retreating steps, she moved quickly into the open, hoping to confront whoever was walking away. But Dedjet stood alone with drooping head.

"What is this I've just heard?" Bekhet demanded.

Dedjet's startled eyes, still filled with misery and now mixed with guilt, looked up at her. "I didn't lie, Bekhet!" Dedjet backed away a little. "I saw it, truly."

"You're spreading nonsense." Bekhet seemed unmoved. "Shame on you for carrying such tales," she scolded.

Bekhet was silent a moment observing the look on Dedjet's face and wondering who had been with her. She felt a little sorry for Dedjet's situation, recognizing it for what it was.

In a more friendly tone, Bekhet said, "if the queen is really able to do magic, I wouldn't wish to let everyone know I saw her casting a spell. The next spell might be on you, in punishment for spying. In any case, you show little loyalty gossiping about your queen in this fashion. Go on your way and watch your tongue."

Dedjet was relieved to be dismissed, and she backed away, thoroughly frightened, remembering again what she had seen in the night, stammering apologies.

As Bekhet continued on her way to Nefrytatanen, she considered Dedjet's story. She wondered who had been with Dedjet. Dedjet had certainly been frightened, and her story was too complicated to be a lie. Finally Bekhet decided to tell Nefrytatanen. The news of this incident would be spread quickly, and Nefrytatanen should be warned.

When Bekhet entered the royal apartment, she saw Nefrytatanen sitting near Amenemhet in the sunlight by the window opening. As Bekhet approached, Nefrytatanen turned to her and smiled. Bekhet knew she couldn't be evil, magic or no magic. She motioned that she wished to talk to Nefrytatanen in the dressing room. Giving Amenemhet's hand a pat, Nefrytatanen rose to follow her servant.

When the door was closed behind them, Bekhet said, "My lady, I'm sorry to disturb you, but I have some news you should hear."

"Yes?" Nefrytatanen's eyes were puzzled.

"I heard just now one of the maids gossiping to someone I couldn't see, telling a wild story, which, though I scolded her, will surely travel fast."

Nefrytatanen's heart fell. She had been afraid someone had seen or heard what she had done.

"A foolish tale, no doubt, and a figment of her imagination, or perhaps, a mistake—perhaps too much wine, although the girl has never shown such tendencies before," Bekhet spoke rapidly in her embarrassment. "She was in the garden last night and claimed she saw you cast a spell—of all things—even summon a spirit and converse with it!" Bekhet spoke even faster now. "She said you received directions to some place where they might heal the king. I'm sorry to bother you with her delusions, but such a story makes exciting gossip and is bound to spread quickly."

Nefrytatanen's face had grown pale, and she sank slowly to the couch. "Bekhet, please sit beside me," she said quietly. Bekhet obeyed, wondering at her expression. "The story is true, Bekhet," she admitted. Bekhet stared. "I'm sorry I was seen. I would have made all the arrangements for the voyage, saying that my mother had told me of Atalan, and everyone would have assumed she had told me long ago, before she died. Now I don't know what to say. Whatever story is spread cannot change what I must do. We must make the trip. It's the only chance to save him," she finished softly. She looked at Bekhet. "Are you afraid of me now?"

Bekhet had composed herself with some effort. She said quietly, "I am startled by this news, but, my lady, I know you too well to fear you." Nefrytatanen took her hand, smiling a little. Bekhet went on, "I'm glad you know a way to save him. You mustn't think of what tales are spread. I'll get Yazid, and he'll help me do what we can to smother this story."

Nefrytatanen stood up. "Bekhet, you are precious," she said, relieved. "You may tell Yazid the truth. He'll hear it anyway, and it's best he hear facts instead of rumors. I think he'll understand, and it will make him happy to know there's a chance to save the king. Will you also find Kheti and bring him to me? I'll need his help with the preparations I must make." Nefrytatanen paused a moment, and her small smile bloomed into a radiance that filled her eyes. "Bekhet," she said, "the king awakened last night. Although he still cannot speak or move, he can hear and feel and see." Her smile took on a mischievous cast as she finished, "Take care what you say in his hearing."

Bekhet's face lit with happiness. "I'll be careful," she promised. "I'll find Kheti and Yazid and send someone with your morning meal." When they reentered the bed-chamber, Bekhet glanced at Amenemhet and smiled, then left them alone.

Bekhet walked swiftly through the hall, her steps quick with excitement. She decided to have Dedjet bring the meal to them. The girl could look at Nefrytatanen face-to-face and see how unfearful the queen was, then be ashamed to tell her story.

After Bekhet had left, Nefrytatanen considered the situation. She finally decided that if everyone in Tamera knew what she was, it might be easier for her. She was everything she had always been, and they would see no difference in her now. Perhaps the noblemen's behavior might even benefit from hearing the old rumors confirmed.

When Dedjet brought the meal, Nefrytatanen took one look at her and knew she was the one who had spread the story. She said nothing, but smiled at Dedjet and directed her to place the food. Seating herself near Amenemhet, Nefrytatanen began to feed him, dismissing Dedjet quietly. When Dedjet had left, Nefrytatanen related to him this latest development.

Glad to escape, Dedjet hurried down the hall. She thought of how Nekhen had laughed at her and vividly remembered the way the queen had looked last night. She thought of Nefrytatanen feeding Amenemhet so tenderly. Dedjet hadn't missed the look in the king's eyes whenever the queen had been near. Dedjet considered what she might do if she were Nefrytatanen and decided that if she knew any spells, she would use them to save him. She reflected on the emotions behind such looks. It wasn't often, she decided a little bitterly, that one found such happiness in love. She thought again of Nekhen and paused to stamp her foot. She would choose more wisely the next time.

At Nefrytatanen's voice, Kheti entered the room. Glancing at Amenemhet, guilt rushed over him again. He sat near Nefrytatanen.

"Kheti," she said softly, "he's awake again. He cannot speak, but you may talk to him."

Kheti's face brightened a little, but his grey eyes again became bitter. He mumbled, "What can I say to him? How can I even face him?"

"Say what you will." Nefrytatanen smiled. "He doesn't blame you. Besides, I have good news." Startled, Kheti looked up at her. She added, "There's a way to save him."

"What way? What can we do?"

"We must take him to Atalan, my mother's birthplace, where they know how to save him. It's a long and dangerous voyage, but it's the only chance."

"I'll go," Kheti said quickly. "Where is this place?"

"Beyond the opening to the ocean in the Great Green Sea." Nefrytatanen watched Kheti carefully, but his eyes never faltered. "We must build a papyrus ship modeled after those painted on the tomb walls. It's the kind of ship my father used when he journeyed to Atalan. It's the only ship we know of that can withstand the trip."

"I'll go, however far it is, if we must travel on an open raft. I'll get Sepa to build the craft, if you wish. He's the best shipbuilder in the land."

"That's a good suggestion, Kheti. There will be other things I'll have to ask your advice about." She was quiet a moment, thinking.

"Whatever I can help you with, you need only tell me," Kheti offered quickly. "Surely you know that."

"Kheti, I give you no order to go with us," Nefrytatanen said slowly. Her fingers played absently with a small enameled hippopotamus on the table beside her. She looked up at him. "There will be great danger, and you may see some strange things. . . ." She knew she must tell him, but she didn't know how. "Oh, I might as well just say it!" she exclaimed. "It's no use trying to tell anything but the truth of the matter. If you have to make a decision, you must know what you'll face." Kheti stared at her in bewilderment. "Kheti," she said, "I can do magic—just as the rumors say—though it's not quite what most people think. In Atalan these things are spoken of without fear, and my mother taught me long ago what she knew." Kheti had paled slightly, but he said nothing. His surprise was obvious, but his eyes remained steady. "The powers, Kheti, which are called magic, are forces of nature, unlocked and used with intelligence. I called on my mother for help last night, and I was seen. There will be rumors about it soon, if they haven't already begun to spread. Yes, Kheti," she sighed, "my mother is dead, but she came to me to tell me what to do. On the voyage I may need her again. If I do, I'll call her, and she'll come. On such a craft as we'll make, there will be no way to conceal what I do. You'd see it, if you go. So I warn you before you decide."

"It's the only way to save him?" Kheti glanced at Amenemhet.

"So she told me."

"Then, I'll go. Sorcery, spirits, or demons though we

meet, I'll go." Kheti's eyes again grew angry. "After all, did I not bring the viper who stung him?"

"And you killed her."

"I brought her," he said stubbornly. "But even if I hadn't, I would go to help save him."

"And Rakkor?" she asked cautiously. "Do you think he'd agree? I'd like to have him with us."

"I'll tell him what you said, but he'll go, too." Kheti smiled. "He wouldn't miss the chance for such an adventure even if his king weren't dying."

"Tell Rakkor if you wish, Kheti, but send him to me to give his answer," she said.

"I'll do it now. Afterwards, I'll find Sepa and bring him to you," Kheti promised.

After the noon meal, when everyone was sleeping, Nefrytatanen was too restless to lie down. Amenemhet slept peacefully, but each time he closed his eyes Nefrytatanen was afraid he wouldn't reopen them and would drop again into that fearful deep sleep she couldn't awaken him from——or worse. So she sat watching him. His breathing seemed normal and his face was peaceful. She leaned to put her ear on his chest. His heart was strong and steady, and she listened a moment, happy to feel his warmth.

After a time she stood up and looked around for something to distract herself with. The fountain in the garden whispered to her, and she smiled, remembering Noph one afternoon, when they had lain half-sleeping, listening to the fountain in the courtyard. Amenemhet said it was then he had decided to have a fountain and lotus pond close to their room at Ithtawe, because its music had been so pleasantly soothing.

Nefrytatanen went out on the terrace then down into the garden where she sat in a shady place in the grass, not far from the stairway. She looked at the pendant Amenemhet had given her on their wedding day. The delicate silver lotus sparkled while the deep blue stone in the blossom's heart glowed with its strange star. The stone

was the color of her eyes, he had said, and the color of
the twin stars he had seen the night before she had first
come to him. She thought of the matching pendant he
wore. It was a link between them. Like her, Amenemhet never removed his pendant.

Nefrytatanen didn't hear the gate being opened or
the approaching footsteps. She finally noticed two pairs
of legs standing before her. She glanced up and saw
Kheti and Rakkor waiting patiently. She put out her
hand, and Kheti helped her to her feet.

Rakkor spoke first. "Kheti told me what you propose.
If you have any doubt I'd go, banish it now. My only
fear would be that you wouldn't ask me."

Nefrytatanen looked into Rakkor's eyes, and she
realized he really was afraid she might refuse him.
Surprised, she asked, "Rakkor, are you so anxious to
face all these unknown dangers? You're a man of the
desert, and the ocean is quite different. And has Kheti
told you everything?"

"Everything," Rakkor answered meaningfully, his
black eyes snapping. "I wouldn't be frightened away by
such things. Desert, sea, demons, spirits—death comes
when it will. If the movement of a camel doesn't bother
me, the sea won't either."

"When you fall off a camel, you hit the sand," Nefrytatanen said. "When you fall off a ship, you drown."

Rakkor looked affronted. "I never fall off my camel,"
he declared.

Nefrytatanen took a deep breath. "How can I refuse
you?" she laughed. "I can only be thankful for a friend
like you." Although Rakkor seemed a little embarrassed, he continued to look steadily at her.

Kheti said, "Rakkor helped me find Sepa, and we've
brought him here. He waits in the palace now."

Nefrytatanen turned to the doors and motioned for
Kheti and Rakkor to follow her into the sitting room.
There she summoned a servant and sat down, saying
nothing until Dedjet came and poured a cool drink for
them.

After Dedjet had left, Nefrytatanen signaled that Sepa be brought in. She rose and paced around the room until a guard opened the door.

Nefrytatanen thought Sepa looked as timeless as the sea he knew so well. The sun and water had lined his skin, but his movements were young, and it was impossible to tell his age. Large hands, callused with pulling the ropes of many sails, swung at his sides. He came toward her, stopped, and bowed deeply. Tired of courtly rules and impatient with the time they wasted, she motioned Sepa to rise, and she began at once.

"Sepa," Nefrytatanen said, "I'm told you're the finest shipbuilder in the land." Sepa stared at her not knowing what to reply. He knew he was the best, but it seemed immodest to agree. She went on without waiting. "I need a ship made as quickly as possible. It isn't one you've made before, Sepa. Its design is painted on the tomb walls. It must be made of papyrus reeds."

"But papyrus is for scrolls, not sailing!" he declared, forgetting his place. Now he was a shipbuilder, and she his customer. "Reeds are too fragile. The ship will sink."

"There's a way to manage it," Nefrytatanen said. "You'll study the designs on the tomb walls and ask the high priest to locate the records of such ships. This vessel must sail the open ocean, and papyrus is supposed to withstand salt water. The ship must not sink, Sepa, for the king and I will be on it."

Sepa's heart was what sank then. "My queen, if such a ship can be made and will float, I'll make it, but I have doubts as to its strength."

"It can be done, and it will float," she insisted. "My own father made such a craft once. He must have found directions somewhere. It must be done quickly. Each moment is precious beyond your dreaming." Sepa stared at her, speechless. She said, "Whatever materials you need, how many and which workers, choose freely. No cost, no effort will be spared. When you've succeeded, your reward will make your family rich forever." Sepa's eyes grew wide with astonishment as his queen took his hand in hers and urged, "Go quickly, Sepa. Forget all else and begin now."

"Yes, my queen, of course," he stammered and began to back away.

She turned to Rakkor. "Rakkor," she said, "go with Sepa and see that he gets immediate cooperation from others." Rakkor nodded, and they marched out.

Nefrytatanen turned her attention to Kheti. "Kheti, perhaps you should talk to Sepa about supplies for this voyage. When you've determined what we need, would you also see to it that they're ready when we need them?"

"We probably won't require anything for ourselves very different from what we'd take on a desert trek, but there will probably be other things necessary for the ship. I'll ask Sepa about all this," he promised. He smiled at her. "I'd rather be on the desert than the ocean," he admitted, "but it will be a new experience for me to learn from."

"It will be no newer to you than to me," she declared then added, "or to Rakkor, or to Yazid either—if he's willing to go. As I recall, Yazid doesn't like traveling at all."

As he left, Kheti thought of Yazid's probable reaction to an ocean voyage and laughed. Then he hurried down the hall and out of the palace. He had many lists to compile and many questions to find answers for, in a very short time.

During the days that followed, the noblemen were given permission to leave Ithtawe, but Semerkhet came to Nefrytatanen as their spokesman, again, asking permission to stay and see the ship launched on its voyage. She gave her approval, and most of them remained, dispatching messengers to their provinces with instructions concerning their continued absence.

The work on the ship proceeded at a lively pace, and one day Nefrytatanen visited Sepa's work area to inspect the progress. She was amazed at how much they had already accomplished and complimented Sepa. He replied that it was the men who deserved her praise. They had volunteered to divide themselves into shifts so they could work not only during the day but by torchlight in the dark. Nefrytatanen was deeply touched by their loyalty and ordered that they all be given extra pay as reward for their efforts. This gesture on her part, accompanied by her personal thanks, moved the men to even greater inspiration and speed.

Sepa explained in detail how the papyrus was processed. He showed her how the reeds were soaked in water, bound into bundles, and attached with intricately knotted ropes, then bent to desired shapes and allowed to dry. She had been interested in the shape of the ship, and he demonstrated carefully how the sections of the vessel were attached together in a springlike action to give the craft resilience in the rolling waves. Sepa pointed out that the wooden parts were made of cedar imported from Retenú, and he assured her there was no better wood for their purpose, cedar being extremely strong. She was lavish with praise to them all, and she left tired but satisfied.

The visit to the shipyard made Nefrytatanen so anxious to begin the voyage that she couldn't rest that night. After hours of sleeplessness and unusual discomfort for the first time during her pregnancy, she called for Horemheb. He mixed a potion of herbs to calm her and sternly forbade her to leave the palace grounds until the voyage. Then he softened and begged her to rest. The danger of losing the child was, in itself, sufficient to obtain her obedience. After he left in the morning, she stayed in bed.

She was in a gloomy mood until she was told that Ankheneferu had come, bringing a friend to meet her. Hoping for something to distract her from her restlessness, she dressed and received them in the round room off the garden.

As the high priest greeted Nefrytatanen, she could see his concern for her. Although Ankhneferu made no reference to her health, those sharp eyes missed nothing. His friend, Senbi, was a young priest on his way home to Wast from Anu where he had just completed extensive studies. Senbi's lean face was bronzed from his journey, and he smiled pleasantly at her.

Senbi took in Nefrytatanen's pallor at a glance. With a sympathy revealed in his eyes, if not in his manner, he tried distracting her from her worries with descriptions of Anu. Ankhneferu congratulated himself for bringing Senbi. Nefrytatanen's color began to return as she grew more absorbed in Senbi's interesting stories. She asked many questions. They had been talking for some time when it was announced that Sepa requested an audience.

"Send him in," Nefrytatanen directed the guard then turned to Ankhneferu and Senbi. "Please stay, if you can, while Sepa talks with me. I doubt it will take long."

Although the queen's invitation would not ordinarily have been theirs to refuse, Nefrytatanen made it obvious they might decline if they wished. Though Senbi had been in a hurry to resume his journey home, he smiled and immediately accepted for them both.

Sepa came in and, bowing, looked at the priests suspiciously. He remembered only too well what Sinuhe had done. Nefrytatanen smiled in understanding. "Sepa," she said, "meet two friends, Ankhneferu and Senbi. Ankhneferu, Senbi, this is Sepa, the best shipbuilder in Tamera."

They greeted him cordially. He looked a little disconcerted by her praise. After a moment, Sepa said, "My queen, I have good news for you. Your visit so greatly inspired the men that they've worked like never before. I think it's likely the ship will be finished by tomorrow night. If this is true, we'll launch it in the river to test it and load it during the night. If you wish, it can be ready the following morning."

"Sepa, that's wonderful!" Nefrytatanen exclaimed. "When will you know for certain?"

"Tomorrow morning we'll know," he answered.

"There's only one more thing we're unsure of, and once we know about that, then we'll know we're almost finished."

"Sepa," she said, "I'll need someone to sail this vessel. How many men do you think I'll need, and who would you suggest?"

Sepa carefully gathered his thoughts before answering. "The ship will have space for supplies and eight people. More than that number will become too crowded. The vessel's design is such that three people can handle it easily. Actually one person could guide it, and the others would assist him." Sepa considered the matter a moment and then added, "If you had to, one sailor could even teach the others."

"Counting the king and myself, we would take four others, leaving space for two more." Nefrytatanen looked at Sepa meaningfully. "I wish to have these four along for particular reasons. Could they learn to sail this ship, though they're unfamiliar with sailing and the sea?"

"Yes." Sepa was firm. "I make no empty boast, my queen. It's very simple to guide once it's understood. I'm making a fine ship, perfectly balanced, strong and responsive. No effort has been spared. I believe I could have made a larger craft, now that I've seen it, but I followed the directions I found. I think it's the best ship I've ever built, strange as its design was to me." He smiled proudly. "If these people you mentioned are reasonably able and strong, they could learn to handle the ship easily. What you need now is a sailor to teach and supervise them. You also need someone who can read the stars when you sail at night. Some sailors can do both, but they're few. They would have to have had experience on the Great Green Sea—not only on the Nile. The two are very different, you understand."

Ankhneferu and Senbi had been listening carefully. Now Senbi came forward, his eyes gleaming with excitement.

"May I speak?" he asked.

"Yes, Senbi. What is it?"

"I would like to go on this voyage, if I may be so honored," he said hesitantly, Nefrytatanen looked at him in surprise. "I studied astronomy at Anu," he added quickly. "Although I'm not a sailor, I could be useful in several ways. Being a priest, I might help with spiritual matters. This voyage is long and uncertain and may be difficult for people unfamiliar with extended isolation. I've also studied medicine; although I'm not a physician, I can help in case of an emergency. Ankhneferu can assure you of my loyalty. When we reach Atalan, I might study some of their knowledge and record it to bring back to Tamera."

Nefrytatanen considered this proposal. She knew Senbi could be useful. She said, "Senbi, there are some other matters you need also consider. You're aware of the dangers? We don't know what we may face." He nodded vigorously in answer. "Then, Senbi, there's just this one more thing," she said. "You have, no doubt, heard certain stories about me? The latest concerns how I managed to learn the way to Atalan?"

"Yes, I've heard all the rumors about you," Senbi answered. He smiled faintly. "If you hesitate to give me permission to go because you think I'd be afraid or scoff—I am not afraid, nor would I scoff. I know a little about many things, and I know something on the subject of magic. I'm curious to learn more. If you found it necessary to call upon your knowledge in my presence, I'd cooperate in any way I could. I'd like to witness such a thing and, if possible, learn more about it."

Nefrytatanen turned to Sepa. "You know what we're talking about, Sepa. Do you know any good sailors who would answer as well as Senbi? I must be sure he's loyal for I will not—dare not—risk another attack. He'd come of his own choosing because I'm ordering no one on this voyage."

Senbi stared at Nefrytatanen and interrupted, "Do you, then, give me your permission?"

Nefrytatanen addressed Ankhneferu. "Is Senbi all he claims?"

Ankhneferu smiled. "He's modest. Senbi is many more things I'm proud to list. He's intelligent, reliable, unafraid of work, and not easy to panic. Above all his good qualities, Senbi is loyal."

"Then pack what you'll need, Senbi," Nefrytatanen said, "but make your bundle as small as possible."

Senbi smiled widely. "Thank you, my queen. I'll try not to disappoint you in any way."

"I think you won't disappoint me," Nefrytatanen replied.

Senbi and Ankhneferu left immediately, Senbi happily anticipating what he would bring. He seemed to have completely forgotten about going home to Wast.

Again, Nefrytatanen turned to Sepa. "Have you thought of a sailor?" she asked.

"I've considered it carefully," he replied. "I know of one who's not only a good Nile sailor but also has experience on the sea. He can navigate by the stars, and I know he's fond of adventure. He's a great admirer of the king's and would consider it not only an honor, but a privilege, to be allowed to accompany you."

"Who is this man?" she asked. "How do you know him so well? Are you sure he's loyal?"

"I can assure you he is. I trust him with my own life." Sepa smiled proudly. "I'd go myself, if I were a little younger, but I'm retired from sailing and now can only build ships. I've taught Necho all I know. Necho is my son."

Nefrytatanen was silent a moment, much impressed with his offer. Finally she said, "I thank you, Sepa. You know better than any of us what dangers are involved, and I'm deeply touched. I'd like to speak to Necho, if you'd send him to me. I want him to tell me himself that he wants to make this voyage. I say this, not because I don't believe you, but because I've done so with all the others."

"I understand," Sepa replied. Smiling he added, "I'll

leave now, if I may. You can be sure Necho will be here soon—eager to go."

Nefrytatanen watched Sepa leave. When she was alone, she thought over what he'd said.

Recent events had brought much sorrow and she had wondered about the people's loyalty. Amenemhet had tried to bring order so they might rule justly and peacefully, and they had thought, before this had happened, that they had gained the good will of their subjects. Since Amenemhet's poisoning, and after learning of the bitterness of so many of the noblemen, she had often felt despair. But after seeing the eagerness of the builders, after having Senbi volunteer, and after Sepa's offering his son, Nefrytatanen began to feel hopeful. Perhaps, after all, they weren't hated. Perhaps it was only a few who wished them evil. She made a mental note to tell Amenemhet these things. It would cheer him.

Nefrytatanen decided to go to the throne room and see what progress had been made on the work she'd recently ordered. When she arrived, the room was empty. While she inspected the throne's trim, she was informed that Sepa had brought Necho. She told the guard to admit Necho alone.

When Necho entered the throne room, she could see he was awed at being received and felt self-conscious in her presence. She stepped from the dais and smiled at him. She thought he seemed very young for such a voyage, but when he came closer, she noted a look of courage and intelligence advanced for his years. She extended her hand cordially.

Necho was surprised at his queen's friendliness and was unsure for a moment what to do with her hand once he held it. He finally decided to kiss it, which he did, and she withdrew it tactfully.

In a casual tone, she said, "Necho, I've been indoors for a time, and I'd like some air. Let us go into the garden while we talk."

Necho gratefully followed Nefrytatanen from the impressive room. She led him to a bench in the shade near a small lotus pond, where a fountain made rainbows in the sun. Then she sat and motioned for him to sit beside her. Before speaking, she leaned slightly over the pond and dangled her fingertips in the water, gazing at the blossoms floating there.

Turning to him at last, she said, "Your father told me you might be interested in traveling with us. He said you're well-qualified. I trust his judgment. I've asked everyone who will go to tell me, after considering all things with great care, whether they truly wish to go. There will be many dangers, and it's possible you won't return. Please think about this. If you have any doubts, say so now. I won't be angry. I wish only the truth."

As Nefrytatanen spoke, Necho thought of Amenemhet dying somewhere in the palace, and he contrasted this picture with another he remembered very well.

When Nefrytatanen had been kidnapped, Necho—who had been visiting relatives in the area—had been present as Amenemhet arrived at the barge. Necho could see again the look on Amenemhet's face as he'd slid from his horse. Amenemhet had searched frantically through the burned and half-sunken ship, and when he had emerged he'd worn an expression of despair. Necho remembered Amenemhet's quiet voice as he had questioned the people standing about. Amenemhet had asked questions, given orders for the search, and had personally arranged for the proper burial of the victims. Necho had seen the misery in Amenemhet's eyes as he had examined the hacked and burned bodies, searching for Nefrytatanen.

While Necho was thinking of these things, Nefrytatanen watched him, wondering at his strange expression. Necho finally looked up at the face of the woman for whom Amenemhet had searched.

"I will go," he said.

Nefrytatanen took Necho's hand and led him silently to the gate. Her eyes were filled with gratitude and respect. "Thank you," she whispered and turned away.

As Nefrytatanen approached the doors to the royal apartments, she heard Bekhet's usually calm, low voice raised in anger. Startled she stopped to listen, hesitating to intrude on a private moment.

"I will go, and you won't stop me!" Bekhet's angry voice said sharply. "My lady will wish to care for the king, and I'll care for her and cook. You—prepare the meals? May Tehuti in his wisdom spare us such delights."

Yazid's voice carried through the door. "I cooked for the king on the desert. I cared for him then."

"He was able to take care of himself then, and still he returned with little more than skin covering his bones." In a lower tone, Bekhet continued, "Besides, the queen's condition must not be ignored. A woman needs another woman at such a time. No man can know how she feels. If this voyage lasts beyond her time, what would *you* do if the child came? *I know* what to do."

Yazid was silent a moment, and then his voice was softer, with a hint of sadness in it. "There must be something I could do."

"You could bail out the waters that are sure to seep in," came the tart reply.

Now Yazid was angry again. "You talk smartly for a servant—"

Nefrytatanen decided this had gone far enough. Rattling the door first to warn them, she walked in. They went about their tasks quickly, suddenly silent. But Yazid's face was pale and Bekhet's flushed.

Nefrytatanen pretended she had heard nothing and entered as if she had been lost in thought all the time. After wandering around the room awhile, she said, "Sepa's son has just agreed to go on the voyage. There's space for two more and I'd like you to come." She looked at them. Their expressions held both guilt and joy. Nefrytatanen said, "Yazid, I need your strong arm and your love for Amenemhet. He thinks highly of you, and your presence would surely ease his mind on many accounts. Bekhet, I'm not anxious to be the only woman on this ship, and your company would be most welcome. I only *ask* if you'd go, and if either or both of you decline, I'll understand."

"I'll go. No one shall take my place!" Bekhet declared immediately.

"Thank you, Bekhet," Nefrytatanen said. "I prayed you'd agree. And you, Yazid?"

"Can there be any doubt I'd go?" he exclaimed.

"Thank you, my friend." Nefrytatanen's relief was sincere. "Thank you both. This is a burden off my mind." She smiled. "If you're finished with your work here now, I'd like to be alone with Amenemhet. After a time, send the evening meal to us."

Nefrytatanen went to Amenemhet's side. He was awake. "You heard them?" she asked, smiling. He blinked in confirmation. His eyes held humor. "They forget that you can hear them. This morning Ankhneferu brought Senbi, a young priest, who will go with us. He'll be helpful, as he's well-educated in several useful subjects. Ankhneferu assured me of his loyalty. Beloved, Sepa volunteered his son to come with us! Necho's a good sailor and can teach us to manage the ship. So now we have our crew, beloved. Kheti, Rakkor, Yazid, Bekhet, Senbi, and Necho."

Nefrytatanen bent to kiss Amenemhet's forehead, and she lay her cheek against his. "I'd begun to fear we were hated, but more and more have I seen evidence that we are loved. "It makes me proud that so many are loyal. Such a quality never seems apparent until an emergency because it's normally the complainers whose voices one hears."

She smiled. "The ship is almost finished, beloved. It reminds me of a bird, so light and graceful. It does look like the tomb paintings—like the crescent moon with a single sail. The workers have voluntarily toiled day and night, and Sepa will soon be able to tell us for certain how much more time they need. If it's as he hopes, then the ship will be loaded tomorrow night, and we can leave the following dawn." She paused, thinking about the voyage, then said, "The trip won't take too long. Soon, beloved, you'll be well. My mother said you've found favor with the divine beings, and surely she must know."

Amenemhet was wishing that Nefrytatanen would hold his hand, but he was unable to indicate this. As if she knew his thoughts, she took his hand in hers and, bringing it to her lips, slowly kissed his fingers one by one. The soft touch of her lips sent a sweet pang through him.

Still holding his hand, she looked into his golden eyes and whispered, "I have missed you deeply. I fear that, by the time you're well, I'll be too near my time, for lovemaking."

As she kissed him gently on the lips, he wished he might kiss her back, put his arms around her, and draw her close to him.

"I know what you're thinking, beloved," she said. "Often I've lain awake remembering our first night together and how long we'd waited for it. It seemed then as if we'd never find each other. I comfort myself now remembering our joy." She smiled slightly. "That helps. But when I waited for you then, I had no memories of love, as I have now."

She kissed his forehead lightly, and he felt her perfumed hair brush his face.

"Perhaps I should not say such things," she murmured, "for if you also feel this way, it may only make your longing harder to bear."

Amenemhet would have liked to tell Nefrytatanen of his many long hours of silent dreaming. Her touch and her words were sweet.

"Should I say such things, beloved, or should I remain silent?" she asked.

He stared, unblinking, at her.

"Does hearing such things give you comfort?" He blinked rapidly several times. She caught his wry humor and laughed. "Oh, beloved, it's you I long for and no one else," she said. "I seek no other arms and never will. I doubt that, even if I were inclined to do so, anyone would have me. I'm becoming shapeless. Before very long, if I wished for a lover, I'd have to give him a royal command!"

Amenemhet's eyes glowed in affectionate humor and then slowly grew more serious.

When Bekhet brought food, Nefrytatanen sent her away and fed Amenemhet herself.

Later, as Nefrytatanen lay wakeful, she got out of bed and tiptoed to Amenemhet's couch. As sleepless as she, his eyes glowed topaz in the shadows.

She whispered, "Beloved, if I lie beside you, would I trouble you?"

Amenemhet's steady stare was her answer. He felt her get onto the couch next to him. She lay close to him and sighed. Had he been able, he, too, would have sighed. Had he been able, he would have done much more. He let the nearness of her be his caress and the scent of her his comfort. She gave him dreams.

Chapter Fourteen

Nefrytatanen awakened in darkness to Bekhet's insistent prodding. It was the day they would begin the journey. She leaped from her bed and washed and dressed quickly. After a hurried breakfast, she watched the final preparations, and wondered whether she would ever see her beloved palace again.

When the servants came to carry Amenemhet to the dock, she requested a moment alone with him and spent that time holding him close, pressing her cheek against his neck, unable to speak during what might be their final time together in this room. She had no illusions about the dangers of the voyage.

After the servants had carried Amenemhet out, Nefrytatanen paused in the silence, looking one last time at the room he had so lovingly designed, and at their beloved garden. After a time, she turned away and walked through the empty halls stopping at each room to take one final glance. Tears ran freely down her cheeks. Amenemhet, who had made Ithtawe, could not now see it one last time, and she memorized details to feed him later, when he might need cheering. She stood in the hall, her back against the main doors, composing herself and wiping away her tears. Resolutely, she turned—not daring one more glance—and hurried outside. Bekhet and Senbi waited with understanding in their faces.

As Nefrytatanen walked silently with them to the

quay, she fixed her gaze on the ship in growing wonder. The current, not the sail, would carry them down
the river. But the sail had been run up earlier for testing and, while the men prepared to take it down, it
shimmered gold in the morning light.

Nefrytatanen looked at Bekhet beside her and found
no expression on her face. At Nefrytatanen's other side
was Senbi, whose lips moved soundlessly in an ancient
prayer of homage and welcome to Ra at dawn. Nefrytatanen knew that Ankhneferu was now making an
offering in the temple. To these, she added her own
silent pleas.

The breeze from the north ruffled Nefrytatanen's
hair, and she turned again toward the ship, which
floated like a swan on the silver water. She listened
to the gentle lapping of the waves and the cries of the
circling gulls. She breathed the clean, fresh air of
Tamera, storing its scent for future recollection.

Finally, thinking herself in good emotional order,
she turned again to look at Ithtawe and found she
was not. Tears welled again, and blinking them away,
she quickly turned back to the ship.

The nearby waiting crowd watched the loading, respectfully silent. Not even the whimper of a baby could
be heard among them. The morning air seemed to
magnify each sound. When any one of the loading
crew spoke, he did so self-consciously, in whispers.

Finally Sepa approached Nefrytatanen and she
greeted him, hoping conversation would distract her.

Taking in her sadness at a glance, Sepa smiled with
a cheerfulness he didn't feel. He pointed proudly to the
graceful little ship. "See, my queen?" he said in a
falsely bright tone. "She floats like a swan although
she's filled with cargo. Ten heavy men boarded her and
sailed up the river and back, as a test. Still she was high
and light. I'm sure that if the reeds withstand the salt
water, she can easily sail to Atalan and return. I have
made certain each knot was well-tied, each detail
looked over by many experts. Necho finds her simple

to manage. He says you can learn to sail her yourself in three days."

"The ship is beautiful," Nefrytatanen said quietly, "and I know you've made her strong. Go to Meri for your reward as I promised you. He has my instructions."

Seeing that everyone but Necho and herself were already on the ship, Nefrytatanen turned to Meri, Seti, and Nessumontu, who waited to see her off. A little behind them stood the many noblemen who had delayed their return to their provinces, and behind them was a crowd of people from the surrounding countryside.

Nefrytatanen addressed Meri, Seti, and Nessumontu softly. "Thank you for what you've already done and for what you'll do in our absence. It won't be easy for you, but I know you'll do your best. I trust you." Their faces blurred before her, and she whispered, "Pray our voyage is successful." Abruptly she turned to the ship, and Kheti wordlessly helped her to the deck.

Necho cast off the lines and leaped aboard. Nefrytatanen raised a hand to those on the quay, while the ship drew slowly away. Nefrytatanen saw that Ankhneferu had arrived at last. He waved to them. The crowd gradually grew smaller and eventually disappeared.

Nefrytatanen watched the shores of Tamera glide past, and she was deeply moved by the crowds of silent, watching people who lined the banks.

The travelers passed the night watching bonfires on the shore. They knew that, in the darkness, crowds watched their dying king's ship sail by.

At dawn the ship reached the mouth of the Nile. A breeze sprang up and the sail stiffened and tugged the ship toward the Great Green Sea. Necho steered to the west.

The water was silvery green in the pale light, and, as they moved over it. Bekhet wondered if this was to be the final time they would see Tamera. But she turned a smiling face to Yazid and commented on the fair weather.

Necho beckoned to Rakkor. Taking a few moments to explain the guiding of the vessel, he let Rakkor steer for awhile and went to Nefrytatanen.

"My queen," Necho said, "I must give everyone some general instructions before we go farther."

"Of course, Necho," she answered. "I'll listen as carefully as the others. None of us is a sailor, I least of all." She called to the others, and they gathered near Rakkor so he, too, could listen. Then Nefrytatanen said, "Necho will now tell us something of sailing this ship. Afterwards we'll divide our chores."

Necho began, "The ship is easy enough to sail. Once I've taught you the way it works, you should have few problems. A turn or two with me at steering will teach you. There's little to learn other than steering and lowering and raising the sail."

"It's like riding a living creature," Yazid declared. "It undulates over the water like a serpent."

"You'll become used to that movement and forget it."

"Not I!" Yazid looked pale.

Necho smiled faintly and went on, "Whenever the water gets rougher or the waves higher than they are now, we cannot count much on swimming if we fall overboard. There are many creatures, hungrier than crocodiles, beneath these waves, who would consider people a fine meal."

Everyone shuddered, and Necho was satisfied by their reaction.

"When the sea is rough," he said, "you must fasten a rope to your waist and attach it to something solid on the ship, every time you leave the cabin. Remember, no matter why you're leaving or how short a time you expect to be on deck, attach your rope!"

Necho paused to let this warning be fully absorbed and then continued, "We must use the fresh water only for drinking. Sea water will be used for all other pur-

poses. We'll stay a distance from land—though we'll
keep it in sight—until we turn to the open ocean. We
don't want to become beached or caught on rocks. We'll
put into shore only where it's unpopulated. People may
be unfriendly. On this journey we'll find few civilized
peoples, and the more primitive peoples have some
fearful ways of treating visitors. We can take no
chances." Necho looked at them meaningfully and
added, "I'm not exaggerating, and I hope you're
frightened. I've heard stories, from reliable sources, of
headhunters, cannibals and even worse!" They all
looked properly sober.

After a moment Nefrytatanen said, "The men will
take turns guiding the ship, but Bekhet and I will learn
in case of emergency. Necho and Senbi will have to
take turns reading the stars to guide us at night when
we can't see land. Although I'll attend to Amenemhet,
I'll need help from time to time. I'll also help others
when needed. We must share our chores willingly,
despite rank or inclination. We must live in this small
space together for some time, and we must cooperate
if we hope to survive. Necho will give all orders regarding the sailing of this vessel. I'll obey him, as we
all must."

Nefrytatanen paused then said firmly, "Privacy is
going to be difficult, and we must be considerate. Whenever someone is in the cabin with the door-hanging
pulled down, anyone wishing to enter must first seek
permission." She smiled faintly at this. Then her smile
faded as she quietly added, "All of you came of your
own choosing, and Amenemhet and I cannot thank
you enough. While we're on this adventure, we'll observe a minimum of formalities." Her smile returned
as she finished, "Please don't bow or kneel on this ship.
One unexpected lurch may send you over the side! We
need you all."

They soon settled into a routine—awakening at
dawn and going to bed at sunset—except for Necho

and Senbi, who took turns at the rudder at night and slept when they had the opportunity. There was little else to do so little lamp oil was consumed at night.

Nefrytatanen cared for Amenemhet with help from Yazid, while Bekhet cooked and did other light chores. Rakkor often fished for their meals. As Sepa had promised, the ship nearly sailed itself. Eventually all of them grew bored. Being used to exercise and activity, the abundant supply of unfilled time and the close quarters made them increasingly irritable.

Once a ship was spotted far in the distance, and Rakkor and Necho held a heated argument over its design. Kheti became embroiled in the discussion even while attempting to quiet them. Yazid finally shouted for silence, and Nefrytatanen's glare withered the last echoes. It was Senbi, taking a final glance at the ship, who announced that it was coming in their direction.

Necho said, "I don't know who they are, but I don't think we should wait to find out. There are too many unfriendly ships cruising in lonely waters looking for slaves and loot. A ship minding its own business doesn't go out of its way to meet another unless it's in trouble. That one doesn't look in need of help."

He leaped to the rudder and motioned Yazid aside so he could take over the steering himself, meanwhile directing Kheti and Rakkor to run up the extra sail they carried. Because the ship had only a single mast, Kheti and Rakkor quickly attached the extra sail to lines in the makeshift fashion Necho had previously taught them.

The extra sheet immediately took the wind, and the little ship leaped lightly forward. Nefrytatanen went to the side to watch the other ship. She was amazed that their fragile bird flew so fast. The other ship immediately began to lose distance.

"It was as I thought," Necho said grimly. "Such pirates as I anticipated have clumsier vessels than this one, heavier and not as trim." He patted the papyrus side with affection.

Everyone breathed a sigh of relief as the other ship gave up the chase and turned away. They hadn't been near enough to see what banner, if any, their pursuers flew. Rakkor grimly watched it through the increasing distance and counted them fortunate. Such a ship would be heavily armed and well-manned. Had it caught up with them, they wouldn't have had a chance.

The next day Nefrytatanen was standing at the rail passing time by watching the shore. They were closer to land than they had been for a time, and she could see the dunes and rocks clearly.

"What's that?" she suddenly asked.

Kheti hurried to her side because, in her absorption, she had leaned precariously over the rail. Following her pointing finger, he saw great stone blocks piled in an artificial fashion among the natural rock formations on the sand.

"It looks like an old building that's falling apart," he said in surprise.

Senbi hurried closer. "It's made of stones so massive you'd think they'd stand forever," he noted. "It must be ancient to be crumbling like that."

Studying the structure, Kheti remarked, "It doesn't look unlike our own buildings."

"You're right," Nefrytatanen agreed, leaning even farther over the water.

Kheti could no longer endure seeing her dangerous position. Hesitant to touch her but afraid she would fall overboard, he gingerly put a hand on her shoulder. Startled, she moved away. He was about to explain why he had touched her, when she smiled.

"Thank you, Kheti. In my curiosity, I forgot myself," she said. "I have no wish to swim here, but I think I was about to do just that." She turned again to look at the shore. "Can we go a little closer?" she asked.

Necho turned to Yazid, who was steering. "Get a little nearer to shore," he called, "but not too much or we'll land on the rocks."

Rakkor joined Nefrytatanen and Kheti. "It does look

much like our own manner of construction," he remarked. "Has anyone from Tamera ever landed in this place?"

"Not that I know of," Senbi answered, "but we did copy this ship's design from the tomb walls. Perhaps someone long ago sailed here."

"I've wondered since we began this trip why these ships were used," Nefrytatanen admitted. "I've also been curious why we've never bothered to sail very far in exploration of the world. My father did a little, but he seemed to have been an exception. Surely, it wasn't lack of courage, and it wouldn't seem to be lack of knowledge."

They watched the ruins silently for a moment. Then Kheti commented, "I'd like to have a closer look at them."

Necho shook his head. "We cannot land and take the risk."

"Neither do we have time to spare on this voyage," Nefrytatanen said quietly. "Perhaps we can come back one day."

"I wonder if, at some remote time, explorers did come here from Tamera, and their stories have been lost to us," Senbi mused. "What could they have found, that they built that place? Even now, there are few civilized lands except those near us."

"Perhaps," Nefrytatanen said, "but my father found Atalan."

Rakkor turned from the ruins. "Maybe the explorers found that there were few really civilized places, and the ones they did find were so distant it wasn't worth the time and cost to keep contact with them. Maybe that's why we no longer explore."

"You have a point," Senbi agreed, "and, besides, Tamera is too inviting to leave behind for very long."

"That's logical," Kheti observed. "But why would we build something here?"

Senbi was wondering about that, too. "I don't know,"

he admitted. "Of course we don't know that we did build it," he added.

"I'm going to tell Amenemhet about this place," Nefrytatanen said abruptly. "He'll be wondering what we're looking at. I think he'll be interested in stopping here one day to investigate further." She took one more look at the ruins. They would be seen only dimly now for they were far away, and the light was fading swiftly. It felt strange to think that others had been here so long ago that all records of them were lost. Still wondering where else their ancestors might have traveled, she hurried to Amenemhet.

After almost ten days of sailing in smooth seas with a fine wind, there arose before them a mountain that appeared to be formed from one huge rock. The travelers stared as they approached the mountain, marveling at its height.

Necho steered the ship into the strait, and, while he kept a sharp eye for hidden currents, he kept his other eye on the mountain. The sea was calm, and they glided peacefully toward the end of the strait continuing to admire the strange mountain. As they approached the opening to the ocean, Necho turned to them.

"We are leaving the Great Green Sea," he said slowly. "The ocean is before us, and we'll begin sailing south. When you steer, be careful to stay near enough shore so we're not carried into the open water accidentally. Now we must be even more alert that no one falls overboard—I don't know *what* lives beneath these waves."

The warning wasn't necessary. They stared at the silvery expanse that merged with the western sky, marveling at the enormity of it.

As the days passed, the novelty of sailing on the ocean also passed, and the dull routine of their lives began to hone their tempers to a sharper edge. Nefrytatanen was at a loss to keep Amenemhet occupied when she had so little occupation herself. There was little she could tell him because he knew, from where he lay, as much as they all did. To talk too much about the past seemed morbid and to look too brightly toward their future was almost like teasing him. She constantly searched for something to distract him and help pass the time because, she reasoned, if it dragged slowly for her, it must seem endless to him.

Amenemhet although often almost unbearably bored with inactivity, spent many of his hours in deep contemplation. He reflected on his philosophy of living, the customs his people followed, their religious beliefs, and often he considered death. He didn't turn from this in fear nor did he look forward to it. He was curious what might follow the experience, but he was too involved with life to look forward to satisfying his curiosity. When he considered the possibility of his dying, he was filled with anguish. He wanted to do many things in this lifetime. He wanted to see and learn so much. Dying would cheat him terribly. He wanted to spend more time with Nefrytatanen, and he was frustrated tht he could do nothing to help himself.

He wanted to raise the sail higher or make the wind blow more forcefully. He wanted to put out oars and row to Atalan. If he could have, his spirit would have leaped out of him and towed the ship by itself. This thinking stimulated him even further in his resolution to fight the poison in his body with his own will, if he could do nothing else.

Amenemhet had never been a stranger to quiet moments or to contemplation, but he now had greater opportunity than ever before, and he found it rewarding. He felt that if he survived this experience he would have learned much from it. He was, curiously, less bored than the others.

After a day when they had all seemed to reach the limits of patience, Bekhet spilled a bowl of food on the deck and, much unlike her, began to cry. Nefrytatanen knew that she was at the end of her control.

Yazid, his own nerves worn to shreds, leaped at the

sound of the bowl hitting the deck, then turned to Bekhet, ready to reprimand her.

Although Nefrytatanen felt like weeping or screaming, she rose from her place beside Amenemhet and, marching to Yazid, stared almost nose to nose with him, commanding him to be silent. Then she turned to face the others, her eyes allowing no interruption or protest, while she told them in no uncertain terms that they were like children and must practice some restraint. The next one whose temper flared over nonsense would be punished.

Although Nefrytatanen couldn't imagine how she would accomplish such punishment, her vehemence was enough to impress them. She went to sit by Amenemhet, her darkly tanned face almost white with anger.

Senbi, who seemed to have remained calmer than the others, came to Amenemhet and Nefrytatanen. He settled himself beside Amenemhet while Nefrytatanen, glad for his distraction, took a moment to gather her wits and compose herself.

Senbi smiled pleasantly. "You have the best view of us all," he commented, not bothering with Amenemhet's title. "In the daytime, we see only water and must twist our necks to see the clouds. At night we must cramp our necks to see the stars or have only blackness to look at. You can watch the ever-changing heavens in comfort. It is beautiful on these clear nights."

Senbi drew up a pallet and stretched out beside Amenemhet. "I often wonder what is on those specks of light," he said. "If they were closer, would they look like our moon, be fiery as Ra, or something so different we cannot imagine it? Have you studied astronomy?" he asked companionably. Amenemhet blinked. "Very much?" Senbi inquired. "No? Well, something, then? Good. Then you understand some of what I mean." He paused then exclaimed, "Look, there was a comet! Did you see it?" Amenemhet blinked. Senbi continued, "Did you know that, according to the ancient stories, Asar came from Sahu and Aset from Sept?" Amenemhet blinked. Senbi mused, "I've often wondered if there are other worlds out there with living beings on them." He sighed. "Anyway, the heavenly bodies follow predictable paths, and they are reliable to set a course by at night."

Nefrytatanen, now curious, said, "Senbi, you know more than we do of such things. Perhaps you can answer a question I have. The night before Amenemhet and I were to meet for the first time, Amenemhet saw two blue stars streak across the sky. He was puzzled by this and said later that their color matched my eyes. He felt they were an omen of my coming. Can you explain them if, as you say, the paths of heavenly bodies are predictable?"

Senbi was silent as he considered this. Finally he said, "I've never seen or heard of such a thing as two blue stars or comets traveling together. How strange! Perhaps it was an omen at that. Many believe the stars predict destinies. No. I cannot explain such a thing. I've never heard of it before." He sat up and looked into Nefrytatanen's eyes "That color, were they? Do you know your eyes glow very strangely in the dark sometimes? Perhaps it's because of your magic. Perhaps that was what the omen meant." He smiled at Amenemhet. "A beautiful, blue-eyed daughter of Aset was coming to you."

At this, Amenemhet blinked enthusiastically several times.

Nefrytatanen smiled and said in a soft voice, "And she fell completely in love with you—so who has magic, after all?"

Senbi smiled. "All love is enchantment. It creates its own spell." He stood up and stretched. "Now, it's my turn to guide the ship and put my knowledge to practical use." He sighed. "Sometimes, though, I'd prefer dreaming of romantic omens. Good night," he said, and left them.

Nefrytatanen brought her blanket to the pallet where Senbi had lain and stretched herself out by Amenemhet's side. "Who did cast the spell?" she murmured. "Or is Senbi right in saying love itself has magic? Perhaps those stars came from Asar and Aset." She turned to kiss Amenemhet lightly. "We must hurry on this voyage, beloved. You've barely begun the things you're destined to do, and even a lifetime of one hundred ten years seems too short to accomplish them all."

Nefrytatanen nestled close to Amenemhet's side, and they both fell asleep more easily than they had in many nights.

At his lonely post, Senbi looked at the sky and was again struck with awe at its vast beauty. He had never seen nor heard of blue stars traveling side by side across the sky. Neither, he reminded himself, had he ever seen human eyes like Nefrytatanen's eyes.

Chapter Fifteen

At mid-morning Yazid, standing on the cabin roof to adjust the sail, called down to them, "There's a group of small islands ahead! If we continue in this direction, we'll land on one of them, I think." He climbed down to the deck and they gathered to discuss this.

"It might not be a bad idea to stop there," Necho observed. "We could get fresh fruits and be sure our water containers are filled. It won't be long, I think, before we'll have to turn toward the open ocean."

Nefrytatanen looked at the approaching islands with some doubt.

"What of those primitive peoples you mentioned?" Kheti reminded.

"I, for one, have no desire to end in someone's cooking pot," Yazid commented. Bekhet nodded vigorously in agreement.

"We're armed," Rakkor said. "We could stay close to the ship if there's even a hint of danger."

Nefrytatanen knew they all longed to get off the ship, even for a short time. Thinking that such a visit might benefit their tempers, she made the decision. "Let's take the chance," she said. "It's important to have supplies enough to last to Atalan. Let us be watchful as we draw nearer."

The closest island had an undergrowth that began almost at the edge of the beach, and, not far into the bushes, there appeared trees of many varieties, promising fruits and nuts. Although they strained their eyes, they saw nothing to indicate any living things other than the vegetation.

Necho looked at Nefrytatanen, and, at her nod, he turned the craft toward the island.

When the ship's botton scraped the sand, Kheti and Rakkor leaped out and, pulling with ropes, dragged the ship to where the water reached only their knees. They waded out of the water and carefully tied the ropes to trees.

While the others carried baskets, water jars, and other containers to the beach, Nefrytatanen paused to stand in the shallow sun-warmed water. She held the hem of her robe above the surface, enjoying the feel of smooth, soft sand beneath her feet. It was good to stand on solid ground instead of undulating papyrus, but it took her a few minutes to get used to it. A breeze brought the fragrance of flowers, warm earth, and green growing things, and she felt sharp pangs of homesickness.

On the beach, Yazid said softly, "I don't like this place."

"It's but an empty island," Bekhet scoffed. "You're afraid of bushes." When Yazid moved away, however, she glanced around nervously. She didn't like it either.

"This place makes me uneasy," Yazid said, approaching Rakkor. Rakkor looked up.

"I'm not happy to stop here either," he admitted, "but you can see it's a good place to obtain fresh food. It seems wise, too, that we replenish our water. We don't know how long we'll be on the ocean." He watched as Kheti approached.

"Although this jungle isn't inviting to me, either," Kheti said, "Rakkor's right about food and water. Innocent as it looks, this place makes my scalp creep. But let us not express such ideas to the queen. Let us only keep as near the ship as possible and stay alert."

They all muttered agreement and continued gathering their respective share of baskets and bundles. They glanced up from their tasks as Nefrytatanen approached them.

"Kheti," she said, "we won't take Amenemhet off the ship. Also, I think Yazid should stay nearby to guard us. I'm not comfortable on this island. I don't want anyone to go farther from the ship than absolutely necessary."

Rakkor gave Kheti a look of chagrin.

Nefrytatanen's head went up as she listened alertly. "Do you notice the silence?" she asked in a hushed tone. They stopped moving and listened carefully. They heard nothing but the waves washing up on the beach and the wind whispering in the trees. "I don't like this," she whispered.

"Perhaps nothing lives here," Bekhet offered hopefully, feeling that her lowered voice was a loud as a shout.

Nefrytatanen shook her head. "I hear no birds, and I don't like that at all," she whispered. "Take care not to speak of this near Amenemhet so we don't worry him needlessly. While you're getting water and gathering whatever food you can find, Bekhet and I will take what's on the edge of the beach. If we find it necessary to flee, I'm too large to race through the bushes. Yazid, I think it best you keep your full attention on guarding us. While all of you are getting ready, I'll tell Amenemhet what we're doing."

Nefrytatanen splashed through the shallow water back to the ship and got on board. She made her way to where Amenemhet lay in the shadow cast by the sail. At the sound of her footsteps, his eyes opened. "Beloved," she said softly, taking his hand, "we've stopped on an island which seems to be uninhabited. It looks like a good place to get fresh food and refill the water containers before we go to the open sea. Yazid is staying near the ship to guard us in case of danger. Bekhet and I will stay on the beach so we won't be far away." She squeezed his hand and left him.

Amenemhet lay staring at the sail and the sky above

him. He knew none of them were aware of how acute his senses of hearing and smell had become. Since he was unable to move or speak or see much farther than straight ahead of him, his ears and nose had become almost all he could rely on, and these senses had sharpened like a wild animal's. He even heard whispers from some distance, and he had heard their conversations on the beach.

Now he, too, listened to the absence of normal sounds on the island. He could recognize Nefrytatanen's footsteps, even as she walked quietly on the wet sand. Yazid coughed nearby on the ship where he had taken his post as sentry. He heard Bekhet call to Nefrytatanen that she had found a bush covered with berries. He could hear the others at a greater distance beginning to make their way into the undergrowth. Amenemhet wondered about the lack of other sounds. He didn't like this. He wished either that they might have his hearing or he their mobility. He lay silently alert.

After a time Amenemhet heard Kheti and the others return, drop their bundles, and pick up empty containers. There was some further hushed discussion about their uneasiness. Then they crashed back into the bushes. Time crept slowly by, and Amenemhet still lay listening and sniffing the air, so attuned to the outside that he felt as if his very pores could hear.

Presently the breeze brought, along with the scent of plants and flowers, another smell—strange to him, something he couldn't identify. It was, in some way he couldn't have described, a scent of warm-blooded creatures. With a growing sense of alarm, he listened. He heard nothing suspicious. He wondered at the scent.

Nefrytatanen, evidently still wary and unwilling to waste time, called Bekhet to help her carry the refilled baskets and bundles on board.

Amenemhet still wondered about the unfamiliar scent. Each of his companions, he had noticed, had a distinctly different personal scent, and during the voyage he played games with his eyes closed, identifying each of them when they would come in range. This strange scent from the island seemed different, but not very different, from theirs. When Bekhet left the ship to gather more fruit, the scent drifted again to Amenemhet and brought a shiver of fear to him.

Bekhet's scream was a knife through his heart. He heard Nefrytatanen drop something and Bekhet's racing feet. Yazid leaped off the ship, splashing through the shallow water. How Amenemhet wished to be at Yazid's side! Frustrated beyond endurance, he listened to Yazid's sword scrape from it scabbard.

"What is it?" Nefrytatanen cried. Yazid's footsteps moved slowly, cautiously, a little farther from the ship.

"I see nothing!" Yazid called.

Bekhet's panting voice came clearly to Amenemhet. "I saw a face—in the bushes—staring—at me!"

Amenemhet heard Kheti's voice call to them over the sound of running feet and the clanking and bouncing of their burdens.

"Get on the ship—all of you!"

There was a sudden uproar in the distance now, a screaming which, in whatever language, Amenemhet immediately recognized as a cry to attack. He knew only too well the swishing sound of flying spears and the lighter zing of arrows.

First Nefrytatanen and Bekhet scrambled onto the ship, dropping baskets and containers on the deck. Then Rakkor and Yazid leaped on board and immediately turned to face their pursuers with a barrage of their own arrows. Amenemhet was reassured by several answering screams of pain amid the fierce cries. Senbi clambered on, and the ship was pushed into the water. Necho leaped aboard and ran to take the rudder.

"Get in the ship, Kheti!" Amenemhet heard Nefrytatanen scream. Behind him, Necho shouted to Nefrytatanen and Senbi to run up the sail. Amenemhet heard them scramble to the cabin roof and heard the creaking of the sail being raised. He felt so utterly useless and helpless he could hardly endure himself. He saw Bekhet almost fall over the side, reaching down to someone's groping hand. Her feet were actually off the deck, knees hooked under the roll of papyrus, as Kheti climbed over the rail, dripping water. When he was inside, he scolded Bekhet for exposing herself to the arrows, as she had, to help him onto the ship.

Bekhet answered coolly. "Now you scold me, but now you are also on the ship."

The sea wind cleansed the air of the peculiar scent of the island people as it filled the sail, tugging the ship to safety. In the distance, the screaming of the natives could still be heard, but their cries were growing fainter.

Nefrytatanen asked if anyone were wounded. Seeing that they were all unharmed, she stood quietly a moment, too shocked to move.

Yazid said, "While we straighten out this mess, why don't you describe that glorious battle to the king, especially my heroic part in it." Nefrytatanen's laughter floated to Amenemhet. She soon followed it and, kissing his nose, sat on an overturned basket. Her face was flushed and damp from exertion, and Amenemhet silently thanked Yazid for distracting her.

"The people of the island were dark-skinned, like those to the south of Tamera," she began, "and they must have been observing us all the time, trying to decide how much of a threat we were. Perhaps they hesitated because of our strange appearance, but they attacked when Bekhet saw one of them staring at her. . . ." As Nefrytatanen described, with lively expressions and energetic gestures all that had happened, Amenemhet became less worried about her and wondered if it hadn't been a good diversion for them all!

The decision to land at the island had been wise, despite the attack. When the supplies were counted, they found they had saved almost everything they had gathered.

Not long after they had left the island behind, the current began to carry them rapidly west and, they hoped, toward the final stage of their voyage. The ocean's blue stretched before them, seeming to merge with the sky, and it wasn't difficult for them to wonder if they would *ever* reach Atalan. Neither was it comforting to remember that, according to ancient stories, it was in the west that Tuat, the land of the afterlife, lay. Necho, looking over the water toward the setting sun, reflected on this, and he fervently hoped they reached Atalan first.

After the island adventure, they fell into their old routine. But tempers had cooled by this time. Nefrytatanen continued to stay near Amenemhet, and the others visited him often, although Amenemhet realized his company left much to be desired. He knew how difficult the one-sided conversations must be for them, and he wished he could speak.

He began to recognize, with a growing cold fear, that he was weakening. His power to concentrate seemed to be lessening, and he found himself making a conscious effort not to show it, an effort which became more difficult each day. He knew he slept more. Whenever Nefrytatanen asked anxiously if he were all right, he blinked vigorously, but it was only to reassure her. He recognized his drowsiness as the continued assault of the poison on his body. He now struggled to stay awake as much as possible because he was afraid that, if he slept too deeply, he might not awaken.

Nefrytatanen grew larger and became less graceful in her movements. Amenemhet worried that she would deliver the child on the ship. Although Senbi had studied medicine and Bekhet was ready to help, Amenemhet had no desire for Nefrytatanen to bear the child under these conditions. Thinking of Nefrytatanen renewed Amenemhet's strength, and he struggled to maintain his fight against the advancing poison. Often he thought about his unborn heir and longed to see it. He spent many hours wondering how the infant would look, speculating on whether the child was a son or a daughter, wondering how the child would look when grown. From time to time, when Nefrytatanen spoke of the child, she revealed the same thoughts.

With a faraway look, Nefrytatanen spoke of Ithtawe, describing it so vividly that Amenemhet saw it clearly in his mind. She seemed to recall every detail, and he was newly proud he had designed it because he could tell how deeply she loved the place. He found himself thinking of Ithtawe as an extension of themselves, filled with sun in the day and gently whispering shadows in the moonlight.

Small fish leaping from the water captured Nefrytatanen's attention one afternoon, and she told Amenemhet of them. Necho pointed out other fish following the ship to pick up scraps of food from the waste they dumped overboard, and Nefrytatanen described them to Amenemhet as well.

Amenemhet noticed Nefrytatanen's sometimes too-eager smile and her bright eyes, knowing their brightness was often from unshed tears, and he tried to respond with more liveliness than he actually felt, hoping to hide his fears from her.

He didn't succeed. Nefrytatanen knew he was growing weaker. In unguarded moments, she read his eyes. She clearly saw the golden lights in them gradually fading. Often, when he slept, she feared he wouldn't awaken. These times she wept quietly into a pillow, and before she went to him she splashed sea water on her face to hide the marks of her tears.

The cold came suddenly, with a wind that stiffened their faces and penetrated deep into their bones. The wind pulled at the sail until Senbi and Rakkor finally managed to draw it down and tie it. The waves rose higher until they seemed to tower over the small ship. They were terrified, but as each massive wave reached them, the reed swan lifted its throat and deftly swooped over the crest to slide into a valley and face the next wall of water.

Necho took the rudder, shouting that the disturbance was from a number of currents, all meeting here. The sun continued to shine brightly on him while he shivered and struggled to steer. Ra's light gave no warmth.

Bekhet became seasick and lay moaning helplessly in the compartment, her tanned skin assuming a greenish tint. Nefrytatanen was surprised that she felt no particular discomfort from the rolling sea. She was cold, however. Her teeth chattered audibly. All of them put on extra layers of clothing and wrapped themselves in blankets. Fearing that the chill would weaken Amenemhet, Nefrytatanen wrapped him in blankets and lay over him to give him as much of her own warmth as possible.

When they thought they could endure it no longer, the ship was sent flying out of the tumult into calmer waters, and the wind decreased to a brisk breeze. Kheti and Rakkor immediately put up the sail to take advantage of it.

The sun's warmth reached them again, and Nefrytatanen rolled off Amenemhet, joking through chattering teeth that it was his good fortune she hadn't squashed him. She reassured him that she was all right and then went into the sunlight. Having taken the coldness of the air herself, she was shivering, and she walked briskly in the sun, trying to get warm.

Bekhet dragged herself from her pallet, pale and shaky but able to walk. When Yazid offered her herb tea, she firmly refused. Even one sip was too much to consider. Instead, she walked unsteadily beside Nefrytatanen, trying to turn her mind from her misery. Beginning to feel warmth creep into her body, Nefrytatanen was unwrapping her blanket when Kheti, a grim look on his face, approached.

"I've been checking our supplies," he said, "and although nothing was washed overboard or blown away, I've found a number of cracked water jars."

"How much did we lose?" Nefrytatanen asked.

"Too much," Kheti replied with an expression that chilled Nefrytatanen. "I hope Atalan isn't much farther, or we won't have enough," he added.

Remembering the horror of her thirst on the desert, she shuddered. "We must ration the water strictly," she directed. "I'm terrified to think what will happen if we run out. I remember too well the way it affected me on the desert. After a time, one becomes quite mad. "

"I know." Kheti shook his head. "Though I've never reached that point, I've seen those who did. On a ship, it would be terrible."

Kheti told the others how much water they would be allowed each day. They grew thirsty just hearing the news. And when the threat finally became reality, they couldn't disguise their alarm. They spoke little and went about their tasks slowly. Their lips became cracked, and their tongues seemed swollen.

Amenemhet lay stoically silent, wondering how long he would last. He wondered how long they would all keep their sanity. There hadn't yet been a sign of panic, though everyone was terrified.

Finally Bekhet drew Nefrytatanen aside and pleaded in a hoarse and croaking voice, "My lady, can you do nothing for this? Can you cast no spell to save us?"

"Spells cannot make miracles." Nefrytatanen's voice had become a whisper. "To obtain a thing, it must first exist. No spirit from Tuat will come with water for us."

"I thought anything was possible with magic!" Bekhet was dismayed.

Nefrytatanen shook her head sadly. "I would have done it already, if that were so. There's no water here and no way I know of to make it."

Necho had approached and heard some of the conversation. Suddenly he said excitedly, "But there is water! Perhaps we can be saved!"

"What water?" Bekhet asked crossly. "Would you extract the salt from the ocean?"

"No," he said slowly, "but what of rain?"

"What is rain?" Nefrytatanen looked at him with interest.

Necho suddenly realized they had probably never seen rain! Having lived in Tamera all their lives, they had known no water but that of the Nile, springs and wells, and the moisture lightly coating the plants in some places in the early morning.

"Necho, I cannot obtain something I know nothing about," Nefrytatanen said. "I would have to concentrate with great strength on my request. Describe rain for me," she begged.

"I had forgotten rain doesn't fall much in Tamera," he said slowly. "Rain is sweet, fresh water that falls from the sky."

They stared at him. None of them had seen such a phenomenon.

"Why does this happen?" Nefrytatanen asked hopefully.

"I don't know," Necho admitted. "Perhaps someone more educated could tell you."

"It falls from clouds," Senbi suddenly advised.

Nefrytatanen thought about this, trying to picture it. "Describe it more fully," she said. "What kind of clouds? Does the sun shine at the same time?"

"Sometimes it does," Senbi answered. "It depends on how thick the clouds are, I think. I've read about rains that are heavy, steady streams and also light sprinkles. It's moisture that somehow collects in the sky, and, under certain conditions, falls to earth."

"Gentle, steady drops would be preferable for us," Nefrytatanen seemed to say to herself. She looked up at them. "We don't wish to fill the ship and sink."

"You can do it, my lady," Bekhet encouraged.

"I must think about this," Nefrytatanen said softly. She looked up at the sky trying to imagine how it might appear, how rain might feel and smell. She decided it could be like the spray from a fountain blown by the wind. She had an idea. "If the rain comes from clouds,

there are none now." She turned to Necho, her face
slowly brightening. "The wind might bring such clouds,
and wind is something I do know about. Perhaps I
could do this yet."

Nefrytatanen turned a large basket upside-down and
sat on it while she thought. She closed her eyes and saw
against their lids a sky as clear as that above her. In her
mind she saw a cloud come swiftly—a white tower of a
cloud—little spirals of moving currents tumbling at its
edges, a grey and purplish base. She imagined a rising
breeze, turning the silky surface of the waves into
shivers. She could feel the cool wind on her skin and
leaned forward into her imaginary wind—it became
so real to her. She saw the rain falling and felt its
cool drops on her scalp. She turned her face up to
feel the moisture.

While Nefrytatanen was doing this, the others gathered close, curious at her strange motions and expressions. She rose from the basket seat and, with her eyes
now open, she climbed quickly to the cabin roof and
looked out over the north horizon.

Nefrytatanen loosened her thick hair and flung her
arms toward the sky, palms upraised, and cried out,
"Hail, O Shu, the winds come forth from thy nostrils.
Homage to you, O Nut, the celestial water comes from
thy mouth. Thou makest water to appear on the mountains and give life to men and woman. O great Shu,
breathe upon the air currents and bring a cloud, I beg.
If we die, the heir to the double crown dies with us, and
Tamera will have no king."

She plucked a hair from her head and tossed it into
the ocean. Then she turned to the west and repeated
her words, and gestures. She did the same facing the
south and, last, the east.

The others, who stood below her, saw a breeze ruffle
the hem of her robe slightly. It came from the north,
and a large cloud came with it. They stared incredulously at its approach. Senbi smiled as the breeze rose
and the water's surface became shimmers. The sun was

still shining when the first droplets fell, and they stared in wonder at the glistening water on their skin. Bekhet licked the back of her hand and cried out in joy.

Amenemhet was savoring the touch of the water on his skin while he remembered a time when he was yet prince and had led an expedition in search of stones for his parents' sarcophagus covers. The men he led had been numerous, and they had run out of water while on the edge of the desert. In desperation, he had prayed aloud to find water. As he finished the prayer, a young doe had sprung up in their path to fall on the very stone they dragged, where she gave birth to a fawn. Shortly afterwards they had found a spring. Although no expression now crossed his face, Amenemhet was smiling.

"Help me down," Nefrytatanen said, "and get every container that will hold water out on deck, so they can fill." Senbi put his hands on her waist and lifted her down to the deck. She laughed softly. "Thank you, Senbi," she said. "I was like a cat up a tree. In my condition, I could climb up, but I couldn't get down again."

"I thank you!" he said. "I also believe every story they've told about your magic. We must discuss this in further detail sometime."

Her eyes looked up at him sparkling. "You may learn what you can as a priest," she replied, "but there are some things I think I can never tell you. Get some containers, Senbi, so we may reap this wonderful wet harvest." She turned to hurry for a bowl or jar to fill.

Necho stared in awe as she passed. "How did you do it?" he asked, water sparkling on his eyelashes.

"You're the one who really did it," she answered. "You told me about something that was always there. It simply came to us."

As she walked away, Necho watched her, wondering. It didn't come by itself, he was thinking. What had she done to entice it to them?

When Nefrytatanen came on deck carrying a jar, she

smiled at the arch of a rainbow that stretched across the sky.

The night brought fog, something else Tamera never saw except on its northernmost coast, and they were fascinated and a little frightened. Although the current continued to carry the ship silently on its course, it was a strange sensation to seem to stand motionless in this hushed world, empty of everything but the ship and the dense, slowly swirling fog.

The greyness became lighter as morning approached. When the sun turned the fog into a golden veil, the ship suddenly broke into clear air, leaving the fog behind like a living thing reaching harmlessly with soft fingers, streaming in ragged wisps behind them.

"Land!" Necho cried, laughing. "I see land ahead! We're almost upon it! Land, land!"

They hurried out on deck and saw, directly before them, a very large island. They were afraid to hope it might be their destination and not merely some unpopulated body of land. But as Issella had predicted, the current seemed to take the ship directly to the island. With pounding hearts, they stood in a silent group at the bow of the ship, watching the place come nearer, afraid to believe.

As the ship approached the island, rays of the rising sun touched the tops of white mountains in the island's center. They glowed like pearls in the soft light. Over the ship, in a sky slowly becoming bright blue, white gulls circled and dipped, calling.

As the ship drew nearer, a bay stretched before it, and beyond the bay a town awakened to the morning. On a hill above the town, tall, white walls surrounded a stately building large enough to be a palace. On the gently rolling hills of the countryside were cultivated fields dissolving with the distance into green forests.

The current continued to carry the travelers directly toward the island, and Necho called to Yazid and Rakkor to adjust the sail, for the breeze blew toward the town. Smiling happily, he busied himself guiding the vessel into the bay.

Nefrytatanen ran to Amenemhet to tell him the news. She was shocked at the unfocused look of his eyes. She didn't hesitate but told him brightly that their voyage was ended at last, describing what she had seen. Her news seemed to awaken him a little. His eyes became more alert, and the golden fires glowed again behind them, although faintly.

Chapter Sixteen

As the tiny craft swung into the bay, Kheti saw a silver-grey ridge of stones reaching into the sea. He stared in amazement, for at the edge of its uttermost point stood the slender figure of a girl. Her wispy garments gleamed in the early sunlight, as translucently silver as her long, loose hair, and clung to her body in a manner that made Kheti catch his breath. She waved at the ship as though welcoming expected visitors. Kheti rubbed his eyes and blinked. Still she was there, her head thrown back as if in triumph.

Senbi, observing Kheti, asked curiously, "What do you see, Kheti?" Kheti pointed to the crag and, looking again, found it bare.

"I think my eyes fooled me," he muttered, disappointed.

"It may be," commented Senbi, "but from your expression, the illusion seemed most pleasing."

Rakkor joined them, interrupting the conversation, and Kheti was relieved. "If this place isn't Atalan," Rakkor said, "the queen's heart will surely break." They turned to see Nefrytatanen kneeling beside Amenemhet. Tears were shining on her cheeks as she spoke to him with forced cheerfulness.

"It had better be Atalan," Kheti said softly. "I don't know how much longer he can fight that poison gnawing at him. He has become much weakened, and, although he tries not to show it, I'm afraid we'd better get him help without delay." Kheti turned quickly to help Necho guide the vessel toward land. He didn't care to think too much about how weak Amenemhet had become. He knew Nefrytatanen wasn't fooled.

As they drew nearer the moorings of the town, a crowd of people began gathering. The people looked and dressed like those of Tamera.

When Necho leaped upon the stones to secure the ship with lines, Kheti and Rakkor watched the reaction of the crowd. Yazid remained close to Amenemhet and Nefrytatanen, his hand on his sword. The people did nothing other than look speculatively at them and converse among themselves. Kheti and Rakkor relaxed a little when they saw a man helping Necho with the lines. Necho spoke to the man who gestured toward the white walls and turned away to call to a young man. The young man ran to a horse and raced up a street. Waving his thanks of the man, Necho returned to the ship and went to Nefrytatanen.

"That man said this is Atalan," Necho said immediately. "They speak our language, though their accent is different. He asked who we were and, when I told him, he sent his son to the palace. He advised that we wait until someone comes."

"They don't seem unfriendly," Rakkor said, hopefully.

Looking over the crowd, which had by this time grown to quite a number, Nefrytatanen remarked, "They seem curious."

"Such was my impression," Necho said. "They seem curious enough to overcome any wariness, as if they seldom have visitors."

"We'll do as that man suggested and wait," Nefrytatanen said.

"I hope they haven't gone for guards to take us prisoner," Yazid ventured.

"If they did," Necho declared, "all I have to do is slash the lines and put out to sea again."

"Be ready with your knife, Necho," Nefrytatanen

said slowly, "but don't openly display it. We can wait and see what happens." She tried to ignore a fear that these people might not help them. She comforted herself, remembering Issella's promise. She knew that Amenemhet had all but lost his fight against the poison and needed treatment without delay.

Once more, Nefrytatanen went to Amenemhet's side and leaned to kiss him lightly on the lips. The golden eyes followed her dazedly as she turned again to the ship's bow. Watching them Kheti was reminded of once when he had seen a wounded lion, proud but helpless, watching his mate protect him. Kheti turned away.

After a time, a group of horsemen arrived. The crowd parted, and a man walked toward them, followed by several guards. Nefrytatanen stood as near the landing as she could, but she didn't leave the ship.

"Be ready," she whispered to the others gathering near her. She noticed the crowd moving respectfully from the man. When he faced Nefrytatanen, he stared at her, saying nothing.

"I am Queen Nefrytatanen of Tamera, daughter of King Tefibi-Siut, triumphant, and Queen Issella, triumphant, who was a princess of Atalan. Have we landed in that place?" Nefrytatanen asked firmly.

The man's eyes had slowly crinkled with his smile. "Welcome," he said. "You're in Atalan, daughter of my sister. I'm King Sahura and your uncle." His dark eyes clouded then, as he realized what she had said. "My sister is dead?"

"She traveled to Tuat hand in hand with my father several years ago. They had an accident. But they are not dead-things. Her spirit pointed the way to Atalan for us," Nefrytatanen answered.

"I'm sorry I stared at you, but you look so much like her, I couldn't believe my eyes. For a moment, I thought she'd returned, untouched by time," Sahura said slowly. "You have, evidently, inherited more than her physical resemblance. Your reason for coming must be of great importance, if you had to ask spirits for guidance."

Nefrytatanen's eyes filled with tears. "Uncle," she sadly said, "my beloved king has been poisoned and is slowly dying. I've come to you for help. My mother said your physician might heal him. There is no other help." Her tears began to fall. "Does your physician have an antidote?" she begged. "Is his knowledge sufficient?"

King Sahura turned quickly to the soldiers who stood behind him, giving one of them orders to hurry ahead and advise the palace physician to prepare himself. He instructed the others to help the travelers unload their belongings and get Amenemhet's litter.

As they carefully lifted Amenemhet, Nefrytatanen leaned over him and whispered, "My uncle is king here, beloved. He'll help us." She took Amenemhet's cool, unmoving hand in both of hers and walked beside the litter through the crowd. King Sahura glanced once at Amenemhet and ordered the soldiers to move faster.

"He cannot speak or move, uncle," she explained, "but he can hear and feel and see." Sahura patted her arm as she added, "I have, in that chest, a vial of the poison he drank."

"My physician, Apuya, will do anything that can be done," Sahura said. He added firmly, "My child, get upon my horse with me. They'll place your husband in a cart which will follow us. More comfortable transportation would delay us too much, I think, so we'll make do with what's available here. I think it best you ride with me. I'll hold you carefully. You've been through much, I can see. At the palace, you'll rest while Apuya examines him. The heir you carry will surely meet his father too soon if you don't. My horse is very gentle and you'll find the ride passably smooth."

"The child is not due yet." Nefrytatanen smiled weakly. "But you're right. I'll rest when I know Amenemhet is being cared for."

As they rode through the streets, which were lined

with curious faces, Nefrytatanen explained how Amen-emhet had been poisoned. Sahura shook his head sadly. She had barely finished when they were at the gates of the whitewalled palace. She was glad the ride was over; though she said nothing, she didn't feel well at all.

When they stopped in the palace courtyard, Sahura helped Nefrytatanen from the horse and led her into the shady hall. He made her sit down while the others dismounted and Amenemhet's litter was carried inside.

Kheti entered the hall and came quickly to Nefrytatanen, inquiring after her health. She said she was only tired. Noticing he was staring beyond her shoulder, she turned and saw a beautiful young woman standing in the hall, holding a cat in her arms. The cat's silver fur matched the girl's shining hair. Amazed, Nefrytatanen looked at Sahura.

"Come here, Neferset," Sahura said, smiling proudly. "Meet your cousin, who's the daughter of my sister, Issella." Nefrytatanen continued to stare at Neferset, fascinated with her strange coloring.

"Queen Nefrytatanen, my daughter, Princess Neferset," said Sahura as the girl stopped before them. Nefrytatanen realized, then, that Neferset was only a little younger than herself. Neferset's ethereal look made her appear younger than she was. Neferset dipped her head slightly in polite acknowledgment, but her eyes were on Kheti.

Seeing that Kheti also stared at Neferset, Nefrytatanen broke the growing silence. "I'm glad to meet you, Neferset. This is Kheti, Khnumhotep, lord of Orynx Province and count of Menet Khufu. Kheti, Princess Neferset," she said quickly.

Kheti continued to stare at Neferset, unable to trust his eyes, wondering. Was this creature with her cat real, or was she, perhaps, Bast?

Wide, slanted eyes, grey as her cat's looked at Kheti, openly curious, examining him. Kheti observed that she seemed to find him pleasing. When she stepped closer, he saw she was very small. Her face was more triangular-shaped than oval. Under her pale, silver-green garment he noticed her body was well-curved despite its slenderness. While he noted these things, her skin bloomed a trifle pink, and she looked at him a little more shyly. From some hidden well in the soft grey eyes, a green color bubbled up, and shortly her eyes turned green altogether.

Sahura smiled at Nefrytatanen and commented, in a tone meant only for her ears, "My daughter looks upon him with favor. It's seldom her eyes turn green unless she's angry or sad. It's obvious she's neither of those now," he observed.

Nefrytatanen watched Kheti and Neferset wander toward the garden, knowing they had forgotten Sahura, herself, and everything else for the moment. She remembered how she had felt when she had met Amenemhet. She wondered what sort of person Neferset was. She wouldn't like to see Kheti disappointed again. She noticed that he looked at Neferset with more interest than physical attraction.

Neferset's soft laugh was the sparkle of a brook, as she led Kheti to the garden. They strolled in Ra's warmth to a bench. The cat stretched out on her lap while she fondled its back thoughtfully.

"I saw you on the rocks when we entered the bay," Kheti said softly. "You looked like you were made of silver, and I thought you were an illusion conjured up by my own seasick imagination. I've never seen hair that color on a person your age."

"I'm real enough," Neferset said serenely. "I have often sat by the sea waiting for you. Today you arrived, and I was very happy."

Kheti stared at her. Her strange beauty was matched by her strange words. Were all these people magical, he wondered?

"Do the women of Tamera speak plainly of such things?" she asked. "It's not my way to tease and flirt." Her eyes were now a little shy. "Never have I said such things to a man, openly revealing my thoughts. You are the one I have dreamed of, however, and I felt I could say them to you."

"You dreamed of me?" Kheti couldn't absorb all this so fast. "I've had many dreams that seem similar to incidents that happened upon awakening, but I've never had such dreams as you describe. Are you magical, like my queen?"

"I have such dreams often." Neferset smiled. She looked at him with mischief in her eyes. "Are not all women magical—in their own way?"

"No." Kheti shook his head slowly as he thought of Amenardis. "Some women are nothing so pleasant. And the few who seem to have magic have not the powers I mean. I have seen only one like that, and she's my queen."

"I merely have dreams that often come true," Neferset murmured. "Princess Issella, your queen's mother, knew the secrets of Aset and was truly powerful." Nefersets's brow held a slight frown as she added, "Magic or not, however, when love called to her she was powerless to do anything but follow it."

When the soldiers carried Amenemhet's litter into the hall, King Sahura directed them to a bedroom, and Nefrytatanen rose to follow. Although Sahura chided her for her persistence, she wouldn't leave Amenemhet's side. When he was in bed, a couch was brought for her and placed next to the bed. She sat down.

"Apuya is here," announced a servant from the doorway.

The words were hardly spoken when a short, slender man with greying hair and alert eyes brushed past the servant and hurried to the bed. The physician shook his head as he glanced at Nefrytatanen.

"I cannot save your husband and deliver your child at the same time," he said tartly. "Lie down. Do not merely sit, or I'll administer a drug to make you sleep."

With a sigh Nefrytatanen obeyed him. "I must explain what happened," she said. "The vial in my little chest holds a sample of the poison. My physician said

Amenemhet drank too little to kill him immediately, but he is dying slowly."

Apuya examined one of Amenemhet's eyes. He shook his head. "I think I know what it is, but I'll make some tests before I mix the antidote." Apuya glanced over his shoulder at Nefrytatanen, who was again sitting up. He turned to push her shoulders firmly back. "Lie down," he commanded. "Shut your eyes."

Nefrytatanen obeyed, closing her eyes, but she had no intention of sleeping. She only wished to placate Apuya. She heard him speak softly to Amenemhet.

Nefrytatanen didn't feel comfortable. She knew something was wrong with her besides plain weariness, but she decided to keep silent about her vague aches. She didn't want to distract Apuya from his task. Amenemhet needed every second of Apuya's attention. Her exhausted body won the struggle, and, without realizing it, she drifted into sleep.

Pain wrenched Nefrytatanen with a violence that made her gasp aloud, and her eyes flew open in surprise. A strange woman came to her side, and, after glancing at Nefrytatanen, ran out of the room calling for Apuya. Nefrytatanen was terrified, but she fought down her panic and forced herself to lie quietly, her fingers gripping the edges of the couch. An eternity passed before Apuya looked down at her. Dimly, she perceived his fear.

"Amenemhet!" she gasped. "Is he dead?"

"No, no," Apuya said gently. "He's resting while my medicine conquers the poison. We must move you from here so he's not disturbed."

Apuya turned and gave orders to two servants who lifted Nefrytatanen carefully. The movement brought fresh shudders of sharp pain, and she gasped again. The servants hurried with her into another room across the hall where they carefully laid her on a bed. She looked imploringly at Apuya, and he answered the question in her eyes.

"I'm glad you waited until I took care of your husband," he said quietly, then added, "Yes, the child does come too soon, but not so early it cannot live—I think. Do as I direct you and be hopeful. It won't be easy, but if you trust and obey me, I believe your child will arrive before dawn."

The door opened, and Nefrytatanen heard an unfamiliar voice say softly, "We cannot find him. She'll have to go through it without the waking sleep."

Nefrytatanen shut her eyes. Apuya need not have told her it wouldn't be easy. She knew this was no normal birth pain. Fear gripped her. She opened her eyes.

"Apuya," she whispered. "Senbi is a priest in Tamera. Ask if he knows the skills of hypnosis."

"I've already inquired, and he doesn't," Apuya answered quietly. "You and I will do it alone. If it gets unbearable, I may have to give you a potion, but I cannot let you be too drugged. You must stay conscious."

Nefrytatanen closed her eyes, dreading that her will was not strong enough to endure this. Fear sat beside her, coldly watching, and only Apuya stood between her and it.

The hours that followed were a pit of anguish, and Nefrytatanen lay trapped at its bottom. All thoughts were blotted from her mind but one—to listen to the quiet, steady voice of Apuya, to obey him and to endure.

Kheti, Rakkor, Senbi, Necho, and Bekhet had spent the remainder of the afternoon waiting with King Sahura and his family. Yazid had stayed with Amenemhet and the physician. Although they had been offered rooms in which to rest and refresh themselves, they had declined. Comforts didn't interest them. After introductions had been exchanged, there was little conversation. On all their minds was one thought: Amenemhet would live or would die. They waited.

With trays of food for the evening meal, word came of Nefrytatanen's labor, and Bekhet, hearing that Senbi didn't know hypnosis, paled, and wordlessly rushed out to be with her mistress. None of them touched the food, and it sat cooling until servants carried the dishes away.

As the night dragged on, they grew restless. King Sahura paced the room from time to time. Prince Sarenput, a quietly dignified man, wandered into the garden and waited in the darkness. Princess Neferset sat, holding her cat in her lap, occasionally glancing at Kheti and looking quickly away. Queen Nesitaneb stared sympathetically into space, obviously sharing Nefrytatanen's pain.

Sahura urged them all to go to bed, promising word would be sent immediately, but no one left. They heard servants hurrying in the hall; occasionally, Queen Nesitaneb called to one of them, asking if anything was needed. Nothing was. There was only waiting to be done.

Bekhet wiped Nefrytatanen's face gently with a cool cloth while Nefrytatanen looked up gratefully and refused to scream. Apuya had finally given her a drug, which had done nothing more than clear her mind. Her thoughts had turned to Amenemhet. She would not make a noise to disturb and worry him. This idea obsessed her.

Through the fog of pain that surrounded her came a dim, wavering cry. It confused her. She couldn't believe it was a child, for the pain hadn't decreased. After another eternity had passed, there was another wailing, like the first. She decided she was delirious.

Apuya's voice was faint and came from far away. "Queen Nefrytatanen, you have two children. First a son and now a daughter." Through her pain, she realized what he was telling her, and she smiled. Watching her, Apuya added softly, "It's good you have two. There will be no others."

Before unconsciousness took her, Nefrytatanen heard Apuya gently tell her to rest and not move at all.

Amenemhet slowly rose from the blackness into which he had fallen, to partial awareness. He hadn't awakened fully, when he was startled by a cry. He saw Yazid leap up from beside him and race out of the room. Time passed, and he wondered if he had been dreaming. Then he heard another cry. Without thinking, he sat up and swung his feet off the bed. When he stood up, he felt dizzy and leaned against the wall, dazed. He was perspiring, yet cold, as if he had awakened after a fever, and he sat on the edge of the bed, confused.

Yazid raced through the door, stopped suddenly, and stared.

"Sire!" he cried. "You moved!"

Amenemhet stared back at him, slowly remembering. He looked down at his feet in amazement. He wiggled his toes, watching them in delighted surprise. He held his hands before him and stared at his moving fingers. He looked up at Yazid, whose face was wet with tears. Amenemhet had never seen Yazid weep. Still disoriented, he stared at the servant.

"I heard a cry," he said vaguely.

"Sire," Yazid whispered, "the queen was taken from this room to have the child. I had just gone to see if the child was born yet, but no one answered the door."

Amenemhet suddenly alert and cold with fear, paled. He knew it was not yet Nefrytatanen's time.

Apuya entered the room, looking weary. He smiled at Amenemhet.

"Everything happens at once," he sighed. "Lie back and rest some more. You're still too weak to be up." Apuya smiled. "You have a son for your first-born. Your daughter came shortly after."

"Two?" Amenemhet stared at Apuya. "A double birth? And Nefrytatanen?" The physician was gently pressing him back into bed.

"It was too soon," Apuya replied. "It was very difficult for her. Now she's weak, but she'll recover in time. The infants are somewhat small, but they're well-developed and seem strong." Apuya added drily, "Their voices are particularly strong."

Amenemhet closed his eyes in relief. Finally he whispered, "When can I see her?"

Apuya's smile grew wider. "Perhaps if she has a good night we can move her here tomorrow to be with you. You can recuperate together. There's no use in separating you any longer than necessary. You can see the infants in the morning, after you've slept the rest of the night—what's left of it."

Almost numb, Amenemhet gazed at Apuya in awe, trying to absorb all this. He whispered, "You have saved my life and Nefrytatanen's. You have given us not one—a wonder enough—but two children. All in one night! What can I do to thank you? What is precious enough to offer in gratitude?"

Apuya shook his head sadly. "There's one thing I could not do tonight. She can have no other children."

Amenemhet was startled. "It was that bad?" He saw Apuya's eyes and understood. Quietly he said, "I'm glad. If it were possible to have other children, I'd prevent it, for I can see in your eyes what she has suffered. Two are sufficient."

Apuya stood up and said a little sternly, "Your family has kept me busy all this day and night. Please go to sleep and trouble me no further for a while. I'll sleep across the hall next to her room in case I'm needed. Rest now, so I may rest—or next I'll need treatment!" He turned and left, sighing slightly, but Amenemhet and Yazid could hear him hum softly as he closed the door.

Neither Amenemhet nor Yazid knew what to say. Both were overwhelmed. Amenemhet finally grasped Yazid's hand and squeezed it. To do this, just to be able to squeeze his friend's hand, was wonderful.

There was a soft tap at the door. Amenemhet released Yazid, and the servant went to answer it. Yazid opened the door a bit and Amenemhet heard him say, "Yes, he is well. Yes, he was almost standing, but he must rest. Two! A son and a daughter both! The queen is weak but will recover."

Yazid closed the door, still smiling, and came back to settle himself on the couch beside Amenemhet's bed. Before he closed his eyes, he mumbled. "That was Kheti. He's been up—as the whole palace has been—waiting for the news." Then Yazid promptly fell asleep, snoring softly.

Amenemhet smiled and settled himself more comfortably. What a wonder it was to be able to turn over in bed! He wiggled his toes again and remembered how Nefrytatanen had clung to him all during the voyage, keeping his hope alive. He decided it was she who had kept him living. It had been the dread of losing her through death that had made him continue fighting for his life. He thought of the children and was filled with wonder. His smile widened. Then, thinking of his family, he fell asleep.

After hours of silence, the group waiting downstairs had been startled by the cry of a child, and Kheti had leaped up. Without asking questions, almost running, he hurried toward the sound. Confused for a moment in the unfamiliar corridors, he hesitated. Hearing another cry, he sped on.

As he raced around a corner, he saw Apuya leave one room and enter another across the hall. Kheti waited a moment until the physician came out, looking tired but humming softly. Apuya didn't notice him and went into another room, closing the door behind him.

Now Kheti didn't know where to turn, and he decided to try the door the physician had just left. After a hesitant knock, the door was answered. Yazid's face peered at him from the crack.

When Kheti heard the news, he felt that a stone had been lifted from his chest. He turned, his wonder and joy shining in his eyes, to face Neferset, who had followed him. She said nothing but took his arm and led him toward the others who were waiting behind her.

Kheti said brokenly, "King Amenemhet is saved. He awoke to hear the cries of the newborn children—a son and a daughter. They're small, but Apuya said they're healthy. Queen Nefrytatanen is weak, but she'll recover."

After the tension of the long wait, no one knew quite what to say. They stood smiling wordlessly at each other until Sahura cleared his throat and said, "Come. Let us drink a goblet of wine to celebrate this news."

They followed him immediately, still dazed, Neferset clinging unshyly to Kheti's arm, her silver cat at their heels. When they had drunk their wine and were more at ease, weariness washed over them. Watching Sarenput smother a yawn, Nesitaneb sighed and put down her goblet. "Tomorrow is almost here, and the day holds much," she said. "Let us go to bed now. We can get better acquainted when we've rested. There are many things we'll be curious to hear, and I'm sure you have many questions you wish to ask. As soon as your king and queen can receive visitors, we'll all want to see them and give them our congratulations." She paused to take a breath and stifled her own yawn. "I must say, I don't plan on rising early," she said. "Please don't feel you must rush from your beds either. We'll be informal and have our morning meals in our rooms when each of us feels ready." No one protested.

Kheti found himself being shown to his chamber by Neferset. When she stopped at a door and indicated that it was where he would sleep, he said, "It's hard to believe this ordeal is finally ended."

Neferset smiled. "When you awaken, it will seem as if today was a dream, but I'll still be here to make it real again for you."

He was suddenly struck by a strange emotion as he looked at her, and she smiled a little shyly at his expression.

"We can talk of such feelings later, Kheti, when we're both more awake," she said softly.

Kheti looked at her silently a moment, realizing he

wanted to take this girl into his room this very moment, not from physical desire, but to have this creature near him through the night to insure she wouldn't disappear with morning. The sentiment was new to him, and he smiled at himself. He said, "I think we'll have a great many things to discuss."

"I'll dream of them tonight," she promised and then added, "I hope your dreams are as pleasant."

"They will be," he said softly as he watched her glide away.

Nefrytatanen awakened during the night. She lay in the darkness of the strange room, marveling at all that had happened, Although she still ached with exhaustion, she didn't notice it. They now had a son and a daughter! Amenemhet was well again! She smiled. When she had thought their marriage was merely for political reasons, she had been embarrassed to think of producing an heir. She laughed softly. What fools we can be, she thought, to come to conclusions too soon and worry about the future. She thought of her mother and lay staring into the darkness remembering how Issella had sent her here.

"Thank you," Nefrytatanen whispered.

Moonlight flooded the room, and she could almost see Issella's spirit-body looking at her with its silver eyes. Nefrytatanen thought that if souls could converse without words and disregard time and distance, then Issella surely knew what had happened here tonight.

A breeze from the garden filled the room with the scent of flowers. Nefrytatanen fell asleep breathing the fragrance, her aching gone. She dreamed of Issella giving her a bouquet. When she awakened, just as dawn was beginning to light the room, there were flower petals scattered across her bed.

Amenemhet's eyes opened to look curiously at a golden ceiling. For a moment, he didn't know where he was. As memory of the night's events returned, he wondered if it was all a dream or if he had truly been awake. He decided the only way to prove its truth was to move, if he could, and as he cautiously turned his head, he saw that Yazid and Apuya were watching him.

"Now that you've rediscovered you can move, don't think you can get up," Apuya warned. "You'll find yourself weak and dizzy yet. You'll need to regain your strength gradually."

Amenemhet smiled and stretched, enjoying the luxury of muscles obeying his will. He said, "I stood up for a moment last night."

"And you were dizzy enough to sit down immediately," the physician concluded. "I don't mind if you get up now and race down the corridor. I warn you only because you're likely to feel faint and perhaps will fall and crack your skull."

"You show little respect for a king," Amenemhet muttered smiling with good humor.

"I treat the royal family and have found them to suffer the same ailments as any other," Apuya returned. "You're my patient and it matters little to me at what profession you earn your living. If you get up too soon, you may fall, and your royal head will need sewing."

Amenemhet could see Yazid was enjoying this, and Apuya's eyes sparkled despite his scolding manner. Amenemhet scratched his head, and this simple moment was pure, undiluted pleasure. He stretched again and yawned. "Have neither of you any hint of human kindness for a man who has subsisted on nothing but broths and milk for several months?" Amenemhet asked. He sat up too quickly, then waited a moment for his head to clear.

"I told you you'd be dizzy," Apuya said smugly.

"I'm dizzy from hunger," Amenemhet retorted. "How late in the day is it?" He could see the sun was high from the absence of shadows in the room.

"You're going nowhere," Apuya replied coldly. "Food is already on the way. You are, in fact, going to have the noon meal."

Amenemhet had been delaying asking about Nefrytatanen, though his thoughts had turned to her immediately. He was afraid the news of last night had been a
dream.

The physician said softly, "Your queen will be having
her meal also. She's feeling as well as can be expected
and asks about you."

Amenemhet looked startled. "She's feeling as well
as can be expected? Is there something wrong you
haven't told me?" The golden eyes bored into the physician.

"No," Apuya said emphatically. "She's weak, that's
all. She slept well and was in a most cheerful mood
this morning."

Although Amenemhet said nothing, his relief was
obvious.

When his tray came, he was newly delighted to face
the prospect of eating without help. It had been humili-
ating all this time to have to be fed and cared for like
a baby. Now even to be able to chew was a wonder.
As he slowly ate, Nefrytatanen crept again into his
mind. Was Apuya still hiding something from him?

"Last night you said you'd bring Nefrytatanen here,"
Amenemhet said a little anxiously. "Is there some
reason you cannot?"

Apuya looked at him, shook his head, and smiled.
"No." Apuya sighed and stood up. "I'd better give the
orders for this to be done, or I'll have no peace from
either of you."

When Apuya had left and the tray had been removed,
Amenemhet sat up and waited tensely for Nefrytatanen
to be brought. Ignoring his dizziness, he reflected on
finding the words he would speak. Knowing he would
see her in a few moments filled him with too much
happiness to allow much concentration.

A tall, broad-shouldered man carried Nefrytatanen
to him. She was wrapped in a blanket, and Amenemhet
was shocked by her pallor. When she was laid carefully
beside him, she smiled, and he couldn't speak. He only

took her hand and gently kissed her fingers. They looked at each other wordlessly for a long time.

Amenemhet was vaguely aware of two women entering the room just as Apuya said, "Now you may meet your son and daughter. We won't leave them beside you for long. They've already found this world to be tiring, and they sleep often."

Amenemhet stared at the tiny creatures placed between them while Nefrytatanen smiled and silently watched his face. Bewildered golden eyes looked up at her. "Which is which?" Amenemhet finally asked, hesitant to touch the fragile-looking beings.

"Which do you think, beloved?" Nefrytatanen laughed softly. "The blue-eyed one is your daughter, the golden-eyed your son."

He stared in amazement. "They're like you and me?"

She smiled. "So it seems. But often, children of double births don't look like each other."

He couldn't take his gaze from the tiny faces. He put out a finger cautiously to touch a miniature hand, and his eyes rose to meet Nefrytatanen's. He was filled with wonder. He could say no more. His throat was stopped. She smiled at him a little shyly now and pulled the wrappings carefully from them exposing the diminutive bodies for his inspection.

"Although they're earlier in the world than was intended," she said, "they seem to have all the necessary parts."

Amenemhet was curious and amazed at these small and perfect creatures. That they could be so small, and yet whole, fascinated him. Until this moment, they had been only a promise. To have them alive and before him to touch and look at astounded him.

"Have you nothing to say?" Apuya demanded.

Amenemhet glanced at him then, looking into Nefrytatanen's eyes, replied, "I have many words to say but only for her ears."

"Then you can say them now," Apuya said, "for we're going to take the infants and let them sleep."

The women took the babies and left, following Apuya. Though Amenemhet was unwilling to let the children be taken away, he was also eager to be alone with Nefrytatanen.

He turned to kiss her softly on the lips, and she smiled and closed her eyes.

"If you kiss me too often, I will be tempted." Her words were teasing, but she was very pale.

"I can resist your attack," he whispered. Then he grew serious. "I've thought about what I might say to you at this moment, but now that I can speak, words are too little."

"Say whatever you wish," she murmured, "and just let me listen to the sound of your voice again. Let me watch the movement of your mouth and know you are well, that you're alive and the nightmare is ended."

"What more can I ask?" Amenemhet said softly. "My life has been given back to me, and I have a son to follow me and a daughter whose beauty will be surpassed only by her mother's."

Nefrytatanen smiled with pleasure. "And what more could I ask?" she said. "The gift is mine as well as yours." She was quiet a moment and then said, "Apuya told you there will be no other children?"

"Yes, he told me." The golden eyes again met hers. "For that I'm also thankful." Seeing her surprise, he added, "I would not have you go through that again." He turned her face to his. "I would not risk losing you. I would not subject you to more pain." He was quiet a moment looking at her. Then he smiled. "Have you considered their names?"

"We've never had a chance to discuss it, so I confess I've thought only briefly on it. Have you?"

"Yes," Amenemhet replied. "What would you think of naming the boy Senwadjet? Someday he'll be king, and I'd like to remind the people of Tamehu that he's your son as well as mine. To name him as the son of Wadjet, the northern goddess, would assure them, by his name, that he rules both lands."

"You are always the wisest of kings," she said softly. "And the girl?"

"I don't know," he confessed.

"I have an idea, then," Nefrytatanen said. "From the beginning, you've tried to follow your dream. As the prophecy foretold, you've tried to restore order, maet, to the land, and I think you'll succeed. What do you think of naming her Maeti, after the double goddess?"

"She would be a reminder, then, of what we wish for the kingdom." Amenemhet smiled. "It's a beautiful name." A sudden wave of dizziness washed over him, and, for a moment, he looked at her with unfocused eyes.

Alarmed, she asked, "Beloved, are you well?"

"Yes," he answered slowly. "Apuya said I'd be dizzy from time to time, but this will diminish eventually."

"Let us rest," Nefrytatanen said hastily. "Let us both heal quickly."

Amenemhet smiled at her worried expression and pressed her hand. Content with each other's nearness, they fell asleep quickly.

Amenemhet awakened to see Nefrytatanen's face near his, her eyes yet closed in slumber. He lay quietly, looking at her. When he had thought his death was certain, he had so often dreamed of being well and awakening next to her. He kissed her eyelids softly, a little impatient, hoping to speed her awakening. As he drew away, feeling guilty for disturbing her, her eyes opened, and she smiled.

"We've slept some time," Nefrytatanen murmured. She smoothed his rumpled hair from his forehead.

"All afternoon," Amenemhet replied, turning his face to brush his lips against her palm. "I suspect someone will come soon with the babies."

As if his words had been overheard, a servant tapped on the door, then entered carrying a tray. She placed it near the bed and rearranged their pillows, her serene dark eyes filled with warmth.

"I am Amset," she said softly. "I've brought food."

Seeing their nod, she organized the dishes for them then stepped back smiling. "My lady, the infants need feeding," she said.

"Bring them after we've finished," Nefrytatanen said.

"You also have many visitors waiting also," Amset said.

Nefrytatanen looked at Amenemhet and smiled at his raised eyebrows. "First things must come first," she said. "We will see the visitors after the children are fed."

After Senwadjet and Maeti had been fed and taken away, people suddenly filled the room from wall to wall. Amenemhet's shipmates smiled happily at them, and he saw many people whom he didn't know.

"Who are all these people who have helped us?" he finally asked, perplexed.

Nefrytatanen laughed. "I don't know all their names." She looked at Sahura, the smile still lighting her eyes. "Please introduce us to our other relatives, uncle," she urged.

Sahura's dark eyes smiled at Amenemhet. "I am King Sahura, Issella's brother." He took the hand of an elegantly slender green-eyed lady, bringing her a step nearer the bed. "This is my wife, Nesitaneb." On his other side he indicated a smiling girl with solemn grey eyes and silver hair and said, "My daughter, Neferset." Then he turned to the young man Amenemhet recognized as having carried Nefrytatanen into the room earlier. "My son, Sarenput," Sahura turned to a man who had stood quietly watching. "This is my friend, Commander Semu."

Amenemhet smiled. "You have a fine family and a generous one." He looked at Semu and remarked, "From the little I've seen, your job must be easy. Your people seem more inclined to kindness than to war."

Semu answered easily. "Atalan is too small to conduct a proper war upon. Since we have few visitors, we fear no invasion. My job is keeping order among ourselves, which is mostly settling such civilian matters as plague any town." He grinned and added ruefully, "However, an irate wife in hot controversy with her husband, thus disturbing the neighbors, can be a formidable foe."

Amenemhet laughed. "Have you met the friends who came with us?" he asked.

Nesitaneb answered, "We didn't stand on ceremony and have introduced ourselves." She glanced at Kheti. "We seem to find ourselves becoming well-acquainted."

Noting the look that passed between Kheti and Neferset, Amenemhet said smoothly, "I'm glad we're so congenial. I have not, nor can I really, express our gratitude for all that was done for us."

"Have you decided what to name your new prince and princess?" Sahura asked, shrugging away the thanks.

Amenemhet smiled and settled back. "Yes, we've decided. Nefrytatanen was heir to the crown of our north kingdom and I to the southern. With our marriage, the two kingdoms were united. By our son will they be ruled, and we would like to assure the people of the north that their next king rules for us both. We've decided the boy's name will be Senwadjet. Wadjet is a divine being especially revered in the north."

"And the girl?" asked Nesitaneb. "Have you found an equally fitting name for her?"

Nefrytatanen answered. "We have a word—maet—that means the perfection planned for the earth by the One Alone. The divine being who symbolizes the meaning of this is Maeti, and we've decided to name our daughter after her." Nefrytatanen paused. "It is Amenemhet's dream, and mine, to restore maet to the land."

"We also have this word and belief," Nesitaneb said. "It's a fitting name as well as a beautiful one. I hope you can achieve the reality of it in Tamera."

"We'll continue trying." Amenemhet sighed.

"We've exchanged enough social amenities," Sahura decided. He turned to the others. "I'm sure they'd like to visit with Kheti and their other friends before they're overtired. Let us leave them now." The group said their good nights promptly and left without lingering.

"I cannot tell you how relieved I am," Kheti said. "Often I have lain awake all night thinking it was I who brought this whole thing upon you."

"It was Amenardis, who did it, not you. How could you have known who she was?" Amenemhet asked. "I surely wouldn't have guessed. It's difficult to imagine Sinuhe's being with a woman, much less having a child."

After Kheti had left Amenemhet and Nefrytatanen to return to his bedchamber, he glanced around the halls but saw nothing of Neferset. Although she had spoken of having many things to discuss with him, Kheti now found it impossible to locate her. Their meeting, with the others in Amenemhet and Nefrytatanen's room, had been their first since the previous night.

He was beginning to wonder if she deliberately avoided him. He was anxious to see her again, but he was afraid, too, that he would be drawn to her beyond his power to resist.

In this disturbed state of mind, he wandered into the garden. The night air was cool and seemed to clear his head, which ached from introspection. The moonlight cast shadows among the bushes and trees, making cloudy masses of the flowers.

He sat on the edge of a low stone wall some distance from the door. He looked at the building. Idly comparing the palace with Ithtawe, he suddenly realized what was troubling him most. If he became too deeply involved with Neferset, as he suspected he might, would he have to choose between this land and his own? Would Sahura allow his daughter to leave her home for him? Would she want to go to Tamera? He recalled what Neferset had said about Issella, that she had been powerless to do anything but follow her love. He wondered about this. Issella, like Neferset, had been a princess unlikely to become queen. But by marriage to

King Tefibi-Siut, Issella had become queen in Tamehu. Neferset could never aspire to be even a princess in Tamera. Her status would be lowered with Kheti. She would have to leave her home, family, and title to go with him. Would she give it all up? He wondered. Only a few short years ago, Kheti never dreamed of marriage, and he smiled a little bitterly as he thought of these past months. Though he was awed at the idea of marrying a princess, he considered that he had earned his own title and was proud of it.

Kheti decided he was getting ahead of himself. They had only hinted at love and hadn't even made any declarations. Perhaps Neferset had disappeared because she regretted her earlier impulsiveness.

Kheti's thoughts were interrupted when he saw a figure in the distance walking silently over the carpet of shadowy grass. When the moonlight struck silver hair, he knew it was Neferset. He stood up. Neferset paused in her steps, put down her cat, and sent it padding toward the palace. Then she began to walk toward Kheti.

When she reached him, she said, "I avoided you, I know." She was silent a moment then added, "I wished to think over all the possible problems and decide on them before I allowed my emotions their freedom."

Kheti looked at Neferset steadily, and she wasn't sure what thoughts lay behind his grey eyes. After a moment she realized it was pride. It was triumph, too, and tribute accepted gladly. She had offered him a gift, and he accepted it, wordlessly, in that look. It was a moment of supreme triumph for them both.

Kheti's voice was low and calm when he finally spoke. "The moment I first saw you standing on the rocks I decided I would have you, if you weren't an illusion. Prophetic dreams or not, you stayed away from me to consider the powerful feelings we share—which shows your wisdom. Since last night, when you left me at my door, I have wandered around filled with dreams of you when I should have had my mind on other things.

I've argued with myself, listing all the reasons we shouldn't let this emotion grow. Now you're here, silencing my questions with nothing but your presence. I was just thinking about whether you'd be willing to come to Tamera with me, afraid you wouldn't leave your family, your land, your birthright."

Kheti took her in his arms, and she lifted her face to his and moved closer. He stared into her grey cat-eyes. She looked steadily back at him and let him see through her eyes what her soul contained. He held her face between his hands and kissed her softly. When he drew away to look at her again, her eyes were a blaze of green. He kissed her again, holding her tighter. She didn't hesitate or restrain her kiss in any way. She clung to Kheti of her own accord, and no question was left unanswered.

Before Kheti left Neferset at her door, he held her close to him a moment, knowing he was no longer alone, knowing he had followed the drift of an unknown current and had found his destination just as the papyrus ship had found Atalan.

Later in his room Kheti stared out his window at the sea below. The moon shimmered on its waves, looking much like Neferset's hair. Suddenly there was a knock on the door, and Rakkor entered without waiting for an answer. Preparing to settle himself for a visit, Rakkor noted the look on Kheti's face and whistled softly. "Something very interesting has happened to you, I think," he commented.

Not yet wishing to share his news, Kheti replied quietly, "Don't tease me or make jokes, Rakkor. I'm in no mood for them."

"Has she said yes or no?"

"Who?" Kheti, being deliberately obscure, hoped Rakkor would drop the subject. He didn't.

"That child of Bast," Rakkor said, "is not so much a child as might be thought at first glance."

"She is no child at all."

"There seems to be more to this than I'd thought,"

Rakkor remarked. "Are you in love with her?" Kheti said nothing. Rakkor became disturbed by Kheti's silence. He was making no progress at all. "Have you managed to persuade her to your bed?" Rakkor asked, hoping to get some reaction. Seeing Kheti's face, he abandoned that subject. After a moment he commented, "The beautiful little kitten-princess looks fragile and helpless, but I think she's very strong-willed underneath."

"I have no taste for pliant women who have nothing behind their eyes," Kheti snapped.

Rakkor was thoughtful for a time. Then he observed, "Perhaps I'll yet bounce your children on my knee."

Kheti glanced sharply at his friend, but his eyes gradually softened. He made no reply and turned back to the window. Rakkor now knew all he had been curious to know.

As Rakkor closed the door, he heard behind him Kheti's cheerful whistle and the sound of the window hangings being pulled. Rakkor smiled as he continued down the hall to his room.

Yazid, leaving Amenemhet and Nefrytatanen's room, met Rakkor and paused to comment, "You look most cheerful, Rakkor. What happy matter do you contemplate?"

Rakkor sighed and rolled his eyes airily. "I dream of love and romance," he said and went on his way leaving Yazid staring in bewilderment at his retreating back.

Chapter Seventeen

Amenemhet rapidly regained his strength and in a few days he was able to walk unassisted if he didn't move too impulsively. Any sudden motion still brought a wave of dizziness so he was careful while the weakness slowly faded. It wasn't as easy for Nefrytatanen to recover. She tired easily, although she refused to stay in bed. She spent much of her waking time seated.

Two decans had passed since their arrival in Atalan. Amenemhet was with King Sahura, discussing the repairs to the ship and supplies for the voyage home, when Amenemhet learned that Atalan's ships were almost identical in design to their own papyrus vessel.

Sahura smiled. "Living in a land surrounded by water, it's natural for us to be at home on the ocean," he said. "We've sailed east and traded at ports in the place you call the Great Green Sea. The people we've dealt with probably thought us from Tamera. Tell me, why must you leave us so soon?"

"There's still much unrest in Tamera," Amenemhet replied, "and when I consider the possible developments in our absence, I shudder. As much as I'd like to visit with you longer, we must return and get Tamera in order."

Sahura nodded agreement. "I understand, of course. Now that we're acquainted, perhaps we'll visit you sometime. If you wish, I can send a ship of our own to guide you back. You won't have the current to carry you home."

"I dislike troubling you further," Amenemhet said.

"It would be no trouble." Sahura's quick smile flashed. "After all, you are really part of my family. It would also be a good way for us to learn the exact location of Tamera." Sahura fell silent a moment, trying to decide whether or not to mention something. Amenemhet waited quietly. Finally Sahura looked at him, his eyes both sad and contemplative.

"Amenemhet," Sahura said quietly, "before the first king, what do you know of Tamera's past?"

Amenemhet was thoughtful then answered slowly, "I know of records, which date to our first king's time. I know of other writings, which are supposed to be much older, but we have only copies of them. I know of some stories passed from generation to generation of priests. From time to time, a farmer will dig up a bit of pottery or a relic of a more remote past, but these articles are, in my opinion, questionable. In no way I can see do they bear any resemblance to our present styles. They wouldn't seem to have evolved into what we have today in Tamera."

Sahura smiled humorously, and Amenemhet was surprised at his odd expression. Sahura said, "What you know, then, is only that which dates to your first king. Doesn't it seem strange to you that the tales the priests tell of earlier times weren't recorded someplace? The relics you question as being part of Tamera's past may have no real resemblance because they aren't really things of your people. You have no evidence of previous civilization, but your first kings are credited with having built pyramids? Tamera seems to have no beginning in rudeness and savagery, with a gradual building up of knowledge. It would seem that your civilization of culture and learning, suddenly appeared out of nowhere. Is that not peculiar?"

Amenemhet lifted his golden eyes to Sahura and nodded thoughtfully. He knew what Sahura said was true. He had never thought of it quite this way before.

Sahura studied his reaction intently. "Amenemhet, no civilization suddenly appears from nowhere. The customs, the architecture, the religious beliefs, couldn't evolve overnight. Such things don't happen."

Amenemhet's curiosity was thoroughly aroused, and he leaned forward slowly, "Sahura, tell me what point you make. I follow your thinking and find it reasonable."

Sahura smiled, gratified. He said softly, "Have you noticed how similar our people are? Have you not wondered why we speak the same language though we live so great a distance apart? Do you not question why we build much the same structures, dress with only minor differences, even follow almost the same religion? Tamera's beginnings, I think, are here."

Amenemhet looked a little startled, but he said nothing and waited for Sahura to continue.

"We have very little—merely shreds and small bits— of what Atalan once was," Sahura said. "What we would regard as extraordinary and magical now, according to legends, was commonplace then. There are stories that adepts and magicians abounded; that apparatuses worked marvels we can never duplicate; that there were fabulous crystals, small and huge, which drew power directly from Ra; that there were metals whose secrets we no longer possess. It is said that at that time gods and goddesses walked in Atalan in the flesh, and we are their children's children. Would this not explain our religious precepts telling us that we're descended directly from the gods? Isn't that what Tamera's religion teaches?"

Amenemhet nodded but remained silent.

"Why do we look like no other people on earth?" Sahura asked. "Why do we have this religious philosophy and knowledge like no other people you and I know about?"

Amenemhet still said nothing, but he listened intently.

Sahura leaned forward in his chair and said, "Because Tamera's roots are deep in the dim past of Atalan—because we began in a time that would be called ancient by those who lived in the time we call ancient."

Amenemhet finally asked, "Why would some of Atalan's people have gone to Tamera while the others remained here?"

Sahura took a deep breath and sat back in his chair. He looked at his lap as he answered. "At a time further in antiquity than we can imagine, there was a catastrophe in Atalan. According to the records and legends, Atalan was a series of large islands, like a necklace of jewels in the ocean. I am not sure why the catastrophe occurred because the stories have been shrouded in the mists of passing centuries. Volcanoes suddenly erupted. There were earthquakes and tidal waves and most of the land collapsed into the ocean. What you see is all that remains of Atalan. When Atalan's beauty was taken from the earth, it was replaced, I think, by that sphere which now adorns the night sky."

"The moon?" Amenemhet asked in amazement.

"Yes," Sahura replied. "The records show no mention of earth as having had a moon before that time. I think the moon's coming so upset the earth that Atalan was destroyed."

Amenemhet considered this possibility and mumbled, "That may be." He was silent a moment, absorbing this fantastic story. Finally he asked, "How many people were living then, do you know?"

Sahura shook his head. "The records only recall absolute terror and chaos. Some were reported as having managed to launch a few ships and escape the devastation. They never returned, and, I assume that if they did survive, they settled elsewhere."

Sahura sighed. "When Nefrytatanen's father came and spoke with my father, they also discussed this," he said. "They finally decided it was possible some of the survivors landed in Tamera and settled there." Sahura looked at Amenemhet and continued, "The people of Atalan and Tamera have so much in common, their small differences could easily be accounted for by differences in natural resources and time itself."

Amenemhet nodded. "That could explain why Tamera has no past beyond our first king. If survivors from Atalan went to Tamera, they had barely escaped with their lives and had little to begin with but memories. After what would have been a time of struggle for mere survival, they would have built their first cities slowly, but they would have been a people founding a colony fully developed as a culture. When they crowned their first king, they would have been establishing a new country, but it would have been based on what they'd known in the past."

Sahura got to his feet. "Amenemhet, they would have had no reason to believe any part of Atalan had survived, so terrible was the destruction," he said. "With the passing of years, when they might have been able to return, they probably thought there was no place to return to. And with the passing of generations, their beginning could have been lost to their descendants. Memories would have become stories, and the name of Atalan could have been forgotten except in legends." Sahura took a breath and sat down again. "Neither Atalan's nor Tamera's people are inclined, it seems, toward exploration or conquest. Until Nefrytatanen's father came here by accident, we had no contact. Neither land knew the other existed. There may even be other such colonies in the world, but we don't know about them either."

Amenemhet digested this idea in silence. He couldn't argue with Sahura's logic because he brought forth questions for which Amenemhet had no answers. The similarities of the two kingdoms were unquestionable. Amenemhet couldn't help but ask, "How did Nefrytatanen's father come here?"

"He was curious and traveled farther than your people are inclined. His ship was accidentally caught where the currents meet, and he was brought here by the same current as you." Sahura chuckled. "When they were carried out to the open sea, they thought themselves doomed. How amazed they were to find us! While they were repairing their ship and getting supplies for the return voyage, King Tefibi-Siut asked many questions. He also met my sister, and they loved each other from the first. They were married before they left. I never saw her again, of course."

Sahura grew thoughtful, and Amenemhet sensed a great sadness in him. Slowly Sahura said, "It is possible Atalan will one day sink completely beneath these waters. The land is very unstable. It's honeycombed with volcanic tunnels, and some of the volcanoes are still active. I'm privately convinced they'll again erupt someday and destroy the island completely."

Amenemhet stared at him in horror. "What of your people?" he asked.

"If any of us escape, it would be comforting to know we could find a home, as our ancestors likely did so long ago in Tamera."

"You'd be welcome," Amenemhet answered promptly. "My children will know their family has beginnings here, that friends are here. If so terrible a day ever comes, you may enter Tamera without fear. Even if it never happens, we would welcome your visit."

Sahura smiled and grasped Amenemhet's shoulder warmly. "The words you speak, and the invitation they extend, repay many times over what we've done for you. My heart is much lighter because I'm convinced this catastrophe will happen. Neferset has prophetic dreams, usually of bad news; and she has told me many times of Atalan's doom. I hope it's only personal nightmares, but she has seldom confused one dream with another."

Amenemhet stared at the beautiful room in silence. His eyes traveled out the window opening to the landscape beyond while he thought of these things destroyed —the loss of lives.

Before they spoke again, the door opened, and they

turned to see Nefrytatanen standing on the threshold, Kheti and Neferset stood behind her, each carrying a child. Sahura didn't miss the light in Amenemhet's eyes as he looked at Nefrytatanen. Amenemhet immediately rose and went to her, brought her to his couch, and carefully seated her beside him. She smiled affectionately at his efforts.

"Beloved," she said softly, "be less worried for me and more careful you don't become dizzy. Babies are born daily, and I'm well enough."

Amenemhet looked at Kheti, who seemed completely at ease with the burden he held, and laughed. "You're more used to carrying my son than I," he said.

Kheti grinned and handed Amenemhet the child. "It's your daughter I hold—a little damply, I might add."

Looking at Maeti's face, Amenemhet was again filled with wonder at the elfin creature. Neferset gave Senwadjet to Nefrytatanen, and Amenemhet peered at his son's golden eyes, silently marveling at them.

"If you're able to distract yourself a moment," Kheti said, still smiling, "Neferset and I have some news."

A little surprised at Kheti's tone, Sahura and Amenemhet glanced from one face to another, though Nefrytatanen remained serene.

Kheti went on, his eyes soft as he spoke, "Neferset would like to sail with us." He nodded at Sahura with formal courtesy. "With your permission, we wish to be married."

Sahura shook his head slowly. "I knew I would someday lose her, and I suspected the winner would be you. That she goes so far away is an added loss. My heart, however, is filled with joy for your happiness."

Amenemhet knew Sahura was saddened that Neferset would leave Atalan, and he also knew Sahura was also relieved that she would be safe. Thinking to lighten the moment for Sahura, he said dryly, "At least Neferset is unlikely to poison me." When he saw that Sahura smiled, he added, "I'm happy for you both. Kheti, you've made a good choice. Tamera will be richer for your presence, Neferset, also even more pleasant to look at."

Neferset's eyes held green sparkles of mischief as she asked, "Would you care for a little wine, my king-to-be? I'll pour it."

They laughed without hesitation, relieved at being able to view the past without flinching.

Amenemhet said, "Yes, Neferset. A goblet of wine to wish you love—as I've found." He looked into Nefrytatanen's smiling eyes, feeling yet again the strange power they held for him, and added, " though I wonder if such love has ever been before, or can ever be again."

Looking into Amenemhet's golden eyes, Nefrytatanen silently wondered at this herself. Softly she said, "A goblet of wine—and our wish that you know increasing joy."

"Call the queen and the prince," Sahura ordered a smiling servant. "We must share this happy news with them."

Nesitaneb came quickly, followed soon after by Sarenput. Kheti repeated the announcement, and Nesitaneb embraced her daughter.

"This doesn't surprise me," Nesitaneb said, "but I'm saddened you'll leave us."

Kheti took Nesitaneb's hand. "You'll visit us," he urged.

Nefrytatanen smiled. "It's not really so far when you know the way," she said.

Sarenput, who had been silent all through this, remarked, "A ship must surely accompany you home, and I, for one, will be on it. I won't miss my sister's wedding—and I admit I'm curious to see Tamera."

Nesitaneb's relief was obvious, but she said calmly, "You may take Amset with you, Neferset, if she's willing to go."

Neferset's eyes lit. "Thank you, Mother. You knew

I'd want her, and I'm sure she'll be willing. Having Amset will be like having part of Atalan with me."

Nefrytatanen smiled. "You won't find Tamera so different. I think you'll be surprised."

"Who else will go?" Sarenput asked.

Sahura chuckled. "I think that depends on how much Neferset takes with her and what she can be persuaded to leave behind. I'd say take Susu, your own servant. And for sailors, Arek and Nehemu are the best."

Nesitaneb added quickly, "Semu will go." She turned to Amenemhet and explained, "He really is an old friend and has always regarded Neferset almost as his own daughter. If we don't let him go on this ship, he'll launch another for himself."

The preparations for the ship's departure made the next two decans a flurry of excitement. King Sahura revealed that he couldn't go because of his health, but he didn't elaborate. It was clear he and Queen Nesitaneb yearned to be included on the voyage and that only a serious problem prevented them. Amenemhet wondered what Sahura's trouble was, but he said nothing.

Kheti and Neferset briefly considered having the marriage performed in Atalan before they left, but they soon decided they would rather spend the time after their marriage on dry land together, not on a crowded ship. There was no time to dwell on sad farewells or weeping. Everyone was too busy.

On the night before the ships were to leave, Amenemhet, a sly look on his face, entered his and Nefrytatanen's room.

"I arranged to obtain something for you to take back to Tamera," he said in response to Nefrytatanen's suspicious look. "It will replace something you lost," he added. At his signal, a servant entered. She carried an armful of shimmering silver cloth.

Nefrytatanen sank to a couch in surprise, speechless. Amenemhet took the cloth from the servant and dismissed her. Then he held up the cloth, which sparkled like spray from the ocean. Softly he said, "It's an exact copy of your wedding dress. I thought you might like to have it, but if it brings you sad memories, thoughts of Sira, I'll destroy it."

"Beloved," Nefrytatanen whispered, "I cannot dwell on what Sinuhe did to Sira. I can remember only the happiness I knew when I wore the dress, and you watched me come through the temple to you."

Amenemhet smiled and whispered, "I never was able to tell you how you looked in that moment, but perhaps you realize now what I thought. I'd like to see you wear it again."

Nefrytatanen's eyes glowed as she remembered the temple and the slanting light shining on them, the flowers and the clouds of incense, Amenemhet's soft voice, and his eyes on her. Quietly she said, "I have put away the sadness and think only of the joy of that day." She took her gaze from the dress and looked at Amenemhet, promising, "When we return to Ithtawe, I'll wear it for you again."

Amenemhet laid the gown on the bed where it became a mass of twinkling stars in light of the lamp. He was smiling happily when he asked, "by that time, I expect you'll have recovered your health—I hope?"

Nefrytatanen understood his meaning, and her eyes became sapphire smoke. "Oh beloved, yes. I surely hope so."

The golden disk of the rising sun generously poured its fire over the water, and the reed swan sailed straight into the face of Ra. The last good-byes had been said, the last embraces given, and the golden light reflected on bright tears.

For the sake of balancing weight and saving emotional strain, Neferset had decided to sail with Sarenput on the Atalan ship while Kheti remained on Amenemhet's vessel.

The sails filled with wind, the lines sang, and the

calls of the seabirds seemed sad. Looking back at Atalan, Amenemhet considered what that land meant to them all. He remembered Sahura's fears and shuddered as he gazed at the receding island.

As the pearly mountains faded in the distance, Amenemhet and Nefrytatenen turned to look eastward. Ahead of them at last, and growing nearer with each tug of the sail, was home.

Nefrytatenen realized Sarenput's ship must have the same appearance as their own. Though it was greater in size, she wondered at its size compared to the ocean's vastness. The ship looked fragile, vulnerable, lonely, yet brave. It was fitting, she decided. Courage usually was a lonely thing.

Amenemhet slipped his arm around her waist and, after a time, commented, "I guess I'll have to learn from Necho how to steer, now that I can. It'll be interesting to take my turn and feel the movements of the ship." The wind blew his thick hair into little wings flying from his temple as he turned to look at her. "I think I might even enjoy this voyage," he added.

Nefrytatenen smiled and smoothed his hair. "Being able to get around may make it less boring, but after we've spent a few nights with crying babies and no privacy, you may be less enthusiastic."

"No," Amenemhet said thoughtfully, pulling her a little closer to his side, "because we're going home." He laughed softly and remarked, "I have less privacy on the way here." He looked at the horizon quietly for a time, and Nefrytatenen laid her head against his shoulder in contentment. "Although Amenardis's poison took my body for a time," he said softly, "it didn't take my mind, and I spent many hours contemplating serious subjects."

Amenemhet deliberately continued looking at the water as he said, "I spent some time thinking of dying. Dying had, of course, become real to me as it cannot be unless you face it. I wished many times to tell you not to bury me in my parents' tomb." He shivered as he thought of the mountain containing his family's burial vault. "I wish no monument after all," he said. Nefrytatanen looked at him in surprise, but he continued as if unaware of her look. "I thought of the generations to come, not those immediately following us, but those far in the future. Long after we're gone, the world may change many times over in its beliefs and customs, and I realized that those who come may be disrespectful of the dead or curious of our ways. They may not realize that our tombs are houses of silence for human beings and may look at the tombs as mere curiosities of a long-dead past. There will, no doubt, be those who are lured by the personal possessions we bury with us, and they might break into our chambers and disturb our bodies."

Nefrytatanen said nothing, but she knew he was right about the possibilities.

"If you're agreeable," he said, "I'd have both of us —or if you're not agreeable, only myself—buried differently from our customs. It's distasteful to me, in any event, to think of being handled by others, soaked in natron, preserved like a fish, and wrapped. I wish you'd only have me washed and laid in my coffin as if I'd fallen asleep and might reawaken on another day. I would have my vault sealed and carefully hidden from other eyes." He looked questionably at her.

"These sentiments are not strange to me," Nefrytatanen said slowly. "I've considered such things myself, especially when I was afraid you'd die. To hand you over to the knives of the priests was distressing to me, and I thought I would have your statue take the place of your body in the wrapping and preparations." She paused a moment and then promised, "I'll do as you say, if I outlive you. And I would have my own body laid with you in the same manner."

Amenemhet was satisfied at her agreement. He said, "If we continue to live after our bodies die, as I believe we do, we'll be gone from that place. But out of respect for this body which has served me so well,

I would wish it might be undisturbed. People touching you as though you were an object is an insult. However, if we're buried as I have it in mind to be, it's possible our names will be lost and all memory of us forgotten."

"Does that matter?" Nefrytatanen asked. "What we will do will have been done. The results will have been achieved. Hundreds or even thousands of years from now, our names would only be marks on stones that no one may know how to read. What we have now, this one moment, is all we have. Beloved, I don't care if I'm remembered by a carving on a piece of stone. Besides I've told you before that your name will live forever, though what I am will be forogtten."

"Perhaps the name of Amenemhet will appear on some list of kings someday," he said, "but Nefrytatanen will be beside it."

Nefrytatanen shook her head. "No one will know I was queen," she said, "and what does it matter? As long as you know me, what else is important?" She smiled up at him. "If you're likely to forget who I am, I'll have to make very sure to remind you often! I think I'll begin this effort the first moment we land in Ithtawe."

Amenemhet smiled faintly for a moment, but when he turned his golden eyes on her, the smile faded. "Beloved, of all the things I would regret when I die, your loss would make mine the loneliest soul in eternity."

Nefrytatanen was silent as she put her arms around him. After a moment she whispered, "I've already thought of this. I've decided it won't be so." She looked up at him solemnly. "As I have no wish for another man in this life, so have I no wish to be without you in the next life. Tuat would be no reward for me if you weren't beside me. If we're fortunate, as my mother and father were, and die together, we can go holding each other's hands to the afterworld. If the divine beings decide I'll precede you, go to the high priest, beloved, and tell him what we wish. He'll know what to do—I'll leave instructions for him. If the change should come upon you first, merely wait awhile for me. I'll work a spell for us, and I'll find you soon after."

Amenemhet stared at her in amazement. He hadn't known such things were possible.

Nefrytatanen smiled at the stunned look on his face and said, "I'll follow the path of stars you've scattered after you, and you'll hear my laughter like small, silver bells coming nearer. Never fear, beloved. The way to find you will be easy. I'll search to the uttermost corner of eternity, and I will find you."

Soon enough, the lives of the voyagers fell into a monotonous routine, though their tempers weren't as sharp as before. The thought of home sustained their serenity, this time. In idle moments, it was possible to relax on the swaying, sweet-smelling deck and look at the sky and dream happily of Ithtawe and Tamera.

Senbi had recruited Yazid to help him sort out the many notes he had made about Atalan, and they spent much of their time at this task.

The weather was so clear and perfect there was little they had to do for the ship but steer. A lively wind pushed them swiftly on their way, tossing an occasional spray of salt water, which fell, a cooling mist, over them. The sun turned their skin deep bronze. The nights were clear and filled with stars.

Nefrytatanen's energy soon returned, and with the renewal of her vitality, came other feelings.

Amenemhet and Nefrytatanen had both faced death, not only their own, but each other's, and the instinct to reaffirm and celebrate life's gift began to rise in both of them.

Amenemhet noted Nefrytatanen's lively expressions and lissome step; under his often intense looks, she instinctively found herself drawing nearer him, brushing close, compensating for their lack of privacy by being near or by touching. The small gestures gradually became, instead of compensation, a sharply growing need for more. Their awareness of each other's physical be-

ing was heightened until it obscured their other thoughts
while awake and filled their dreams while sleeping.

On one of his many sleepless nights, Amenemhet lay,
restless and lonely, looking into the clear and star-filled
sky. He had fallen asleep after a long while, thinking of
Nefrytatanen so close and, because of the others, so
impossibly far. In his dreams he ached for her but was
unable to touch her. He had awakened to continue the
aching, and he arose to walk to the bow of the ship and
watch the foam, blooming in streaks of white over the
blackness of the water, to trail behind in streamers of
small bubbles. He listened to the wind sighing in the
sail and singing in the ropes overhead.

Nefrytatanen emerged from the cabin pulling a cloak
over her sheer robe, and Amenemhet watched her
stand in restless uncertainty, as he had. Softly he called
to her, and she looked in his direction, unsurprised. She
glanced quickly around to see that everyone slept save
Senbi, who was engrossed with watching the stars and
steering. Stepping carefully in the darkness, she joined
Amenemhet who looked at her with glittering golden
points in his eyes.

He drew her against him and held her tightly for a
long while, as he enjoyed the warmth and the feel of her.
Into her hair, he finally whispered, "When we land at
Ithtawe, I'll lock us in our chamber for a decan. I'll
allow no state problems, no reports to disturb us until
I've had you to myself long enough to end this aching."

"Not since Amenardis came have we been together,"
she said softly, "except in many dreams."

"Many dreams," he murmured, "and dreams are not
enough for me." He put his mouth to hers, and caressing her lips gently a moment, he was suddenly overcome with desire and kissed her so hard and so long it
might have been painful, had she not welcomed it. The
magic he had always awakend flared within her, and he
could feel her body melting against him. Trembling,
they clung to each other in the fire they remembered so

well. The ship undulated sinuously, the moon of Aset surrounded them with silver, and the salty breeze caressed them with its warm fingers. Nefrytatanen exalted in the hard muscles of the now-healthy body that pressed hers, and all her senses sang, vibrating with his touch. Amenemhet's mind was sent spinning, throwing sparks, until he felt their figures must glow in the dark.

"Beloved," he sighed against her neck, "it has been so long—so long."

She twined her fingers in his hair and pulled his face to hers to cover it with kisses in answer. His mouth crushed hers again, and he thought he would surely die of desire. His dizzy mind traveled to each corner of the ship as he wondered if a private place might be found for them, but there was none. His need of her was so strong he couldn't find the resolve to back away but reached instead between the folds of her cloak to feel, at least, the warmth of her flesh through the sheer cotton gown.

She shivered at his touch and whispered faintly in his ear, "Is there no place we can go?"

After he kissed her again, he said softly, "Not unless we command them all to turn their backs and cover their ears."

He put his face against the curve of her throat and inhaled for a while her warm scent. Then he raised his head, and staring at her with eyes glowing gold fire, he stepped reluctantly a little away.

"If we continue this, I'll go mad," he said. "Go back to your bed and get all the sleep you can tonight and all the other nights on this ship, for, by Aset, you'll have little once we reach Tamera's shore!"

"I've already had too much of sleeping," she murmured, swaying toward him. He held her back, smiling ruefully. She sighed. "When we're in Ithtawe again I'll need no sleep for a long time" she added.

He took her hand and, laughing softly in the darkness, led her back to her blankets. "When we step off this ship," he warned, "I promise I'll take your hand and race with you to our chambers."

"It would shock those who await us," she commented. She smiled serenely and added, "But they would know for certain that we're both alive and well."

Chapter Eighteen

Although dawn had promised a fine day, it grew more apparent with the morning's passage that Ra had become uncertain. By late afternoon, the sky had turned to impenetrable grey, and, when night came, the darkness seemed to fall faster than was normal.

Necho looked at the sky and shook his head. A storm was coming. Although he said little, he wondered how the others would react. The soft rain that had fallen at Nefrytatanen's bidding was far different from what he expected to happen shortly. The water had grown still. A strange yellow glow seeping through the murky clouds gave the only light.

Amenemhet remarked on the tension in the air. Everyone felt uneasy. Even Senwadjet and Maeti were fitful and short-tempered, crying often without apparent reason.

Slowly the sea began to rise, like an animal awakening, each wave growing taller and blacker than the wave before it. Necho told Bekhet to take Nefrytatanen into the cabin and make her comfortable. Bekhet asked no questions. Looking fearful, she obeyed.

The air, which had seemed to lay heavily on their skin, suddenly became alive. It pummeled them in surprising, staggering gusts that rocked the ship crazily and sent them flying for their waist ropes.

Before Necho could give them directions, the rain began to fall so violently that they lost sight of Sarenput's ship and could hardly see each other. They fought to stand upright.

Rakkor, who had been steering alone, called desperately to Kheti for help. Yazid and Senbi, rushing to tie down the supplies more securely, arrived just in time to see most of them slide overboard. Staggering helplessly, they tumbled one way and then another.

In the cabin, Nefrytatanen and Bekhet stared at each other, growing more terrified with each shudder of the papyrus ship. Waves pounded fiercely on the back of the thatched cabin. The ship was no longer their serenely obedient bird. It became a screeching, writhing serpent, angrily struggling to rid itself of its passengers. Nefrytatanen held Senwadjet close, trying to shield him from the leaking water. Bekhet, with Maeti clasped to her breast, was pale and silent. They listened to Necho screaming orders to lower the sail.

Even Kheti and Rakkor struggling together couldn't control the ship, and Amenemhet shouted to take the steering blades from the water before they snapped off.

Finally Yazid and Senbi staggered into the cabin and stood, panting and dripping water, staring at each other, unable to disguise their terror. At last the others came through the door.

"There's nothing more we can do," Necho shouted over the noise. "We can only wait for it to end."

"Most of the supplies, and the water, have been lost!" Yazid said loudly.

"When this is over," Senbi shouted, "we can see where we are and perhaps put into shore for water and repairs. I only hope we're not blown too far off course." He was relieved they were in the Great Green Sea at this point and not in the ocean where they could be blown so far that they would wander endlessly.

"I hope the other ship is safe." Kheti looked worried. "We couldn't see it in the darkness."

Bekhet silently breathed a prayer for all of them. She was convinced this was the end.

Throughout the night the storm continued tossing the

papyrus ship like a toy. Nefrytatanen said nothing. She wondered if all their struggles would bring them to so useless an end—drowning near their destination. Amenemhet watched her for a long time then finally said close to her, "We will come through this."

She smiled hopefully to reassure him, but she was sick with fear. Amenemhet knew it. He took Senwadjet from her and gently rocked the terrified infant, thinking meanwhile of Ithtawe and its sunny halls. He looked at Senwadjet and Maeti sadly. They were now beyond crying and only stared with round eyes at this strange, uncomfortable, damp world. The wind struck the cabin with a new force, and water trickled coldly on Amenemhet's shoulder. He barely noticed it because he was looking at the others. They couldn't die now.

Waves smashed against the ship, but again and again the little swan bobbed over or through them, and up in triumph. The noise of the storm was unlike any they had heard before. Even the shrieking of the deadly desert storms seemed fainter than this. The travelers spent the night huddled together in unrelieved terror.

The rain crashing on the roof of the thatched cabin began to slow. After an eternity, it stopped. Light began to creep in tendrils through the woven walls and roof, and the travelers stood up slowly in silence, hoping this wasn't merely a pause. They were afraid to consider the possible damage to the ship or to guess where they might have been carried.

Finally Amenemhet and Kheti looked at each other. Amenemhet gave Senwadjet to Nefrytatanen and he and Kheti stepped cautiously outside.

Kheti's joyous cry burst forth almost immediately. "They're waving! They're safe! It's over!"

Nefrytatanen, hair dripping in her eyes, gave Senwadjet to Yazid and was next out the door. She couldn't believe the sight before her. Amenemhet took her hand and said softly, "We're almost home."

The silver-gold fire of dawn sparkling on the wet papyrus turned the Atalan ship to crystal. Purple clouds were glowing red and gold at their edges in a sky lit once again by the sun. The Nile was before them, and they watched Sarenput's ship glide unhesitantly into it. Shafts of sunlight broke through openings in the clouds, sending transparent columns of pale gold to touch the sea. The others, now grouped behind Amenemhet and Nefrytatanen, stared at the shore, speechlessly beholding the welcome the divine beings had arranged for their homecoming.

"How are we alive?" Yazid finally said in wonderment.

"We needn't worry about fresh water now," Amenemhet said softly, "for we've been blown to our own sweet Nile."

Necho laughed with relief and delight. "We'll be home tomorrow," he said. He leaped to the cabin roof and Kheti followed him to help put up the sail. Immediately, the wind filled it, and the little ship leaped forward, just behind the Atalan ship.

Bekhet pointed toward the shore. "Look!" she cried. "We've been seen!"

A group of people on the bank were shouting and waving at them. Farther in the distance more people were running toward the shore. Amenemhet climbed to the top of the cabin and ran up the banner of the Royal House. The people on the shore shouted at them, and someone on a horse raced south toward Ithtawe.

"They'll know we're coming now," Amenemhet said smiling widely. He dropped lightly to the deck.

Throughout the day people continued running along the shore, waving to them; during the night, bonfires winked cheerfully from the darkness. Finally Amenemhet urged Nefrytatanen to lie down and get what sleep was possible before dawn came. She obeyed but lay awake with sparkling eyes, thinking of morning and Ithtawe: home.

As the papyrus ship approached Ithtawe's moorings, pulling beside the Atalan ship, a great roar rose from the waiting crowd. Flowers and fragrant leaves showered

over the decks of the royal ship and the Atalan ship.
When Bekhet, smiling with triumph, raised Maeti high,
urging Yazid to show them Senwadjet, the noise was
deafening. Trumpeters on the top of Ithtawe's walls
lifted their golden instruments and announced the return
of Tamera's rulers. From every direction, bells chimed.

When Nefrytatanen felt the ship gently bump the
quay, her heart leaped. She could hardly restrain herself
from leaping onto the solid ground.

"We are home," Nefrytatanen whispered, "—home."

Smiling, Amenemhet took her hand and helped her
off the ship. Tamera was beneath their feet at last. They
straightened to look at Ithtawe. Nefrytatanen felt she
could throw herself on the ground before it. She looked
at Amenemhet and saw the same impulse shining in his
face. Amenemhet looked down at Nefrytatanen, and
another light began to fill his eyes. She stared at him in
shock. He smiled, and his eyes began to glitter. He took
her hand firmly in his, and as the crowd parted for them
he began to walk quickly toward Ithtawe's gates.

Amenemhet barely nodded to Meri, who stood ready
to welcome them. Meri looked after them, startled that
they had passed without a word. Amenemhet marched
past the soldiers, past Seti, Ankhneferu, the noblemen
and their ladies, all the crowd—with Nefrytatanen
hurrying to keep pace with him. She took an undignified
little skip with each step, almost running, and he
smiled at her again—but didn't slow his stride. As Nefrytatanen's amazement subsided, she began to smile,
though she was breathless. Guards opened the doors at
Amenemhet's impatient signal, and the bewildered
crowd watched their king and queen march from sight.

Only when the doors had closed behind them did
Amenemhet pause and look again at Nefrytatanen. For
a moment they stood smiling into each other's eyes.
Then they laughed. Hand in hand, like children in a
contest, they raced down the hall to their private apartments. Slamming the door behind them, they paused
in their room. Amenemhet joyously threw his arms

around Nefrytatanen. They stood holding each other
and trying to catch their breath, laughing.

Meri's cautious voice came through the door. "Sire,
when will you hear our reports? There's much trouble!"

Amenemhet took Nefrytatanen's face in both hands
and, looking intently into her now darkened and smoky
eyes, cried, "Tomorrow, Meri, tomorrow!"

Meri's footsteps slowly faded away, but Amenemhet
was covering Nefrytatanen's face with kisses and neither
of them heard him.

Chapter Nineteen

Amenemhet awakened with the early sunlight on his face, and the garden's fragrance pouring through the room. His golden eyes traveled over the room to rest on Nefrytatenen standing by the doors. Her naked body was silhouetted against the light, every curve outlined in sunshine. She stood in profile, and he watched her breasts rise and fall gently. Her black hair falling to her hips gleaming in the light, and he lay thinking of the silken feel of it spread over his chest in the night. His eyes followed each curve of her, and he could feel again the softness of her skin. Her lips moved soundlessly; he realized she gave welcome to Ra, even as he thought of those lips pressed to his, warm and eager and hungry as his own. Her eyes closed, and he recalled their dark and smoky blue color.

All of yesterday and last night, since they had landed at Ithtawe's moorings, they had been locked in their chambers as if they were newly married, making love in a burst of emotion finally set free after so long a time restrained. As Amenemhet watched Nefrytatenen he found himself wanting her again. As if she concurred, she turned from the doorway and came to him. Saying nothing, she sat on the edge of the bed, as unconscious of her nakedness as a bird of its wings or a flower of its petals. She lay across his chest and kissed him with such passion that the day and night just past might never have been. He put his arms around her and she drew her

325

legs onto the bed to entangle with his. They entered again their private realm of love.

When she lay against his side, and her racing heart and quickened breath had slowed, he held her close to him with great tenderness. "Beloved," Amenemhet murmured, "we will have to rise soon. Meri is still waiting."

"Yes," Nefrytatanen sighed, "I'm sure he's paced the floor all night, mentally enumerating all the troubles he'll relate to us. But, my beloved, how I wish to stay here close to your heart!"

After a moment he chuckled softly. "Think of poor Kheti and Neferset. They're still waiting for their wedding and the fulfillment of their love. Perhaps it will be easier to face our trying duties if we remember the happy one of arranging their wedding and celebration."

"I'm selfish, beloved," she whispered. "Even their plight finds me reluctant to leave your side." She stretched slowly, like a cat, not moving away from him, and he could feel the silken movement of her muscles.

"There will be tonight." Amenemhet smiled. "And all the days and nights to follow." He patted her buttocks playfully. "Get up, my little spell-caster," he coaxed.

Nefrytatanen's eyes turned to him, and he couldn't resist kissing her and holding her tightly one more moment. Then they rose slowly. Signaling for Yazid and Bekhet, they wrapped each other in their robes and waited hand in hand.

After washing and dressing as slowly as possible and dawdling over the morning meal as long as could be done without being too conspicuous, Amenemhet and Nefrytatanen finally could not put Meri off any longer. Before they entered the room where they would receive him, they paused and took a deep breath. Then, sighing, they went in. He was not there. Though they were surprised, they used the extra time to inspect the newly finished room.

Where they had left rough stone walls, they now saw white limestone panels; where the floors had been unfinished wood planks, now they were smoothly shining ebony covered with rugs of red, gold, and black. Instead of cloth window hangings, the openings were covered with white reeds woven into latticed designs allowing the sun to enter in lacy patterns. The crimson couches were covered with pillows of animal skins— tawny gold and black spotted furs, long, silky-textured black fur, shaggy white skins, short-haired white and black striped hides. The wood in the room was ebony, trimmed with gold and inlaid with deep-toned amber.

Amenemhet and Nefrytatanen had settled themselves on a couch when Meri entered. He seemed surprised to see them waiting, as if he had concluded they would never arrive. His perpetual frown grew even deeper now. He hadn't been joking when he had said there was grave trouble. He didn't know where to begin.

"Come in, Meri," Nefrytatanen said, smiling. Meri thought that if she knew what he had to tell her, she wouldn't smile so warmly.

"Sit down, Meri, and tell us what you have to tell," Amenemhet said, his eyes glowing with humor as if he had read Meri's mind. "I know the news isn't good, so begin where you will."

"Ithtawe was completed while you were gone." Meri thought he might begin with something happy. "I hope you find it to your liking."

"We do," Nefrytatanen answered enthusiastically. "From what we've seen of it so far, we're well pleased."

"Thank you," said Meri politely. "I'll tell the workers you're satisfied, and they'll be happy." He looked at Amenemhet, who was smiling slightly, waiting patiently for the pleasantries to be over. Meri wished the task of relating the worst news didn't always have to fall on him. He took a deep breath and began, "The surveying hasn't been completed. In fact, it's been stopped."

Amenemhet was dumbfounded. Nefrytatanen stared. Meri wished fervently he could go away on an excursion, very far in some direction—any direction.

"Why? Why was the surveying stopped?" Amenem-het demanded.

"That's the least of it, sire." Meri's stomach felt terri-ble, and his head ached.

"Tell us all of it, whichever way is best." Amenemhet now settled back with an expression of resignation. But as he heard Meri's hurried description of the state of the kingdom, he sat up stiffly again.

"Some of the noblemen continue to quibble over every measurement made which has caused no end of trouble. Furthermore, the thieves have returned in even greater quantities, and even the surveyors are afraid of them. They've harassed the farmers, who have had to contend with a low flood besides, and the crops are poor, very poor. I truly fear a famine. And there is also the matter of a priestess who has gained a large following and has used these disturbances and her own seductiveness—which I understand is considerable—to gain power. Even now, Ankhneferu is anxious to dis-cuss this with you."

Amenemhet stood up and walked back and forth, dis-gusted. "Have we been attacked by the Hyksos again?" he asked.

"No, but they haven't forgotten us," Meri admitted.

"It's a marvel that Ithtawe was finished and that we have a roof over our heads," Amenemhet muttered sar-castically. He looked at Nefrytatanen. "I'll have to see them all, and it will, no doubt, take the rest of the morn-ing to hear the reports." He shook his head.

"I would stay with you, beloved," Nefrytatanen said, "but I must be with the children for a time. Will you need me?"

"I'll see what can be done this morning," he said. Suddenly he smiled. "I'll keep in my mind the picture of you with Senwadjet and Maeti. I can soothe myself with that when I get too upset. I'll come for the noon meal with you; while everyone is resting, I can relate what has happened."

As Nefrytatanen rose, she stood close to Amenemhet

and squeezed his hand encouragingly. He brushed her cheek with his lips and whispered, "Don't worry about coming back this morning. All this will be untangled eventually."

"I know," she murmured. "We'll solve it somehow." When she left, she considered all the new problems with disgust. How she had hoped they would have some peace together!

When Nefrytatanen entered the nursery, Bekhet and Dedjet looked up from their handwork. Bekhet sensed that Meri had given his report.

Nefrytatanen sighed. "We seem never to have any peace, so Amenemhet and I can relax and enjoy our family."

Bekhet said, "It is a pleasant thought, my lady."

As Dedjet laid Senwadjet in Nefrytatanen's arms, she smiled and remarked wistfully, "However many are the troubles that plague you, my lady, others would take them gladly to have a loving man and such beautiful children as you have."

Nefrytatanen looked at the girl, a little surprised. Dedjet was usually reticent with her despite her own friendliness.

"You're right, Dedjet. I'm fortunate and shouldn't complain." Nefrytatanen smiled at the servant and then lifted her golden-eyed son to gently rub noses with him. "I am very fortunate," she said softly.

Bekhet answered a soft tap at the door. Neferset entered, followed by Sarenput and Semu. Neferset walked quickly to Dedjet and, smiling, took Maeti from her.

"I'm sorry we haven't paid more attention to you," apologized Nefrytatanen, a little embarrassed. "It's not at all hospitable to ignore guests as we have."

"We can understand this." Sarenput smiled faintly. "You have many matters to attend to."

Neferset was less tactful than her brother, and her eyes sparkled as she said, "Oh yes, many matters of great importance."

Nefrytatanen smiled faintly at Neferset's thinly disguised humor. "Amenemhet is now confering with Meri and some others about what's happened in our absence," Nefrytatanen said. "I don't know how long it will take him, but I suspect he'll be busy all day. What have you been occupying yourself with meantime?"

Sarenput was serious. "I've discovered your library and I've spent my time reading about Tamera. I hope I haven't presumed."

"Feel free to read all you like." Nefrytatanen put Senwadjet in Bekhet's arms. "If knowledge isn't shared, it means little." She turned to Semu. "Have you also been reading, or have you found other ways to pass the time?"

"I've been acquainting myself with Ithtawe and its grounds."

"I've spent my time waiting," Neferset remarked pointedly.

"Kheti, too, is no doubt busy." Nefrytatanen considered the matter. "We'll have to begin making arrangements for the wedding despite all the problems we're suddenly faced with. You'll want to be married here?"

Neferset's eyes grew soft as she thought of it. "If that's an invitation, I would like it very much. I'm sorry if I was rude." Neferset looked down in embarrassment. "I can't help but be anxious."

"Of course you're anxious!" Nefrytatanen declared. "Who wouldn't be? I'll talk about it with Amenemhet. We'll have to do something about this immediately. Neferset, you and I will plan it together. You'll enjoy it." Secretly, Nefrytatanen didn't look forward to this chore, but she hoped she smiled convincingly.

"I'm so excited at the idea I can hardly contain myself!" Neferset's immediately radiant face brushed aside Nefrytatanen's gloomy anticipation of organizing so complicated an event. She saw Sarenput's smile at his sister and resolved that plans must be made at once.

"Let them in," Amenemhet muttered gloomily as soon as Nefrytatanen had left. He felt as if she had taken the sun with her. As he watched Ankhneferu, Nessumontu, Kheti, Rakkor, and Semerkhet troop in, his eyes were wary. He realized Meri's explanation of the problems hadn't been exaggerated. Their expressions confirmed Meri's report.

"You may as well admit Taka and Hera too," Amenemhet said. "We can discuss the whole muddle together." Meri opened the door again, and Taka and Hera entered, also wearing worried faces. "Sit down, all of you," Amenemhet grumbled. "It looks as if this will take some time. Ankhneferu, you tell me first about this priestess."

The high priest's eyes were cold as he began. "Kuwait has the instincts of an actress, the beauty of a leopard, and the heart of a viper. She's obsessed with power, and she's very clever."

"She sounds like a paragon of something or other," Amenemhet remarked sarcastically. "Why do you say these things?"

Ankhneferu's anger showed clearly. "She's a paragon of evil! A flower whose outward beauty hides a venomous insect in its heart. She's used the misfortunes of the day to gain stature. She's turned the temple service into a personal display, dancing in a way calculated to draw male followers. I know she accepts large payments for private consultations with the richest of them. 'Private consultations' she calls it," Ankhneferu sneered. "I tried to reason with her, and she ignored me. I reprimanded her, and she laughed. I could do nothing in your absence, and she knew it and used the time to gain all she could. She degrades the temple. She's an acute embarrassment. To denounce her now and throw her out would shake the confidence of the genuinely faithful. They would wonder how she could get this far if she's a fake. She wouldn't go quietly, and, after what Sinuhe did, the priesthood already has too much to live down. To list her alliances publicly would cause many di-

vorces, mostly in high places." Amenemhet raised his
eyebrows at this. Ankhneferu finished, "The scandals
would rock the kingdom."

Amenemhet ran his hand through his hair, perplexed.
"Perhaps I'll have to pay a quiet visit to the temple and
see what she does. In the meantime, perhaps I can find
out more details about the people involved with her.
I'll think about it, Ankhneferu. I'd like you to give me
a list of the names of some of her friends, if you can.
Of course this must be kept absolutely confidential."

Amenemhet looked at Hera, who had sat waiting
patiently, staring at his feet. "Hera, tell me why you've
stopped measuring the boundaries," he said.

Hera looked up, startled, his darkly tanned face
flushing with embarrassment. "My hands are tied, sire,"
he exclaimed. "The lords argue with every measurement
we take. They have, on some occasions, come out to
the area where my crew is working to argue right on the
site of our work. Sire, if these measurements are to be
accurate, they require some concentration. How can we
concentrate on our work if we must listen to them argue
and sometimes even get embroiled in it ourselves? Also
my men are afraid to venture to more remote areas because of bandits. No noblemen bother us in these places
because they're safe at home behind their walls. But the
bandits are like a horde of locusts! We've been attacked
on several occasions. I realize Nessumontu can't have
his men everywhere, but we've become afraid, truly!
We carry only our supplies and the equipment for our
work, but the thieves seem to believe we have valuable
articles and stalk us!"

Amenemhet looked at Nessumontu. "What of these
bandits? Are they so terrible?"

The military commander answered softly, "I've never
seen so many." Nessumontu's slanting eyes, which had
always reminded Amenemhet of a wolf's, were gleaming orange with controlled anger. "They're like flies—
and they're bold. I have patrols returning weekly, telling of sighting bands and often pursuing them. It's not

unusual when they return with bodies: when there's combat, it's difficult to get them alive."

Amenemhet was silent a moment as he absorbed this news. He finally said grimly, "Although I dislike such displays, any of them now captured alive—and I ask you to make a special effort to get them alive—will be questioned carefully and then executed publicly in the nearest town, village, or crossing to warn others I won't allow the continuation of lawlessness. Perhaps this will help reassure the people that something is being done."

Amenemhet paused to think a moment. He said, "I know we're barely touching the top layers of these problems, but I'm anxious to hear all of you now because I want to get a general view. We can talk in detail later." He turned to Taka. "Tell me about the problems of the farmers. Is there real danger of famine?"

The look on Taka's lined face would have been answer enough, but Taka began to describe the farmers' plight. "The flood was low. While fighting locusts and other pesty insects and chasing hippopotami from the fields, the farmers have been beset with the additional distraction of fighting off these robbers. . . ." Taka continued to give his disgusted king more details.

Nefrytatanen delayed the noon meal for Amenemhet until the dishes grew cold. Then she left their apartment and approached the library. Standing silently outside the door, she could hear them talking. She listened a moment then, shaking her head, slipped away. Meeting Yazid in the hall, she told him to see that a meal was served to all of them without disturbing their meeting and to give Amenemhet a message that she would talk with him later.

Amenemhet was surprised when the trays were carried in. He had forgotten the time and realized only now that Nefrytatanen had been waiting.

Leaning close to Amenemhet, Yazid whispered. "The queen sent these to you so you wouldn't be interrupted. She said she'd talk with you later."

Amenemhet was relieved to know that Nefrytatanen wasn't angry with his forgetfulness, and he was grateful for the food she had sent. As deeply engrossed as he had been with the reports, he had heard his stomach grumbling. From the look of the others, it was evident they had made the same discovery.

While they ate they relaxed somewhat. As he finished, Semerkhet said, "I think we've loaded enough troubles on the king's head for now. Perhaps we'd all have clearer minds if we returned to this discussion tomorrow."

"That's an excellent suggestion, Semerkhet," Amenemhet quickly agreed. "My head is spinning." He turned hopefully to Meri, anticipating spending what was left of the afternoon with Nefrytatanen. "There's nothing else of immediate importance to occupy me now?"

Without hesitation Meri trampled Amenemhet's hopes. "There are a number of ambassadors waiting to see you. Perhaps it would be a change of pace to receive them now?"

Amenemhet was sarcastic. "It will be a great pleasure that will surely refresh my mind and body." He gloomily poured another goblet of wine. "I'll see them in the throne room as soon as I can drag myself there," he said. "Advise the queen of this so she can be present if she's able." He stood up and walked with the others to the door. "I'll see you tomorrow about the same time," he confirmed.

Amenemhet walked slowly to his dressing room where Yazid was ready with a red and gold robe. Amenemhet sighed, thinking the garment ought to be splendid enough to impress the ambassadors even if his somber expression wasn't. Yazid put the double crown on Amenemhet's head and, without a word, handed him his scepters.

As Amenemhet stepped into the hall, he nearly bumped into Nefrytatanen. She, too, wore the double crown and a robe of gold and crimson. He smiled. "If they aren't overimpressed with my quick and witty remarks, I doubt it will matter," Amenemhet commented, "because they'll have their minds on you anyway."

Nefrytatanen laughed. "I thought it was time I gave you some help," she replied.

"The ambassadors can wait a moment longer," Amenemhet said suddenly. "I want to visit Senwadjet and Maeti." He turned at their door.

"They're sleeping," she warned, as they entered the room.

Amenemhet stood over them, looking first at one, then at the other. He whispered, smiling, "I hope someday I'll be able to see them when they're awake or they'll grow up without recognizing their own father."

"They'll know you," Nefrytatanen whispered.

Amenemhet laid down his scepters and, turning to Nefrytatanen, put his arms around her. "Did I say, only this morning, that we'd have time to ourselves? I think I should have stayed with you behind locked doors."

As lightly as he kissed her, they found themselves drawing closer and clinging to each other, and he stepped away with glowing eyes. "We'd better go to the throne room now," he said, "or I won't go at all."

"I wouldn't mind that," she said putting her cheek again next to his.

"A fine queen you are," Amenemhet mumbled in good humor. "You would let the ambassadors wait and the whole kingdom fall apart while we stand around kissing."

"Only if I have *you* to kiss," Nefrytatanen laughed. She handed him his scepters. Holding her own scepters formally crossed over her heart, a haughty look on her face; she was suddenly queen. "Shall we proceed?" she asked icily. Abruptly the coolness melted into merriness. "Do you think I can fool them into thinking I'm concentrating on royal business?" she asked.

From the noise they heard even before they reached the doors, Amenemhet and Nefrytatanen knew the throne room was filled with people. Trumpets announced them, and they quickly glanced over each other in the hall, making sure they had forgotten nothing.

As Amenemhet and Nefrytatanen paced toward the dais, they passed people of all sizes, shapes, and colors, clothed in the variety of fashions from their lands. Next to the gracefully draped togas of blond-haired representatives from Troy stood the stocky, dark-complexioned Hyksos and the Babylonians with their long, elaborately curled beards; the simply dressed, slender Minoans clustered near heavily-jeweled Phoenicians and elegant representatives from Ur. Bright robes on the black-skinned ambassadors from Kush, competed with the jeweled capes of Far East representatives and fur-trimmed garments on nobles from the north. There were the hawk-eyed, sharp-featured sand-dwellers in white burnooses and somber bearded representatives from Retenú.

Amenemhet took special notice of some unfamiliar faces and, particularly, of a whole group from the Far East he had never seen before. The face of their leader was serenely lined with age, his robe a complicated arrangement of elaborately embroidered silk. Those who accompanied him were more plainly dressed and possessed a look of fierceness.

Amenemhet noticed one man from Troy with beautifully symmetrical features and a body to rival even a Tameran athlete's. He was boldly inspecting Nefrytatanen, who ignored him as she glided past. Amenemhet did not fail to note that the Hyksos ambassador didn't seem overjoyed at the king's obvious good health. And the Hyksos, also, looked at Nefrytatanen with exceedingly warm eyes. Amenemhet felt his neck grow hot with anger. He thought contemptuously that the Hyksos might well look because Hyksos women wore many layers of clothing to hide their clumsy and ungraceful bodies. Before sitting Amenemhet glanced at Nefrytatanen to confirm her cool and regal expression. Filled with pride at her poise, he thought she looked like an untouchable goddess placed among barbarians.

Meri, who had begun to look weary, came forward to call the Hyksos delegation. The one with bold eyes was introduced as Gobryas, their ambassador. Gobryas bowed before Amenemhet, expressing little respect, and, looking over Nefrytatanen again, gave his greeting. Nefrytatanen leveled her sapphire eyes on him coldly. She was as silent as a statue.

Quietly Amenemhet said, "My wife is queen, not consort. She will be greeted as ruler also, and not ignored." His golden gaze was brilliant with anger.

"Forgive me, most beautiful of all queens," Gobryas said in a deliberately sarcastic tone. He knew well enough who she was. She was his old enemy.

No smile or hint of one was in Nefrytatanen's eyes as she stared at Gobryas and answered sharply, "You are forgiven, Gobryas, considering how rarely you meet a queen."

The ambassador from Troy raised his eyebrows at this. The Hyksos's dark face flushed with anger, but, smiling like a crocodile, he turned to Amenemhet. "I've been instructed to bring you my king's congratulations on your recovery and on the birth of your son."

Amenemhet rose, looking at Gobryas with menace. He said softly, "Let us have no pretense, Hyksos. You've come to confirm that I'm still alive and to see how strong Tamera is. You can see that I'm in excellent health and that the queen and I have complete charge of the Two Lands. Go and tell your king we're no easy prey for his ambitions. The hawk of Heru lives, and the double crown is safe. The banners of Ithtawe and Tamera fly proudly, and the walls are firm. If your king looks for lands to conquer, he'd be wise to look elsewhere."

Gobryas stared, taken by surprise. He had anticipated the usual diplomatic maneuvering. His dark eyes burned hot with this public humiliation. He gave no answer to Amenemhet but turned away, his short beard almost quivering with rage. The rest of the Hyksos delegation followed him to the door, where, at Amen-

emhet's signal, the crossed spears of Nessumontu's men
stopped them. They turned slowly back toward Amenemhet and Nefrytatanen, hands on their swords.

The room was so quiet that, although Amenemhet
spoke softly, his voice was clearly heard by them all.
In a falsely pleasant tone, he said, "To assure your safe
return to your country, Gobryas, Nessumontu will send
an escort with you as far as the border. The guards are
waiting for you now."

Gobryas glared at this additional insult. He knew very
well that Amenemhet was little concerned with his
health and safety but wanted everyone to know he
trusted them so little he was assuring their immediate
and direct departure over Tamera's border. The Hyksos
looked at each other furiously. With all the others
watching and with the spears before them and more
ready in the hall outside, they had no choice but to
obey. They turned to stalk angrily out of the throne
room.

Amenemhet smiled slightly and whispered to Meri,
"Next bring that Trojan here, the one who looks at the
queen so boldly."

Although the Trojan seemed unruffled by Amenemhet's aggressive treatment of the Hyksos delegation, his
manner was subdued as he approached and formally
saluted Amenemhet and Nefrytatanen.

"Greetings from Troy, King Amenemhet and Queen
Nefrytatanen," he said pointedly. "King Melanpus sends
congratulations and all good wishes. He'll be pleased to
know you're both in good health and seem to have matters under control." He smiled slightly at his own words
and added, "I also bring a gift from him." He signaled
an aide who handed him a beautifully carved box. Meri
took it and passed it to Amenemhet who opened it
and gave it to Nefrytatanen. It contained a large gold
medallion in the design of a sunburst. It was beautifully
carved.

"We understand you hold the sun in great reverence

in your religion," the Trojan said, "and we hope this small gift is appropriate."

Amenemhet looked thoughtfully at him, thinking that this Trojan was exceedingly courteous and respectful and might be forgiven for staring so boldly at Nefrytatanen. Amenemhet had heard of the frequent scandals in Troy caused by their reckless appreciation of beauty. Too, Amenemhet concluded, it was difficult not to stare at Nefrytatanen.

Amenemhet said, "Our religion is considerably more complicated than that, but the gift is most appropriate. I'll send a message to King Melanpus thanking him for his generosity. We are pleased with his gift." Amenemhet paused a moment then asked, "What is your name? I haven't seen you here before, have I?"

"I have just been appointed," the Trojan replied. "My name is Acetes."

"You're welcome here," Amenemhet said, "as long as you wish to stay. Before you return to Troy, request an audience with us so I may give you a message for King Melanpus and also a gift for him."

Recognizing his dismissal, Acetes inclined his head and moved back to a place where he could stare at Nefrytatanen less conspicuously. He hadn't missed the look of warning in Amenemhet's eyes.

The representative from the Far East was summoned next. The man in the beautiful silk robes came forward to bow with elegant courtesy. He was so small in stature, he had to tilt his head up to look into Amenemhet's face. When he spoke in his strangely accented language, it was through an interpreter.

"We heard of your poisoning," he said, "and I came with a possible antidote to find you already well, for which I'm most happy. I humbly apologize for my tardiness, but it was necessary to travel very far, and I came as quickly as possible." At the end of his speech, the Oriental bowed again.

"You certainly have traveled far," Amenemhet said, greatly impressed. "To undertake so long a journey to help someone you don't even know is no small gesture. I'm very grateful. While you're in Tamera, I invite you to stay at Ithtawe as my guest, if you wish."

"That is most generous of you," the man replied after the interpreter had translated Amenemhet's invitation. "We can stay only a few days before we must return. As a humble token of our good wishes, I offer you this carving." From somewhere in his complicated garments, he produced a small statue, gracefully carved from pale green stone. He handed it to Meri and bowed again. Then he explained, "She's our goddess of inner tranquillity. Whenever your mind is anxious and your thoughts seem scattered, take the statue and handle it. The stone she's carved from has soothing qualities and will give you serenity."

Amenemhet took the statue from Meri and admired its exquisite workmanship. The goddess had so peaceful an expression, Amenemhet thought, that merely looking at her face long enough might calm a troubled heart. He thanked the delicate-looking little man sincerely. The ambassador smiled faintly and, once again, carefully bowed then moved silently away on his soft, silken slippers.

Amenemhet passed the fragile statue to Nefrytatanen and whispered, "Keep this little goddess within easy reach. I think we'll find her useful."

Thinking again of Senwadjet and Maeti, Nefrytatanen told Amenemhet she must leave the court. He stood up as she rose, and Meri announced to the crowd that she had to attend to other matters.

Nefrytatanen paused by Amenemhet before leaving and said softly, "I probably won't be able to come back, though I'd like to. This certainly isn't the dull session I'd expected." She smiled. "If I don't return, I'll wait for you, whenever you finish. I'll be anxious to hear about the rest."

Glancing at the roomful of people, all straining to hear, Amenemhet whispered, "It isn't necessary for you to come back unless you really want to."

"I can see you handle them easily without my help," she replied, "perhaps more easily if I'm not present."

"Your absence might make their minds turn more quickly to business," he observed casually.

The waiting ambassadors and their delegations were a little startled by Nefrytatanen's soft laugh as she pressed Amenemhet's hand and left, her eyes dancing merrily. Amenemhet, however, noticed Acetes's clear eyes follow Nefrytatanen as she disappeared through the side door.

When Amenemhet had finally finished his audience with the ambassadors, the time for the evening meal was long ago passed. He gave Yazid his heavy crown and scepters and, dismissing him, walked alone to the royal chambers.

Senbi turned a corner and walked ahead of Amenemhet with long strides. He was carrying an armload of scrolls. Amenemhet called out to him, and, turning quickly, Senbi dropped a scroll. Struggling to pick it up with his arms full, he dropped two more. Amenemhet retrieved them, and replaced them on the stack in Senbi's arms.

"Thank you," Senbi said, more than a little embarrassed that his king bent to pick up his burdens.

"Are you making progress sorting the information you gathered in Atalan?" Amenemhet asked as he began to walk with him slowly.

"Some progress," Senbi replied, "but if I had more knowledge, I could make more sense of what I brought back. I'm not a mathematician, nor do I know much about chemistry. This makes it difficult to interpret many things. I'm afraid I'll miss something important in my ignorance."

"Let me look at some of this," Amenemhet suggested. "I'm very curious about how much they know that we do not."

They entered a room where Senbi dumped the scrolls on a large table. He began to straighten them out, and Amenemhet picked one up, unrolling it. After some time looking at it, turning it slowly, stopping from time to time to read details, he put it down and chose another.

"Horemheb could be helpful with the information concerning chemistry," Amenemhet commented. "His knowledge of chemistry is second only to his knowledge of medicine." He studied yet another fat scroll.

Amenemhet spent some time looking and reading, and Senbi wondered how much Amenemhet really understood. But his question was quickly answered for, at regular intervals, Amenemhet made comments that demonstrated he understood as much as Senbi did.

Finally Amenemhet straightened and stretched with weariness. "Why don't you also consult with Meri on the people who could help you with these?" he suggested. "I can see why you need assistance. Tell Meri I told you to ask him." Amenemhet sighed. "I'm going to my room now to rest."

"I'm curious. You seem to know so much about these," Senbi said. "If you don't mind my saying so, I wasn't aware that you were interested in these subjects."

Amenemhet smiled. "I'm interested in many things. My father sent me to Anu, just as you went. He wanted me to learn as much as I could absorb before I took the throne." Amenemhet seemed to travel backwards in time as he said softly, still smiling, "I plagued my parents with many questions from the time I could first talk. At the time they decided to send me to Anu, they thought it a wise change because I was becoming too involved with a certain girl." He turned to walk slowly to the door and then stopped to look at Senbi with mischief in his eye. "Anu did distract me from that girl. There are many lovely ladies at Anu."

Senbi smiled. "Yes," he agreed, "and they are distracting."

"I think I'd better leave now," Amenemhet said, "or another certain lady will think I'm never coming back." He yawned.

"You must be very tired," Senbi said. "I've delayed you, and I'm sorry."

"I delayed myself. Those scrolls are very interesting, but my eyes are seeing double. Have a good night," Amenemhet said and left Senbi to his task.

Nefrytatanen had waited for Amenemhet long after all sounds in the halls had ceased. When he entered their chamber, he looked very weary. He dropped into a couch and sighed. Nefrytatanen bent to kiss his forehead, and he smiled up at her. Then he sighed in pleasure and humped his back like a cat while she rubbed his neck and shoulders.

As he ate almond cakes and drank warm milk, he related the troubles he had heard that day. Then he said, "Kheti didn't mention the wedding, but his face looks a little strained. I suppose he's afraid it will be delayed."

Nefrytatanen laughed. "I spoke to our guests from Atalan this morning. When I asked what they'd been doing, Neferset remarked most pointedly that she'd spent her time waiting. I assured her we'd make immediate arrangements for the wedding."

"I'll be glad to have that off my mind." Amenemhet took a deep breath. "I'll send Kheti up the river to see if his new house is ready to receive him and his bride. If he takes three days to get there and three to return, will ten days be enough time for you?"

"I'll manage it," Nefrytatanen said firmly, though she shuddered, remembering the intricate details of her own wedding. She wondered how she could do it, but she kept that thought to herself, whispering, "Go to your bath, beloved. You'll be better able to sleep."

As she watched Amenemhet walk slowly from the room, she resolved she would arrange the wedding without troubling him, however desperate she grew.

When Amenemhet returned, he was so relaxed he fell asleep even as he lay in her arms kissing her good night. Sighing, Nefrytatanen pushed their headrests aside and adjusted the pillows more comfortably, careful not to disturb him. Then she lay a long while thinking of their troubles. Finally her eyes closed with weariness.

His initial exhaustion worn off, Amenemhet awakened in the night and couldn't fall asleep again. He lay listening to the silence of the palace, which was broken at intervals by the regular tread of the guards through the halls. Amenemhet was still tired and knew that he would need a clear head to face the next day. Thoughts buzzed through his mind like a swarm of bees. He could neither sort them out nor stop them. Over him hung vivid pictures of thieves attacking the helpless peasants. He shuddered. Did his people really sleep locked up in their houses? Although he realized he could do nothing for them at this particular moment, he couldn't put their terror from his mind.

He decided to get up for a breath of night air. Moving slowly so Nefrytatanen wasn't disturbed, he got to his feet. For a moment he stood looking at the lines of her body beneath the light covering. Then he silently moved around the bed to her side.

Sitting back on his heels, his face on a level with hers, he looked at the black hair spread over her bare shoulders, a lock flowing over the edge of the bed. Gently he brushed his fingertips against it, gazing at her peaceful expression.

How beautiful she is, he thought, even with no cosmetics on her face and her hair all disarranged, the fans of her black lashes spread against her cheeks, the soft mouth slightly open and relaxed in slumber. Remembering the fiery anger in her eyes when he had lain poisoned, he marveled at how serene she looked now.

Amenemhet began to feel cramped, and he stood up carefully. He stepped out on the terrace. The stones were cool and smooth. He looked out over the courtyard and past the walls toward the Nile, which was a pale golden ribbon in the moonlight. His gaze traveled to the far horizon, climbed into the stars beyond, and swept across the breadth of the sky until he looked above the palace, wondering at the beauty of the night. He considered the possibilities of building a pyramid of his own, nearby. Then, when his current troubles were over, he could learn more about the heavens.

Did his fatigued brain deceive him, or did he see again the double stars? They were there! The blue stars streaking from beyond the palace room suddenly swung in an arc over him—higher and higher. He tilted his head to watch them ascend into the blackness. In an instant they had vanished. What was this thing? What were these stars that followed no prescribed pattern unlike all the rest? He touched the silver lotus with its blue stone glowing on his chest. What omen was this now?

Amenemhet remembered that, before, the stars had come from the north, just as Nefrytatanen had come from the north. Now they had risen over Ithtawe. He mused. Here was where Nefrytatanen was sleeping. Did the stars foretell the ascent of their personal fortunes? It was peculiar, he decided, that the stars seemed connected with Nefrytatanen, but it was only he who saw them. He wished Nefrytatanen could see them because they were a beautiful sight. Doubtless, he thought, neither he nor anyone else would view them again. To have seen them once was marvelous enough. Twice was truly unbelievable.

Amenemhet yawned. His heart was lighter. Taking a deep breath of the cool air, he stretched and yawned again. Now he would sleep. When he slipped silently beneath the bed cover, Nefrytatanen still asleep, turned and put her arm around him. He smiled, moved closer to her warmth, and closed his eyes.

Chapter Twenty

The wedding had finally been arranged. After ten days of planning and endless details, Nefrytatanen sat on the terrace wall drawing deep breaths of cool night air. Everything had been done. She could enjoy tomorrow's celebration without further problems. Anything that went wrong now would be the fault of the servants, and she had given them explicit orders.

Kheti had floated up the river to his new house, not on a boat, but on his dreams, she was sure. It was fortunate this task had taken him from Ithtawe. If she'd had to endure his aimless wanderings all that time, as she had during the two days since he'd returned, she might finally have gone mad. Now she could smile, remembering his unfocused eyes and absolute bewilderment.

Neferset, too, had been of little help, though she had meant well. She had raced around the palace in excitement, like her silver cat, silently appearing in unexpected places, getting underfoot. As Nefrytatanen had carefully avoided stepping on the cat, she had also carefully avoided giving Neferset any hint of her irritation at endless questions. Nefrytatanen remembered the preparations for her own wedding and forgave Neferset her interruptions. Getting the two of them together with Ankhneferu to arrange the wording of their marriage contract had been Nefrytatanen's only easy task.

For this, Kheti and Neferset were clear-minded, and they cooperated enthusiastically.

During this turmoil Nefrytatanen had never bothered Amenemhet with her many problems. Once only did she ask his opinion, and this had been after Yazid had told her of rumors. The people, fearing famine, had begun to ration themselves strictly, in hopes that their supplies would last until the next harvest. When they heard of the elaborate celebration being planned for the wedding, many grumbled. Hearing this, Nefrytatanen decided to enlarge her plans to distribute food and drink so that the people could not only join the celebration as they had at her own wedding, but also have extra food left over for their future use. She had asked Amenemhet about this, listing what she hoped to distribute, and he had immediately agreed.

Amenemhet told her of plans he had set in motion to begin solving Tamera's troubles. His ideas were in accord with hers, and she encouraged him without interfering. It gave her satisfaction that his spirits seemed lighter these last few days. Although the problems were far from solved, she could see he was satisfied to have made a beginning. She perceived that he enjoyed rising to the challenge of untangling them. He made a point of discussing state matters with her during any free time, but she made it clear she was content to let his decisions prevail. The wedding had been a way for her to demonstrate, tactfully, not only to Amenemhet, but also to the others close to him that she wished to hold her scepter lightly.

Nefrytatanen made a mental note to think of some way to thank those who had helped during these last few days. She wanted to do something personal for them, rather than simply reward them with gold, and she considered this carefully.

The night sky was black, and the stars seemed to be chips of crystals suspended on invisible threads. She put aside serious thoughts and stood up, smelling the spicy-sweet scent of the garden. The moon rose in a silver arc, reflecting its glow in her eyes. She decided there was no peacefulness more profound than a secret moment of wakefulness when everyone else slept. Even Amenemhet hadn't heard her rise and seemed to be sleeping soundly.

A warm, soft breeze flicked the torches in the courtyard into the swirlings of some secret dance, while the swaying palm fronds made soft music.

In this time of utter privacy and peace, Nefrytatanen had an impulse to take a walk in the garden. She turned to look again at Amenemhet. He hadn't moved. For a moment she hesitated, the white, silk-draped room inviting her return. The warm, familiarly intimate scent of the room tempted her, but another breeze from the garden touched her with gentle fingers. She decided to follow it.

Not bothering to cover herself—she knew the garden would be deserted at this hour—she tiptoed down the steps feeling the texture of the cool stones under her bare feet. The soft wind brushed her legs, luring her to continue.

As Nefrytatanen passed the fountain, the playful breeze turned a mist her way, and her hair and skin were were covered with crystal droplets, as if the stars sprinkled dust on her. She glided through foliage that reached out to brush her hips in greeting as she passed and entered a small clearing enclosed with flowers and shrubbery. In the moonlight, everything appeared covered in gossamer. The grass was as soft as human hair, fresh and sweet-smelling.

Nefrytatanen sat, then lay on her back, smelling the earth close to her, feeling rooted in Tamera's soil. She lay quietly, looking at the stars and the shadows of the swaying branches overhead. Amenemhet came so silently that he disturbed no branch or twig, to catch her there, pale ivory in the moonlight, unaware of him.

When Amenemhet knelt at Nefrytatanen's side and leaned over her, she wasn't startled. Anything was possible in this magical night. He asked no questions, spoke not at all. Gleaming topaz eyes looked into hers a moment, and his lips spoke for him, as he left a path of kisses from her toes to her chin. He softly kissed her countless times before his hands even touched her.

Under the attraction of the silver light and with the scent of Nefrytatanen rising all around him, Amenemhet heard within himself a quiet voice telling all the divine beings that now two mortals joined their ranks, becoming, in this night, immortal and eternal. The night's sighs combined with their own, and the calls of the nightbirds were unnoticed. Only when the stars had begun to fade did he lead her back to the palace, and the little glade was left forever haunted with their love.

The scent of flowers filled the temple, joining with clouds of rich incense. The aromas brought Amenemhet vivid memories of Nefrytatanen standing quietly on the threshold of another temple, wearing her translucently shimmering silver gown in the slanting golden light. The memory of their own wedding was so real to Amenemhet that it wasn't necessary for him to close his eyes to see her again glide soundlessly toward him in the hush that had fallen over the crowd.

Where Amenemhet's father and mother had sat, Amenemhet sat today with Nefrytatanen. Amenemhet missed his parents with a sudden pang. He wished they could know how happy he was with Nefrytatanen. He wished they could see Senwadjet and Maeti. How amazed they would have been at two children! In Tamera, unlike other, ignorant, lands where the phenomenon was thought of as a curse, a double birth was considered a blessing.

Nefrytatanen wasn't reflecting on the past as Amenemhet was. From the corner of her eyes, she was watching him in his contemplative mood, thinking how dignified he looked, seeing the wisdom that grew daily in his eyes. She looked down at his hands, one lying quietly in his lap, the other grasping hers, and considered their gentleness and strength. She wondered

what he was thinking. The copper color of his robe
made his sun-bronzed face a trifle deeper and his eyes an
even more brilliant gold. She thought of last night and
the garden, which now seemed almost a dream, and
she wondered if she would ever cease to marvel at his
endless variety.

Kheti stood with Ankhneferu where Amenemhet and
Sinuhe had stood. What happened, wondered Kheti, to
the spirits of such evil people as Sinuhe? To what re-
gions had Sinuhe's soul traveled? It was strange to reflect on memories of so evil a being on an occasion of
such joy, Kheti observed. His thoughts were stopped
abruptly.

The doors had swung silently open, and Princess Neferset of Atalan stood on the threshold of the temple
like the goddess Bast, gentle and warm with ethereal
beauty and cursed by her dreams to deliver messages of
evil prophecy. Her hair, intricately plaited in many silver strands, fell past her shoulders. Her garment, a
sheer Atalan cloth, flowed pale green over every curve
of her like a wave running over sand. On her brow was
a crown of silver, like intertwining delicate vines gathered into a circle. Small, green, flowerlike gems were
caught in the strands, the green the same as her eyes. It
was her personal crown as Atalan's princess, and, after
marrying Kheti, the only crown she would wear.

Kheti saw Sarenput smiling at his sister as she walked
forward.

Amenemhet and Nefrytatanen listened to the ancient
words they had barely heard on their own wedding day.
As they themselves had done, Kheti and Neferset scattered flower petals. They could taste again the sweetness
of the almond cakes and the cool sips of wine. At the
memory of that moment Nefrytatanen's eyes filled blurring the scene. Amenemhet smiled at her and her tears
evaporated in the warmth of his gaze.

As kings and queens had done countless times before
in weddings of high rank, they rose to bestow official approval and blessings on the union. Nefrytatanen recalled

the words Sira had spoken to her and she whispered them now to Neferset. "May your love compare in joy to that of Asar and Aset." The echoing drafts in the temple seemed to murmur and repeat the words, as though Sira confirmed the sentiment.

When the company emerged from the quiet temple into the gay and laughing crowd, they were pelted with flower petals and the leaves of fragrant herbs. At Amenemhet and Nefrytatanen's wedding the crowd had burst into a spontaneous song of celebration and now Senbi began to sing that song aloud, encouraging, with gestures, the others to join him. When Amenemhet and Nefrytatanen began to sing, the others followed their example, and the music soared through Ithtawe. Lord Kheti of Tamera and Princess Neferset of Atalan looked into each other's glowing eyes. Smiling, she removed her crown and gave it to Kheti.

As Kuwait entered the banquet room, she wondered what King Amenemhet looked like. She hoped he wasn't ugly or, at least, that he might be tolerable, if not pleasant to look upon. She had plans for him. While he had been absent, she had taken what she could. But now he was alive and, from all reports, healthy and ruling all the kingdom's affairs. She wasn't sure how long it would take before he investigated her. She knew Ankhneferu had wasted no time in reporting her activities. She hoped to inveigle her way into the king's favor, thereby assuring her continued prosperity and, perhaps, increased power. She only hoped he wasn't repulsive. There was a limit to her abilities as an actress, although this talent was formidable.

Kuwait's saffron gown had been specially made for this wedding party. Her gleaming black hair was arranged in the most elegant fashion that her slave, a girl of considerable talent, could devise. Her jewels were dazzling, and she walked forward with confidence, coming as close to the front of the room as she could manage.

Kuwait wanted to get a good look at Amenemhet; if he wasn't unbearable, she wanted him to see her. She also intended to examine her competition, Queen Nefrytatanen. And she wanted to watch them together, to see if any look or gesture passing between them might indicate a rift she could help widen.

Kuwait found a place amid many warm and smiling faces, whose smiles she returned as warmly. She was thinking she was after far bigger prey than these people, but, if she didn't capture it, she would keep her present friends within reach.

Hardly had Kuwait settled herself when the trumpets announced the arrival of the royal party. She arose with the others, aranging gracefully the folds of her gown and giving her hair a final pat.

When Amenemhet entered with Nefrytatanen on his arm, Kuwait looked at her king and smiled, her black eyes glittering. She had hoped to find him tolerable. Now, she decided it would be no distasteful task to lure him to her. She would like to see those strangely tilted eyes glow with a fire of her own making. His golden eyes swept slowly over the throng, and, as they passed her, she shivered slightly. The face of the king held a certain sensuality that greatly intrigued her.

The royal couple had mounted the low platform where they would dine and stood to face the gathering. Kuwait turned her attention to her queen.

Nefrytatanen's simple white robe was long and flowing but concealed little of her graceful curves. Her hair fell loose and shining, straight and unstyled as a ribbon of black satin. Suddenly Kuwait felt that her gown was too bright and her hair overcontrived. Nefrytatanen's one piece of jewelry was her lotus pendant, and she wore no formal crown or elaborate headpiece. Only a slender silver band carrying the cobra of the north circled her hair. Looking at those serenely confident sapphire eyes, Kuwait's envy turned to fires of white heat. When Nefrytatanen looked in her direction, Kuwait was undone. Never before had she felt overwhelmed by another woman, but this slightly smiling queen awed her. Nefrytatanen was unquestionably the daughter of Ra, Aset incarnate, and Kuwait felt helpless. Those eyes glowed on her a moment, and Kuwait remembered the stories of Nefrytatanen's magic. She shivered. Nefrytatanen's glance traveled past her and over the others, but it seemed to Kuwait as if she had been personally inspected and found of little significance.

When the royal party was seated, Amenemhet signaled for the music to begin, and the crowd sat while servants began bringing platters of food and fresh containers of wine.

Kuwait watched closely, hoping for some sign of coldness between Amenemhet and Nefrytatanen. But she saw him lean toward Nefrytatanen to smilingly whisper some comment and heard the queen laugh softly. Kuwait couldn't lift a bite to her mouth. She felt sick. The easy camaraderie of the royal couple, their glances and gestures which clearly demonstrated their affection, made Kuwait feel defeated already. Nefrytatanen's cool and regal beauty became warm and responsive to Amenenhet's slightest glance and touch, and Kuwait was devoured by jealousy.

Kheti, Neferset, and Sarenput now gathered closer to Amenemhet and Nefrytatanen to exchange some conversation and smile, while Semu laughed softly. Kuwait acutely felt her status as an inferior. She was shut out, an alien, for all her scheming and her beauty. She was furious.

Kuwait resolved she would lure Amenemhet to her bed somehow and humiliate the queen in the worst way possible. In all her experience, she must have learned something of love that Nefrytatanen didn't know, and she would find the opportunity to use it. She took a sip of wine. She would continue to watch them for some weakness, some fault. She would see if Amenemhet's eyes wandered at all, if Nefrytatanen had some flaw. . . .

During a lull in the conversation, Nefrytatanen felt eyes upon her—they were not the usual curious eyes.

These eyes made her scalp prickle with warning, as if a
hostile being was studying her menacingly. Startled, she
glanced up and slowly looked over the crowd. She felt
foolish to find herself examining the faces at each table,
but she couldn't stop. The feeling was too strong to be
ignored. She trusted her instincts because they had
served her so well in the past.

Nefrytatanen's gaze fell upon glittering black eyes in
a beautiful, but overly sensual, face. The woman wore
a bright yellow gown. Were those the eyes she'd felt?
No, they were smiling pleasantly at a man who sat next
to her. Still, Nefrytatanen looked at Kuwait, studying
the elegant hair and gown, the beautiful jewelry, concluding that whoever the woman was, she must be
wealthy.

The feeling had subsided, and Nefrytatanen turned to
Neferset who was telling a story. She tried to put aside
the memory of that powerful feeling, but her scalp still
prickled, and she couldn't forget it.

A dozen dancing girls, each wearing a different colored floating veil, appeared to fly into the room like
bright and graceful birds and began to swirl rapidly,
moving about the open area in front of the royal table
in a strenuous, but charming, dance filling the air with
the sound of many tiny bells. They obstructed the view
of the royal table from the rest of the room. While
Amenemhet and Nefrytatanen watched the gay dance,
Nefrytatanen wondered who in the crowd wished her ill.

While Kuwait listened distractedly to the noble who
sat beside her, smiling and trying to pretend interest in
his conversation, she resolved to be careful. She hadn't
missed Nefrytatanen's studying her, and, although she
had quickly turned her attention to the man beside her,
she wasn't certain Nefrytatanen hadn't noticed her
scrutiny. She wondered why the queen had suddenly sat
up stiffly and looked so carefully over each face in the
room. Had some sense warned her of Kuwait's
thoughts? Could she read minds? Kuwait suddenly felt
a cold shiver of fear pass through her. Could Nefryta-

tanen make magic, as the tales told? If it were true, how could Kuwait overcome her?

Kuwait pushed her fears from her, disgusted with herself. Wasn't she, herself, a priestess? Did she not know a few things about such matters? As reluctant as she was to leave this party and her study of the king, she decided she might be wise to go as soon as she discreetly could. She had hoped for a chance to meet Amenemhet personally, but perhaps that would be better delayed for a time. She ought to concern herself now with some protection, in case Nefrytatanen did have magic secrets or even held the favor of the divine beings.

Kuwait began to consider the possible ways to affect such protection. Even tonight she decided, she could do something. She stared into her goblet, looking at the ripples in the wine, thinking what she might do. Then she smiled.

As the evening wore on, Amenemhet began to feel sleepy. He had been working very hard these past days and last night had given him little rest. When he thought of the moonlit garden, he smiled. What strange things Nefrytatanen did and caused him to do. What beautiful and delightful things, he thought. For a moment he reflected on them. Then he suddenly yawned. He began to wonder if he would be able to keep his eyes open all through this celebration. He yawned again. What is one yawn if it isn't followed by another, he decided. The next he struggled against and won. He turned to Neferset, who sat at his side. Her eyes were laughing.

"I saw you," she whispered. "If you fall asleep and commence to snore, my king, do I have your permission to awaken you?"

Amenemhet stared at her a moment then smiled. "By all means," he said softly. He grew serious. "I don't wish to fall asleep at your wedding party, but I seem ready to do that anyway. I'm sorry."

Neferset's eyes lost their laughter, and she whispered, "You would never be rude. You're exhausted." Slowly her eyes began to sparkle green again. "I wouldn't mind an early ending to this evening. I'd like to see Kheti yawn too—after a time."

Amenemhet laughed aloud at this, and Nefrytatanen looked at them curiously. "What's going on here?" she said lightly. "Are you flirting with the king?" She was smiling.

Neferset laughed. "I've decided I prefer King Amenemhet to Kheti after all." At the look in Nefrytatanen's face, Neferset added quickly, "I was really suggesting the party might drag on too long, and I'm anxious to be with Kheti."

Nefrytatanen realized her feelings about the mysterious danger in the room must have shown in her expression and made Neferset uncomfortable. She certainly expected nothing evil of this shining girl, and she hastened to put Neferset at ease. "I can understand that," Nefrytatanen said. "Perhaps we could think of a way to sneak you away. Perhaps we could begin a new custom, beloved," she said, turning to Amenemhet. "Wedding celebrations have always gone on all night, which is a discouraging thing for the newly married couple, as happy as the party may be. Why don't we begin a new custom now?"

At this Neferset's eyes lit, and Kheti smiled. "Perhaps that's a good idea," he said. "How do you suppose we could accomplish it? We might pour the wine a little faster and make the guests tired a little sooner."

Sarenput had been listening and, thinking the conversation merely joking, suggested, "How about someone feigning illness?"

"I could do that," Nefrytatanen said. "It wouldn't be difficult." She already had a pain in her head from the threatening feeling in the atmosphere, and she wanted to escape the crowd. "If I, the queen, were suddenly overcome by a fainting spell, surely the party would come to an end. Or I could be carried away, and the party could continue without the royal family."

"You're a constant delight," Amenemhet said, smiling. His smile faded as he swallowed yet another yawn. "Kheti, what do you think? It's your party."

"I certainly wouldn't protest too loudly." Kheti looked at Neferset and grinned.

"Then I shall immediately faint," Nefrytatanen stated. "Are you prepared to catch me, beloved? I have no wish to fall on the floor."

"I'm not sure I have enough strength left," Amenemhet said dryly. "Perhaps I could manage."

"Well, you'd better be sure!" Nefrytatanen declared. "Kheti, perhaps you'd better catch me. Then you'll have the excuse of carrying me off, and Neferset will have a reason to follow."

"I'll be happy to catch you," Kheti replied. Now he wasn't so sure she was joking.

"Then get ready," Nefrytatanen warned. She hesitated a moment to consider how she could convincingly faint. Finally she stood up and moved around Amenemhet toward Kheti, who stared at her in surprise. She leaned closer to Kheti, as if to converse with him but whispered, "Now, Kheti, stand up."

Wavering a second to give him a chance to get to his feet, she collapsed against his chest. She heard a shocked cry go up from the crowd and people rising quickly. She sensed Amenemhet's silent leap from his chair. As she began to slide down, she opened one eye a little and whispered anxiously against Kheti's chest, "Pick me up, Kheti. Carry me out!" Barely able to control his expression, Kheti scooped her up into his arms.

Recovering from his own surprise, Amenemhet announced, "The queen seems to have fainted. Please stay where you are until we see what this is about."

No one could have left the banquet room because Nessumontu's guards, unaware of the sham, filled the doorways menacingly. Horemheb leaped from his place and came hurrying to look at Nefrytatanen. His heart pounded in fear. As Horemheb bent over Nefrytatanen, Amenemhet whispered, "Nothing is wrong, Horemheb. Just come with us." The look of bewilderment on Horemheb's face was genuine as he followed them. He wondered if they had all lost their minds.

Bekhet and Yazid met them in the hall and hurried after. Bekhet looked reproachfully at Neferset because Neferset was struggling not to laugh. When they reached the royal chambers. Yazid rushed to open the door. Kheti walked inside and promptly put Nefrytatanen on her feet. Then they explained their plot and exploded in laughter.

Finally Horemheb controlled himself enough to ask, "Who will tell the guests the story? Not I!"

Neferset still giggled. "But you must!"

Amenemhet smiled. "She's right. None of us can go. As the royal physician, it's fitting for you to bring the news."

"What could I say?" Horemheb wouldn't lie. Yet he couldn't refuse.

Seeing his consternation, Nefrytatanen suggested, "Tell them to continue enjoying the party. Say I'm all right and the others have stayed with me. Assure them there's no danger. None of that will be lying, Horemheb."

Horemheb sighed. "Perhaps not, but it bends the truth," he retorted. He shrugged his shoulders in resignation and left.

Sarenput smiled at Semu. "Shall we return to the party after awhile?" he asked. "There are some very pretty girls there."

Semu snorted, "I'm going to bed."

"Good night, little sister," Sarenput said to Neferset. He kissed her gently on the cheek, smiled and nodded to Kheti, then left.

Kheti and Neferset looked at each other, wanting to go immediately, but unsure how to take their leave. Finally Amenemhet laughed softly. "What are you waiting for?" he asked. "Bekhet, take them to the room that was prepared for them."

Neferset smiled at Amenemhet and murmured, "Thank you for everything. It has been beautiful."

Nefrytatanen took Neferset's hand and whispered, "Go now and make it more beautiful yet."

When they were alone, Amenemhet turned to Nefrytatanen. "I never believed you'd do it," he said, grinning.

"It seemed the easiest way to get out, and I did have an ache in my head," she replied. Smiling, he shook his head. Then, yawning, he went to prepare himself for sleep.

When Horemheb announced that there was nothing to worry about, the musicians immediately resumed playing, and the guards withdrew in relief. After a moment of hesitation, the guests continued their interrupted conversations. Before long, the party again grew lively.

Kuwait heard the news and prepared to leave. The noble beside her tried to persuade her to remain. She refused firmly yet graciously.

When she was finally in her private quarters, she undressed and speculated on Nefrytatanen's faint. Kuwait wondered if the queen's health had become delicate since the birth of the children and the long voyage. If so, this might be the flaw she sought. A wife prone to fainting and in less than the best of health might not always be anxious for love. From the look of him, Kuwait judged the king to be a man who would grow restless, however devoted he might be.

Now naked, Kuwait ordered her maid from the room. The maid went quickly—she had heard from other attendants that Kuwait sometimes worked evil magic in the darkness.

Kuwait made sure the servant was gone, then took from a hidden place, a small black statue and a scarlet cloak, which she fastened around her shoulders. She had decided she would risk nothing. Whatever Nefrytatanen's health, if the queen knew anything of magic, Kuwait intended to protect herself from its effects. Whatever Nefrytatanen might conjure up, Kuwait

would have Sutekh make powerless before Nefrytatanen got the chance to work her spells.

Long after Amenemhet slept, Nefrytatanen lay awake
with the evil singing in her ears like an insect. The feeling had followed her even into their chambers and
wouldn't be dismissed. Although Nefrytatanen was no
longer particularly frightened of it, she had been alerted,
like an ibex testing some strange scent on the wind. She
was worried.

Nefrytatanen arose from the bed and walked out onto
the terrace, wondering at this feeling. The night seemed
ordinary, but the magic of it had vanished. The evil
thing seemed to hover over her, blotting out the beauty
of the dark skies. Nefrytatanen shuddered. What could
she do against this vile thing whose face and purpose
she couldn't know? It was dangerous to cast spells indis-
criminately, even spells of protection.

Issella had told Nefrytatanen that Aset knew and
favored her. Nefrytatanen thought of this and decided
that, whatever the malevolence was, it could pose no
greater threat than those dangers she had already faced.
She had found help before when she'd needed it. She
decided to trust in her mother's promise and Aset's
protection.

Chapter Twenty-one

As Kheti and Neferset approached his house, Kheti noted the carefully barred gates, the abundance of conspicuous guards, and the deliberate show of weapons. The servants who greeted them smiled at Kheti and their new mistress, but their faces were stiff with tension. Kheti could smell fear, and he knew they were not afraid of him.

After leaving Neferset in their room to direct the unpacking, Kheti walked slowly through the house and its courtyard, observing the guards again. He concluded that his house was as fortified as if they expected momentary attack.

He sent for Susu, his friend and comrade from former days, who now was in charge in Kheti's absence.

Looking anxious and trying to hide it, Susu entered Kheti's sitting room. After greeting him warmly, Kheti offered him a cup of beer, which Susu accepted automatically and drank as if unaware of what the cup contained.

Kheti came straight to the point. "Susu, what's happening? I come home with my bride to find my new house guarded like a fortress, and the servants terrified. It wasn't this way when I came to inspect it before the wedding. This house is on the river, not in a desolate place. We're not far from Menet Khufu. Why are we so afraid? What catastrophe is expected?"

Susu's sun-browned face grew pale. Kheti could see

how afraid he was, and he knew Susu was no coward. Kheti waited patiently for his friend's answer.

"The thieves have been seen in this area," Susu said slowly. "If you think this house is carefully guarded and these servants are fearful, you should see how terrified the farmers are. They're afraid to go out into the fields and leave their wives and families in their own houses." Kheti stared in amazement. Susu continued, "If you wish to inspect the land, I strongly advise you not to go alone. Take a good number of guards with you because you might very well be attacked."

"In the name of Sekhmet, who are you talking about, Susu?" Kheti's voice was sharply angry. "Who would dare threaten me in my own house?" he demanded. "What thief are you all—even you—so afraid of?"

"Yes, me. I'm afraid, too." Susu didn't lower his eyes, and his fear was unconcealed. "The thieves and assassins are led by Shera. They butcher even women and children for a few scraps of food, some garments, a gold piece or two. Don't you think such men would find your house—richly appointed and containing a beautiful princess—a tempting target? Don't you think such a man as rides with Shera would be a hero among his friends if he slit your throat? Would not your new bride be a prize? Wouldn't Shera like to have her?" Susu took a breath and finished, "You're almost as feared as the king is, and killing you would be a great honor—especially for Shera."

Kheti swallowed his mouthful of beer hastily, almost choking in his fury. "I might have known Shera would be one of them," he snarled. "I've heard the situation was serious, but I never realized it was this bad."

"It's worse than you can imagine," Susu said. He stared at Kheti. "The farmers on your land are terrified, so how do you think those who work on the property of other nobles, less able to defend them, feel about going into the fields? They live with terror day and night. Each man who leaves his wife and children in the morning, goes unsure if he'll see them alive when he returns.

The families, while he's gone, stay close to the house where weapons are handy. Many women have learned to use the bow and arrow, the spear, even the dagger and sword for close fighting! Those children who attend the house of learning must be escorted there and back, and they travel in large groups. When night falls, the people bar their doors and pile heavy furniture before them. They cover the windows with thick skins fastened tightly, so they're not attacked unaware in the night. I know large families who post regular guards and make patrols, like military outposts. You ask how bad the situation is? My answer, Kheti, is that it couldn't be worse."

Kheti put his hands over his face for a moment. When he looked up, his eyes were fierce with anger. "I will not have this at my house," he declared. "I'll stop them. They'll know I'm home, and they'll be afraid. I will not hide. I will not fear for my wife in her own house." Kheti was so angry his face was reddening. Susu had never seen him so furious. "Let them come here and we'll kill them," Kheti said in a voice tight with menace. "If they won't come, I'll drag them from their holes. I'll get Shera myself—once and for all."

"That's just what Nessumontu's been trying to do. He has the whole royal army at his command, and he's hardly made a mark on them," Susu said grimly. "You know Nessumontu's no man to fool with."

"Perhaps not, but Nessumontu doesn't know them as I do," Kheti shot back. "Nessumontu doesn't know the secret places to look. He doesn't fully understand the kind of traps to set. I know these things well enough. It was this knowledge that kept me alive all those years."

Neferset, who had overheard Kheti's angry voice, came slowly down the stairs, listening. Never had she heard Kheti use this tone. Never had she heard such terrible things. What kind of place was Tamera? Where had she traveled to from her peaceful homeland? Alarm showed in her wide green eyes as she approached them.

"I heard you," Neferset said, her face pale and her voice shaky. "What will we do, Kheti?"

She ran to him, and he put his arm around her to comfort her. He found she was trembling violently.

"Neferset, they won't touch you," Kheti promised. "They won't harm you, be sure of that. I'll send for Rakkor. We know how to deal with such as Shera. We've done it before. Don't be afraid. My house will be safe."

"But I'm afraid for you!" Neferset looked up at Kheti with tear-filled eyes. "I heard what Susu said about what a prize you'd be. I'm afraid they'll kill you, beloved." She looked away and asked, "Who is Shera?"

"Don't worry about him," Kheti said grimly. "He knows how to fight farmers and kill women and children, but he'll find Rakkor and me and our men a different matter."

They were interrupted by a commotion in the courtyard. Fearing the worst, Kheti told Neferset to stay in the house. Picking up his sword, he raced from the house with Susu close behind.

At the front gates, setting up a clamor with the guards, Kheti saw a band of sand-dwellers. Their white robes were covered with dust, and Kheti could see women, children, horses, camels, goats, even dogs—he was amazed. Aside from a little trading, the nomads never wanted to have anything to do with the river-dwellers. They barely talked to each other's tribes—and yet they now clamored at his gates. He stared in shock.

At Kheti's arm, Susu warned, "Have a care my friend, for their hearts are not mild."

Kheti shrugged off Susu's hand and ran closer. None of the nomads had drawn a weapon, but they argued fiercely with the guards.

"What's happening here?" Kheti asked.

One sand-dweller looked at Khetti with sharp eyes and concluded from his dress and manners that he was someone of authority. The sand-dweller said softly but angrily, "I asked to speak to the nobleman who lives here. He will not allow me inside the gates."

"What do you want?" Kheti asked, "I'm the governor of this province."

"You are Lord Kheti? You're the one who is a friend of the king, who was once a—" The sand-dweller hesitated, searching for a tactful word.

"I am," Kheti said quickly. "What business do you have with me?"

The sand-dweller glanced at his feet then looked not at Kheti, but beyond him, while he talked. His pride didn't allow him to look into the face of a nobleman from whom he asked a favor.

After a long pause, he said slowly, "I am Abba Hasan. I've come to ask if I and my family and friends might settle in your province."

Kheti was too surprised to speak.

The nomad continued, "We're afraid. Yes, I might as well say it, shameful as it is. We're afraid to stay on our desert. We, who have always been proud to defend ourselves, whose home has always been on the sands, we come to a river-dweller and admit we're afraid. We've been attacked several times. Last night three of our group were killed before we beat off the bandits. We've come upon the camps of other tribes who had been attacked, and the sights we've seen are too terrible to describe. I"—he thumped a finger against his chest in anger, "I who have never been afraid, who have seen many horrible sights, have been sickened by what these murderers do." Noting Kheti's expression, Abba said, "What do *we* have that they might want? You may well ask this question. What can I, a poor man, possibly have that a thief might kill for? I have a wife. I have daughters. I have animals. I have food, and a tent to cover me, water." He looked at Kheti with haunted eyes. "That's enough for some of them. The women are reason enough for any of them. I won't describe what they do to women. I cannot."

Kheti was speechless. He thought of Neferset's silver

hair, her soft body filled with love. Her sweet lips. He thought of Shera. He felt sick.

"If we settle on your land, perhaps they'll be less bold," Abba said. "Perhaps they'll be afraid to fight us all." The sand-dweller pleaded, in an agony of embarrassment. "We ask—no—we beg to stay. I cannot let those bandits take my woman and kill my children. I cannot!"

"Stay in peace, my friend, if you can find it." Kheti was grim. "I've just arrived myself and been told how things are. I cannot guarantee your safety here. We have guards and weapons, but our own farmers lock themselves away every night in fear. As my overseer has just pointed out, I may be a choice target myself. You may stay. If you're attacked, my men will try to help you. Now that I've heard the full story, I can promise only that I have no desire greater than that of ridding the land of these demons. Stay where you choose on my province. I hope you'll be safe.

The sand-dweller regarded Kheti silently a moment. "What do you wish in return?" he asked.

"I'm not bargaining with you," Kheti answered quickly. "I'm glad to have you join us. If you've fought them off already, your weapons are welcome. That you survived proves you can use them."

The nomad looked hard at Kheti a moment. Although he had degraded himself by begging, he intended to repay Kheti in some fashion. His sword could serve the nobleman as well as defend his own family. He decided it was fair. He took Kheti's hand in a firm grasp. Kheti knew this was his thanks and asked for no more.

The sand-dweller turned and shouted to his companions, and they quickly set about arranging their burdens. They were much relieved by Kheti's generosity but, in their fashion, they said nothing. Abba Hasan spoke for them.

Kheti watched the nomads disappear through his gates, then he turned toward the house. He had made a decision. Neferset couldn't stay here. He would take her back to Ithtawe. He would have to report all this to Amenemhet, in any event. Kheti shook his head as he walked. That sand-dwellers asked to settle on Orynx Province, afraid of the desert, was final proof. There could be no more powerful testimony than this.

When Lord Petamen had first come, many years ago, to the palace at Wast to petition Amenemhet's father with some complaint, Amenemhet had been fourteen. Upon being introduced to the nobleman, he had looked into the bulging eyes and instantly disliked the man. Now Amenemhet settled back in his chair in disgust and listened to Petamen's long discourse regarding the sundry injustices heaped upon him.

"That's not true!" Lord Mesemneter leaped from his chair to confront Petamen. "You're always complaining about my people, but they've never gone over the boundaries into your land. I've told you time and time again that they haven't."

Lord Niuserra interrupted Mesemneter. "It's only an illusion when I see your warehouses heaped with grain grown in Petamen's province? I seem to suffer the same delusions."

"That's a lie," Mesemneter spat. "I've invaded no one's land. My farmers know very well where my boundary ends and yours begin."

"Perhaps you should then visit your outlying districts more often to supervise them," Petamen said smoothly.

"You aren't going to tell me how to run my province!" Mesemneter exploded. "First you accuse me with lies. Then you get your friend Niuserra to stand with you in the same accusation to lend it credence. Now you tell me I don't know what my own peasants are doing!"

Amenemhet had said nothing through all this. He had remained silent for the last twenty minutes, witnessing the noblemen argue among themselves. He wondered if they had forgotten his presence. Or did they mistake his silence for meekness? As their voices rose higher, his disgust rose in proportion. He decided he had given them sufficient chance to act constructively, and he concluded they didn't wish to be constructive. They dared test him with their increasing aggressiveness. He pushed back his chair and stood up.

"I will hear no more of this." Amenemhet's voice was quiet with menace. "I called you to this meeting because you were here at Ithtawe for Lord Kheti's wedding, and it seemed convenient to try to settle your differences without extra traveling." His eyes blazed with anger. "I haven't come to argue with you or to waste my time listening to your whining. There are other, more serious, matters to be settled than your petty squabbles."

Lord Semerkhet smiled to himself. It was time those fools heard this, he thought. He was disgusted with their quarreling over nonsense, and he welcomed Amenemhet's anger. Perhaps, Semerkhet thought, the king will settle their disagreements for them with a royal command. Then they all could go about their business.

Senbi, who was visiting the palace at the time the meeting began, sat between Semerkhet and Rakkor. He noticed their pleased expressions, and he settled himself more comfortably to see what Amenemhet would do next. Semu sat in a corner, watching silently.

Amenemhet's next words were spoken so softly that it took some concentration to hear him. The faces of some of the lords grew pale.

"When the queen needed to choose a governor, she made sure she chose one she trusted. If I continue to have troubles, I might take her idea a step further." The noblemen were shocked at the implication that he would simply unseat them from their coveted places. Amenemhet smiled humorlessly. "I might find it possible to place assistants at your sides, if you find it so difficult to come to agreements and make decisions."

The guilty noblemen thought of the kind of assistants he would give them, and they swallowed dryly. To have the king's spy constantly at their elbows would render them as powerless as if they had been stripped of their titles. Fear hung over the room like a vulture.

"The surveyors were sent by my order," Amenemhet said softly. "They are like my own arms. I won't have them interfered with." At this pronouncement, Hera silently applauded in relief and gratitude.

Amenemhet continued, "Their orders are to locate the correct borders, and these measurements are not subject to your whims. They're my borders. You merely supervise them." Amenemhet was reminding them of the ancient law that the king owned all the land and distributed it for use among the people.

Semerkhet felt like laughing aloud when he saw Petamen's expression, but he settled for a smug smile. Rakkor sat slouched in his chair like a hunching mountain, though his face was a blank, he was thinking that Kheti would enjoy this.

Senbi was fascinated by this king he had thought he knew. Here was a side he hadn't known Amenemhet possessed, and he was intrigued. It occured to him that it was no wonder they had come through that terrible storm. With Amenemhet on the ship, Sutekh dared not sink it!

Amenemhet stepped around the table and said in an unmistakable tone, "When I was unable to reign, and the queen met with you, she described how she might have to rule the land if she had trouble with you. I think you'd best consider that I, too, could take such steps."

Amenemhet remained silent, allowing them time to consider the possibilities. Finally he said in a congenial tone, "Now, do we have anything further to discuss?"

The noblemen were quiet, afraid to hope he was ready to dismiss them. They didn't want to hear any more.

"No? Very good. I'm glad we understand each other again," Amenemhet said. Then he added, "Have a good journey home. Rakkor and Semerkhet, will you stay a little longer? I have things to discuss with you." Amenemhet looked at the few nobles who still sat silently, not knowing what to do. Sarcastically he said, "I told you to have a good journey home. That meant you can leave."

Semerkhet could hardly restrain his laughter. He smiled openly, to the chagrin of the others, who hastily got up and rushed out.

Nefrytatanen had been in the next room feeding the children. The door between the rooms had been left open so she could hear what was said. Listening to Amenemhet's words had filled her with pride. She gave the children to the waiting servants and quickly refastened her garments. In a gay mood, feeling like celebrating, she took several flowers from a container on a table. Pulling off their petals, she entered the meeting room and tossed the petals over Amenemhet's head.

Surprised, he turned to see her standing behind him with petals still clinging to her fingers.

"Good! Good!" Senbi stood up smiling. "That was a perfect ending to this meeting."

Rakkor dragged himself out of the chair and mumbled, "Let us see if they obey before we celebrate too much."

"I think you're too pessimistic," Semerkhet said, his eyes shining. "I think this has accomplished the purpose. They needed shaking up, and they got it. Don't be surprised if all their complaints suddenly vanish now."

"For a while, anyway," Amenemhet said. He wasn't smiling. "It won't last forever, but this may give us a long enough breathing space to solve some of the other troubles."

Yazid opened the door and stepped in, looking very disturbed. The others turned to look at him questioningly. "Kheti has returned with Neferset," he announced. "She's all packed, as if she plans to stay!"

Semerkhet was startled. "Did they have a fight already?" he asked.

"No," Semu said, rising slowly, "not that. Something else is wrong."

"Bring them in, Yazid," Amenemhet directed. Before

Yazid had the time to reach for the door handle, Kheti and Neferset burst in.

"I'm sorry to interrupt your meeting," Kheti apologized. "I have to tell you something important."

Nefrytatanen, seeing the fury in Kheti's eyes said, "Sit down, both of you. Then tell us."

Neferset sank into the nearest chair, looking dejected, but Kheti threw himself down with force. Kheti first briefly described his guarded house and his servants' fear. Then he told them about the visit from the sand-dwellers. They stared at him incredulously.

Finally Amenemhet said, "Yazid, get Nessumontu. I want him to hear this."

Yazid vanished, and they waited in silence until he returned with the military commander.

"Tell Nessumontu what you've just told us," Amenemhet said quietly.

Kheti repeated the story. When he had finished, Nessumontu seemed unsurprised.

He said, "Although I'm startled by the sand-dwellers' request, I'm not shocked by the rest of it." He looked calmly at them. "I couldn't really describe what's been happening. I've seen the results of these attacks and the terror of the peasants. The bandits have attacked so near cities that people are afraid to walk in their own gardens in the evening. Away from the cities, the thieves are bold enough to strike in the daylight. They were like mice changed into rats during your absence—like swallows become hawks!" Nessumontu's slanted eyes glowed orange in anger. "Each governor is building an army of guards to protect his province. I couldn't tell them not to do this for they have real need of them, but I've been afraid they might use these men for other reasons. The sand-dwellers, who are famous for their unfriendliness, have been forming into larger groups to save themselves from attacks."

Kheti's eyes were grey stones as he heard this. He said, "Well, Rakkor, it seems we'll have to go after them again. Interfering with my time with Neferset puts me in no mood for mercy."

"I've never felt merciful toward them," Nessumontu said coldly, "but I've had to spread my forces too thinly with too little authority."

Semu, who had been silent through all this, was testing the edge of his sword with a careful finger. "In Atalan," he finally said, "I had little need for this. Now it can be put to use." He looked at Amenemhet. "You'll find that lack of activity hasn't weakened my arm or slowed my reflexes." He frowned. "My compassion is not aroused for butchers."

Amenemhet spoke quickly. "It's good to know so many strong arms are eager to help. However, this isn't the only problem needing attention. I can't send everyone to chase bandits. Kheti and Rakkor, you did a fine job of decreasing their numbers before, and I want you to resume your activities. Take what soldiers Nessumontu can spare to fill out your forces. Nessumontu, you'll station men at every outpost and city to insure that the citizens can continue their work. Also keep an eye toward the outside borders in case any foreign enemies think this an opportunity to strike. Make sure that, in all these areas, there are frequent, unscheduled patrols." Amenemhet turned to Semu. "I appreciate your offer, Semu, but I can't have you risk your life in desolate areas unfamiliar to you," Amenemhet said. "You told me that your duties in Atalan were keeping order among the people. From the hungry faces I've seen in the city, we need someone used to civilian problems."

After the others left, Kheti motioned Neferset to go with Nefrytatanen. Then he turned to Amenemhet.

When the doors were closed, Kheti said softly, "I remained to tell you something that will assure you that Rakkor and I can get these assassins."

"I had no doubt that you could," Amenemhet replied. He stood up and walked away a few steps to look out the window opening.

"It's more than just our men's ability to fight well," Kheti said.

Amenemhet turned to observe Kheti. His eyes shone with a cold light. "You have more to say?" he prompted.

"Yes," Kheti answered. "I know Shera personally. I know the way he thinks. For this reason, Rakkor and I can get him. I'm sure of it. It doesn't surprise us that he's the strongest and greediest of the bandits. We know, too, how clever he is." Kheti was staring at the floor as he mumbled, "And probably the most evil among them."

"What is there between you and Shera, Kheti?" Amenemhet moved a cushion and sat down, his eyes never leaving Kheti's face. From Kheti's expression, Amenemhet knew Kheti was disturbed at his question. "If you don't wish to tell me, you don't have to. I ask as your friend, not as your king."

Kheti looked at Amenemhet. For a moment, he had felt a flash of resentment at Amenemhet's prying. But, recognizing his concern, Kheti felt guilty. "I told you once that my mother was a commoner whom my father never married," he said slowly.

"Yes."

"A little background information will make my position clearer to you. My father sent my mother gifts to help us survive when I was a child, but we were poor and had to struggle. I was much affected, not so much by the poverty but by my mother's loneliness. She had loved my father. He was, I think, her only love. She never kept company with another man.

"Shera is a few years older than I am, and we lived in the same area. His story was different. His mother was a less honorable woman. When his father came around, he was cruel to her and to him. If I had only love from my mother, I had more than Shera. He had nothing."

Kheti paused as he remembered his childhood. He continued, "When I was small, Shera was envious of the love my mother gave me, and he tormented me mercilessly. We had many fights." Kheti smiled grimly in retrospect.

"Still, Shera and I were friends in an odd way. Being younger, I looked up to him. And he had no one else but me. Life was hard for my mother and me. At one point, my father either forgot us or no longer cared about us—or perhaps he died—but the gifts stopped coming. My mother did what she could to keep us alive. I was a small boy when I began working in the stables of a noble family. In the little spare time I had, I got an education of sorts from an old man. As I grew older, I took on more responsibilities and worked hard, but I never got more payment. It made me angry. The household treated me like a beggar. I observed the characters of the noble and his wife and grew resentful that my kind and decent mother should have so little respect and should have to struggle as she did."

Again Kheti paused, his eyes focused on a past invisible to Amenemhet. He said softly, "I noted that some people did less than honest work and received goods readily, and I began to think of what I might do. I decided I wasn't inclined, as Shera was, to be a thief or an assassin, but I did know how to fight. It was Shera who taught me. When I revealed how much I'd learned by beating him one day, we parted. We knew we could no longer be companions. It was as if we'd been natural enemies from the beginning, merely pretending friendship from mutual need. I was now old enough to be dangerous."

Kheti paused, sighed to himself, then continued, "I began to hire myself out quietly, without my mother knowing, for work that paid more than my noble did. I collected debts for those who paid me to use more force than they dared—I did all sorts of things like that. Although what I did wasn't exactly unlawful, they weren't things that made me proud. My mother thought I continued to work for the nobleman and was advancing in my position. It wasn't easy to maintain this farce."

Kheti sighed again, and Amenemhet nodded sympathetically. "Shera was a constant menace. He continued to harass me from time to time. It was as if he wanted badly to hurt me in some way, but he didn't know how to do it. After my mother died, I was involved in a scrape that developed into something bigger than my usual activities, and Shera informed on me." Kheti shook his head. "I suppose he hoped for a stiff penalty that would put me out of the way, but I managed to escape. After that, I decided the only way to avoid the degradation of being a criminal was to sell my sword for a higher price than I had in the past. I persuaded some friends to join me, and we became prosperous working together. Like me, they had no other way to live. I knew that if you amass a fortune, you can gain respectability of a kind."

Kheti looked at Amenemhet and remarked, "I hope I don't tire you with my story." Amenemhet shook his head in answer. Kheti smiled faintly. "I think I need to tell these things to someone." Amenemhet nodded but said nothing. Kheti looked at his feet and continued, "It's true that the stories circulated about me were often exaggerated. Shera helped expand and spread them. He wanted to have me declared a criminal—and hunted down. It was done so carefully that I really had no way of challenging his stories. He was like a fly buzzing around my head—constantly irritating, but never close enough to catch."

Amenemhet was silent a moment before he said, "Shera did something more, something you haven't told me."

Kheti's eyes had become ice. "Just before Sinuhe hired me and my men to stop Nefrytatanen's ship, I was on the desert searching for Shera. Yes," Kheti murmured, "Shera had finally done something to give me reason for revenge. Although recent events have distracted me from this revenge, I will now get it."

"I saw the look in your eyes whenever Shera's name

was mentioned," Amenemhet said quietly. "I think that there was a girl involved in all this."

Kheti smiled bitterly and said nothing.

Amenemhet stood up and walked to the door. He opened it a little, gave the guard some orders, then turned back to look at Kheti. "I know you'll get Shera one day," he said quietly.

Chapter Twenty-two

Yazid was rearranging some of Amenemhet's garments when Amenemhet came quietly into the room and addressed the servant in a low voice. Yazid turned from his work.

"Now that the noblemen are settled for a while and the thieves are being pursued, I think I should look into the matter of that priestess," Amenemhet said. He sighed. "Poor Ankhneferu came again today to ask me about this. It seems that Kuwait performs the ceremony tonight, so I intend to watch it. I want you to go with me." Seeing Yazid shrug, Amenemhet added, "We'll dress as nobles and wear cloaks with hoods so we aren't recognized. I don't care to have it known that I visited Kuwait's ceremony, if it's as Ankhneferu claims it is!"

"How would we get there?" Yazid was surprised at this secrecy.

"Like anyone else," Amenemhet answered. "We'll take a quiet walk and stop at the temple to see what Kuwait does. I must know for myself before I can accuse her of wrongdoing."

"Why must we always behave like spies?" Yazid grumbled.

"It won't be difficult," Amenemhet replied. He smiled. "Consider this an evening of devotion or entertainment—whichever it turns out to be. Don't mention this to anyone, though, so my motives aren't misunderstood, and also so Kuwait isn't warned."

This seemed reasonable to Yazid, but, later, when they were walking down dark streets, he felt uncomfortable. If Amenemhet were recognized by an enemy, Yazid would be his only protector.

Amenemhet enjoyed the change. The freedom of being able to do as he wished, without ceremony, exhilarated him. He felt a little reckless and was in high spirits when they reached the temple.

Looking out from behind the drapery to see how many had come and what the prospects for the night might be, Kuwait's eyes fell on a man who stood in the back of the room. He was a stranger but in the way he stood, the set of his shoulders, the way he held his head, he was familiar. She studied him carefully. He was dressed in fine garments and must be a noble, but his clothes were subdued, as if he didn't wish to draw attention. She wondered about this. When noblemen came, they usually wanted her to see them and dressed accordingly. She wondered if this stranger wished to hide. It was difficult to see his face because he wore a cloak and hood, making it impossible to recognize his features in this light.

As the man turned to speak to his companion, similarly dressed, Kuwait saw his profile. In the momentary flash of a torch's sudden flare, she saw the glimmer of a golden eye. There was only one man she had ever seen with eyes like those. She looked again, but the face was shadowed. It didn't matter. She knew.

Kuwait's heart beat faster. If she had plotted for weeks, she couldn't have chose a better way to see him again. Now that she knew he was here, she would be very careful with her part of the ceremony and her dance. She would make it sufficient to shake the coldest man. And she was sure Amenemhet wasn't cold.

Kuwait returned to her room thinking about her dance. What would appeal to this king to whom she had never spoken? She decided not to be too obvious. He might not like that. Perhaps something very slow and subtle would be best, something she could work into the ritual. She decided to wear a modest robe. She would let the robe slide open and, possibly, fall off. If he didn't like that—which she doubted—she could always say it had been an accident. She smiled, very pleased.

Amenemhet stood with Yazid in the crowd waiting for the ceremony to begin. Before the statue of Hat-hor, a flame burned, and Amenemhet passed the time watching the smoke rise in small, grey curls. Ankhneferu didn't have to warn him what this could turn out to be. Amenemhet could sense the anticipation of the others, who were exclusively male and almost visibly panting. He was disgusted that the temple should be turned into such a scene. Although Amenemhet had never suffered from excessive bashfulness, he thought lovemaking had a proper place. The temple of Hat-hor wasn't such a place. The goddess was a woman and, in one sense, represented physical love. But a temple was yet a temple.

Kuwait glided from an opening in the drapery by the side of the goddess's statue. She was completely covered, dressed in a blood-red robe. Amenemhet noted that even her sleeves were long. This surprised him. She was followed by a number of young girls, all dressed in long white robes.

Amenemhet had to admit that Kuwait was beautiful. Even from his distance he could see her large black eyes shining in the light, her full red mouth. Though the robe covered her, it didn't hide the outlines of her rich body. When the part of the ritual arrived in which the priestess offered herself to the goddess, Amenemhet stiffened slightly. For, from behind the curtains, came the sound of a reed flute played as if to charm a snake. This was not part of the usual procedure.

The girls in white disappeared like swallows flown away, and Kuwait knelt alone before the statue. She prostrated herself before Hat-hor. Then slowly, very slowly, she began to rise like a cobra from a basket, moving with the music of the flute. The room was silent.

Yazid exchanged looks with Amenemhet. Here was what they had come to investigate.

For some time, Kuwait swayed slowly on her knees, as gracefully as a serpent. Then she slithered to her feet, and Amenemhet caught the quick and clever movement, disguised by her dance, in which she loosened the fastening of her robe. He anticipated what she would now do.

Kuwait swirled in a slow circle, and the robe became a little looser. She dipped a shoulder, and the robe slipped down around her arm. A very slow turn and a slight, appropriate rolling of her torso, and the robe slipped further. A sudden twist, and, like a snake shedding its skin, the crimson robe fell at her feet. A small kick—and she was free of it. Amenemhet stared.

Kuwait's copper-colored skin was like satin rippling with her movements. Her body was, unquestionably, one of the most seductive Amenemhet had ever seen. Her dance, still slowly following the writhings of a serpent, did nothing to disguise her attributes. Neither did her undergarments. One small bit of shining black cloth was arranged to barely cover her breasts; an even smaller bit held in place with a single, precarious-looking strand of red beads, served as a sort of girdle. Now Amenemhet knew he hadn't been mistaken in the movement he had seen when she had unfastened her robe. Kuwait had not intended to keep her robe on.

Amenemhet thought of the dance Nefrytatanen had performed as the slave-girl Lotus. Her costume had been no less revealing and her body no less tempting, but Nefrytatanen had made her dance an expression of love. Kuwait made hers an invitation—a challenge—to every man there, if he had the courage to accept it—and the price.

The tempo grew neither slower nor faster, but remained all through the dance the same pulsing, throbbing beat. Amenemhet felt his heart matched the rhythm of the music. Despite himself, he could barely endure the temptation much longer. Slowly Kuwait recoiled to the floor, ending the dance like a cobra withdrawing into its basket. Amenemhet was relieved it was over. His whole body was warm and damp.

After a tactful moment of composing themselves, Amenemhet and Yazid exchanged glances. Yazid's skin was shining with moisture.

"Never have I seen such an exhibition!" Yazid took a deep breath. "Never!" he added.

"Nor I," Amenemhet agreed. "A man would have to be a stone not to react to that. I swear she could raise a dead man with that dance if his eyes were propped open to see it!"

"Devotion to Hat-hor," Yazid sneered. "That's a joke. We've just attended devotions to Kuwait and her own appetite."

Amenemhet lowered his voice. "Take a message from me to that guard of hers. Tell him I would converse with her." Yazid looked doubtfully at the gigantic man who stood barring the entrance to the back rooms, then, taking a deep breath and showing the royal insignia he wore, he approached the guard.

Moments later, Kuwait came out and walked toward Amenemhet and Yazid. She again wore the crimson robe, but didn't trouble herself to hold it closed. She walked slowly, not as a humble subject who approached her king, but with her head high. He knew she deliberately exaggerated the swing of her hips for his benefit; with each step, her robe fell open. She evidently thought he would be her companion tonight.

When the crowd saw Kuwait coming, they turned curiously to see who attracted her attention. Seeing the king himself, for Amenemhet had thrown off his cloak, they seemed not to know who to look at first, the king or the voluptuous priestess. Those nearest Amenemhet stepped away, bowing self-consciously. Amenemhet ignored them.

Like well-rehearsed dancers, the others swayed in a long line of bowing heads, as Kuwait approached them. Amenemhet was irritated because they seemed to treat her with as much respect as they did Nefrytatanen but it wasn't actually respect he saw in the eyes that stared at Kuwait. When she paused before Amenemhet, she knelt.

Kuwait's black eyes gleamed as they lifted to meet his, though she stayed on her knees. He realized she remained kneeling so he might have enough time to view the soft flesh that rose and fell with each breath from the top of her well-filled costume. When she rose, gracefully, a musky perfume floated with her.

"My king," Kuwait murmured, "your visit does me honor." Her voice was low-pitched and very soft.

"I would speak privately." Amenemhet's eyes were gold glitters.

Those standing near enough to hear this listened with great interest. Was it possible the king tired of the queen? They speculated on this interesting scandal. What if Nefrytatanen should learn of this? What exciting gossip there would be?

Kuwait led Amenemhet through the crowd, then down a hall, her bangles jingling softly with each step. They entered a small room which Amenemhet judged to be part of Kuwait's private quarters. The inside of the doorway was covered with drapery, as were the rest of the walls, giving the effect of a tent. It seemed to be a sitting room, for he noticed it held only one large lounging couch and a small table or two. Amenemhet was sure he knew how the couch was used. Draped over it, and spread as carpets on the floor, were fine skins of many animals. The room looked like a rich sand-dweller's tent.

"You will share some wine with me?" Kuwait offered. Remembering Amenardis too vividly, Amenemhet eyed the goblet with suspicion and shook his head. "I'm not Sinuhe's daughter," she said. She smiled. "I wish my king a long and healthy life—very long and very healthy." This last became a purring invitation. She was standing so close Amenemhet could feel the warmth her body radiated, and he could see her skin glistening slightly from the efforts of her dance.

"Such dances as I've just witnessed are a titillating experience at a party, but seem out of place in the temple," Amenemhet said softly.

"I'm Hat-hor's priestess, and she's the goddess of women and love," Kuwait replied. She sipped her wine looking at him from the goblet's rim. Her pink tongue flicked her lips like a snake. "Surely, love and its delights aren't shameful," she whispered.

"They aren't, he answered slowly, "but such public displays are better left to other religions."

"I'm sorry if I offended you," she murmured. She didn't like the direction this was taking. "My robe slipped off by accident, and I don't usually dance with such abandon," she lied. She moved a little closer. "I saw you before I came out, and I'm afraid your presence inspired me." Her eyes challenged him as she added, "I didn't realize my king was so attractive." At Amenemhet's slight frown, she realized that flattery wasn't going to have a favorable effect on him. She knew, then, that she hadn't fooled him. He had seen her unclasp her robe, although he didn't mention it.

"The next time I come," Amenemhet said pleasantly, "will be when another priestess presides, unless you can direct your inspiration with more wisdom."

He held the drapery aside and, giving her one more warning look, ducked under it and left.

As Amenemhet and Yazid walked away, they heard a crash behind them. Yazid looked questioningly at Amenemhet, who only smiled and continued walking.

Kuwait stood alone, the shards of a shell-thin goblet at her feet. The slave that hurried in to gather up the pieces heard Kuwait mumble, "I'll get you yet. King or not, you won't walk away next time so calmly." Kuwait's expression was so frightening that the slave finished her job and left hastily, pitying those who must prepare their mistress for bed.

Later, having sent her servants rushing from her room, two in tears and another with a bruise on her cheek, Kuwait lay in the darkness, thinking. Having used her servants as objects for punishment, she felt more peaceful. She closed her eyes and stretched, yawning.

Shera entered the room as cautiously as he entered every enclosed area. He was a shadow moving among other shadows. He was used to walking in darkness and had no trouble seeing clearly with only dim light. He stood by Kuwait's bed looking down at her a moment. Then he put his hand over her mouth.

Kuwait's eyes opened, their whites pearly in the dimness. She lay calmly looking at Shera until he removed his hand. "In case I startled you, I didn't want you to scream," he said softly.

Kuwait got out of bed, undisturbed by his presence or her nakedness. She pulled the window hangings down and then lit a small lamp. Shera watched her movements with admiration.

"Nothing startles me," came her low voice, "and I'm not given to screaming."

"Least of all because of a man in your room at night." Shera was sarcastic as he put his arms around her. His kiss was ungentle. He stepped back a little and said softly, "So King Amenemhet came tonight to watch you." Her eyes met his and glanced away. "I hear the news," he added.

"It surely wastes no time reaching you," Kuwait murmured.

"You outdid yourself in your dance. Was that in honor of his visit?" Kuwait didn't answer and was afraid to look into those pale eyes that watched her. "He came back here with you later," Shera said softly, "but he didn't stay very long. Is he so fast or did he disapprove of you?" At her angry look, he laughed softly. "Your expression would tell me the answer even if I didn't already know it. You reach far, Kuwait," he warned. She didn't take the warning lightly.

"He didn't approve of me or my dance and gave me his opinion on this," Kuwait said sharply.

"Marriage seems to have made him very conservative," Shera remarked. "Or else the queen is a good bed partner." He watched Kuwait's eyes flare in renewed anger and added lightly, "Before their marriage he would have enjoyed your dance, judging from what I've heard."

"Perhaps," she said, trying to be calm, "but he seems dull to me now."

"Your eyes say you lie," Shera whispered, "for there was passion in them you couldn't hide."

"The passion was anger, remembering what he told me," she said quickly, "not desire."

"I could almost believe that, you are so accomplished a liar," Shera replied, "but I know you better. It doesn't matter. What woman wouldn't like to have a chance at the king? Especially you, with your hunger for power and wealth. It doesn't seem likely he'd be interested in one such as you." Shera smiled. "Even before he was married, he was careful who he was involved with."

Shera was deliberately goading her, Kuwait knew. Playing with Shera was like teasing a cobra. "You should scoff at wanting power and riches," she said. "It wouldn't be a bad thing, though, to befriend him, even for a short time. I might learn things of interest to us both." Kuwait wound her arms around Shera and whispered close to his ear. "Did you come only to discuss business?"

"No," he answered softly.

Kuwait could tell she was succeeding in distracting him. She nibbled his ear lobe thoughtfully. "You came for me?" she murmured, pressing closer to him. Now she knew he no longer thought of Amenemhet.

Shera tangled his hand in her hair and pulled her face to his. When his pale eyes met hers, she knew he was under her control. He picked her up and walked to the bed. In one motion, he dropped her on it and laid himself over her roughly.

"Take off your dagger," Kuwait whispered. "It's bruising me."

Rising to kneel over her, Shera unfastened the dagger

and placed it on the table carefully in reach. "Now it will be only me who will bruise you," he said.

Kuwait smiled in triumph and loosened Shera's tunic.

It took no longer than the following morning for the gossip to reach Nefrytatanen. As she sat in the garden with Neferset and Bekhet playing with the children in the grass, two servants passing on the other side of a row of thick shrubs, unaware of the queen's presence, discussed the incident in the temple. When Nefrytatanen realized they spoke of Amenemhet, she was incredulous. If he had gone there, he would have told her. But as she listened to the voices, she realized she had made no mistake. Her heart sank, but in a moment she was flooded with the heat of anger and jealousy. Controlling her expression, she appeared undisturbed, but Neferset and Bekhet stared at her in open shock.

Neferset said quickly, "The king said he was going to investigate that matter, and it seems he has done this."

Trying to seem calm but having tears of anger in her eyes, Bekhet said, "Oh yes, Ankhneferu has been asking him daily for help." Privately, she resolved to talk to Yazid about this matter.

"Of course," Nefrytatanen murmured, staring at the grass. Silently, she cried: why didn't he tell me? Why was a simple matter kept secret from me? Or *was* it a simple matter, after all?

Though Nefrytatanen said nothing more, Neferset and Bekhet were suspicious of her outward calm. They didn't know what to say, and the moment was uncomfortably quiet.

"My family relaxes in the shade, and I, finally, have time to join them." Amenemhet came toward them smiling. He dropped to the grass next to Nefrytatanen and tickled Maeti.

Neferset and Bekhet rose quickly, hiding their anger from him.

"I must do something in the house. Excuse me," Neferset said quickly and hurried away before they could answer.

Bekhet said, "And I." She gave Amenemhet a grim look as she turned and rushed off.

Amenemhet watched them go, a puzzled look on his face. He turned to Nefrytatanen, who still stared at the grass. He held out a small white flower.

"I saw this perfect blossom and thought of you," he said. Nefrytatanen took the flower, forcing herself to look up at him and smile convincingly, wondering if he preferred lush crimson blooms. He plucked a blade of grass and nibbled on it thoughtfully. Then he lay back and stretched luxuriously. Nefrytatanen looked at the body she knew so well and wondered if she now shared it with another.

With eyes half-closed, but watching Nefrytatanen intently through his lashes, Amenemhet asked softly, "Why did Neferset and Bekhet leave so hastily?"

"I suppose they thought we'd like to be alone."

He chewed the grass, thinking. Then he rolled over and tickled Senwadjet's bare chest with the grass. Small golden eyes crinkled with delight and looked at him. The child kicked and wriggled, wanting more. Amenemhet smiled and caught a foot gently in his hand, which produced more happy sounds.

Nefrytatanen felt her heart turn over while she watched. She considered the problem carefully and then made a decision. She felt as if her heart fell in small pieces in the grass.

Amenemhet had turned from the children and lay quietly on his back looking at the leaves above him.

Nefrytatanen took a deep breath and composed herself. She would not think about shadows—she would not.

Amenemhet wasn't as relaxed as he appeared. His thoughts traveled far from the leaves he was looking at. Why had Neferset and Bekhet rushed off so strangely? Why was Nefrytatanen so quiet? Had they heard about last night? Didn't Nefrytatanen trust him? He wondered how he could approach the subject from some unexpected angle to see what she would say. He wanted to know what her reaction might be to a question he had wondered about from time to time but had never asked. It was related to the subject he really wanted to discuss. He decided to try.

"Beloved," he said softly, "I have often wondered about something you alone can answer for me. At least you're the only one I could ask and expect an honest and unembarrassed answer from."

Nefrytatanen looked a little startled and wondered what this was. She waited.

"It's a strange question, but I am curious and now seems as good a time as any to ask," he said. "I've wondered how it feels to a woman to make love." He noted that Nefrytatanen's face paled. "I've wondered if it's the same as a man feels or if it's different. Can you tell me how you feel?"

Amenemhet watched Nefrytatanen put aside the question of Kuwait and concentrate on gathering an answer to this one. Twisting the flower stem between her fingers, she sighed.

"I can speak only for myself and my own feelings with you. Perhaps others are different," she said slowly. "I'll try to tell you, but it isn't easy."

She looked briefly at Amenemhet, and he saw that her eyes were exceedingly shiny. She looked away.

"I had heard love was a beautiful and pleasurable experience," she said. "I had looked forward to such a sharing, trying to imagine what it would be like. But, as with other feelings, it's impossible to imagine what you haven't experienced. With you, beloved, I found more than I dreamed about, and words cannot relate such feelings."

She hesitated, searching her mind so she might make her meaning clear, taking the opportunity to regain control of her voice, which was beginning to tremble. "I found more than physical sensation. In itself, that's indescribable and can be almost unbearable at its height.

But it can be endured because it's such pleasure. Through our bodies, our minds also blend, and my emotions are stirred to even greater heights than the physical sensation, giving more dimension to what our bodies do and even more depth to our minds' meeting. She smiled faintly. "That's the only way I can describe how it is for me, and the words seem so pale."

Amenemhet had dropped the blade of grass and was sitting now with arms clasping his bent knees. He leaned toward Nefrytatanen and tilted her chin with his fingertips, so her eyes met his. "Then we have the same experience after all, and it seems there's no difference between the sensations of men and of women in love," he said softly, still intently watching her expression.

The shadows of gossip hovered over her again and wouldn't be driven away. She withdrew her chin and looked at the grass so he wouldn't see her tears. She said quietly, in a tone she fiercely controlled, "Our marriage contract allows you a harem, and it seems men often desire a variety of women even if they love a wife." Amenemhet's eyebrows raised slightly. Now he was certain what bothered her. "I have wondered if you, perhaps, wish this and say nothing of it. If it would make you happy, I wouldn't refuse you." Her voice trailed off. It had taken all her strength to say this.

Amenemhet knew how much it had cost Nefrytatanen to offer him a harem, and he was shaken. He replied, "What we have I cannot share with another because you are the meaning of it. Imitation would be insult. A mere physical joining without this blending of mind and emotions would mean too little to interest me. The land is filled with charming ladies with shapely bodies, but you're the only one who's beautiful to me. Why would I waste one night, or even an hour, mating with a pretty face and body which is empty of love, when you are here?"

Amenemhet pulled Nefrytatanen into his arms and felt her heart racing against his own. "Beloved," he said softly, "I want only you. I may admire others, as I

would admire a flower, but you're the only woman I
wish to hold in my arms." He smiled into her hair.
"Once, I didn't know this. It was before I'd met you.
Like other young men, I sought the favors of pretty
girls. Now I'm glad I did. They were a preparation for
you."

After sending slanting streaks of red into the skies,
messengers heralding his arrival, Ra himself appeared
on the eastern horizon. As the sun's rim rose from behind the hills, the sky between each streak was filled
with orange brightening to gold until the sun floated
free of the earth's edge, surrounded by its own radiance.

While the shadows separated and became substance,
one shadow moved toward Ithtawe's gates. The guards
watched it carefully as it approached.

A rider on a horse, which seemed to drag each hoof
forward with great effort, finally reached the gates. One
sentry came down the ladder to open the doors a little
and investigate.

Weary eyes looked at him from a blood-smeared,
sand-caked face. A slit of a mouth whispered, "I must
see the king."

The guard saw a large and wetly gleaming red stain
on the man's lower chest and threw open the gates to
admit him. The man slid off his horse and collapsed into
the sentry's arms, and the soldier shouted to the others
to help him.

The guards carried the man inside the palace doors.
He was bleeding so profusely that they laid him on a
bench in the hall rather than carry him further. One
guard ran for Amenemhet and the other for Horemheb.

Amenemhet, still wrapping a cloth around his waist,
raced downstairs two paces ahead of Nefrytatanen, who
ran holding her robe together, hair flying loose.

Amenemhet glanced once at the wound and leaned
over the man. "What is it?" he asked softly.

The messenger's eyes opened slowly. Already they
were slightly glazed over, but he recognized the king's

voice. "Lord Seti has been attacked by bandits," the courier whispered. His voice was lost, but his lips moved to shape, "Help me." Then, there was no way to help him.

Amenemhet looked up as Horemheb arrived, clutching a robe around him. "Go back to your bed, Horemheb," he said. "There's nothing you can do here now." He stood up slowly.

Nefrytatanen glanced at the blood and stepped back. "What did he say?" she asked.

Amenemhet didn't like to tell her for he knew she was fond of Seti. He took a deep breath. "Seti has been attacked." Her face went pale, and she said nothing. "Where's Nessumontu?" Amenemhet demanded, turning to the soldier.

"He's out on a patrol. Lord Rakkor is also gone."

"Get Lord Kheti then!"

It wasn't necessary to awaken Kheti because he was halfway down the steps, wrapped as Amenemhet was, hair askew.

"Seti's house has been attacked, and Nessumontu and Rakkor are both out of the city," Amenemhet said.

Kheti waited for no orders. "Get my horse ready!" he snapped to the soldier, "and get as many men as can be spared. Take supplies for the trip."

Kheti turned to hurry back upstairs and almost ran into Neferset, who had wrapped herself in a robe. "I must help Seti," Kheti said. She nodded and followed him upstairs.

When they were in the room, as Kheti was dressing rapidly, Neferset asked in a soft voice, "Is it far away?"

"Seti's province is three days from here. Of course that's why they've attacked him. If he can hold his house until we get there, we'll teach them something they're unlikely to forget." Kheti adjusted his sword at his hip. Then, taking his other weapons, he hurried toward the door.

Seeing Neferset looking at him silently, he stopped and laid down his weapons. He put his arms around her and held her close to him. She was trembling. He turned her face to his and kissed her, tasting the salt of her tears. With one finger he wiped the tears gently away, while he held her with his other arm.

"I'll come back," he said softly. "Don't be afraid for me. It's Seti we must worry about. He's a statesman, not a military man."

Neferset nodded but made no reply.

Kheti picked up his weapons and, giving Neferset one more kiss, quickly turned and hurried from her, afraid to look back and reveal he wasn't as calm as he tried to appear. Neferset followed him slowly, watching him run lightly downstairs. She was only halfway down when Kheti waved to Amenemhet and Nefrytatanen and went out the door. Neferset had barely reached the hall when she heard the horses thunder off. She stepped out of the doorway to glimpse them go through the gates, then stood watching as the gates closed slowly.

Nefrytatanen's hand on her arm turned her gently. Neferset couldn't look up as she asked, "How long will he take, do you think? When will we know if he's safe?"

Nefrytatanen turned to Amenemhet questioningly.

"Kheti will return, surely, in seven or eight days or ten at the most—if he lingers to help them clean up the mess." Amenemhet answered in a firm tone allowing not even a hint of doubt in his voice.

Nefrytatanen smiled and turned to lead Neferset slowly back upstairs. "You've never seen Kheti in a battle," she said softly. "If you had, you wouldn't be afraid for him. I saw him fight more than once, and I know the thieves would be wise to flee now."

Neferset looked at her but said nothing. Nefrytatanen knew well enough how her friend felt and squeezed her arm a little as they turned into Kheti and Neferset's room.

"I'll send Horemheb to give you something so you can sleep a little longer, if you wish," Nefrytatanen offered.

"No, thank you," Neferset whispered. She

straightened herself and stood away from Nefrytatanen. "It's just that we never had such troubles in Atalan. I've never seen violence and bloodshed. Kheti will be all right. I know he will. He must."

Neferset closed the door and went to the window opening to look in the direction Kheti had ridden. She could see nothing. She went back to the bed and lay in the place yet warm from Kheti's body. She drenched his headrest with silent tears before she finally got up. She couldn't sleep, and his place had grown cold.

Being the wife of a nobleman in Tamera was far more difficult than being a princess in Atalan, Neferset observed as she dressed. She picked up her cat and rubbed her face in its fur.

"It's easy to be brave," she told the cat, "when nothing threatens you or anyone you love. Courage is only a shining word then, not a thing you must reach into your soul and find."

After two-and-a-half days of riding as fast as they could without killing their horses, Kheti and his soldiers came over the last hill to look down at the house of Seti. They stared.

"Great Asar, Lord of Eternity!" Kheti breathed.

The house showed no sign of life, and vultures flew around the place. They could see holes broken through the wall surrounding the buildings. They could see that bodies lay all over the ground by the wall.

Kheti moved his horse forward slowly. It seemed there was no need to rush, and they walked the horses down the hill.

"They got away again!" Kheti exclaimed. He knew no one but Shera would dare raid a nobleman's house. Kheti was furious that the quarry had escaped him. Worse, the bandits would gain courage from this; they would be more ambitious. Who could tell what they might dream of next?

Kheti was thinking about this when the man riding next to him fell forward, an arrow in his chest. Suddenly the missiles flew in a steady shower. Shouting, Kheti turned his horse, and they raced back up the hill. There was nowhere else for them to go. He cursed himself for thinking of other things when he should have been watching for an ambush. He saw a man before him slump over his horse's neck.

"Hold on, hold on," Kheti mumbled. If they might only get to the other side of the hill, they could rest and see what to do next. If they could only get that far. Kheti thanked whichever fool down there had let fly the first arrow. It had been too soon. He was sure the man would pay for his mistake. Shera would have waited until Kheti and the soldiers were at the walls and then cornered them.

They scrambled over the hill at last. Kheti turned to see how many had fallen. Six men lay on the hill facing the house. He saw one of them crawling slowly toward them. Hesitating, Kheti considered the possibility of running down to help the man. He crouched on the hill, wondering if he could make it. He ran.

It hadn't seemed so far away when Kheti had looked down from the top, but as he ran toward the man, it seemed to take forever to reach him—forever, another shower of arrows falling all around him, thumping with unnerving regularity against his shield.

When Kheti reached the man and turned him over, he saw the risk had been for nothing. Cursing, he darted back up the hill, half-running and half-sliding in the sand. He foundered and fell to his knees. He struggled to his feet and, straightening his shield to afford him its best cover, he gasped and climbed on.

His soldiers used their own bows to try to protect him, but it was difficult. They could see no one and took aim by guesswork.

Kheti threw himself over the hilltop and lay catching his breath, wondering what they now might do. The assassins in the house wouldn't be likely to get away with the soldiers watching them. But they also had a well. Kheti's supplies were very limited because they had

traveled light for speed. He couldn't let Shera escape
without trying. The men were looking to him for orders.
He sent them to check their water supply while he considered what they might do. To simply turn their backs
and ride away from Shera was unthinkable.

Neferset awoke screaming in the night. Nefrytatanen heard the sound in her sleep and wondered hazily
what was making such a noise Amenemhet leaped up
beside her and listened a moment.

"It's Neferset!" he exclaimed. Snatching up a robe
beside the bed, he pulled it over his head and ran to
the door. Nefrytatanen was only a step behind him.

Amenemhet threw open the door to see Neferset
sitting up in bed weeping. Yazid appeared behind them
in the doorway.

"Get Horemheb," Nefrytatanen said quickly. She
went to Neferset and put her arms around her. Amenemhet hadn't been sure what to do because Neferset,
like the rest of them, usually slept naked. He was
hesitant to touch her, though she cried like a child.
Nefrytatanen held her to her shoulder and stroked
her head soothingly. The cat slunk against the wall, its
fur standing from fright, its green eyes wide.

Neferset's sobbing had calmed considerably by the
time Horemheb came wearily in, clasping his robe
around him. He looked Neferset over and took powder
from the box he carried. Mixing it with some water,
he gave it to Nefrytatanen.

"Make her drink this," he said. "It will calm her."

Nefrytatanen obeyed, and Neferset swallowed some
of it. Then Nefrytatanen tucked the covers around
Neferset and held her against her shoulder like Maeti,
until her trembling slowed.

"Can you tell me what happened?" Nefrytatanen
asked gently.

Neferset nodded. "Seti is dead," she said in a dull
voice. Her eyes, green and wide as the cat's, stared at
them. "All those in his house are dead."

"No, no, that's not so," Nefrytatanen soothed. "You had only an evil dream."

"I had a dream of prophecy," Neferset said, looking down at the bed linens. Her tears again began to fall. "Kheti knows about the dreams. He's riding into an ambush. The thieves that killed Lord Seti are waiting for Kheti."

Nefrytatanen and Amenemhet exchanged looks of alarm. They turned as Sarenput and Semu arrived.

"What is it, Neferset?" Sarenput asked, sitting on the edge of the bed. "What did you dream?"

"Lord Seti and those in his house are dead. Their murderers are waiting for Kheti."

"Are you sure you didn't dream this because you're worried about Kheti?" Sarenput was very gentle with his sister.

"I'm sure," she said after a moment's pause. "It was one of those terrible dreams."

Sarenput turned to Amenemhet. "You know about these dreams she gets that tell the future?" Amenemhet nodded. "I'll go myself, if you can spare the men and horses."

"How would you find the way?" Nefrytatanen asked. "You don't know where Seti's house is, and it's a three-day ride."

"I'll show him the way." Rakkor, still covered with dust from his patrol, stood in the doorway. "I'll get my men ready while you get dressed, Sarenput. We'll leave right away. No one but Shera would dare such a thing."

After they had watched Sarenput, Rakkor, and the men ride away, they went back into the palace. Amenemhet slammed the door behind him.

"I want to go myself." His eyes were fiery gold triangles.

"If you go, who will protect Ithtawe?" Nefrytatanen asked.

"There are soldiers here," he said sharply. No one will go in my place the next time!"

Four days later, all of them returned, grim-faced. Kheti stalked into the hall looking furious. He threw himself into a chair and stared at the floor.

"Neferset was right," he said. He was quiet a moment and then related what he had found. "We camped on the hill," he said disgustedly, "trying to decide what to do. We hadn't enough men to storm the place and not enough supplies to wait them out."

Sarenput interrupted, "They were still afraid to wait and see what you'd do."

"They crept away in the moonless night like jackals," Rakkor sneered.

Kheti was inconsolable. "I had Shera in my hands, and he got away."

"There was no way to prevent it," Amenemhet said firmly. He turned to look out the window opening at the dark garden. "You'll get him next time."

"How?" Kheti demanded.

"I don't know yet," Amenemhet said slowly. "There will be a way."

"Rakkor and Sarenput met us coming back. We looked like fools with nothing but more dead." Kheti's eyes were grey stones.

Amenemhet turned to him. "Not like fools," he said. "You went with no supplies and too few men. The next dead will be theirs."

"I have some you can begin with," came Nessumontu's voice from the doorway. He pushed several prisoners, stumbling ahead of him, hands bound behind their backs.

Kheti stood up quickly. Amenemhet smiled coldly.

Nessumontu's slanted eyes gleamed. "We managed to get them alive, as you asked. But I can quickly change that state, if you wish it." He drew his sword as he spoke, and the prisoners looked at him fearfully. Now the hall behind them was filled with Nessumontu's men.

Amenemhet went closer to the prisoners to look at them. "On your knees," he said softly. They crashed to the floor. He studied each of their faces and found

what he wanted—terror. He smiled at Nessumontu. "I
think they know where Shera hides," he said, "but they
won't be willing to volunteer the information. Starting
tomorrow just before the noon meal, execute them at
Ithtawe's gates—one each day—until one of them
speaks." The prisoners no longer simply knelt. They
lowered their foreheads to the floor in supplication.
Amenemhet put his foot lightly on the back of one of
their heads. "This one first," he said.

Nessumontu dragged the bandit to his feet, and the
man, paralyzed with fear, stared at Amenemhet.

"By what method should they be dispatched?" Nessumontu asked casually.

Amenemhet considered this. "I'll think about it and
tell you in the morning," he replied.

The bandit saw a variety of grisly visions and threw
himself again on his knees, groveling to kiss Amenemhet's foot, which Amenemhet moved away.

"I don't know Shera. I don't know where he is!" the
bandit cried.

Amenemhet said softly, "That is most unfortunate
for you."

Nessumontu nodded to the guards behind him, and
they dragged the bandit from the floor, holding him up,
half-carrying him as they led the other two prisoners
away. The man was too afraid to walk.

When they had left, Amenemhet said, "Execute him
and the others one by one in the usual way. Don't let
those left alive know how their predecessors died. Let
them think about worse methods than we'll use, and we
might get an answer from them. If not—we would have
executed them anyway."

The prisoners never spoke. They looked terrified
enough as each was led to Ithtawe's gates where the executioner waited with his axe, and a crowd stood watching silently.

After the last of them had been disposed of, Amenemhet concluded they must not have known Shera's
hiding place, after all. He wasn't surprised, but it had

been worth the try. He didn't like making an exhibition of death, but it had been good for the honest citizens to know someone had been caught and punished. He hoped it would also frighten any lesser bandits who had seen or would hear of the executions.

Several days later Kheti came triumphantly back from his patrol with six more men, he had caught attacking a small farm. Amenemhet had them lined against a wall, facing a row of archers. He walked slowly past them before giving the order.

"If any of you wish to live, now is the moment to say where Shera hides." He looked into each of their faces. "If you know and speak, banishment is your penalty."

They remained silent.

Amenemhet shook his head in disgust, knowing that if he could catch Shera and his band, the lesser thieves would scatter in fear. He stepped to the side and gave the signal.

The arrows flew cleanly to their marks.

Amenemhet turned away with Kheti and Nessumontu at his side. As they walked, Kheti said, "Yesterday, Lord Semerkhet's men killed three bandits on his province. The day before that, Rakkor executed five more near Wast."

"A grim business," Amenemhet commented, not looking grief-stricken.

"It surely is," Nessumontu said. His eyes narrowed as he glanced at the bodies being loaded into a cart. "It's too bad Shera isn't one of these."

"He's mine," Kheti replied.

Amenemhet went into the palace and joined Nefrytatanen for the noon meal. He appeared very cheerful.

Chapter Twenty-three

The bands of thieves had become more cautious. Amenemhet's sudden, forceful campaign and the many captures and subsequent executions made even Shera and his band withdraw awhile. During this ensuing period of relative calm, Nefrytatanen decided to travel to Noph. There were some things in her old palace she wanted to bring to Ithtawe, and the journey would take her away only three nights. She left early in the morning, taking Senwedjet and Maeti, Bekhet and Dedjet, and a well-armed escort on her ship.

As the day dragged on, Amenemhet found he missed Nefrytatanen's presence. Although they usually saw little of each other during their day's activities, he suddenly realized he no longer heard her footsteps in the halls, the drift of laughter or her singing from another room. He missed the faint scent of her perfume in the air, and he secretly dreaded the coming night's loneliness.

Amenemhet ate his evening meal and went to their bedchamber, tired from the day and not looking forward to his empty bed. Putting aside his other chores, he sat looking listlessly at the garden.

Just then a message arrived from Kuwait saying she had heard news of Shera, and, as she did not dare to come to the palace, could Amenemhet come discreetly to her quarters at the temple? He thought about this carefully. Was it a trick? Would she dare try to trick him? He wondered awhile. She might know something. Finally, taking a cloak to disguise himself, he left, deciding not to tell even Yazid where he was going. This time he was taking no chance that gossip would reach Nefrytatanen. To prepare for possible danger, he took his dagger.

When Amenemhet entered Kuwait's quarters, he was greeted by a servant who requested his patience for a moment and invited him to sit down and be comfortable. Watching the girl back out, bowing, Amenemhet sat on the couch. He was impatient because he wanted to get out of there as quickly as possible. He tried to soothe his uneasiness by persuading himself that Kuwait very possibly had information for him and wanted a reward. It was understandable that she would be afraid of being seen entering the palace. Amenemhet nervously considered what Nefrytatanen would think if she ever found out that he had been here, especially only a few hours after she had left for Noph. He refused to reflect on this at any length. He was here to obtain information, he reminded himself, and it was perfectly proper to do this, even under these unusual circumstances.

But Kuwait's perfume was a living thing in the air, making Amenemhet almost dizzy with its power.

Kuwait entered the room, and Amenemhet was shocked to find desire rising in him at the sight of her in a gossamer crimson robe. The memory of her dance returned vividly to him—the satin skin, the rhythmic movements of her hips. He took a deep breath. It was that perfume, he decided. It was so heavy it seemed to cling to him. Gathering his thoughts raggedly about him, he was about to ask what her information was, when she smiled and glided toward him. He forgot to speak. The perfume seemed to render him unable to think. He tried to analyze this, but the pulse in his temple pounded, shutting out reason.

Kuwait sat beside Amenemhet, and, to his amazement, she pushed his shoulders firmly back until he reclined on the fur pillows. He couldn't seem to refuse or even resist her. He felt powerless. Her red mouth came closer, and her breasts pressed tightly against the thin cotton of his tunic.

Amenemhet didn't give the kiss. He lay still, feeling helpless as Kuwait took it from him, her warm, luxurious body pressing against him. Her hands caressed his bare arms. Her perfume rocked him. Her long legs coiled around his legs, and her black eyes stared into his until he felt he was being absorbed into their glittering depths. She took the kiss from his mouth.

Kuwait smiled. "You are mine," she whispered. "You are mine, and I'll bring you such delight you'll beg for this night never to end."

Amenemhet couldn't stop his response. He couldn't remember his own name, much less his purpose for being there, as Kuwait moved slowly against him, kissing him again, that perfume drowning his mind to submissiveness. No, not to submissiveness, but to a slowly awakening need for conquest.

What was he doing? What was he thinking? He felt her begin to unfasten his tunic; yet he seemed incapable of protesting.

Protest? Submit? No. Like lightning flashing, he felt the sudden, eager desire for conquest, to make this female creature moan and writhe with his conquest of her.

In a rush of unexpected violence, he held her away from him, angrily tearing the gauzy gown and throwing it on the floor. Then, suddenly twisting his body, he rolled over until she was under him, feeling her nakedness, crushing her mouth with his. He heard her startled gasp, and his head spun with the desire that poured through him.

From nowhere, a silver cat leaped between them, pushing its body against Amenemhet's face, screeching a warning, staring at him with fiery green eyes. He stopped.

Neferset's cat. How was it here? By Heru, Amenemhet thought, what am I doing? For an instant, his brain cleared, and he leaped up. With eyes of fiery gold, he stood over Kuwait. It took a moment to refasten his tunic.

Then Amenemhet picked up Neferset's cat, and, without looking back—not daring to look back—he marched out of Kuwait's quarters into the cool, clear night. The air cleansed her perfume from his senses.

"Thank you, my friend," he said softly, stroking the cat. He carried it in his arms, like a protective amulet, all the way to the palace.

In the royal apartments, he hurried to bathe himself, to wash Kuwait's touch from him.

Later, Amenemhet lay in bed staring at the shadowy ceiling and wondering what had made him do such a thing. He hadn't been merely aroused. He'd been like a madman. What had Kuwait done to make him that way? Was it her perfume? Was there a drug in it? He couldn't understand what he had done, but he realized how the others became enslaved by her. Even now, he had only to think of her, and he could feel the desire rising again in him.

Amenemhet thought about Neferset's cat and wondered where it had come from. He sighed, thankful the cat had appeared, however strange its behavior had been. Had it not come, nothing would have stopped him from taking Kuwait.

Amenemhet thought of Nefrytatanen; her image was a spring of cool water in the desert, driving away all desire for Kuwait. Nefrytatanen's perfume was in her pillows. He pressed a pillow to his face, breathing deeply of it, to counteract Kuwait's scent.

Kuwait lay on her couch, still dazed. Amenemhet's violence had frightened even her, frightened and excited her at the same time. She had lost control of the moment. She had been swept helplessly away, and this confused her. She didn't like losing control of what she did. That was dangerous.

Kuwait remembered how he had suddenly torn away her gown, how he had twisted and rolled, the feel of his muscular body on hers, the feel of his hard lips. And when he had risen, her body had ached for him. Kuwait shivered. There was danger in him. He aroused her, and it was impossible to keep a clear mind about a man who could do that. She thought of how he had looked down at her with burning golden eyes, and she trembled at the memory.

What a delight it would be to have such feelings available whenever they were wanted, Kuwait thought. She smiled. She would get him yet. Now that she had had this experience, she would know what to expect and would have more control over herself. Perhaps she could win all of him for herself. Perhaps she could capture his mind as well as his body. Then she would have everything. She shivered. She must have him. She wondered how she might eliminate Nefrytatanen.

Kuwait lay thinking a long time, which increased her passion. It mixed with her lust for power, and the mixture gave life to a demon. She hated Nefrytatanen, and when she thought of her returning to Amenemhet, rage hotly flooded her. She would kill the queen.

Kuwait forgot her ambition to be a powerful priestess. She wanted to be the king's consort. The thought of having him every night aroused so powerful a desire in her that she felt as if something would burst in her.

Perhaps there was a way to stir the people's anger over the impending famine, she thought. If they were hungry enough, they might be encouraged to produce violence during Nefrytatanen's arrival. When she walked from the moorings to the palace, it might be possible that, in the confusion, she could meet with a dagger's blade.

Kuwait decided she would have to get an assassin, one who could be disposed of later so no one would know who had paid him. She thought, briefly, of asking Shera for the name of such an assassin. But she pushed that idea aside. Shera was too unpredictable. She could never tell him her true reason for wanting the assassin, and he seemed to see through too many of her lies. She didn't want to risk losing Shera's friendship because she had decided to save him as a gift for Amenemhet.

Kuwait called her maid and sent the girl to find Unas. He would do the job. She sent enough gold with the girl to entice him, and the message promised additional reward. She smiled as she poured a goblet of wine for herself. Unas would do as she proposed, and he would come to her gladly. She would reward him, ultimately, with poison in his cup.

Nefrytatanen arrived at Noph. Although the faces of her people weren't hostile, neither did they seem happy to greet her. They were thin and worried-looking, and she thought sadly of the food rationing. She wondered if Amenemhet realized how serious the situation had become.

The day she spent at the palace was filled with packing, and the time passed quickly, but the night was another matter. She lay in her bed listening to the fountain, wondering if Amenemhet was as lonely as she.

Suddenly the feeling she had experienced at the wedding party came to her again. It was even more terrifying without Amenemhet beside her. She got out of bed and paced the room for a time, feeling herself near panic.

There was evil in the room, grinning at her from every corner. She paced, trying to think of Amenemhet, of some pleasant memory, but these things eluded her. She was cold with fear. Finally she went back to bed and sat with her back against the wall, knees drawn fearfully to her chest. What was this thing that stalked her? What was this evil? She shivered and held in her hand the lotus pendant Amenemhet had given her. Its silver gleamed in the moonlight. It was her amulet and her link with him, and it gave her comfort. The feeling of evil began to pass.

She got out of bed again and went to the window

opening to breathe the cool air. She pressed her aching temples with her fingertips. "If only I knew what it was," she whispered to the shadows, "if only I knew who hated me, I could do something for myself." She stared at the darkness for a moment, then turned from the silent garden, and padded back to bed. But she did not fall asleep until dawn had begun to light the sky.

During the day, she clung to the knowledge that she would leave Noph that evening. Merely knowing that she would be with Amenemhet the next day gave her relief.

Late in the afternoon, as she rode slowly through the streets on her way to the moorings, she again was disturbed by the listless look on the faces of her people. They were ordinarily a people of spirit, and the dullness in their bearing saddened her.

A woman emerged from the crowd and stepped suddenly in front of Nefrytatanen's horse. The startled animal reared and she struggled to calm it so the woman wouldn't be trampled. Two guards rushed to Nefrytatanen, one taking the horse's bridle to steady it, the other intending to drive away the woman.

"Wait," Nefrytatanen ordered. She dismounted and turned to address the woman who had thrown herself to the ground. "Why did you stop me?" she asked. She noted the woman's thinness and her swollen eyes ringed with shadows. She felt a stab of sorrow.

"My lady," the woman cried in alarm, "I have no wish to harm you."

"Tell me why you stopped me." Nefrytatanen took her arm to gently raise her to her feet.

"Prince Senwadjet and Princess Maeti are beautiful and healthy children and for this I'm glad," the woman whispered. She looked at her feet. "My own son is their age, but he isn't healthy. He's weak and sickly because he doesn't have proper nourishment. We do the best we can for him." She lifted her eyes to Nefrytatanen's face and begged, "Can nothing be done to get us more food?"

Nefrytatanen noted the many attentive faces surrounding them. What she said would be known all over the city by nightfall. She took the woman's hand in hers.

"I'll speak to the king as soon as I return to Ithtawe. I promise. It will be the first matter we'll discuss. There must be something that can be done to ease your trouble until the next harvest. I promise, we will do something."

"Thank you," the woman said, stepping back.

The guard helped Nefrytatanen to her horse, and she turned once again to look at the woman. She thought of Senwadjet and Maeti. Then she turned back to the guard and said loudly enough so those standing near heard her. "Let us return to Ithtawe with all possible speed. Something must be done immediately." How could the people fight thieves when they were starving, she reasoned.

"Are you having trouble here?" came a voice from behind Nefrytatanen. She turned to see the Trojan ambassador smiling at her. "If I can be of help, I'm at your service," he added.

Nefrytatanen studied Acetes a moment. Although his garments looked alien in the crowd, he seemed at ease and addressed her in her own language. She noted that he had the same expression as when he had stared at her in the throne room.

"To kill a demon would be a small task, if it would please you." Acetes' smile had a charm impossible to ignore, and she smiled faintly in return.

"The kingdom is filled to its brim with problems, though none of them seem to be demons," Nefrytatanen replied. "Which of them would you like to try first?"

Acetes came closer. "Name it," he said quietly.

One of Nefrytatanen's guards also moved nearer and watched Acetes alertly. Nefrytatanen didn't wave the guard away.

Noting this, Acetes said, "I understand why your soldier watches me, but you can assure him I mean you no harm."

"What are you doing in Noph?" Nefrytatanen continued to smile, but she didn't recall the guard.

"I'm visiting this city, which I understand was your home." Acetes sighed. "It seems I'm temporarily stranded here. A friend of mine, one of my group from Troy, has been bewitched by one of the beautiful ladies of this city and cannot tear himself from her yet. Although I have business at Ithtawe, I don't like to travel alone, so I must wait for him."

To leave Acetes standing on the shore when she was ready to sail to Ithtawe would be inhospitable. "We're getting ready to sail there now. You may join us if you wish," she said.

"That's very generous of you and an offer I can't resist," Acetes replied smoothly. "I would never refuse an invitation from you, anyway." Acetes knew she was aware that he had deliberately maneuvered her into the position of having to offer. He didn't mind that she was hesitant. He'd known many cautious ladies. "I'll go immediately to prepare the few possessions I brought with me and will be at the ship quickly."

"I recommend you move quickly," Nefrytatanen said coolly. "We're in a hurry and cannot delay for you." She turned her horse away, ignoring his undisturbed smile, and continued toward the river. This Trojan might be pleasant company on the voyage, she decided, if he conducted himself properly. And she knew she could rely on her position to make sure he was proper. She wasn't misled by his easy smile. He wanted to be much more than friends.

Nefrytatanen had barely had time to supervise their settling into their quarters when she heard Acetes come on board. She had already directed one of the guards to show him to a compartment as soon as he came, thinking this might occupy him awhile. She considered staying in her cabin to avoid him as much as possible, but she decided his presence wouldn't make her a prisoner on her own ship. She wished to enjoy the fresh breeze blowing from the north and she instructed Bekhet to take the children on deck with her. Smiling to herself, she thought there was probably nothing as effective in smothering romance as one's own small children.

Acetes wasted no time in his compartment but quickly joined Nefrytatanen on deck. After a brief and very polite greeting, he spent some time admiring the children—seemingly undisturbed that their royal father was her husband—and charming Bekhet with small pleasantries.

Nefrytatanen purposely stayed a distance away during this time, hoping to make him further understand her disinterest.

Soon Acetes moved toward her, his dark blond curls rumpled by the wind, and engaged her in an innocent commentary on Tamera and its people. By this method, he managed to engage her in a conversation, even causing her to laugh at one of his remarks.

"It's good to hear you laugh," Acetes commented. "You seem too preoccupied with problems."

Nefrytatanen had forgotten herself a moment, and Acetes had moved a little nearer. She glanced at him. Her smile faded, and she stepped back.

He looked out toward the shore and said quietly, "I meant no disrespect. I admire your courage and strength in enduring all you have with unwavering poise."

There was a hidden meaning in Acetes's tone, and she looked at him intently.

"What do you mean?" she asked. "Every queen has problems."

"So do many wives," he replied, "but to have both kinds and to bear them all with such dignity is no small task."

"What are you talking about?"

"Forgive my impertinence," he said quickly. "I'd heard certain stories." He hesitated a moment before adding, "They're so widely known I assumed you were aware of them. I'm embarrassed because I brought gossip to you. I'm sorry I spoke." He could see, from the taut look of her face, that he had found a vulnerable area.

"What did you hear." It wasn't a question, but a command.

Now Acetes was sorry he had tried this approach. It grew clumsier with each attempt to extricate himself. Obviously, she felt more strongly about such matters than a Trojan woman would have. He didn't know what to say.

"Do you mean when the king went to the temple to investigate that priestess?" Nefrytatanen's voice was sharp. "That's old gossip. There was nothing more to the incident than that, but it was blown out of proportion by wagging tongues."

"And nothing in his visit to her two nights ago?" Acetes couldn't resist asking. Nefrytatanen's eyes revealed her shock. "She called for him as soon as your ship was out of sight. And he went," Acetes added.

Nefrytatanen's voice trembled slightly. "If he visited her again, it was for good reason." Her head was high, her chin lifted in defiance.

"No doubt," Acetes agreed slowly. Seeing her wounded, but still loyal and proud, he felt a new respect for her. "He'd be a fool to risk losing you," he said. He looked away from her and stared at the shore. "I've been a fool," he said quietly, "to think I might trifle with you like any other woman. I've been disrespectful." He looked at her with a serious expression. No longer were his eyes flirtatious. "I beg your pardon and ask that we might be friends." Nefrytatanen was startled by this sudden change in him, and she looked at him suspiciously. He said, "I would be honored to have you think of me as a friend."

She looked at him a moment. He seemed sincere, his offer genuine. She said, "I forgive your mistake in judgment. As long as you understand how I feel then, yes, I would like to consider you a friend."

"Good." Acetes smiled, much relieved. "Someday when you're able, please come to my city for a visit. I'd make sure you'd be warmly welcomed." He saw her cautiousness returning, and he laughed softly. "The invitation extends, of course, to King Amenemhet and your children." She smiled at this, and he added, "But whatever your situation—even alone and in trouble— please know that you do have a friend and a place to go where the gates will always be open.

"That is a kind and generous offer," she said thoughtfully. "Too often those you think are friends are unwilling to open their doors in case of trouble."

"I am willing, whatever it is," Acetes said. He was quiet a moment, thinking. Then, abruptly, he asked another question about Tamera and changed the subject. By the time she had answered him the awkwardness of the moment had passed.

Later, they had a relaxed and pleasant evening meal together. Acetes was not only charming, but an intelligent companion. Nefrytatanen asked him many questions about Troy. He answered carefully and also told her stories and made jokes, capturing her complete attention. When it was time to go to their own compartments for the night, he thanked her for her hospitality, and she found it easy to compliment him on the pleasure his company had given her. He bid her fair dreams and went on his way without delay.

When Acetes was in bed, he lay awake for some time, thinking about Nefrytatanen. He decided that Amenemhet would be a fool to risk her loss. If the king ever happened to be such a fool, Acetes would gladly open Troy's gates to her. Picturing such a situation, he smiled.

When Acetes awakened the next morning, he realized once again how small a chance he had with Nefrytatanen. He resolved he would be her friend as he could be nothing more. When the ship had landed at Ithtawe's moorings and was being tied, Acetes again formally thanked her for her hospitality and couldn't resist adding, "I am your friend. Please don't forget me."

"I never forget a friend," she answered solemnly.

Acetes left the ship quickly, and Nefrytatanen wondered about him as she watched his toga disappear into the crowd.

The people were in an ugly mood when Amenemhet went with Nessumontu and an escort to meet Nefrytatanen. He had never seen anything like this. Not only were they openly grumbling, but many of them looked openly hostile.

Nessumontu's eyes shifted warily along the line of people they passed. As usual, he looked undisturbed; privately, he felt uneasy, and kept his hand on the handle of his sword as did the guards.

Above the heads of the crowd, Amenemhet saw Nefrytatanen on the ship speaking to Acetes, and he wondered what the Trojan was doing on the ship. He remembered, with a slight stab of jealousy, that the voyage had been an overnight journey, but thinking of his close escape from Kuwait, he put jealousy out of his mind.

When Nefrytatanen stepped from the ship into Amenemhet's embrace, she was alarmed at the tension in the crowd and was glad that Ithtawe's gates were so close. When Amenemhet released her, she urged Bekhet and Dedjet, who were carrying the children, to hurry to the palace.

When they were only halfway to the palace gates, a fight broke out between two men, and it spread like a fire, until it surrounded even the royal party.

Nessumontu and his men formed a protective circle, occasionally cracking a head, as the crowd surged and struggled around the small group. The palace guards started working their way through the crowd to the royal party.

Immediately in front of Amenemhet and Nefrytatanen, one of their personal guards sank to the ground, blood gushing from his throat. Nefrytatanen's face went white with fear, and Amenemhet drew his sword. In the gap, where the soldier had stood, an evil face appeared, clutching a gleaming blade. The man stared directly at the queen.

Amenemhet looked sideways at the same moment and, stepping back against her, raised his sword and struck in a shining arc. The man fell at Nefrytatanen's feet, a great cleft in his skull, blood splashing on her robe.

In shock Nefrytatanen stared at him and at the fallen soldier until the guards from the palace reached them. Forming several more layers of bodies between the royal family and the surging crowd, the soldiers forced their way to the gates. Nessumontu pushed the dazed Nefrytatanen roughly through the entrance, and the gates slammed shut.

After confirming their safety, Nessumontu panted, "That was no accident. He was an assassin."

"It was me he was after." Nefrytatanen was aware, again, of the evil hovering over her.

Amenemhet glanced at Nessumontu, whose expression confirmed his own fear. The blade had been meant for Nefrytatanen. But why?

"With as little bloodshed as possible, stop that fighting out there," Amenemhet directed. "This was all deliberately planned to cover the assassin's movements."

Nessumontu said nothing and immediately went back outside, calling orders to his men. They pushed through the crowd, separating individual combatants, shouting, and waving their swords, until the people gradually quieted and drifted from the streets.

Inside the palace, Amenemhet and Nefrytatanen went immediately to their private apartment. She took off her blood-spattered robe and, with obvious relief, dropped it on the floor. Then she looked at Amenemhet.

"Beloved, whatever the motive behind the attack, it couldn't have been accomplished if the people weren't so hungry," she said. "I didn't know how severe the food shortage was until I rode through the streets of Noph. The people weren't violent, but they were sullen and looked thin and sickly. One woman threw herself at my horse and begged me to do something because her small son was ill from poor nourishment. Beloved, is there *nothing* we can do? We can't expect the people to resist thieves if they're weak from hunger. It could eventually cause them to turn to robbery themselves!"

"I know how serious it is," he said. "I never mentioned its full extent because we had so many other worries. I know that hunting and fishing is no longer a pleasant pasttime, but a serious matter. And it's not only meat they need. They need grain and vegetables." He shook his head. "The only way I can think of to help them would be to give them our own stores. What do you think? Shall we distribute our own food and keep only a minimum for our household and the army until the next harvest?"

"Yes!"

Amenemhet smiled. "That means you can give no parties until this emergency is over. It may get a little dull for you."

At that moment Nefrytatanen was holding Maeti balanced on one hip, and she reached deftly for Senwadjet as he crawled under a table. She looked at Amenemhet meaningfully as she swung Senwadjet off the floor.

"I doubt it will be dull with these two," she panted. "Now that they're big enough to crawl, they are both swift and sneaky. I dread to think where their curiosity will lead them when they can walk."

Amenemhet laughed and took his wriggling daughter from her. "I don't mind forgoing the parties because I can see there's ample excitement and entertainment right here," he said.

Nefrytatanen looked at the ceiling and made a face. "You're welcome to share some of this amusement whenever you wish to indulge yourself," she replied.

Amenemhet swung Maeti gently before him. She was ecstatic at this. Nefrytatanen looked at him, perplexed. Why did he never see them when they were bad-tempered? Whenever he had them, they were all charming giggles and endearing smiles.

Amenemhet handed the child to Dedjet and kissed Nefrytatanen on her cheek. Bekhet stood waiting to help her mistress put on another garment.

"While you're dressing—" Amenemhet began, then stopped. He had been ready to ask about Acetes but changed his mind. "While you're dressing, I'll hold Senwadjet," he said. "Then we can go downstairs and decide how we'll distribute the food."

He reached for his golden-eyed son, who was suddenly tranquil and smiling. Nefrytatanen handed Senwadjet to him with relief.

"Senwadjet seems to be taking after me quite a bit, don't you think?" Amenemhet remarked. "At the prospect of watching you dress, he becomes quiet and attentive." Amenemhet settled in the chair and looked up at Nefrytatanen. Two pairs of golden, tilted eyes watched her expectantly, and she laughed.

Chapter Twenty-four

Mid-morning the next day, when the streets and market-places were filled, messengers were dispatched to announce that Amenemhet would speak. Expecting to be penalized in some way for yesterday's disturbance and fearful of the king's anger for the attempt on the queen's life, the people gathered slowly. They whispered among themselves, wondering why the assassination had been attempted and whose hand had directed it. But no one knew.

There was a fanfare of trumpets, and Amenemhet and Nefrytatanen appeared. They were surrounded by the most skillful of their personal guards. After Meri had announced them, Amenemhet came forward alone, gesturing Nefrytatanen back with an arm.

He came dangerously near the edge of the Platform of Appearances, close to the crowd, and Nessumontu felt that he grew ears and eyes all over his body as he listened and watched for possible trouble.

Amenemhet said, "I'm dispatching messengers to every corner of the land to bring the news I have for you. We don't know who attempted to take the queen's life or why. We know you were used by the plotter; the confusion gave the assassin an opportunity to strike. Although we don't hold you responsible for that, we warn that such disorders will be severely dealt with in the future.

"We are aware of your troubles. The land cannot be

strong unless these problems are solved, and we have already taken steps to accomplish this end. The queen and I have worked out a plan to provide food from our own storehouses. Feed for your livestock will also be distributed among you. We've set rations for our household and the army. We divide the rest with you."

The people were stunned.

"Each storehouse in every province will be opened and the food distributed each month to every family, in proportion to need. This distribution will be carefully supervised so that none can cheat or be cheated. But we will levy a price for these supplies. While the season is right, and at every future season until the project is complete, every man who is able will work on an irrigation system I've been planning. The system won't be finished quickly, but it can have a good beginning by next spring. If Asar brings a good flood, our next harvest should be abundant."

Recovering slowly from their surprise, the crowd began to smile. Presently there was a shout from someone that he would happily work on the irrigation project. There was another shout, and another, until they came enthusiastically from every direction.

Nefrytatanen smiled as Amenemhet rejoined her. "The noblemen won't be overjoyed at having to open the storehouses," she remarked.

Amenemhet continued smiling at the noisy crowd as he replied, "They'll do it anyway."

After Kheti and Rakkor had dispatched messengers to their provinces instrucing their overseers to obey the order, nobles began to gather at Ithtawe.

With governors absent from their provinces, the bandits grew bolder. Reports of raids increased—as did reports of captures and executions. Kheti and Rakkor went on regular patrols.

Semerkhet and a number of loyal governors remained in their provinces, continuing to stand firm against the thieves, obeying without question or complaint the order to distribute food. Other governors loitered at Ithtawe, grumbling among themselves.

Several days after his announcement, Amenemhet arose in the morning to stretch, yawn, and smile at Nefrytatanen. She noted the look in his eye, and knew his outward relaxed appearance contradicted some inner purpose. Those eyes foretold a plan.

As Bekhet was combing her hair, Nefrytatanen asked casually, "Beloved, what is it you're planning today?"

Amenemhet smiled at her question and replied, "I think all the lords who are grumbling have had time to arrive by now."

"I see."

"What do you see?" he asked.

She laughed. "I see that you are about to give them another glimpse of your temper. Shall I wait again in the next room with flower petals?" Bekhet had finished her hair, and Nefrytatanen rose to examine the results in her mirror. Amenemhet stepped behind her and put his arms around her, laying his cheek against hers. She settled back against him.

"No," he answered, inhaling her perfume. "I want you beside me, not in the next room." He turned her around and kissed her eyelids. "After the morning meal, I'm going to send messages to all the governors in the city to come after the noon resting time. They may be surprised that I know exactly who's here because most of them have never come directly to me. After their naps, they should be refreshed and ready to discuss their problems."

"What will you do this morning?"

"After our messengers have been dispatched," he said softly into her ear, smiling at the faint tremor he felt go through her, "we're going into seclusion with orders not to be disturbed."

"Where?" she asked, her eyes wide in bewilderment.

"In this room," he answered, resting his cheek against hers.

She smiled. "Undoubtedly, that will be to plan what will be said to the noblemen?"

He drew her closer and whispered, "No. It will not."

Although Amenemhet and Nefrytatanen entered the meeting room with a regal air, their eyes were soft with matters far removed from politics and famine.

When everyone was seated, Amenemhet's expression changed.

"We haven't named a successor to Seti yet, hoping this might be done when the thieves and assassins had had been brought under control. However, this seems a lengthier task than we'd foreseen," he said. "The task hasn't been made easier by laziness—which has become obvious, or pomposity—and we call that cowardice—or quarrels among those we've placed in positions of authority—which we call a struggle for private power. Every order we've given has been diluted in direct proportion to the distance of the province at which it's aimed. Conversely, these are the first lords who find it convenient to come here to argue and mutter together. If their provinces are so distant they cannot manage to understand direct orders, they're also too far away to constantly travel here to quibble and beg favors while bandits run loose in their lands. We say it once again and this is the last time. The Hyksos haven't given up, and we can't discount their ambitions to take Tamera. They must be shown we're united and strong. The thieves are a disgrace. They must be put down. The walls of our land can't be built unless the borders are measured, and this must be done. The people are hungry, and I intend to make sure they're fed." He looked sternly at the faces before him, particularly letting his eyes rest on those nobles he knew had opposed opening the storehouses.

"We've given the order that the people are to be fed. We aren't asking, and we aren't arguing. We are commanding." He paused a moment to allow his meaning to be absorbed, then continued. "The last time I spoke to you, I made our intentions clear. My words seem to have fallen on deaf ears. We've had enough of patience. You appear to mistake patience for stupidity. We have decided to make action speak for us. Tuamutef will replace Lord Seti."

The noblemen's mouths fell open. Tuamutef was a commoner. He had risen through the army ranks because of his excellent combat record. It was an insult that he was not of noble bloodlines like themselves!

Amenemhet continued, "Grumbles of protest have reached our ears from those of you who continue to dispute the borders and have delayed distribution of the food supplies. You sit, instead, on your fat bottoms, moving only your mouths to complain and to eat. Far be it from you to face a bandit, even if he's in chains!"

The noblemen gaped, shocked at Amenemhet's plain words.

"It's well you look at us," Amenemhet said sarcastically, "and it's time you opened your eyes as you do so. It's well past time for some of you. We've already made some decisions for those of you who need lessons on how to supervise your provinces, as well as lessons on obedience. And we have decided who will teach and assist you. Ankef will travel home with you, Lord Qebshenuf, to help you with your problems at Hatweret Province. Setme will go with Niuserra to Yuna Province. Hesyra will go with Makeru to Khent. Akeset will go with Lord Petamen to Erment Province. Saneha will return with Mesemneter to Xois."

The noblemen were speechless. They hadn't believed he would go so far. He had, in this announcement, taken their authority from them. He leaned over the table toward them.

"Stare all you like," he said softly. "Those I've named will have authority over you until you've learned where your responsibilities lie. If you don't learn well, you'll be called to Ithtawe for further discussions. We don't wish to see you at the palace again unless you're called here. Nor do we wish to hear from you except by official reports, and we expect these reports to be frequent and truthful. You'd best take good care of your companions for if any misfortune befalls them, you will answer for it."

Amenemhet straightened and stood back from the table, smiling coldly. "Do you have questions?" he asked.

The noblemen were silent with indignation they dared not voice.

"No questions? Good, then my intentions are clear to you all." Without another word, he and Nefrytatanen left the room.

The noblemen rose slowly from their places. They had been so stunned they had forgotten to stand when Amenemhet and Nefrytatanen left, a discourtesy Amenemhet graciously chose to ignore. Now they turned silently to leave, afraid to speak to each other lest their comments be heard and interpreted as further complaints.

In the corridor they were joined by their smiling "assistants," who stayed at their sides until they left Ithtawe, an event they didn't delay.

Now they wanted to go home and fight thieves. They wished they had never come to the city. It was clear that Amenemhet carried out his threats without second warnings. They hadn't expected that.

Chapter Twenty-five

Although Kuwait had been greatly disappointed by the failure of her plan to kill Nefrytatanen, she hadn't been very surprised. Such ventures were always difficult to bring to success, and her plan had been hasty. She had hoped the very simplicity of having Unas stab the queen in the street might make the attempt successful. Since Sinuhe's daughter had tried to poison Amenemhet, he had been too afraid of treachery for Kuwait to slip someone into the royal household. Unfamiliar servants were never allowed near any of the family.

Last night Shera had come to Kuwait in the darkness. Although he had amused her and had rewarded her handsomely, making love to the leader of the assassins hadn't given her the excitement she craved. All during the time Shera spent with her, she had wondered what he would think if he knew she planned him as a gift for Amenemhet.

In the past, Kuwait had been tempted by Shera's potential power. Too, he was neither unattractive nor an inept lover. Now, however, she kept Shera coming to her merely in the event that her plans for the king failed. And if they were successful, she expected to be richly rewarded by Amenemhet for helping in Shera's capture.

Since that night Amenemhet had come to her and the cat had interrupted them—Kuwait still wondered where that beast had come from—she spent much of her idle time dreaming of him. She was unable to forget him, violent though the encounter had been. She often wondered if he were so ungentle with the queen, or if it had been the conflict in his feelings that had made him so forceful. Kuwait wouldn't mind if he was that way with her from time to time. Remembering his eyes looking down at her, brilliant gold and filled with desire, Kuwait shivered. As many visitors as she had since received, she'd had no relief. She couldn't forget Amenemhet, and she knew that only he could ease the ache she lived with permanently.

When news of Amenemhet's meeting with the noblemen and its results reached Kuwait's ears, she pictured Amenemhet commanding their obedience. She laughed at the thought of those lazy cowards trying to defy him. Her longing for him spread through her with renewed fire, and she was sick with hatred for Nefrytatanen.

Why had Amenemhet not returned to her, she wondered. She had given herself protection against Nefrytatanen's magic. Did the queen have so much power that she could deflect her spell? Kuwait walked aimlessly from room to room as she thought about this. She dropped articles from lifeless fingers. She had never been gentle, but now her servants were in dread of each contact with her; they crept silently from her at their first opportunity.

Finally Kuwait could endure waiting no longer. She couldn't call him to her again. She would never meet him, as she might a noble, casually in the streets. She decided she must go to the palace.

She considered the possibility of meeting Nefrytatanen, and decided she could use some temple matter as an excuse. She considered the possibility of managing to see him alone, and if he succumbed to her, he would surely be able to find privacy in his own palace. Kuwait also thought about the chance of Nefrytatanen's discovering them, and she decided it would simply hasten the end of whatever affection might yet live between the king and queen. Kuwait was sure that he must be growing tired of Nefrytatanen, particularly so if the queen were prone to weakness and fainting. If what Kuwait had seen was any measure of his passion, then one woman could not hold him for very long.

Kuwait could endure it no longer, and set her slaves hurrying to prepare her for a visit to the palace.

As Nefrytatanen walked toward the royal bedchamber to prepare for sleeping, she met Neferset wandering in the corridors, looking lonely. Kheti was seldom in the palace, being kept busy with his relentless pursuit of the bandits, and she reflected on how little company Neferset had. Semu and Sarenput were small comfort to a newly-married woman abandoned of necessity by her husband for his work.

"I see you also put off going to a lonely bed," Nefrytatanen said, smiling faintly.

"I find it difficult to sleep with Kheti gone, not knowing what danger he may be facing at the very time I'm resting," Neferset murmured.

"Visit with me awhile, and we'll comfort each other," Nefrytatanen offered. "I also find myself too often alone, and danger is always near a king. At least Kheti knows from where he can expect attack—and let me assure you, Neferset, he also knows what to do if it occurs."

Neferset's dull eyes became lively with interest at the queen's praise of Kheti. Eagerly, she said, "Tell me how you know these things. Tell me all you know about Kheti that I have not yet had the chance to learn."

"Let's walk in the garden," Nefrytatanen, invited. "I'm tired of the stuffy air inside, and the night is beautiful."

"When did you first meet Kheti?" Neferset asked. "Did you know him long?"

Nefrytatanen laughed. "I met him when he kidnapped me." At Neferset's shocked expression, she laughed even more merrily. As they walked in the garden, Nefrytatanen shared her memories with Neferset. Much later, at an hour when most of the palace was dark, they strolled upstairs to the terrace outside the royal apartments.

Nefrytatanen intended to enter the room where she knew Amenemhet still worked. She and Neferset were quiet as they walked, lost in their own thoughts. Their bare feet made no sound as they approached the doorway.

Nefrytatanen was about to step from the shadows into the room when she saw Kuwait enter and Amenemhet stand up. From his sudden leap, Nefrytatanen could see he was surprised. She stopped. She put out a hand to stop Neferset and then stepped silently back into the shadows. Her heart pounded as they watched and listened.

Amenemhet stared at Kuwait. She closed the door softly behind her. She was wrapped from head to toe in a crimson cape and, even from where he stood, he could smell her perfume. Her black eyes glittered at him. Slowly she unfastened her cape and dropped it. It fell, looking like a pool of blood on the floor. Surely, Amenemhet thought, she had persuaded a spider to spin a web around her body. He could see almost every line and curve beneath. Red beads draped over her forehead twinkled as she moved closer to him.

"I came to you," Kuwait whispered, "for I could not help myself. I could wait no longer for you to come again to me."

Amenemhet stood, arms at his sides, staring at her in confusion as her perfume, like a snake, spread its coils around him.

Kuwait watched his expression carefully and noted his eyes glowing with the well-remembered golden light as she put her arms around him, swaying closer, her warm body pressing tightly against him, offering herself.

Amenemhet stood silent and unresisting, drawn to her and repelled at the same time. Her mouth took his, and she poured her full meaning into a kiss. She was shaken by it and pressed even closer, trembling with all the desire she had felt throughout these last days.

Finally, no longer able to breathe, she stepped back, looking dizzily into eyes that burned on her.

Amenemhet put his hands on her shoulders and firmly pushed her away. He said nothing, only stared at her a long time. Kuwait shivered, her desire mixed with uneasiness.

Kuwait found her voice at last. "I have dreamed of you and longed for you until I ache with desire. Since the night you left me so suddenly, I have had no rest. Were you so unaffected that you could forget me?"

"I was not unaffected," he answered. "Even a stone would have been affected. I have put you out of my mind only after much struggle."

Kuwait's temper flared a moment, but she quickly suppressed it and said softly, "Why do you struggle? You're king and can have a harem if you wish. You've been married for some time now; surely, the newness has worn off. Still, you have no harem and, apparently, no lovers. Perhaps it's time you did." Her black eyes met his, gleaming with the passion she couldn't hide.

Amenemhet continued to look at Kuwait with that strange expression. He said, "I omit a harem out of kindness to those ladies who might inhabit such a place, for they would die of loneliness waiting for me. I have neither need nor desire for a harem, with your queen for my wife."

Hope had caused Kuwait to hold her temper, but at Amenemhet's answer, her anger burst through. "There are others who are rich, who are of noble blood, rulers from other lands who beg for just a warm look from me! I offer myself to you, and you turn away. Are you a man, after all?"

Golden sparks rose in his eyes. "I am your king," he said softly. "You are no priestess. You're a woman of the streets, like those in the Hyksos cities, selling herself to any passerby. You offer nothing I desire. You make love a bargain, nothing more." He turned contemptuously and walked out, slamming the door behind him.

Seeing the kiss go unresisted, Nefrytatanen's heart had fallen, but hearing his answer she was filled with pride. Neferset looked at Nefrytatanen in uncertainty. Nefrytatanen had forgotten her friend. She stepped from the shadows into the room her eyes glowing with triumph.

"The last priest," said Nefrytatanen sweetly to Kuwait's startled face, "who tried to reach beyond his domain now resides in another land. The last Tamera saw of him was his receding back hurrying away, for if his shadow falls on this soil ever again, he'll meet his final destiny." She stared full at the priestess, and Kuwait shrank away a little from the impact of the blue fire in the queen's eyes. "I suggest you pack without delay or such will also be your fate." Nefrytatanen smiled in an unfriendly fashion, showing small white teeth. "Perhaps you'll find Hathorbes—who knows? And you may comfort one another." Nefrytatanen gathered her gown together and, turning, swept past Kuwait.

Before following Nefrytatanen, Neferset paused befor Kuwait to say, "I wouldn't delay if I were in your place. The moon rises full tonight, and the queen is very angry."

Kuwait stared at the silver cat in Neferset's arms and said nothing. Neferset turned to follow Nefrytatanen, leaving Kuwait looking pale and shaken.

Neferset's eyes were merry as she caught up with Nefrytatanen, but one glance at the queen's expression quickly erased all hint of humor from her eyes. The moon was indeed full, and Nefrytatanen wasn't angry—she was furious.

Nefrytatanen marched down the corridor. She had forgotten Neferset, and walked directly into her chamber without a word. Neferset stood outside the door a moment, shrugged, and went her way.

Inside the room, Nefrytatanen sank into a chair and stared blankly into space. Kuwait, she knew now, was the evil that had haunted her. Kuwait was also, certainly, the hand behind the assassin.

Bekhet came to Nefrytatanen carrying the magic powders and the blue gown Nefrytatanen had worn the first night she had spent with Amenemhet. Nefrytatanen looked up at her in surprise.

"I smelled the perfume of the snake that slithered through here," Bekhet said grimly, "and I can tell something has happened requiring strong measures. My lady, will you put a curse on her? Or will you lure the king back to your arms? Or, perhaps, he deserves reward?"

Nefrytatanen stared at her then began to laugh. "Oh, Bekhet, you're surely high among the favorites of Aset. Save the curse, unless I find need of such methods at another time. I should reward the king, for he must be made of bronze." The smile faded and she added slowly, "However, I intend to make certain of this." She stood up and began unfastening her robe. "Get every oil, powder, and perfume I use," she directed. "Make sure we overlook nothing. Tonight I'll assure that he forgets everything except me!" At this last, she had the robe undone, and she threw it to the floor with a violence that made Bekhet jump. Then Nefrytatanen went to the bathing chamber.

Bekhet directed Nefrytatanen's bathing with soothing efficiency, so calmly perfumed, combed, and dressed her that Nefrytatanen was prepared to meet Amenemhet with confidence in her appearance and in her bearing. The bath and massage had given her the sleek composure of a cat.

When Amenemhet wearily entered the royal bedchamber, he was pleasantly surprised to have Nefrytatanen greet him with a smile and offer him a goblet of spiced wine.

When he sat down, she loosened his tunic and gently rubbed his neck and shoulders until he felt his tension subside. Only one lamp lit the room, and her perfume crept over him with as much stealth as Kuwait's. He smiled at her cautiously, and she kissed his forehead.

"You are tired," she said softly. "I've had a relaxing bath prepared for you." Amenemhet moved to stand up, and her hands pressed him gently back into the cushions. "Don't get up," she said. "Rest a moment and finish your wine slowly."

Amenemhet was suspicious. It wasn't that Nefrytatanen was never attentive, she frequently was. But such elaborate arrangements, at this particular time, alerted him. Although he had never seen her really angry with him, he wondered if this was the prelude to such a moment. Had she seen Kuwait? At this idea, he shuddered, speculating on whether Nefrytatanen planned to drown him in his bath. She did have a strange gleam in her eyes.

With a sinking heart, he wondered if she had witnessed the entire scene. How could she have done so? She had been nowhere near the room. Even so, he wondered. He smiled to himself as he sipped the wine. If Nefrytatanen was preparing to seduce him tonight to turn his mind from Kuwait, he wouldn't speak of it now and spoil the pleasant prospects!

After his bath, he cautiously entered the bedchamber. Nefrytatanen put her arms around him and tilted her face to his. Her lips were soft, caressing his, sending a warm tingle through him. His weariness and doubts drifted away. A hundred Kuwaits could never match these feelings, of this he was certain.

"You are beautiful," he whispered, his eyes gleaming gold. "To have a woman, only mine, whose body brings me this perfection, whose smile stops my tears, whose soul strengthens me, and whose words bring me joy and comfort—how is it that you know which moment I need each of these?"

She sat on the bed and smiled at him. "The way *you* know when *I* need strength and you give me this, when I need gentleness and you're gentle, when I need love and you love me without question." Still smiling faintly, she lay back on the cushions and looked up at him.

Amenemhet leaned over Nefrytatanen and looked at her for one single moment, and then forgot about Kuwait and the reason for Nefrytatanen's special preparations.

Amenemhet awakened slowly, warm and content. Even after he was completely awake, he kept his eyes closed, looking at the orange sunlight filtering through his eyelids. He stretched slowly and reached for Nefrytatanen, but her place was empty.

He remembered Kuwait, and for a moment he thought the night of love had been a dream, that Nefrytatanen was gone. He opened his eyes. Her soft laughter floated from the terrace. Amenemhet saw her wrapped in a light robe, crouching in the sunshine, coaxing a bird with crumbs. Relieved, he smiled. She hadn't seen Kuwait after all. It had been merely a coincidence that she chose last night to wait for him with kisses, wine, and love.

Or was it just coincidence? Perhaps she had witnessed Kuwait's scene, and chose silence for some reason for her own. He wondered. If she knew, would she mention it?

The sun was high, and heat had begun to creep into the room. It was late, and he began to get up. As he moved, the bird fled to a nearby tree and landed on a swaying branch, watching. Nefrytatanen looked at it a moment longer and then, spreading the crumbs for her cautious friend, came in smiling to Amenemhet.

He wondered what she would say.

"Good morning, beloved."

That was all. A greeting given in a light and cheerful tone. He considered it carefully. She kissed him and lingered in his arms a moment, as she often did in the morning.

She left him to signal for Bekhet and Yazid. To his amazement, she told them they wouldn't be needed, that she and Amenemhet would come down for the morning meal after a time. Bekhet and Yazid smiled knowingly and left.

Nefrytatanen came to Amenemhet, dropping her robe as she walked. "Let us repeat that morning at Kheti's house by bathing alone." She smiled. "Do you remember it?"

He remembered. She laughed when he reached out for her, and she fled down the private hall to their bath. He heard her bare feet running lightly across the stone floor and then a splash. He followed her.

They repeated the morning, as she had suggested, with a bath of laughter, ending in puddles of scented water on the floor and more lovemaking in the bed, their skin damp and sweet-smelling skin, their bodies warm in the sun.

When they went, casually dressed, for the morning meal, she held his hand, and there was no trace of anger or sorrow in her eyes.

They were midway through the meal when Yazid advised them that Ankhneferu was waiting to speak with them. Amenemhet's heart sank. He knew what Ankhneferu had come to discuss. What would Nefrytatanen do when Kuwait's name was mentioned?

Her eyes rose from the food before her. They held no hint of unpleasant thoughts. She said, "Tell Ankhneferu to join us now."

When the priest apeared in the doorway. Amenemhet smiled stiffly and invited him to sit with them. Ankhneferu shook his head at the offer of food and sank slowly into a chair.

"I don't know what happened," Ankhneferu said immediately, "but during the night Kuwait packed and left without a word." Ankhneferu shook his head, obviously relieved. "I don't care where she's gone, for this is a great burden off my mind. Do you know anything of this?"

Nefrytatanen's eyes met Amenemhet's over her cup,

but they held no expression. Now he was sure she knew it all.

Amenemhet looked at her, not at Ankhneferu, as he said, "She came to see me last night." Nefrytatanen's eyes remained serenely blank. "We had a talk, and I advised her to leave." Ankhneferu stared at him. Nefrytatanen looked down into her cup.

"I don't know how you did it, and I ask no questions," Ankhneferu said. "I only give thanks, however you persuaded her."

Nefrytatanen said lightly, "The king has his ways of getting things done." She glanced at Amenemhet. "Neither do I question them, especially if the results are the right ones." Looking at Ankhneferu a little sternly, she added, "Just be sure to watch for any new development like that one. It should be stopped before it has a chance to grow dangerous as this did. Is that not wise, beloved, to be alert?" She turned to Amenemhet with raised brows, but he saw no anger in her face. He realized she would say no more.

"Yes," he agreed solemnly. "It's wise to see danger before it's upon you."

Ankhneferu stood up. "I must go now," he said cheerfully, "but I wanted to tell you the news and thank you. It has removed a great pain from my head."

And mine, thought Amenemhet. Aloud, he said, "Have a pleasant day."

The sun felt hot on his neck, and he finished his meal hurriedly. When they left the table. Nefrytatanen took his hand. "Let's go to the garden and sit in the shade awhile, beloved," she invited. "Perhaps Kuwait's leaving is a happy portent for the end of our other troubles."

"Perhaps it is," he murmured. In the garden, he bent to pluck a small, star-shaped white flower.

Sarenput was standing quietly under a tree that dripped fragrant, violet blossoms. When he saw them coming, he raised a hand in greeting.

"You looked so deep in thought, I was hesitant to approach you," Amenemhet remarked.

When Sarenput smiled, his eyes lost their troubled look and grew warm. But Nefrytatanen wondered why this young prince was usually so solemn.

"You seem given to grave thoughts, Sarenput," she commented, as she settled herself in the grass among the fallen blossoms. Amenemhet sat beside her, put the white blossoms in her hand, then kissed her fingers closed.

Watching them, Sarenput sat down nearby. "The garden smells sweet," he said. "It reminds me of home."

"You miss Atalan." Amenemhet made his question a statement. "As I missed Tamera." After a pause he added, "Does a girl wait for you?"

Sarenput smiled. "No." Nefrytatanen wondered why a girl didn't wait for him. He was certainly attractive. Sarenput added, "But I miss it all the same." He tilted his head to look at the cloudless skies. "I'm concerned about Neferset, not my homesickness. I don't like to leave until all these troubles are settled, and I'm assured I don't leave my sister a widow."

"I think it's unlikely she'll be a widow," Amenemhet said, "but she's too much alone. Even if Kheti were not sorely needed, he still would want to help seek out these bandits and assassins. Shera is an old enemy of his."

"I know." Sarenput threw a pebble in the bushes. "Nothing can be done for it." He looked at them sadly. "It's not a sight I like to see—Neferset wandering around with only her cat for comfort. I've done what I could to distract her, as Semu has. I know you're both busy, and you've been as kind as you were able. The children have helped fill her time—"

"But no one can replace Kheti," Nefrytatanen finished. She sighed. "It would be the same for me—and often is."

"I've seen her eyes light with love and watched her step quicken and her mood become cheerful because

Kheti's there," Sarenput said softly. "I'd like to see her that way all the time."

"I'd like to see all of us smile more," Nefrytatanen observed.

Amenemhet got up, and they followed his example. He remarked softly, "I think it won't be much longer before these troubles come to an end." His golden eyes turned toward the rainbows sparkling in the fountain.

Sarenput smiled humorlessly. "When they do, please excuse me if I leave quickly for home, before the next ones come along."

Amenemhet chuckled. "You may yet be only a prince, but you know already what it means to be king."

Chapter Twenty-six

After a hot, fruitless patrol that took several days, Nessumontu and his men were returning to Ithtawe. As they came within sight of their destination, they saw a group of riders approaching Ithtawe from the south.

Nessumontu called a halt and stood up in his saddle, narrowing his eyes against the sun. He examined the riders ahead, and his eyes widened in surprise.

The riders were sand-dwellers, and they seemed not to be traders. They carried weapons and rode their small horses at a rapid pace.

Nessumontu considered the possibilities. The sand-dwellers were too few to attack Ithtawe. Never having trusted sand-dwellers in general, however, Nessumontu decided to learn for himself what they were doing at the palace. He signaled his men forward at a gallop.

When Nessumontu's patrol arrived at the gates, the nomads were engaged in a heated discussion with the sentries. Nessumontu approached them cautiously. The leader of the sand-dwellers stopped arguing with the guards and turned to Nessumontu.

"I don't know your name," the sand-dweller said quietly, "but I can see your rank is high. I have come to speak with Lord Kheti of Orynx Province, where we now live.

Nessumontu studied the man. His eyes held an easy authority, and he sat straight and relaxed on his mount. There was pride in his bearing, and he looked at Nessumontu with a steady gaze.

"I'm Commander Nessumontu. I know Lord Kheti well. Why have you come here?"

The nomad stared unblinkingly at Nessumontu, unimpressed with his identity. "I have news for him. I think he'll hold it in high value, and I wish to tell him personally."

"I don't know if he's here now or out on patrol," Nessumontu answered softly, looking over the group and estimating their potential danger. "I'll find out." The sand-dweller nodded agreement. "What is your name, so I can tell him, if he's here?" Nessumontu inquired.

"Say Abba Hasan comes to return his favor."

Nessumontu waved to the sentries, and the gates were thrown open. As they all rode through the great doors, Nessumontu's soldiers discreetly merged with Abba Hasan's men and quietly surrounded them.

Dismounting, Nessumontu invited the sand-dwellers to rest in the shade while he searched for Kheti. Abba Hasan thanked him courteously but remained on his horse. His men followed his example. Shrugging, Nessumontu marched through the dusty courtyard and entered the welcome coolness of the palace halls.

Just inside the doorway, he heard voices coming from the room where Amenemhet set his seal. He recognized Kheti's and Rakkor's voices. Saluting the guard casually, Nessumontu entered the room.

Greeting Amenemhet and Nefrytatanen, Nessumontu gave his brief and disappointing report.

"Nothing from anyone," Amenemhet said. He stood up and began to pace the floor. "It seems as if they've all gone into hiding for neither Kheti nor Rakkor have brought a clue."

"I've brought something," Nessumontu said as he sank gratefully into the softness of a couch. "I've brought visitors. Just outside the walls we met a group of sand-dwellers, who wish entrance. Their leader's name is Abba Hasan. He said he lives in your province, Kheti."

"It was he and his family and friends who came to ask protection from the thieves." Kheti sat up alertly. He hadn't heard from Abba Hasan since, and he was surprised that they had traveled here to find him. "Where is he?" Kheti asked. "Did he say why he came?"

"He and a small group of men are waiting just inside the gates. He said he has news and wanted to return your favor."

"Send for him," Amenemhet said quickly. "Perhaps his news will be of interest to us all."

Nessumontu called the guard and told him to bring the nomads. He looked at Amenemhet wearily. "If you don't mind, I'll sit where I am," he said, "The ride was long and hot and tiring."

"Especially when it brings no results," Amenemhet observed.

Nefrytatanen had signaled for a servant, who brought a wine jar, its outside temptingly coated with moisture. At his first sip, Nessumontu nodded his appreciation.

Covered with dust and looking tired and hot, the sand-dwellers entered the room. Nefrytatanen ordered the servant to pour goblets for them. They accepted gratefully, though they appeared surprised by her hospitality.

Abba Hasan didn't recognize Amenemhet and Nefrytatanen, and Kheti prompted him softly, "My friend, you stand before the king and queen." The nomad was startled. He knew nothing of court procedures and didn't know what he should do. Amenemhet came forward and saved him the decision.

"Would your news be of interest to us?" he asked easily.

"Yes, it would." Abba's eyes met Kheti's proudly as he added, "Now I can repay you as I promised. Although we live in your province, we haven't lost contact with our brothers in the desert. There are ways in which we are able to communicate. I've learned you search particularly for a thief named Shera."

"If we could get him," said Rakkor tensely, "the others would scatter in fear. Shera would be a great prize."

Abba smiled. "So I thought. I can lead you to his hiding place."

Kheti stared, unable to speak for a moment. The others looked at the nomad suspiciously. Noticing the looks, Kheti turned to them and said firmly, "There's no trickery here."

"Where does Shera hide?" Amenemhet asked quietly. His heart pounded.

Abba said softly, "Much closer than you'd think. In the mountain, where there are many old tombs, they've broken an entrance and then hidden it carefully. There is Shera's den."

Nessumontu was disgusted. "The place is a honeycomb! How can we get at them? We can't chase them through every passage, one by one. And there's no way I know of to coax or trick them out."

"We could frighten them out," Nefrytatanen suggested.

Amenemhet turned to her. "How?"

"Tell me when you would have them come out. I'll arrange such visions for them that they'll gladly throw themselves on your swords to escape the place." Her eyes were cold, for she was remembering stories of their bloody crimes.

Abba shivered slightly as he stared at her.

Amenemhet was silent a moment before he asked, "You can do this to them as you gave me your vision in the tomb?"

"Yes."

Amenemhet turned excitedly to Nessumontu and directed, "Send for Sarenput, Semu, and your commanders. This must be carefully planned. Call back every man you can reach, without suspicion being cast on their movements. We'll need everyone you can spare."

Nessumontu regretfully put down his goblet and turned to leave.

"We won't move for several days," Amenemhet added quickly. "I know you and your men will need time to get ready. I have no intention of bringing you into a battle tired and unprepared."

"Thank you." Nessumontu smiled faintly and left. His weariness was apparent in the unusual heaviness of his steps.

Amenemhet turned to Nefrytatanen. "There will be many of them scattered throughout the passages. Are you sure you can manage this thing?"

"I have told you I'll do it. It doesn't matter where they are or how great are their numbers. They'll see such horrors they'll flee," she promised.

"What horrors can you show these men? They fear nothing!" Amenemhet couldn't imagine what visions she would be capable of creating that would frighten the assassins.

"I'll bring them visions of their own victims," she said coldly. "They'll see those they've murdered as they were when they murdered them."

They stared at her in horror. Amenemhet said nothing, but his scalp prickled at the prospect.

Abba Hasan let out a breath. "So the stories are true," he said.

"They're true." Nefrytatanen looked at him and smiled. "You have nothing to fear, unless you're thieves in disguise."

Amenemhet said abruptly, "Abba Hasan, are you sure of all your men?"

The sand-dweller looked at Amenemhet with unwavering eyes. "I'm sure of them all." He turned to them and spoke rapidly in their own language. At his words, the men came closer. They all stared at Nefrytatanen with awe.

"I must go upstairs awhile, beloved," she said softly

to Amenemhet. "Tell me when everyone has come so I may hear your plans and so decide what I'll need to do."

As the door closed behind her, Amenemhet smiled and commented, "The fearful spell-caster goes to tend the children." Abba smiled at this.

"Sit down and rest," Amenemhet offered. "Tell me how you learned of Shera's hiding place."

"Our friends were camped not far from the tomb cliffs. In the evening, after the meal, one boy slipped away. He took his sling with him, hoping to find some small game and thereby bring back food and prove his marksmanship. He had gotten a fair distance from the camp when he heard riders. Not knowing who they were, he hid himself and watched. When he realized he'd found something more valuable and far more dangerous than hare, he followed them, and they led him to the tombs. He watched them hide their horses in a place among the rocks and saw the thieves pass into a hidden opening. He was afraid to move, but before dawn came, he crept away. When he told the others in his camp, they moved away immediately. Thus, the story was passed to me. No camp of sand-dwellers could face Shera's men and hope to vanquish them. But knowing of my acquaintance with Lord Kheti and knowing his high rank in court, they hoped the army itself would take the robbers. Even now, among themselves, they're quietly preparing to fight. All I need do is pass the word, and they'll meet to join the battle." Abba's eyes were angry as he finished, "They all have good reasons to want Shera and his men dead."

"We've all been searching everywhere, overturning every rock," Rakkor said, "and they're found by a boy hunting for hare." He whistled.

"Nothing happens by chance," Amenemhet said thoughtfully. "I'd like to meet that boy one day. He has great courage."

"I can arrange that when this is over," Abba said. He smiled. "He's my youngest brother, Amru."

Ten days were spent gathering the needed men. As each patrol returned to Ithtawe, men from other garrisons joined their ranks. No new patrols left the palace.

Shera was aware, from his spies' reports, that soldiers were gathering at Ithtawe, and he wondered why. It was hinted that the king recalled many to give them a rest. Shera thought this was possible. The new vigilance of the previously lazy noblemen had made him and the others cautious, and this had probably enabled part of the regular army to withdraw and rest for a time.

Shera also considered the possibility of a secret plan of the king's, but he couldn't imagine what this might be. He was sure no one had ever learned the secret of his hiding place. He had made certain his own ventures had followed no pattern. He could not have been trailed.

"I don't like this place," Kuwait said as she raised herself on one elbow beside him. "It's evil to stay here among the dead."

"It may not be cheerful," Shera chuckled, "but it is safe. Who would ever suspect we would be found in the old tombs? This place has served us very well, and the dead aren't likely to bother us." He slapped her bare hip. "You're a fine one to think of evil. You seem to have few qualms."

"What do you mean?" her eyes were guarded.

"Just what you think." Shera's soft laugh held no humor. "When gossips whisper everywhere, first about your pursuit of the king, then about your sudden disappearance, I'd be a fool not to surmise what happened." Kuwait looked at him fearfully. His smile faded as he continued, "And why shouldn't you have tried? I don't blame you for your ambition. I've had no illusions concerning you, so to pretend jealousy would be ridiculous. Besides," he smiled again, "you know I've never promised love."

Considering this a moment, Kuwait asked cautiously, "Do you mean to leave me stranded somewhere then?"

"No," Shera answered. "When the time comes for us to part ways, I'll tell you. I think you wouldn't dare go to Amenemhet to let him know where I am now. I'm sure you were ordered to leave Tamera. That's the only way they could have gotten rid of you. You probably risk death if you're seen. I will give you escort to the border when I'm finished with you. I think you can take care of yourself. Women like you can always manage as long as there are men." Shera's hand took Kuwait's chin roughly to tilt her face to his. She shivered at his expression. "But, Kuwait, whatever happens," he said softly, "don't even think of trying to make a bargain for me. If the king didn't kill you, I would."

After darkness had fallen, the guards at Ithtawe were given orders to let no one leave its gates. Amenemhet wanted to be sure no spies escaped to report what went on behind the walls. He had finished assembling his forces, and they now were openly preparing to leave.

Amenemhet was in his dressing room. Yazid helped him change his garments for the battle.

"I wouldn't trust this sand-dweller too far," Yazid remarked, "nor any of them. They aren't river-people, and they think in altogether different terms. He repays Kheti; he will help us fight the thieves in order to make his own way safe. This doesn't necessarily make him loyal to you."

Amenemhet smiled. "You speak harshly of one of your own blood."

Yazid was serious as he added, "I can see these things for that reason. I know how their minds work. They play their own game. Trust none of them too far."

Amenemhet couldn't let this pass, and he teased, "And you? Do you play your own game?"

Yazid was aghast. "Have I not served you faithfully almost all your life? I am not a sand-dweller in my outlook. Besides, my interests are the same as yours."

Amenemhet raised an eyebrow in mock suspicion. "You've been loyal in the past, but you still have their suspicious mind." He was still teasing his friend.

"I suppose you've never met a devious river-dweller," Yazid returned.

"You're looking at one," Amenemhet said softly, a warning in his tone.

"That's why we understand each other so well," Yazid muttered.

"Just be sure your interests remain the same as mine," Amenemhet commented, fastening his cloak.

Yazid's eyes opened wide at this. Although it was said in a light tone, he was being reminded of who he conversed with. He had overstepped his place. Yazid said quietly, "The day I'm disloyal, I won't have to be dragged to the executioner. I'll open my own veins, from shame."

Amenemhet put a hand on his shoulder. "I know, Yazid. I accused you of nothing. My comment sounded more harsh than it was meant to be. There's no question in my mind about your loyalty. I repent my stupid jest."

Yazid was near tears.

"Come, my old friend," Amenemhet said. "We can't be late on this occasion." The two embraced.

Amenemhet and Yazid walked quietly down the hall and through the courtyard into the area outside, where the soldiers waited. Amenemhet was making a final inspection of their ranks when Nefrytatanen came from the courtyard with Bekhet.

"My lady," Bekhet was saying softly, "if Yazid can go with the king, why can I not go with you? You can't be alone in that place of darkness. I won't be afraid when you do this thing."

Nefrytatanen's voice was patient and gentle, although she had said this already many times. "Bekhet,

I must be alone. I know you're not afraid, and I appreciate your offer. It is I who am afraid for you. I can protect myself from what will happen, but I can do nothing for you. It's very dangerous. I'm sorry, Bekhet. I cannot explain. I'll be safe." Nefrytatanen turned to Amenemhet.

"We're ready." He answered her unasked question, then helped her mount her horse.

Nefrytatanen bent to pat Bekhet's cheek, which was moist with tears. Then she turned her horse to face the soldiers and said in a voice that echoed through the stillness, "When I leave you to ride into the darkness, no one must follow me. I need no protection. Of us all, I will be most assured of safety. What I'm going to do will bring great danger to anyone near me. As well-meaning as your intentions may be, if you follow—even to keep me safe—you will endanger yourselves." She turned to Amenemhet and nodded.

He gave the signal, and the gates swung open. The sentries on the wall watched carefully as the soldiers rode past, making sure that no spies tried to sneak out by mixing among the soldiers. When the last of them was gone, the gates closed, and the guards bolted them. Then they began their regular pacing, keeping watch.

The night was moonless, and the black of the sky was relieved only by the cold light of the stars. It was a suitable night for what they intended to do, Amenemhet thought. The breeze carried a chill that penetrated to his bones. He knew it was fear, and not the wind, that made him feel so cold. Although Nefrytatanen had assured him countless times of her safety, the thought of her walking alone in that desolate place with murderers nearby made him shudder. And the knowledge of what she was preparing to do caused him to forget all thoughts of his own danger.

Nefrytatanen's mind was on Amenemhet. She was afraid of the approaching battle, but she knew she must control her fear because of what she would shortly do. Her full concentration would be necessary. All thought of danger must be driven from her mind. Emotions were more treacherous than thoughts. One thought could deliberately be replaced by another, if the will was strong enough. But emotion was another matter. She decided, finally, that she might turn the love behind her fear for Amenemhet into a positive force and incorporate its power into her spell. She began to consider ways she might add protection to her petitions, not only for Amenemhet, but for all those who rode with him.

Bekhet paced impatiently up and down the length of the room. Finally, a determined look on her face, she turned to Dedjet.

"Dedjet, watch over the children for me. I must go after her."

Dedjet grasped Bekhet's arm. "You mustn't!" she exclaimed. "The queen told you to stay here. She commanded you to stay. It is dangerous. I don't know what she's planning to do this time, but I remember well enough the night I saw her confer with her dead mother!" Dedjet shivered. "That was frightening enough. This time the queen goes for an even more terrifying reason. Oh, Bekhet, you can't go!"

Bekhet took from her robe a small, silver object. "If my soul stands in danger by my witnessing what happens, I'll wear the amulet of Aset for protection. I don't wish to look at what my lady does. I go to be on the watch for others, mortal beings, who might come upon her. I'll bring a dagger for them."

"Bekhet," Dedjet pleaded. "She said that merely being there is enough to bring disaster."

"Not while I carry the amulet." Bekhet appeared confident as she put on her cloak, but, privately, she was concerned as to whether the amulet would be sufficient. "I think my silent presence will delay others' access to her."

Dedjet grasped Bekhet's hand. "She said she'd be safe. Her spell will protect her. I saw her call on the spirits that time in a spell which carried no danger. I assure you, Bekhet, she doesn't play games with magic. I've seen others throw powders on fires, pray, and claim this to be magic. She throws her powders on a fire, and the stars come down to her! She speaks to the company of divine beings and they answer her! You are not trained in these matters. You cannot go, Bekhet!"

Bekhet's eyes revealed the fear she was trying to hide, but she said firmly, "I must, Dedjet. If anything happened to her while I sat safely in the palace, I could never forgive myself. What is the worst that may happen to me? That I might die? To die in the service of my lady isn't the worst of fates. Although I disobey her, surely this wouldn't condemn me in Tuat." Bekhet embraced Dedjet briefly. "Watch over the children while I'm gone," she said softly. "We don't know if there are spies prowling in the palace. This would be a good opportunity while almost everyone is gone, to harm the children. If I don't return, take care of them. And from time to time, offer a prayer for me."

Bekhet turned quickly and left Dedjet standing alone, tears streaming down her face.

Dedjet, heeding Bekhet's warning about spies, carefully bolted the door. She went to each window opening, pulled the covering down, and fastened it securely. Still unsatisfied, she decided not even to trust the guards in the hall. She would take no chances because, she reasoned, it was entirely possible there *were* spies in the palace.

Carefully, she carried the sleeping children into the room where she could stand guard over them. From Amenemhet's cabinet, she gingerly took his ornamental sword. Although it was used only for ceremonial occasions, its edge was kept as sharp as the one he wore to battle. She was awed at her effrontery in handling the king's sword. She sat, finally, with her back against a wall, where she could see every entrance to the room.

Laying the glittering golden sword across her lap, she shuddered at the thought of using it. But she asked herself if she could do less than Bekhet, who offered her life. She began again to weep, as she thought of Bekhet. She prayed earnestly for her, and for the safety of them all.

In the meantime. Bekhet had managed to obtain a horse, and she approached the main gate. She had decided there was no way she could sneak quietly out. Moving openly would be least suspicious. She hailed the sentry before he had a chance to hail her. When he began to tell her she couldn't pass, she interrupted him.

"Do you not know who I am?" Bekhet demanded. "I'm Queen Nefrytatanen's personal attendant, Bekhet. I know you have orders not to allow anyone outside, but she has forgotten something essential to her safety." Bekhet gestured as if she held something beneath her cloak. "I must catch up with her and bring this."

To the sentry's offer of an escort, Bekhet shook her head vigorously. "It's unnecessary," she called. "You need the men you have, for the royal children remain within these walls. Take care not to overlook their safety," she scolded him. By this time, the soldier had come to stand beside her horse, and they recognized one another.

She said softly, "I'll be all right. If I hurry, I should be able to catch up with them. They can't be too far ahead, and I know the way—but I must bring this to the queen."

The guard shook his head. "You're taking a chance," he warned.

"I'm taking no greater chance than those I follow," she answered tartly. "Just don't forget about the children's safety."

"I won't be likely to do that," he said, a little irritated. He knew his job. He decided he had best allow Bekhet to pass. He didn't doubt her loyalty for a moment, and he knew he would pay heavily if he prevented the queen from accomplishing what she had set out to do. He opened the gate just wide enough for

Bekhet to pass. "Good luck," he said, glad he could stay within the walls.

Bekhet rode off into the darkness without hesitation. She hadn't really lied to him, she thought. She was bringing the queen something she might need—Bekhet brought her own self, and her dagger.

Nessumontu raised his arm to stop the column of soldiers. He turned his horse to approach Amenemhet and Nefrytatanen. "I think we're close enough," he whispered.

"Now I leave you." Nefrytatanen took a firm grip on the cloth sack she had brought. It contained the articles she needed. Amenemhet dismounted and walked around her horse. She slid from the saddle into his arms.

He held her close to him a moment, and she whispered, "I'll be safe, beloved. Don't distract yourself with worry for me. I'll meet you here where we'll leave my horse." She held him tight and added, "I'll do what I can to keep you safe. But, my beloved, return to me—return to me!"

"I'll be back," he promised. "Be very careful so you're here when I do return."

She kissed him, lingering as long as she dared, then broke away and ran soundlessly into the shadows. As Amenemhet watched her disappear, he felt that his heart as well as his arms had emptied.

Nefrytatanen walked quickly and silently between the rocks. Now all her attention was on what she did. Discovery here would destroy all their plans. It was an eerie place and, she decided, appropriate to her purpose.

The night creatures, seeing Nefrytatanen's dark figure and glowing blue eyes and scenting impending death in the air, swerved from her path to avoid notice.

Nefrytatanen saw an opening in the cliff's wall, in a place which would shelter her fire. She traced the opening with her fingertips, carefully examining it to assure the shaft was clear all the way into a passage. When a cool draft of air brushed her searching fingers, she knew she had found what she sought.

She put her sack on the sand and then sat down beside it to open and spread it flat. The purple lining of the bag became an altar cloth on which she placed the articles. She got up and removed her dark cloak and robe and carefully laid them on a flat rock, where she could find them later, then took off her boots and placed them beside her garments. The sand was cool and soft under her feet, and the night air sent a chill through her naked body. Shivering a little, she loosened her hair and spread it free to the night wind.

She filled her silver dish with oil and ignited this with a coal she had carried in a sealed container. The small flame seemed to float over the oil's surface without touching it. She turned her face to stare quietly into the darkness for a while, clearing her mind and gathering strength. Then she turned again to her fire. From the swaying crown of the flame rose a coil of black smoke which climbed to mingle invisibly with the night sky.

When she cast her powder on the fire, a shower of blue sparks burst in a spiral and soared into the darkness toward the stars. Her fragrance rose over her head, spreading over the area to protect her from intruders as an awning would protect her from the glaring sun.

Raising her arms to the darkness, she spoke clearly into the shadowy hush of the night. The edge of her words struck the rock faces and were multiplied. She spoke to the whispering winds. Three times she spoke, and a thousand times the echoes murmured with her voice.

She continued, "I have used the Words of Power. I have come wearing the cobra and the hawk on my brow, for I am the queen of the Two Lands, daughter of Ra. I am the servant of Aset, Mistress of Magic. I have told you your secret names in proof of what I am."

Nefrytatanen paused a moment, and her expression-

less face became fierce. Then she said, "My eyes are the
eyes of Asar. My face is the face of Aten. My hands
are the hands of Heru. My teeth are the teeth of Sekhmet. I am one with you, according to the Law. Hail,
O Heru, he who was bidden to rule among the gods,
whose scepter I carry. This House of Silence had been
defiled by the presence of evil-doers. Homage to thee,
Asar, Lord of the Universe, release the souls of those
the desecrators of these tombs have sent to Tuat before
their appointed day, so the murderers may look upon
the truth and flee."

Purple vapors began to rise in soft billows and hung
over her fire, as if waiting.

"Behold, O Sekhmet, Lady of Flame, Amenemhet
and his army who go to destroy the evil ones," she
directed. "Give them the strength of thy fires to vanquish the evil and avenge the murderers of the innocent."

She took feathers plucked from a hawk and waved
them over the purple vapors leading them obediently
to the open mouth in the cliff wall. They went where
she directed them, and the fire fed the darkness into
which the purple vapors vanished.

Kuwait watched Shera, who stood before the camp-
fire gazing into the flames. As he stirred the ashes,
causing sparks to leap and dance, she studied his movements. His body, she was thinking, was like Amenemhet's; they seemed nearly the same in height and
proportions. She wondered why Shera's touch couldn't
arouse the same feelings in her as Amenemhet's had.
His mouth might be as soft as the last kiss she had
stolen from the king or as hard and demanding as the
one Amenemhet had once given her. Why did Amenemhet's kiss make her feel so much and Shera's kiss
make her feel nothing? She had often shut her eyes to
those peculiar pale eyes of Shera's and thought of
golden eyes, trying to pretend it was the king she kissed.

But it wasn't the same. Why, she wondered, had Amenemhet turned from her?

In the darkness outside the tombs, Amenemhet and his army had hidden their horses far enough away so that no noise from the animals would warn the thieves. Then they had walked toward the dark mountain. As they approached the tomb's entrance, Nessumontu, Kheti, Rakkor, Abba—even Semu and Sarenput—gave gestured orders to the men assigned them.

Amenemhet hadn't been happy to have his guests from Atalan come with them, to return the peaceful hospitality of Atalan with this violence, but they had insisted. As he walked, Amenemhet remembered Neferset, standing in the palace corridor, refusing to go out with Nefrytatanen, watching her brother and her friends go by, her face filled with grief. When Kheti stopped before her, she managed to control her expression. Only her eyes gave her away. After he had kissed her and left, she turned aside and quietly wept.

Yazid crept soundlessly beside Amenemhet, and they went closer to the dark opening on the hill before them. Amenemhet could hear Yazid softly muttering about Shera's choice of a hiding place. Yazid may mumble, Amenemhet thought, but he was no more unhappy to fight before the tombs of the dead than the rest of them were.

When they were as close as they dared go, Amenemhet crouched behind a pile of stones. He turned to see other silent shadows finding dark places and merging with them, and wondered how so many men, wearing and carrying so many weapons, could move so soundlessly. Not one soft clink of metal betrayed them.

"I wonder how long it will take the queen to do what she must," Yazid whispered, shivering as he considered what she was doing even at this very moment.

"I don't know," Amenemhet murmured. "She didn't think it would be long after we were settled that those inside would see the visitors she sends them." Now it was he who shuddered. It was a gruesome thing to think of seeing the victims of your own evil-doings come to you in the ancient tombs. The sight would send anyone screaming.

Shera had considered the possibility of how much danger Kuwait could be to him, and he had decided he would kill her at the first hint of betrayal. But he hadn't become tired of her lush body. Until he did tire of her, or found another to replace her, he would keep her happy. He knew that greed was the best path to her happiness. He turned from the fire to tell her again of the riches these passageways held.

Shera was about to speak when Kuwait's eyes stopped him. Black pools of horror, they turned his own blood cold with their expression. Her eyes stared past him. Shera found himself afraid to turn and see what she beheld, and he stood looking at her. Her shaking hands reached the rough wall, and she dragged herself to her feet, still staring.

Kuwait's scream was a sword slashing at the air again and again, tearing it, and she turned from Shera and bolted, stumbling, farther into the black passage. Her screams echoed, growing fainter with distance.

Perspiration shone on Shera's face, and he drew his sword and turned, slowly. In the chamber were grotesque faces that seemed suspended, separated from bodies that yet stood upright beneath them, glowing luminous purple. Slashed and hacked, jagged wounds showed on the men and women. They hovered a little above the ground, still bleeding from gaping wounds, their hands smeared with a wet and sticky-looking shadow. The face of a young girl, twisted perpetually in the agony of her death, floated before him, so close he could have touched her with his hand. He remembered her.

Now he recognized some of the others. Gradually he began to realize what he saw. Backing away in horror,

Shera felt himself against a wall. Afraid to look away from the figures, but more terrified to stay, he turned and ran down another passageway.

The place was filled with the creatures. Every tunnel held more of the glowing purple figures, and he ran faster through the passages, brushing aside spiders and stumbling over ancient crumbling coffins. He was barely aware of his men. They ran shrieking all around him, some carrying weapons, many waving bare hands in panic as they fought to escape the place.

One man in front of Shera, turning a corner to see yet another lurid figure, groaned and collapsed with fright. Shera leaped over him and swerved to another tunnel forking toward the outside. He stumbled, almost losing his balance, catching himself on a statue.

On the statue he saw the golden face of the goddess Sekhmet; it was filled with anger, and she appeared to be directing the things that followed him. He groaned and ran from her.

The thieves had brought vermin to the place. Now rats scurried between their feet, fleeing even as the bandits fled.

A man crashed against one of four funeral jars holding the embalmed inner organs of some long-dead noble, and its contents smashed upon his sandaled feet. He fainted.

Others trampled over him in their own terror, blind to what they ran upon. When another group followed, they recognized nothing of the man with whom they had only a short time ago shared the evening meal.

An opening to the dessert night stood before them, and Shera looked at it as though it led to Tuat. He ran, gasping for breath. He glanced back and saw that the awful things still followed them and fresh horror washed over him. Would these things follow them into the desert and devour them when they fell from exhaustion?

He needn't have worried, for, as he and the remnants of his band emerged from the tunnel slipping and sliding on the hilltop, a storm of arrows greeted them.

Long training acted now for Shera, and he ducked low and leaped behind some stones. Who was shooting arrows? He looked back at the black tunnel and saw no more purple figures following. Yet the terrified men of his much diminished band continued to shriek and flee the tomb.

"Get down! Get down!" Shera screamed. "It's a trick. Get down and fight."

A few of them obeyed his order. Others, used to reacting instinctively, ducked their heads and ran low among the rocks, finding hiding places. The rest continued to run into the night, down the slopes of the hill. These men were struck down by figures who rose suddenly from shadows. The few who escaped, who were now near madness, ran into the desert.

When no more of his men fled the tomb, Shera and the others left hiding among the stone piles were alone with this invisible enemy.

The night had grown quiet. The last mad screams had faded. Shera could hear no sound from the attackers who waited below. He considered the situation, able, at last, to think clearly.

Not for ten times the treasure stored in that tomb would he set foot in that black maw again. And there weren't enough men left to face those waiting below. He reasoned that the enemy must be the king's army. Now he knew why patrols had gathered at Ithtawe. He wondered how they had learned where he was hidden. He decided he would save himself and let the others fight, if they chose. No—he would send them to fight. Their dull brains could not think beyond his orders. Let them fight the king's army, covering his own escape.

Rising a little, Shera shouted for his men to fight. He called them cowards who ran from illusions. As those of his thieves who were still alive rose in obedience, he slipped quietly away.

When Amenemhet saw how few men rushed at them, he pushed his bloody sword into the sand to cleanse it.

"Stay here, Yazid," he said. "Attacking those poor wretches with all our forces is unnecessary. Let them fall on other swords than ours. As Nefrytatanen predicted, they'll be glad enough to do it."

"I wonder what it looked like," Yazid whispered.

"I wouldn't wish to know," Amenemhet replied, "not when I see the way it affected those men." He stood up, for the last cry had faded. The others were rising from their hiding places, looking at the bodies that lay strewn thickly over the ground.

Abba Hasan came toward Amenemhet. He wiped blood from his sword as he walked. Nessumontu was walking slowly among the bodies, turning them over with his foot and looking at them closely. He was relieved to see Rakkor, Sarenput, and Semu approaching, but glancing around, he realized he didn't see Kheti.

As Rakkor came near, Amenemhet asked, "Have you seen Kheti? Surely, he must be around somewhere." He couldn't believe that Kheti had fallen. With a rising alarm, he thought of Neferset. "Has anyone seen Lord Kheti?" Amenemhet called, frantic now.

"Don't mourn for me yet." Kheti came around another slope, sheathing his sword as he walked. When he reached Amenemhet, he was smiling. "Your plan worked," he said.

"With all the horror here, how can you smile?" Amenemhet demanded.

Kheti's smile was not a pleasant one, but it was triumphant. "I can smile because, beyond that slope, I met an old acquaintance. Shera tried to escape by sneaking away in the confusion. When I saw how few of his men were left and heard him call to them to fight, I knew he'd not fight with them. It was as I thought, and I found him creeping silently toward the horses." Kheti's grey eyes gleamed. "He creeps no more."

Amenemhet said nothing. Kheti's expression left

nothing for him to say, and he gave his friend no more than a satisfied nod.

Yazid asked in a hushed voice, "Who will go in there now? There may be other bandits remaining hidden. Surely that must be where they kept their hoard, but I, for one, am not anxious to meet what chased them out!"

Amenemhet turned to Nessumontu, who was gazing calmly at the tomb's entrance. "Nessumontu," Amenemhet said, "whatever was in there wasn't our doing. The spirits who haunted the bandits should now be gone or, at least, will mean us no harm. You look as if you think the same. Come with me to investigate the place."

Nessumontu made no reply but began to climb the slope without hesitation. Kheti and Rakkor followed them. Yazid looked at Sarenput and Semu.

"I'm too curious to stay here," Sarenput said, "but why don't you two direct the others with the mess out here?"

Yazid looked at Semu. "I don't think gathering up the dead is a happy task, but it seems less unpleasant than going into that place." Semu nodded agreement readily.

Abba Hasan, who had been silently listening, commented, "Save your pride with excuses, if you wish. I freely admit my fear. Nothing will make me put one foot in that place." He turned, throwing his hood back over his shoulders, and went down the hill, calling orders.

Amenemhet and Nessumontu entered the tomb first. The darkness was relieved by still-burning torches. There seemed to be nothing more mysterious than the shadows any ancient tomb would hold.

Nessumontu turned to Amenemhet. "I cannot say I'm enthusiastic about exploring this place now," he said.

Amenemhet was a little surprised at this because he had long ago decided that Nessumontu feared nothing.

"I'm not anxious either," Amenemhet agreed, "but if any of them are still hiding here, I intend to find them tonight before we leave this place." He drew his sword and continued into the depths of the tomb's passage. His boot brushed something, and he glanced down at a corpse, its terrified eyes still staring. "What awful thing did he see?" Amenemhet remarked before going on.

Nessumontu didn't reply. He didn't care to reflect on this.

A little farther down the echoing tunnel, they entered a chamber. Kheti, Rakkor, and Sarenput were now right behind them. Rakkor had taken a torch from the wall and carried it for light. He held the torch high and they saw, in a far corner, the grisly remains of a trampled man. Rakkor shuddered and lowered the torch. They marched on grimly.

After some time walking, their caution began to ease. Finally Amenemhet stopped and faced the others. "I see no reason to go all through this place," he said. "Nothing seems to be here now. Nefrytatanen will be waiting and worrying about us. Let us return to Ithtawe and send more soldiers in the morning to explore the tomb."

"What of the stolen goods?" Nessumontu asked.

The sound of Amenemhet's soft laughter echoed through the darkness. "If any loot is here, I think it will stay until tomorrow. Place guards at the entrance if you like, but it seems unlikely anyone will dare enter this place to hunt for it."

"What is this?" Kheti bent to pick up a tangle of scarlet cloth. He held it up to the light.

"That looks like Kuwait's cloak!" Amenemhet said. "She must have come here instead of leaving Tamera. Where could she be now?"

"I saw no woman come from the entrance with the others," Nessumontu observed, "and I think I would have noticed one. If she were here, then she either left before the battle, or she's still around."

"Let us search a little further," Sarenput said, "as a mercy to her if she's still alive."

They walked quickly now, calling her name down each passage, but only echoes answered. After a time they turned back and left the place.

Bekhet rode slowly, keeping to the sandy places where her horse's hoofbeats would be muffled. She was approaching the rocky hill where he old tombs had been dug, and she listened carefully, alert for thieves. Where would Nefrytatanen be? Straining her eyes to peer into the darkness, she saw no sign among the rocks and shrubs of the fire Nefrytatanen would need. She knew she hadn't lost her way and began to wonder if another plan had been made and the queen hadn't stopped alone but had gone on with the others.

Bekhet's hair almost stood on end when her horse whinnied at another horse he sensed but couldn't see. For a moment she was undecided whether to conceal herself or continue forward in the hope that her own horse had found the one Nefrytatanen had ridden. In her indecision, her horse continued slowly toward the sound, and she was relieved to come upon Nefrytatanen's horse.

Bekhet dismounted. Her mistress couldn't be far away. She stared into the shadows wondering which direction Nefrytatanen might have taken, but she could see nothing.

A branch snapped sharply in the silence. Bekhet leaped in fear. Then she hurried behind the shelter of some rocks and, trembling, drew her dagger.

The shadowy figure of a woman emerged from the darkness. Upon seeing the horses, the figure paused in surprise then hurried toward them as if relieved by their presence.

Bekhet stepped from her hiding place. "It's only me, my lady," she whispered. "Are you all right? Is it all over?"

The figure whirled around to face Bekhet.

"What are you doing here?" Kuwait hissed, her eyes wild with fear.

Bekhet stopped and stared.

"The queen's maid!" Kuwait whispered. "I should have known this was her doing." Kuwait reached for the reins of Nefrytatanen's horse and prepared to mount it.

"Take your hands from those reins," Bekhet said clearly. "Why you're sneaking around in the dark I don't know, but you'll wait and explain this to the queen."

"I will not wait." Kuwait tightened her fingers on the reins. Her voice was nearly hysterical. "I won't wait for those things back there to get me!"

"What things?" Bekhet laid one hand on Kuwait's arm, still concealing the knife in her other hand.

"Back in those tombs I've seen every form of death and torture there must be!" Kuwait's voice rose a little higher, and she trembled. "Sekhmet surely has sent every demon to us." She tried to pull her arm away, but Bekhet held it fast. "Let me go, handmaiden of a sorceress! Wait for your mistress alone. I won't stay to meet her and her demons."

"Get away from the queen's horse," Bekhet commanded. "My lady will come shortly, and we will wait for her."

Kuwait stared at Bekhet, her fear becoming desperation, her hatred of Nefrytatanen transferring to Nefrytatanen's servant. With a snarl, she threw herself at Bekhet.

Surprised, Bekhet lost her balance, falling and rolling on the sand as Kuwait tore at her face with her long, sharp nails.

Kuwait was taller than Bekhet, and supple and strong from dancing, and Bekhet felt she grappled with a wild beast. She couldn't, in the struggle, free her arm to use the little dagger.

Kuwait saw the shimmer of metal, and she threw her weight to the side, rolling until Bekhet was under her.

She straddled the maid, wrenching the knife from Bekhet's hand.

Bekhet twisted and struggled as the knife came slowly down toward her. If she died, then Kuwait might wait in the shadows for Nefrytatanen. She struggled harder to keep the knife from her breast.

Kuwait loosened her knees and, raising herself slightly, brought her body down with all the force she could manage on Bekhet's stomach. For an instant, Bekhet's breath was knocked out of her. And in that instant, her grasp on Kuwait's wrist loosened. Kuwait struck, driving the knife, to its handle, into Bekhet's chest.

Nefrytatanen, making her way across the rocks toward her horse, heard a noise and stopped to listen. A voice mumbled something and then moaned. Soundlessly she raced through the darkness and, coming around a large rock, stopped. She could see someone standing over a form on the ground. The shadowy figure, seeing her approach, turned quickly to dart away.

"Hold!" Nefrytatanen commanded.

Kuwait froze, paralyzed by the voice. She stared in fresh terror at the approaching dark figure and glowing blue eyes. What fiend did she now face, Kuwait wondered, shivering.

It gave Kuwait no comfort to hear Nefrytatanen's voice exclaim, "Kuwait, it's you!" Nefrytatanen stood before Kuwait now, looking at her with piercing eyes. "You were with Shera?" Nefrytatanen asked. She was silent a moment, considering this. Then she heard another moan and looked toward the fallen Bekhet.

When Nefrytatanen recognized Bekhet, she hurried to her. Understanding her condition, she sat down in the sand and lay Bekhet's head in her lap.

"Stay right there," Nefrytatanen ordered Kuwait. Kuwait had been ready to run again, but now she stood obediently, convinced that, if she moved, the queen would send demons after her.

Bekhet whispered, "I didn't see what you did. I came too late. Kuwait tried to steal your horse, and I stopped her. Forgive me for my disobedience." Nefrytatanen knew Bekhet was dying. Tears blurred her vision and stole her voice. Mistaking Nefrytatanen's silence for anger, Bekhet begged, "My lady, will you forgive me, so my soul may go in peace?"

"Oh, Bekhet," Nefrytatanen finally murmured, her tears dropping on Bekhet's face, "you've done nothing, ever, that I need forgive you for. I'll pour out prayers to Asar for you and will beg favors for you from Aset."

"Ah," Bekhet smiled weakly, "if you ask these things for me, surely my soul will be spared!"

"You'll journey to Tuat on your own merit," Nefrytatanen whispered, barely able to speak, "but if it can be made even more happy for you, I'll ask every favor possible." She bent to kiss Bekhet's forehead. As Bekhet closed her eyes, she heard her queen addressing Aset in her behalf, and smiled, hearing the footsteps of the sacred bird coming for her.

Through all this, Kuwait had stood still, afraid to move. She knew Nefrytatanen had accomplished what she had seen in the tomb. Kuwait gratefully remembered the magic she had done on the night of Kheti's wedding to protect herself from the queen's magic. If Nefrytatanen decided to deal directly with Kuwait by magic, the queen's curse would be turned against herself. Kuwait knew this was her only chance to destroy Nefrytatanen.

When Nefrytatanen had finished her brief prayer, she laid down Bekhet's lifeless head and wiped her tears. Then she stood up and faced Kuwait.

"What you learned, in becoming a priestess of Hathor was given as a sacred trust, to be used with wisdom for good, not for evil," Nefrytatanen said quietly. "The knowledge I possess is also a gift of trust. It, too, must be used for life and truth, and my powers carry grave responsibilities. I'm sometimes tempted to misuse them, and you are the greatest temptation I have ever faced."

Nefrytatanen stared at Kuwait, longing to call down evil on her, trembling inside her being with the need to do this, but she continued, "You are a priestess of Hat-hor, and I have no wish to strike down a priestess. I don't want your blood on my hands or your soul on my conscience. Let Hat-hor decide your fate. If the goddess deems your heart evil, let it be her hand that awakens Wadjet's cobra and Heru's hawk."

Kuwait's black eyes widened in new terror at Nefrytatanen's meaning, and she backed away. Throwing up her hands, she ran screaming and crying, stumbling into the night.

Nefrytatanen watched her go, feeling compassion for her. She knew what Kuwait's fate would be.

Amenemhet took one more glance at the operation of gathering the dead and tending the wounded, and he decided to delay no more. He leaped to his horse and rode quickly toward the place where Nefrytatanen should be waiting. He could no longer endure the thought of her standing alone in the darkness. He was afraid of thieves running loose. To think of one, insane with fear, coming upon Nefrytatanen and her horse, turned Amenemhet's blood cold.

As he thundered around the last turn in the road, he was relieved to see Nefrytatanen standing quietly beside her horse. He didn't wait for his horse to stop completely, but leaped from it and ran to her. They held each other close, pressing one another again and again, unable to believe each was safe. After the first rush of emotions passed, they stood more quietly, still locked in each other's embrace.

"I was so afraid for you," Amenemhet finally whispered.

"And I for you," she replied.

Seeing tears shining on her cheeks, he said softly, "It's over now. You need weep no more." He wiped the tears with a fingertip.

"Beloved," she said, beginning to weep again. "Bekhet followed me, after all." She nodded toward the body which lay in the shadows on the side of the clearing. "She caught Kuwait trying to steal my horse. Kuwait stabbed her."

Holding Nefrytatanen closer, Amenemhet looked quickly at the body. Then he scanned the whole area, carefully examining every shadow. "Where is Kuwait?" he asked.

"She ran away. Where, I don't know."

"She got away?" Amenemhet was disappointed.

"No." At the tone of her voice, Amenemhet stepped back to look at her. "I wanted to curse Kuwait. After Bekhet died in my arms, I wanted this more than anything." Her tears came flooding faster.

"You didn't curse her?" he asked. Nefrytatanen shook her head. "I don't know how you could resist that," he added.

"It was not a thing for me to do. I told her Hat-hor would judge and deal with her." Nefrytatanen could see Amenemhet was still disappointed, thinking Kuwait's punishment would be delayed for years until her death. Softly, she added, "I said that if the goddess deemed her evil, it would be Hat-hor's hand which would awaken the royal cobra and hawk."

Amenemhet stared at her as he realized what was going to happen to Kuwait. Then he shook his head slowly and again drew her close.

They stood peacefully this way until Amenemhet heard a sound behind him. He quickly released Nefrytatanen and spun around to face what he had feared. He pressed his back against Nefrytatanen, forcing her to step farther away. The distorted face of one of the bandits, with terrible eyes, looked at him.

Amenemhet had no chance to take out his sword. The man leaped at him, a dagger's blade glimmering. Amenemhet couldn't step aside and allow the thief past him to Nefrytatanen, so he threw himself forward, grasping the hand that held the dagger. His momentum sent them rolling, and Amenemhet landed on top, twisting the thief's wrist. The thief, like a maddened animal, thrashed around, struggling to bite him. Finally there was a snap, and the thief's wrist went slack. His dagger fell in the sand. Screaming with pain, the wild-eyed bandit pounded on Amenemhet's shoulder with his other fist, unable to reach his face. They rolled over. Amenemhet broke loose and leaped to his feet.

The thief had the knife again, this time in his other hand. He charged Amenemhet, his mouth frothing, making unintelligible sounds. Amenemhet stepped aside, smashing him with an elbow as he passed and catching hold of the dagger. Moving quickly he drove the dagger deep into the thief's back. The man fell in a jerking heap.

"That was what I feared for you," Amenemhet panted. "Whatever you caused them to see was so horrible that many of them ran into the night, shrieking. I was afraid some of them might turn back."

"Looking at the bodies," Nefrytatanen whispered, "they saw only the truth of their own deeds."

Soon the others arrived, leading the few prisoners. Amenemhet told Nessumontu to place Bekhet's body on a horse, while he helped Nefrytatanen to her saddle. Then they rode on, silent and grim, through the fading night. By the time Ra had begun to light the skies, Ithtawe stood ahead, shining in the early light.

Kuwait lay on her back in the sand. The cobra that had bitten her now wound its way among the rocks where Kuwait had tripped and disturbed it. Dimly, she saw a large hawk circling in the sky, watching her. She moaned softly in defeat. Her eyes closed.

Chapter Twenty-seven

The clatter of horses was drowned by the noise of a joyous crowd. The noise filled Ithtawe's walls and spilled from the gates to spread along the roadway.

As they approached Ithtawe's gates, Amenemhet said thoughtfully, "How many more times do you think we'll have to ride home after a battle?" He looked at Nefrytatanen sadly. "What will happen next to shed more blood?"

"No more, for a while." Nefrytatanen's eyes rose to the ascending sun-disk. "For a time, we'll have peace, and we'll build Tamera into a land the world will never forget. Someday there will come those who won't understand what we've done, but they'll look upon us in awe. There will be others after them, who will learn slowly, and when the wisdom of Tehuti is again perceived, they'll understand our work. We have had to destroy, beloved, but now there comes a time for building."

"Maet," he whispered. "Will it ever be?"

"It is now," she replied. "Tamera has its king." She smiled. "You are the bringer and the protector of maet."

"And you?" Amenemhet looked at Nefrytatanen. "You're queen. The title and its meaning are the same as mine."

"I'll follow your footsteps, my king." She smiled sweetly at him and added, "With children to nourish

and protect, I'll be busy enough. I'll follow you forever."

Amenemhet reached over to take her hand, and
they rode through the gates together.

In the midst of the happy crowd, Nessumontu and
his guards dismounted, but, for all their efforts, they
couldn't hold the joyous people back. Amenemhet dismounted in the middle of the throng, undisturbed by
the closeness. Walking among the crowd, smiling, he
went to Nefrytatanen. She slid from her horse into his
arms.

For a moment, they stood looking into each other's
faces. The sun caught the cobra and the hawk on her
diadem, and the design seemed to spew flame. Neferset
had come from the palace courtyard, and seeing the
flash of it she shivered, knowing that the royal cobra
struck the enemies of its wearer with death, to keep the
ruler safe. She felt, oddly, that someone had just now
died.

Shrugging aside the feeling, her eyes traveled anxiously over the crowd seeking Kheti, her heart pounding
with fear. She saw him as he swung from his horse,
appearing tired, his garments smeared with blood.

Kheti looked toward the courtyard and saw Neferset's silver hair shining in the morning sun. Smiling
widely, he began to walk quickly toward her, gaining
speed until he almost ran the last few steps to her
arms.

Later, as the others came through the courtyard to
enter the palace, they passed Kheti and Neferset staring
into each other's faces as if their eyes would never turn
away. They were completely unaware of everything
else.

Sarenput and Semu smiled and paused to look back
at them a moment. Sarenput said, "It's time we thought
of home. She's found hers at last."

They turned and continued into the palace.

Neferset's cat lingered near Abba Hasan's feet, and
he bent to pick it up as he walked. Fondling the cat, he

turned to Nessumontu, who walked beside him. "My friend, do you only fight?" Abba asked. "Though your skill in battle is admirable, surely you have other interests?" He glanced at Kheti and Neferset and added, "Do you never think of marriage, or have you no taste for love?"

Nessumontu's eyes gleamed with humor. "I enjoy love, but I have managed, so far, to avoid marriage. May my success continue.

"Love has its charms and marriage its advantages," Abba commented.

"I'm sure marriage is a most enjoyable experience," Nessumontu answered, smiling faintly. "And I enjoy watching it from a safe distance."

The sand-dweller laughed softly. "I thought you were fearless and needed no safe distance between you and anything."

"A certain amount of caution is wise in some matters," Nessumontu replied.

The Nile had receded, leaving behind water trapped in the many channels of Amenemhet's nearly-completed irrigation system. Where the river had lain swollen in the flood, the ground was now covered with rich, black soil.

On the first day of spring, the Nile flowed obediently through its normal bed. From the terrace, Amenemhet could see the sparkle of the sun on the water's surface and smell the fresh scent of earth. It was as if all the elements waited for the people to scatter seeds so the earth-god might begin the miracle of sending forth the first green shoots. He glanced up at the clear sky.

"It will be a fine day for the planting ceremony," he observed, "and not too hot for being in the fields." He gave a slight tug at his collar, thinking of the discomfort of ceremonial garments.

Nefrytatanen was standing inside the room, patiently waiting while Dedjet adjusted her robe. She was dressed in the feminine version of Amenemhet's ornately embroidered white robe. She wore an identical collar, a sunburst of gold and jewels reaching her shoulders. She, too, was thankful the day wouldn't be too hot.

A soft tap on the door announced Senet leading Senwadjet and Maeti, dressed in miniature versions of their parents' garments. As young as they were, they sensed something special, and they had an air of dignity that made Amenemhet smile.

Yazid came behind them, smiling. "Everyone and everything is ready," he announced.

Amenemhet thought of the workers in every province who waited for the appointed hour when the king would scatter the first seeds on the land. The time was approaching rapidly. Those who were able had gathered at Ithtawe to witness the event, and they were noisily gay in the streets. They were optimistic that the crops would bring a rich harvest because, they reasoned, with such a king and queen, how could the divine beings not smile on Tamera? The king had been home this season to celebrate the rising of the flood and invoke the favor of Asar. The flood had obediently been neither too low nor too high.

The measurements had been made, and the noblemen were no longer weakening the land with their discord. With the destruction of Shera and his thieves, the farmers would be able to tend their crops without fear.

Giving one final adjustment to the gold and white cloth carefully draped in the prescribed folds around his face, Amenemhet took Nefrytatanen's hand and led her into the hall. Meri paced slowly from the beginning to the end of the procession, inspecting it. Then he went to the front, out of Amenemhet and Nefrytatanen's sight, and gave the signal.

The immense copper doors swung open on their bronze hinges. Trumpets announced the beginning of the ceremonies. Their notes held a ring of pride and of triumph. The line of musicians began the procession, instruments proclaiming the beginning of spring.

The royal party stepped forward slowly. Their personal guards, dressed in red and gold, preceded the scribes. Ankhneferu moved with Senbi proudly at his side, carrying incense and the ankh, followed by attendants waving great feathered plumes. Meri and a group of high officials came next, Meri ever alert that all went as planned. The lords of the nearby provinces walked with their ladies, each couple followed by personal servants, all of them dressed in a splendor not even Ur could match.

Rakkor walked beside Abba Hasan. Although the sand-dweller would ordinarily not have participated in such an event, Amenemhet had wished to give him honor, and Abba had been pleased. His people, waiting along the road to watch him pass, would be impressed.

Kheti and Neferset walked behind the last of the nobles. This position placed them nearest Amenemhet and Nefrytatanen, a special honor.

Another smaller group of palace guards followed. These were the highest ranking of Nessumontu's captains. Immediately after them, Amenemhet and Nefrytatanen walked. They were followed by Dedjet and Senet, each carrying a child. Yazid came after them, alongside Taka, who carried the grain. Behind them all came Nessumontu, followed by two captains.

Gazing at Neferset's back, Amenemhet reflected on the previous dawn, when Sarenput and Semu had embraced them all and thanked them for their hospitality and for the adventures they would enjoy relating to their friends in Atalan. They had, with the few who had journeyed with them from Atalan, launched their ship into the Nile and glided down the river toward the Great Green Sea. Amenemhet didn't envy them their long and hazardous voyage, but they had seemed unconcerned and waved, smiling at the showers of flower petals that sent them on their way.

Amenemhet again felt sadness, remembering the sorrow in Neferset's eyes as she had watched the ship move into the river. He remembered that she had had another dream, and she knew Atalan was doomed. She was certain that she would never see her home again. Although Kheti had stood with an arm around her, Neferset seemed alone. She hadn't wept. What she saw in her dreams was beyond weeping over.

The procession continued through the streets and into the fields by the river, followed and flanked on both sides by the crowds who sang and laughed as they walked.

When they reached the designated field, everyone gathered around.

Ankhneferu and Senbi stepped away from the group, and Ankhneferu began a prayer. Amenemhet decided that Ankhneferu was a superior priest. His prayers, though fervent, were short. Sinuhe's prayers had always made Amenemhet's feet ache. They had also been insincere, he reminded himself, and he reflected on this for a time.

After they had sung the spring song, Amenemhet reached into the grain Taka held out to him, and as he scattered the seeds over the rich soil, the people sang to Ra.

Senwadjet, seeing the grain sparkling gold in the sunlight, longed to spread the beautiful things himself. He tugged at Taka's robe insistently. Taka looked down to see the child reaching unsteadily toward the container. He looked at Nefrytatanen, hoping she would take Senwadjet away before the prince lost his balance and became noisy.

Nefrytatanen whispered to Amenemhet, who, in the midst of scattering grain, stopped. He bent to lift the boy.

The crowd stared. What was happening? They watched as Amenemhet motioned Taka to hold the jar in reach of Senwadjet. Senwadjet's gold eyes sparkled with glee, and he leaned into the jar to his shoulder, taking a fistful of seeds and flinging it to the breeze. Amenemhet laughed, and the high priest looked at Senwadjet in undisguised amazement.

Ankhneferu put up his arms to silence the people,

who were whispering as they watched. "Certainly the crop will be a double one," he said, "for have we not had two kings scatter the seeds?"

Amenemhet gave Senwadjet to Ankhneferu and took the jar from Taka. He turned to Nefrytatanen, holding the jar out to her. He raised his voice so the crowd would hear him in the open air. "As king, I've scattered the grain. But two hands should have dipped into the jar as one. The hand of Queen Nefrytatanen should be beside mine for she rules even as I do." He looked at Nefrytatanen and invited, "Scatter the grain so the ritual is not left incomplete."

Nefrytatanen turned toward him slowly, smiling into his eyes as she reached into the jar. When she withdrew the handful of seeds, she turned to look at the sun rising higher in the east.

"As Ra rises and triumphs over his enemies, so does dominion, as the king brings maet to the Two Lands." She waved her hand, sprinkling the grain, as she said, Tamera rise," she said. "The hawk of Heru soars into its "As King Amenemhet commands, I obey." The crowd wondered at her meaning until she made her intentions clear. "Who in the land will do less than I, who am queen?"

Ankhneferu, setting down Senwadjet, was the first to kneel, bowing his head until his brow brushed the earth. Senbi followed him solemnly. Then, in a spontaneous pledge of loyalty, Meri and Nessumontu and all the court made this most humble of all gestures. Silently the soldiers and the people sank to follow their example until only Amenemhet and Nefrytatanen remained standing, surprised and moved.

Ankhneferu slowly rose and said, "Homage to thee, O divine rulers of the Two Lands, protectors of maet."

The crowd responded, "Praise to thee, children of Ra." They rose quietly, looking at Amenemhet with renewed awe, for his eyes, lit by the slanting sun, were as gold as its light.

Amenemhet whispered to Nefrytatanen, "If I manage

to persuade Asar to give us a good harvest, can you invoke Aset to assist us with peace?"

She smiled and murmured, "I shall do as you wish, O divine ruler."

He took her hand and turned to lead the procession back to the palace. As they walked, he leaned closer to her and whispered, "If my wish is your command and I now tell you I've decided to gather a harem, what will your comment be?"

She smiled sweetly up at him and said softly, "O master of the Two Lands, in my desire to serve your every need, I would spare you time and bother by personally selecting the ladies to fill this harem." The flicker of irony in her sapphire eyes clearly revealed her true intention.

Amenemhet laughed softly. "I would, I think, have the ugliest collection of women ever assembled in one place."

Nefrytatanen stopped walking and looked up at him with a wounded expression. "O glorious son of Ra, would I do such a thing to you?"

He took her arm and resumed walking, considering this. His eyes straight before him, he answered slowly, "I believe you might do that. Yes, I'm sure of it." He looked out the corner of his eye at her as he added, "After a moment of reflection, I'm unsure I wish to take upon myself the chore of training all those strangers. Perhaps I will save my energies for the lady whose experience I now admire so deeply."

Nefrytatanen's eyes were wide and innocent as she gazed up at him. "O radiant protector of maet, your decision fills my heart with joy," she whispered humbly.

"In you," Amenemhet remarked, "this humility is suspect."

Key to Pronunciations
and Meanings

Because the Egyptian names in this novel are authentic, the following explanation will aid the reader's understanding and enjoyment.

Amenardis (Ah-men-ar-dis)—Kheti's fiancée

Amenemhet (Ah-men-em-het)—crown prince of Tashemau, later king of Egypt

Ankhneferu (Ahnk-nef-er-oo)—Second in rank of priest of Tamehu, later Egypt's high priest

Anpu (Ahn-poo)—Divine being ruling over medicine and science and also protector of the dead, more commonly known as Anubis

Apuya (Ah-poo-ee-ah)—royal physician of Atalan

Asar (Ah-sar)—divine being ruling immortality and symbolizing immortal man, more commonly known as Osiris

Aset (Ah-set)—divine being ruling magic and symbolizing women, more commonly known as Isis

Bast (Bahst)—divine being ruling prophecy

Bekhet (Bek-et)—one of Nefrytatanen's attendants

Dedjet (Deh-djet)—one of Nefrytatanen's attendants

Hat-hor (Hat-hor)—Goddess of love and joy

Hathorbes (Hat-hor-bes)—high priest of Tamehu

Heru (Her-oo)—divine being symbolizing the living king or Asar reincarnated, more commonly known as Horus

Horemheb (Hor-em-heb)—royal physician of Egypt

Ithtawe (It-tah-oo-ee)—fortress-palace built by Amenemhet as Egypt's capitol city

Kheti (Ket-ee)—leader of group of mercenary soldiers, later, lord of Orynx Province

Korusko (Kor-oos-koh)—commander of Tashemau's
army

Kuwait (Koo-ate)—priestess

Maet (Mah-eet)—divine being symbolizing truth,
justice and order as planned by the Creator;
perfection

Amen-Ra (Ah-men-Rah)—divine being symbolizing
the benevolent qualities of the sun, such as
life and warmth

Maeti (Mah-ee-tee)—princess of Egypt

Mentuhotep (Men-too-hoh-tep)—king of Tashemau,
Amenemhet's father

Meresank (Mer-reh-sahnk)—queen of Tashemau

Meri (Mir-ee)—prime minister of Egypt

Nakht (Nah-kt)—name Amenemhet uses as disguise

Necho (Nek-oh)—sailor

Neferset (Nef-er-set)—princess of Atalan

Neferu (Nef-er-oo)—prophet

Nefrytatanen (Nef-ree-tah-tah-nen)—queen of Tamehu, later queen of Egypt

Nesitaneb (Nes-ee-tah-neb)—queen of Atalan

Nessumontu (Nes-oo-mon-too)—commander of Tamehu's army, later commander of Egypt's military forces

Noph (Nof)—capitol of northern kingdom (or Tamehu), later known as Memphis

Ra (Rah)—the sun

Sahu (Sah-hoo)—the star Orion

Sahura (Sah-hoo-rah)—king of Atalan

Sarenput (Sah-ren-poot)—prince of Atalan

Sekhmet (Sek-met)—divine being symbolizing justice
or judgment regarding compassion or punishment, mercy or vengeance

Semerkhet (Sem-er-ket)—lord of Uto Province

Semu (Sem-oo)—commander of Atalan's military
forces

Senbi   (Sen-bee)—priest of Egypt

Senwadjet   (Sen-wah-djet)—prince of Egypt

Sepa   (Seh-pah)—Egyptian ship builder

Seti   (Seh-tee)—prime minister of Tamehu, later lord of Ibex Province

Sept   (Se-pet)—the star Sirius

Shera   (Sheh-rah)—bandit

Sinuhe   (Sin-oo-hee)—high priest of Tashemau

Sutekh   (Soo-tek)—divine being symbolizing the evil and violence in mankind

Tamehu   (Tah-meh-oo)—northern kingdom of Egypt

Tamera   (Tah-mer-ah)—Egypt

Tashemau   (Tah-shem-ah-oo)—southern kingdom of Egypt

Tehuti   (Teh-oo-tee)—divine being symbolizing the intelligent principle, more commonly known as Thoth

Tem   (Tem)—the infinite intelligence, the creator, also known as Khepra and Ptah

Tuat   (too-aht)—heaven

Wadjet   Wah-djet)—divine being symbolized by the cobra, also the guardian of the crown

Wast   (Wahst)—capitol of southern kingdom, later known as Thebes

THE SWEEPING ROMANTIC EPIC
OF A PROUD WOMAN
IN A GOLDEN AMERICAN ERA!

PATRICIA GALLAGHER

Beginning at the close of the Civil War, and sweeping forward to the end of the last century, CASTLES IN THE AIR tells of the relentless rise of beautiful, spirited Devon Marshall from a war-ravaged Virginia landscape to the glittering stratospheres of New York society and the upper reaches of power in Washington.

In this American epic of surging power, there unfolds a brilliant, luminous tapestry of human ambition, success, lust, and our nation's vibrant past. And in the tempestuous romance of Devon and the dynamic millionaire Keith Curtis, Patricia Gallagher creates an unforgettable love story of rare power and rich human scope.

AVON

27649 $1.95

CIA 5-76